FABRICATED

A CYBIL LEWIS SF MYSTERY

NICOLE GIVENS KURTZ

CONTENTS

COPYRIGHT

<u>Credits:</u>
Cover art: Natania Barron
Editor: Novellette Whyte

DEDICATION

For Weston

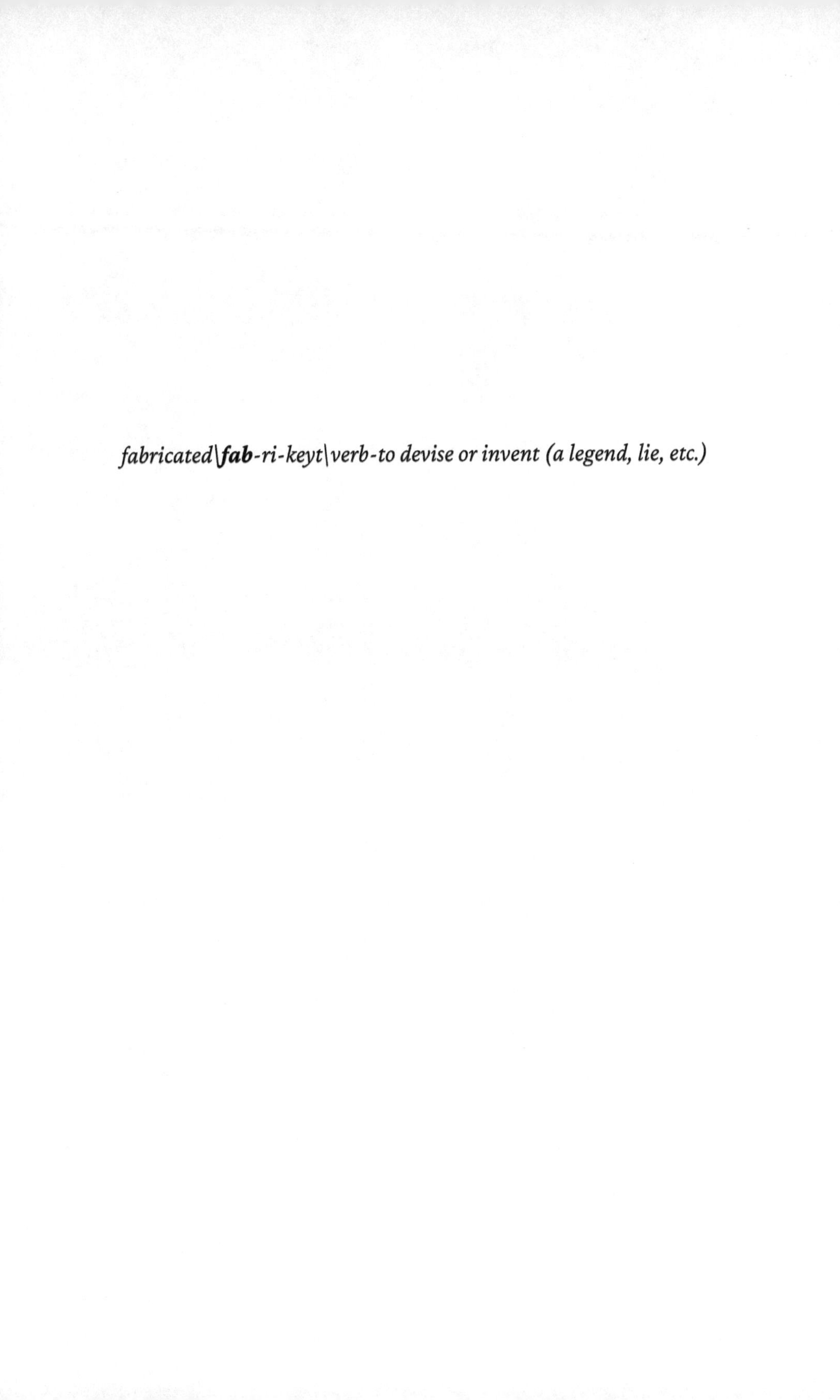

*fabricated**fab**-ri-keyt\\verb-to devise or invent (a legend, lie, etc.)*

CHAPTER
ONE

The person most likely to kill you is the person who loves you.

My grandmomma told me, when my first crush smashed my budding love for him underneath the steel heel of his ranger boots, no one can hurt you like those you love. He had no interest in dark-skinned, teenage girls, and he didn't mince words telling me so. He preferred his partner to have ports and a rechargeable battery.

His words had been filed away and stored in my memory along with the other hurtful adolescent scrapes and emotional bruises. The rejection's sting forced me to bury it there. Yet, throughout my lifetime, they would rise from the depths, returning to the forefront of my mind, tearing open wounds and seeping life lessons in watery blood and bitter tears.

The teenage angst didn't seem too relevant at the time.

If it's one thing I've learned in my nearly forty years is this—trust your gut.

If I had, things would've gone much more smoothly.

Who am I?

I'm Cybil Lewis. Private Inspector licensed in The District Territory. July felt like an oven left on high. The sun's rays rebounded off the pavement, fiberglass, and metal, back into people's faces. An energy nightmare, certain neighborhoods suffered frequent electrical and computer grid breakdowns, leaving thousands stranded without air conditioning, automatic doors, and other necessities. Bots stopped working. Generators and recyclable batteries helped. Still the more tech-rich you were, the greater the potential for damage.

Venture outside at your own risk. Summer snatched victims into its greedy hands and swallowed them whole. Each year an ever-increasing number of people died because they became trapped in their residences without cool air when the grid responsible for controlling the electric crashed or when the generators melted.

Which was why I was leaning over the air conditioning unit when the doors to my office yawned open. In walked two women, one whom I recognized the moment her sleek, dark blonde hair crossed the threshold. I got up to meet them before they came too far into my lobby. Midwest Territory Alliance Agent Lynn stopped. Despite wearing make-up, pockmarks spoiled her attempt at flawless. Cold blue eyes stared out. She grinned, calculated, and cool.

We had a complicated history due to a shared case not too long ago. She tried to get me shot, killed, and sent to the cradle for violations I didn't commit. The entire experience left a bad taste in my mouth.

You can imagine my joy at seeing her again.

"You need a hobby, Lynn. Following me around, showing up at my office, might make folks think you're crushin' on me. You do know, cyberstalking is a regulation violation." Her small mouth became a slash. "You're still a smart mouth, P.I." With her hands on her hips, she stared at me, long and hard. "I go wherever I please."

Perhaps I was supposed to be scared. "I assure you. You won't find any pleasure here."

So, I gave it back, because hard stares don't bother me much, or make me quake in my shoes. My eyes had seen so much horror, my tolerance level for horrific acts was extremely high.

Besides, the only thing horrid here was her outfit. A pantsuit. In July. Both women's long-sleeved suits spoke to a professionalism that the Midwest Territories clung to in hopes of bringing back days long since passed. Thankfully, neither wore stilettos, but rather black books with flat heels and a shiny gloss.

Their laser gun holsters didn't fit quite well under the jackets, but hey, nothing's perfect.

After about a minute, she blinked. "Cybil."

"Lynn."

"You're Cybil Lewis," Agent Winsome walked forward and offered her hand. "I've heard a lot about you. I'm Agent Anika Winsome."

"Oh, I'm sure you've heard plenty." I shook her out-stretched hand. Callouses and a little rough spoke to Agent Winsome's ability to get her hands dirty. "I didn't know Agent Lynn had a partner."

From behind Agent Winsome, Lynn frowned.

Winsome shrugged thick shoulders. "The Territory Alliance responds to the needs of each violation's report. Sometimes we're in pairs, other times we're in groups, and occasionally we're solo."

"I see. So, why are you here?" I leaned back against my receptionist, Kimmila's, desk. "I know Lynn didn't come here just to say hello."

Agent Lynn put a hand over her heart. "That hurt a little Miss Lewis."

I smiled. "Good."

Agent Winsome presented a well-put together killer—big hands, thick body with dangerous curves that hinted at strength any bad guy (or girl) would think twice about approaching as an 'easy target.'

No, Agent Winsome didn't look easy. Her close-clipped hair and nose ring provided a tiny peak into the personality behind the button-up T.A. agent. Her makeup had to contain glitter or something sparkly. She didn't shine, but rather, glowed.

"You have a reputation for being rude, untrustworthy, and violent, especially with authority figures, so I will get right to the point," she said, setting her dark eyes on me with laser focus.

Just as with Lynn, I didn't respond to her hard looks, but Winsome's sizzled like fire brewed in those brown depths. Not only could you drown in her eyes, you'd dissolve into nothingness.

Who are you? My mouth had gone dry.

I coughed.

"I meant no disrespect to you, Agent Winsome," I found myself saying. Those words sounded so strange. I didn't believe they belonged to me.

She smiled, a little uplift of high cheekbone. "We're here because we have a fugitive that's escaped from the Midwest Territories Cradle..."

"I thought Cradles kept people in the floatation gel and in stasis with simulated psych therapy. No one walks out of those without help," I said.

Now they had my attention. Cradle escapes didn't happen. The various territories implemented them to defuse the social storm surrounding the inhumanness of traditional prisons. In some point in our history, the idea of keeping human beings in tiny cages with occasional feedings reached a fever pitch, and prison reform became Cradles. The title alone invoked nurturing and safety. So, the entire point of using Cradles had to do with helping those prison advocates rehabilitate violators. For example, if a violator had an addiction, they placed him in this individual cradle, put him in cryosleep and linked the psychologist A.I. to him. While in stasis, he received simulated therapy.

Agent Winsome shrugged, the act pulling the jacket's fabric tight against her toned arms, back, and butt of her gun. "Right. Well, it so happens, this violator *did*. He's on the run and by all indicators, he's coming this way."

"You mean, here, as in The District?"

Winsome nodded. "Yeah."

"What did he do to warrant a trip to the Cradle? How many sessions did he get?" I interrupted Agent Winsome because she wanted to glide by that information.

Agent Lynn stepped forward with her tablet in her hand, and in her nasal tone, read off his violations. "The violator broke Regulation 187-Murder, Regulation 65-Kidnapping, Regulation 50A-Trafficking of an illegal substance between territories, and Regulation 50F-Trafficking of an illegal substance within the Midwest Territories with intent to inflict harm."

"And you just let him sit up, take a shower, dress, and then leave." I shook my head. "How did you lose him?"

"We aren't at liberty to say," Lynn said with a smug grin, hugging her tablet to her chest.

"In other words, you don't know."

"It's under investigation," Agent Winsome said with a glance at Lynn.

Something passed between them, because Lynn started moving her finger across her tablet, swiping in rapid fashion, her head bowed.

The Midwest Territories didn't share information with other territories. The areas formerly labeled Virginia and Maryland split in the Great War's wake. The District aggressively annexed the land from Falls Church to Silver Springs, Maryland therefore adding critical land to its territory. The Southeast Territory and the District had some heated disputes over Virginia, but they backed off when the District's governor threatened to use the Pentagon's lingering weaponry—as archaic as it was.

If it came out of the Midwest, whatever it was, mind you, it had to be pretty top-secret stuff. Their governor liked things tight and secretive.

So, how did a violator escape?

Agent Winsome continued in her smooth, but matter of fact tone. It rose an octave above the air conditioning's hum. "What we need is your skill set, one that is sorely missing in the Territory Alliance."

"My skillset?" I quirked an eyebrow. "Which one? The violence? The untrustworthiness? Or the rudeness?"

She smirked at that. "None. What we need is your connections to the violator element here, in The District. In other words, you can go places we can't. Places Nico would go."

I sighed. They wanted me to do the leg and grunt work for them.

Agent Lynn nodded at Agent Winsome's words. "The intel says he's coming back to Sector 12."

This has nothing to do with me. I didn't live anywhere near the 12. "What's the violator's name?"

"Nico Benjamin Mars," Agent Winsome answered.

"I don't know him." The name caused an itch in the back of my mind. I didn't have any dealings with anyone named Nico. Jane probably didn't either, but my memory did have its weaknesses.

"We have a team, led by me and Lynn, who are tracking him. What we need from you is to find the reason why he's coming here. Relay the intel to us." Agent Winsome held out her arm. "Here is an image of Nico."

The 3-D sprouted from her bracelet. The sharp full face rotated. Strong jaw. Full mouth and nose. Wide eyes that looked like they'd seen far too much in his life. Dark hair in shoulder-length dread-locks. A ragged scar ran across his forehead. Along his left cheek, a series of marking took over the space between his ear and his nose.

Scarification had been used to create those. I'd seen those mark-ings before. This man would not be easy to capture.

"He's not young." I remarked, thinking of my niece. "Age?"

"35." Lynn checked her tablet and then looked up. "Do not let the image fool you. He's quite smart.

"The facial markings? What do they mean?"

"We're unsure," Agent Winsome confessed.

"There are more P.I.s out there. Some with more nefarious contacts than mine." I crossed my arms over my chest.

The two agents bobbed their heads in agreement. So agreeable it made my skin itch. The uncomfortable warning spoke to their willingness to make me feel like this was some sort of honor.

It wasn't.

My rookie P.I. days had long since passed. The twilight in my hair masquerading as gray didn't come about for being foolish. Oh, but they did a brilliant job of not answering my question. They talked a lot, but the two agents had said little.

After a few rubs of her palms on her pants, Agent Winsome broke the quiet. "We selected you because I am a huge admirer of your work."

"Um, what?" I peered at her. The disbelief most likely mirrored my facial expression.

Lynn sighed in dramatic fashion. "She's been following the stories in the news files about you for months."

Agent Winsome yanked down her jacket. "Not just months. Two major political and high-profile cases solved within this last year. I still remember the governor's case with the souped-up hatchling serum, The Change, a while back. Right?"

"Yeah. Right." My mouth tasted like I'd been chewing leftover tofu. The Change had destroyed the love of my life, introduced me to Trey, and cast me into the spotlight. "Look, agents—"

"I have been following your career since I joined the T.A.," Agent Winsome said. "I admire trendsetters in the field, blazing paths for us to follow."

Did she just call me old?

Well, I *was* waxing poetic about my wisdom and age. What bothered me more was the contradiction. Didn't she come in talking about my rudeness and flair for firing my laser gun at folks? But now, with forked tongue, Agent Winsome admired my work?

This whole thing reeked like the Atlantic Ocean's contaminated banks or the Sector 10 sewer system.

As if to fill the silence, Agent Winsome rushed forward. "But, you're the best P.I. in The District. That's why we want you."

Agent Winsome's round face remained closed off but attempted to be professional. My concern locked on to Lynn. No way she believed a word of the newer agent's words.

That made two of us.

I looked back to Agent Winsome. Outside my office, an alarm sounded, and then sirens wailed. We all stood quiet a few moments while it roared.

"Let me make sure I understand. You want me to scour The District's underbelly for intel you could find on your own or with an A.I. Am I right?"

They exchanged a look. Lynn gave a half-shoulder shrug.

It is exhausting being right *all* the time.

"In a word, yes," Agent Winsome said, breaking the hush. "The AI isn't able to provide any predictions for why Nico would come here. His wife is deceased. He doesn't have any tangible connections to The District."

That you know of. Instead, I said, "What about intangible?"

They both gaped in confusion at me. No wonder Nico remained 30 steps ahead.

"What?" Lynn lined eyebrows raised.

"You two, sit down." I pointed to the chairs in front of Kimmila's desk.

With hesitation, they eased down into the two metal folding seats. Agent Winsome perched on the edge of hers, looked ready to jump to her feet in seconds. And Lynn, well, she shifted this way and that clearly uncomfortable. Good.

I stood behind the desk and called up the District's public internet. The projected image displayed the territory's visible internet connections. A 3-D sphere covered in colorful lines bobbed above the projector. I isolated one public line and traced it to the hub of activity end users were allowed to utilize. I couldn't see what they accessed, or for how long, only that this spot contained the heartbeat of action. There were hundreds of these across The District's public sphere, not counting the private and territory ones.

"Much of our societies live on the web. It may not be the case in every territory, but it is in The District. Entire lives are choreographed from groceries to online medical care to sex. All base human needs are met here. People embedded in the intangible worlds contained here don't leave their homes for much, if anything. Even those that come outside into RL, real life, augment it. So, what if Nico's reason for returning to The District isn't tangible? What if it's in some web fantasy he thinks he needs, and the origins are here?"

"This is why we came to her! I told you." Agent Winsome exclaimed. She shot out of her seat. Then to me, "So, you'll do it!"

"That's a logical avenue to follow, Miss Lewis." Lynn inclined her head.

"No." I sat down in Kimmila's chair and canceled The District's internet sphere.

"No?" Agent Winsome wore an expression I'd seen on many people when meeting me.

Disappointment.

"You're the T.A. You have tons of resources. You won't tell me everything, then, fuck no, I'm not doing it."

Agent Lynn stood as if happy to get out of her seat. As she put her tablet away, she added to Agent Winsome. "I told you. Selfish."

Agent Winsome hadn't moved, even though Lynn reached the lobby doors. They opened in a soft hiss.

"Why?" She stared, in what could be disbelief.

It made sense. She'd played her role to perfection, so why hadn't it worked?

Because I *wasn't* born yesterday.

"I told you," I said.

"Yes, I heard, but you can help capture a violent person."

"And I could die. Plus, I'm not anyone's pawn." I'm already Fate's favorite. I wasn't going to let the T.A. use me.

"Why do you need more intel? We've given you the pertinent details." Agent Winsome scowled.

"I get to decide what's pertinent. It's my neck."

"You're about to make me lose my religion," Agent Winsome huffed.

"I have that effect on others. Don't take it personally." I offered a small grin and gestured toward the door. "Lynn is ready to go."

"Here me out," Agent Winsome said.

I held my tongue but nodded my head for her to proceed.

"You're hard to convince. I've heard this about you. Let me see if I can get clearance. If I do, would you reconsider?" Agent Winsome wrote notes on her tablet, a handheld device, much smaller than Lynn's.

"You get clearance, and I will listen. If I still say no, I'm done. No questions asked. No laser gun blasts to my back," I said. "Or I hit back in return."

Agent Winsome nodded and looked up. "Agreed. We'll be on our way, but this isn't over. We do need you. Let me talk to the higher-ups."

She turned on her heel and stalked out.

Lynn left last with a wide smirk on her face.

CHAPTER
TWO

About half an hour later, Jane, my partner-in-training, and Kimmila, Jane's partner and our office receptionist, arrived with a container of delicious and spicy aroma of curry, rice, and lentil soup. They caught me waiting with my arms folded, still seated in the receptionist's chair. The "fast" trip down to Zipperz didn't go quite as they told me it would. They'd been gone for over an hour.

"Slow service?" I asked, voice set to stern.

"Robots," Jane said with a shrug.

"Robots." I repeated, draping the word with complete and utter disgust it deserved.

Not that I didn't think robots would screw up an order or several. I did. My trust in all things electronic, but especially bots, didn't go far. I detested them. Just last week, a robotic vacuum ran over its owner, who had broken his hip and couldn't get up. The damn thing snagged the owner's hair and ripped large swaths of scalp until someone heard his screams, forced the door open, and came in to save him.

No robots.

"Here's your soup." Jane handed it to me. Delicious, sweet surrender, but she averted her gaze. "Spoon."

"Thank you." I went to stand between their desks. "While you two were out, we had visitors."

"That's why you're crabby." Jane paused between lowering herself into her chair and standing. She looked up at me, then to Kimmila and back to me. "Did you shoot anyone?"

In her typical style of choice, Jane wore black jeans and a black tee-shirt. It read *Girls Love Best.* She wore her dreadlocks tied in a high ponytail. Her green eyes had been decorated with dark eyeliner. Her sunglasses were pushed up to the top of her hair, so it looked like her ponytail wore them.

"How can you wear all that black as hot as it is?" I asked, shaking my head. "But no, I didn't shoot anyone. You should've noticed the lack of blood splatter and laser gun holes, *inspector*."

Jane inclined her head. "I was distracted."

"Distracted will get you dead," I said.

"Yeah, so, new case?" She frowned at my advice. "Finished that boyfriend case."

"Bill the client?" I quirked an eyebrow at her with my mouth full.

"On my list of stuff to do first thing Monday," Jane said with a wide grin that spoke of an ulterior motive for the questions. "I'm done with that for now."

"Try to collect on it in person. Take the bill over there. Don't email it." I was tired of getting stiffed by rogue clients who thought my fees too high when they knew the cost up front. Retainers only went so far. Small claims court wasn't quite worth the expense.

"Got it. What's next for me?" she asked.

"For you?" I lowered my bowl. "You going solo?"

"Testing your ears. That's all." Jane smirked. "There's nothing on tap for now?"

"We do need a client." Kimmila reclaimed her chair and rolled up to her desk. In complete opposite to Jane, she wore a bright orange tank top and jean shorts. Her thick brown hair had been swept into a high bun.

"We do," Jane agreed. "Wait. Who came by?"

"The two of you want the moon." I started eating, opting to let them wait before I gave any additional information.

Jane's body language said it all—she was antsy. More distant than usual, she was hiding something. We'd been around each other enough to know or suspect when the other wasn't being exactly forthcoming. But what? Not everything in her life was my business, private inspector or not. Jane played it close to her laser-proof vest, and I'd respected it.

She'd tell me when ready or when necessary—whichever came first.

Jane leaned back in her chair and folded her hands behind her head. "The moon? Hell no! Been there. Done that. That place's toxic. You know, Cyb."

"I ain't never been," Kimmila said. "Heard the moon made folks crazy. People run in circles, like mutts chasing their tails, especially on the fake illuminated side. Lighting up the dark part of the moon had to make people lose their minds." She stopped, looked up at me, and burst into laughter.

"Does someone have a good beer buzz from lunch?" I looked at Jane for confirmation.

My partner shook her head. "Nope. Sometimes she cracks herself up."

"Speaking of crazy folks," I said under my breath and headed into my private office leaving them to their afternoon work.

What work? I had no idea. We haven't had too many clients since the replicated case. Jane and Kimmila weren't wrong. We *did* need clients.

Despite what most people believed; everything *wasn't* on the Internet.

In that case with Agent Lynn, she'd come to The District from

The Midwest Territories to capture violator Skip Saunders, a human trafficker and a real piece of shit.

Kimmila Barnes had managed to escape him and had started rebuilding her life before the bastard came here. He did some violations in The District and crossed my path while working the Irving case, which is how Agent Lynn and I met. Kimmila had helped Jane and I close a difficult, dangerous, and deadly job. She'd been tending bar when we first discovered her, and true to form, she'd been a long drink of delight for Jane ever since.

You can't judge a person by their profession.

I mean, really. What would people think of me, based upon mine?

Yeah, see, that's why I didn't toss stones at people in glass homes.

But Jane's relationship with Kimmila led to me hiring her as a receptionist.

The negative thing, well, Agent Lynn tried her best to put me, Jane, and Kimmila in the Frazier Cradle for a slew of alleged violations.

I didn't want a long sleep with a mouth full of hibernation gel and a coach's voice whispering into my subconscious to reform me.

I liked my pain. Hell, I needed it. What else could I retool to use as a weapon of justice?

When most people's lives explode in stress or drama, they gain weight or pop out a face full of zits.

Not me.

I break out in a series of personal problems.

Sections of Kimmila's mind had been broken. A psyche A.I. worked on her every Wednesday to untether from the embedded lies and the abusive conditioning.

Yet, sometimes she rolled right off the rails.

My private door hushed close, slicing off their laughter. Now in the air-conditioned drone of my office, I sat down at my own desk and ate the remaining soup. Outside, glorious sunlight poured down on The District. Wautos, wind-automobiles, and hovercrafts sped through the elevated lanes around the former capital. The sun drew people outside the way dead bodies drew flies. They wanted to interact, taste life, dance in the oozing warmth, maybe even mate with others, before giving up that socializing ghost for the inside world of the internet.

Kimmila Barnes arrived on my doorstep about three weeks ago. She'd been cleaned up and wanted a chance to do more with her life. Apparently, she'd been seeing Jane off and on since May. Encouraged by the work Jane did, she wanted to be a part of it, but yeah, I barely had enough funds to keep Jane employed. So, we agreed on a voluntary basis until she proved she could do the receptionist work.

The soup felt good going down and calmed my complaining stomach. Lynn's visit had set off my alarm and my gut kept the warning on high alert.

Who did Nico risk escaping his cradle to come here to see? Or get? I had to admit that I'd been bitten by curiosity. Newly infected, I fired up my computer. My ancient laptop eased onto the web. I pointed my interest on Nico Mars, testing the waters to see what the public had about him. The District boasted scores of mercenaries, bounty hunters, and authorized P.I.s like yours truly. Why didn't the T.A. go to the District's Regulators? They have a tactical retrieval unit (TRU) to track down violators like Nico Mars.

No, there had to be more to it. Lynn's face appeared in my memory as she left today. She knew more.

My door slid back and in walked, District Regulator, Daniel Tom, his hair plastered to his forehead from sweat. His sleek, black helmet under one of his arms.

"Lewis!" He came to a halt just at the corner of my desk. "That smells good. Curry?"

"Yeah, but it's all gone. Sorry."

My air-conditioner blew out a bunch of hot air—just like the man at my desk. No coincidence that Daniel arrived to see me. After all, Agent Lynn had just been here too. Sighing, and feeling already like I was going to regret it, I closed my laptop. The whine of the machine powering down added to the complete eeriness of it all. A tall, ebony-clad District Regulator in knee-high black boots and helmet tucked under his arm and the old-fashion office décor brought it all together. My internal warnings launched into a frenzy.

"You ever gonna update this place?" Daniel searched the room.

"No." Everything in my private office came secondhand or was here when I leased the space years ago. Newspaper and electronic clippings of various cases I had either been involved with or solved decorated the left wall. The yellowing on some of the actual paper ones had chipped and split along the edges. New jpegs had been enlarged and added with updated electronic articles. They scrolled upward in slow, casual, read-me-if-you're-bored cadence.

Kimmila had taken to updating them and transferring them to the blank wall outside the door to my private office. What she literally said was, "You know what you did. The client-to-be doesn't."

Huffing and coughing, Daniel doubled over. He took in great gulps of air.

"Cigarettes," he wheezed out. "Going to kill me."

"So glad to see the District regs have a physical fitness regimen."

"Funny, Lewis." He straightened up.

"I'm tired, achy, and really ready for this day to be over. Speak and be quick."

"Lynn can be a bit of a bitch, but she does know her stuff." Daniel put a cigarette in his mouth. "As your friend, I'm here to drop you some intel."

"Where do you keep those in that tight-fitting uniform?" I didn't even bother asking him how he knew Lynn came by my office.

He shot me a 'wouldn't you like to know' look but didn't answer as he took a drag.

"Stop hanging with the gang unit. Your language is de-evolving." I shook my head. "Why are you back in the Regulator uniform, anyway?"

"I'm undercover. I'm here about Nico Mars. She came by here. Right?"

"She asked the regulators for help." I laughed.

He paused. "You're kidding me, right?"

"I'm not in the mood for kidding."

"She came by?"

"Yeah. She came by."

I planned to ignore Lynn, but then why would she bring the case to me? Because she wanted to see my reaction. When she didn't get any, she stepped back from me a bit smug. Who was being manipulated here? Me, Daniel, or Agent Winsome?

"You know the T.A. can't come into the territory without first consulting us. We have alerts and shit now. So, Lynn had to stop by, do her courtesy thing, but she didn't ask for our assistance. No, she wanted to give us a F.Y.I."

"Wait. She didn't ask you for help. Or for assistance from TRU?"

Daniel shook his head, eyes narrowed against the smoke. "What I heard around the office is she's looking for a dangerous violator, but the kicker is he's a T.A. informant." Daniel puffed. He closed his eyes in pleasure as he sucked on the cancer stick.

"An informant," I repeated. "How you know she came to me?"

"I didn't. I do now." Daniel laughed. "All I know for sure is Lynn's been over here more than in her own damn territory—just for little ole you."

"Then she should come after me, not fabricate ways to get me killed." I put my hands on my hips.

"All things are fair in love and war." Daniel quipped and blew out a stream of smoke from the corner of his mouth. His mustache needed trimming.

"This isn't war, Daniel. We've seen war."

"It is to Lynn," he said, his tone quiet.

"If she had any idea what war looked like, she wouldn't be asking for it, especially with me."

Daniel quirked an eyebrow. "Oh, no. I've seen that look before."

"My grandmomma used to say if you don't start nuthin' won't be nuthin'." I adjusted my pug in its holster.

"Agent Lynn is a Territory Alliance agent. They operate under a whole different set of regulations. You of all people should know that. If she's got something, then it must be solid."

"As solid as cradle foam," I said.

He coughed out a laugh.

"But you didn't come down here to tell me about Lynn's little fishing expedition."

My stomach balled up into a knot at the sight of him. The high collar of the uniform hid his hatchling double-helix tattoo. All hatchlings—artificially created people—had them on their necks. Some wore them proudly, but Daniel optioned to cover his up. I doubt anyone knew he was a hatchling other than me and his ex-wife.

"No. I've got a dead body over in Sector 12." He tossed the butt of his cigarette down to the floor and grounded it out with his booted heel. His hair had grown long and curved under his collar. The helmet had matted it to the top of his head. It hung in his eyes, teasing his hazel eyes and long lashes.

"I can't, Daniel." I heard the whine in my voice and hated it.

"You can't what?" He looked at me directly then.

"Assist you. I'm beat. I'm going home." I leaned on the desk.

"You think I came here to beg you to help me?" He swore. "I mean, damn, I am an *inspector*. I came here to see you." Daniel's hurt seemed palpable. "Try to warn you about Lynn, but she got here before me."

"Look, I'm sorry. Okay?"

But he'd already turned away and started out the door. The smoky trail of a new cigarette wafting behind him.

"Wait. Did you say Sector 12?" I followed him out into the lobby.

I didn't like not knowing things, hence why I was a P.I. Knowing things brought me pleasure and currency. It was what I was good at, and what I knew well.

Daniel paused. "Yeah. I got pulled from my undercover detail to go to the scene."

"I'm coming."

He frowned. "Um, didn't you just say you can't help?"

"Yeah." I smiled. Men liked smiling.

He relaxed, erasing the frown. "Come on, but you don't talk to anyone."

Men also liked silence.

I nodded.

Jane stood up. "You're leaving?"

"Yeah, you and Kimmila should go on home," I said.

They didn't complain.

Once I reached the parking lot, I walked to my wauto. Daniel followed me to the vehicle.

"What's this about? You working a case?" Daniel switched the helmet from one arm to the other.

"No. Agent Winsome said their escaped cradler was headed to Sector 12," I said.

"The 12 is a cesspool. It doesn't mean my body is connected to your cradler," Daniel said.

"Look, can we just go? In this heat, your corpse is melting fast."

"Ewww!" Daniel made a face, but he moved quickly to his aero-cycle. He secured his helmet on his head and started the lift sequence.

I watched the rear blasters glow green, and he lifted into the air, blowing debris and discarded garbage littering the area. He took off to the elevated lanes. I set the flight sequence for my own, wauto. Once I entered the elevated ramp, Daniel's aerocycle was a black blob in the distance. My wauto struggled to keep up, being an ancient model and in need of a maintenance.

I cranked the wind channel to 10 and turned on some old school Sting music.

No point getting a better vehicle. Someone would just smash in the window, shoot laser guns into the body, or get blood all over it. Nope, this one is paid for, so I kept it.

Daniel's point about his violation and the cradler not being connected had validity. My internet search met with a dead wall of nothing. Everyone left an electronic footprint. Every. One. I couldn't find indication of a chip or pathway, but especially cradlers. Trackers are in their very bloodstream. Why couldn't Lynn find Nico? How the hell did he get out of the Midwest Cradle?

Why was he coming to The District?

So many questions. None of them belonged to me. I pushed them away. My musings didn't earn currency.

"Not my issue. Not my circus."

I kept my eyes on Daniel's aerocycle's rear blasters.

CHAPTER
THREE

I saw only legs.

Even from this distance, I noticed the body laid face up, on its back. As I followed Daniel into the apartment, dressed in our protective white jumpsuits and masks, I couldn't help but notice the blood. It decorated the foyer's walls and the telemonitor hanging a short distance in.

Despite the mask, the odor made my throat close. Nothing smelled like death in the summer. The temperature control unit appeared to have failed. The floor complained as people fanned out across the living room. The space, once vibrant and filled to the ceiling with laughter and cries, hugs and fights, loud conversations and whispered secrets, had become a tomb marred by death and the lingering odor of wet pennies.

"Damn." Daniel rubbed his face, dislodging his mask. He shoved it back into place. "Someone turned off the environmental control units."

"They knew what they were doing." I scanned the room.

I kept my voice down. Most of the vioTechs didn't question me being there. They figured I was with Daniel, so I must be legitimate.

Now, if one of Daniel's fellow supervising inspectors arrived, I would have to vanish.

Life in The 12 held the greatest of horrors, but inside this apartment had its own terrors. I surveyed the rest of the place. Gorgeous bright yellow walls with antique art hanging on the walls, not digital prints or electronic pictures. I could see the dried paintbrush strokes. A beautiful space filled with art, literature, and polished wooden furniture. It was like the owner lived in the 20th century.

Despite the exquisite décor, none of us wanted to be here. Regulators didn't come to The 12 often, except for v100s, death violations. Fear was like another person in the room. Shuffling around the shadows, slithering up the walls and slinking around corners, ever elusive and ever present. Its grisly details smeared over every surface. The deceased's photos witnessed the carnage firsthand.

The vioTechs processed the scene. A lot of v100 scenes are messy. They'd fanned out in their similar white suits. Like ants, they crawled over the scene, hoisting books, turning on electronics, and swabbing counters. The tension threated to boil over.

"The system didn't flip off in this heat?" One of the vioTechs asked. Her entire body was wrapped in protective clothing, only her eyes could be seen.

Daniel swore. "I don't think so. Rudy, check it out."

Rudy Chee nodded and rushed out. And not too soon. The dark haired, chubby regulator looked like he was ready to spill his selected lunch choice all over the violation scene.

"Rookie?"

Daniel nodded. He bent over the body. "He's covered in lacerations."

"It's like someone pushed his face through the windows pane." I pointed to the deep flesh cuts with my gloved index finger.

Then I spied shimmering lines on what remained of his face. The violator left what looked like a boot print. I followed the bloody prints to the carpet.

"Look here," I squatted down beside the victim's head. "These look like tattoos."

Daniel squinted. "Maybe. Won't be able to see more until we get him cleaned up. Clark, come capture these images."

Clark came over. She took several closeups of the face. Wordlessly, we watched, fascinated by her careful demeanor, as if the victim remained asleep and she didn't want to wake him.

I tore my gaze away. The tiny rectangular apartment reeked of death. These furnishings and art didn't fit into a tiny home in The 12. No wireless devices, no laptop or personal device to connect to the Internet.

"Quiet!" I yelled, leaping to me feet. "Quiet!"

Daniel whirled around. "Cybil!"

"Don't you hear that?"

The soft meowing pushed through the whirling, beeping, and squeaking of the vioTech's equipment. I started for the sound's origin, careful not to disturb the violation scene. All I could see in my mind was a cat eating its owner liquidating remains. It could also have evidence on it. It may provide some clues.

Daniel stood there, amusement lighting his face, making his already narrowed eyes smaller. Proof that despite the mask, he laughed at me. Bastard.

I turned my attention back to finding the cat. Unlike a dog, no amount of cooing and false cheer would convince them to come to a human being. Their skepticism about human nature was why I always considered them the best of the pet options.

The tight hallway emptied into a bedroom on the left and a bathroom on the right. I peaked in the open doors, and the meowing grew louder as I moved to the bedroom. The first responders cleared the apartment when they got the initial call. So, the doors and closets had been opened. Why didn't the cat come bouncing out when the intruders arrived?

Fear? Maybe she didn't like us being in her territory.

"Here kitty, kitty," I sang beneath my breath.

I inched into the bedroom, making sure my movements communicated my peaceful intention. Stop laughing. I *can* do peaceful.

In the bedroom, yellow eyes loomed in a sea of blackness between the bedframe and the wall. The light from the hallway poured in through the door enough to give me enough illumination to spy the black cat.

"Daniel," I called, not too loud to startle the beast. "I found something."

Daniel's heavy footsteps came into the bedroom. He flipped on the overhead light.

It was like lightning struck the cat. It screeched and shot toward my face, with claws set to ravage. I managed to grab it before it did much more than shred the mask. I held it tight against my chest.

"Whatever evidence it had is now smeared all over the suit." I said, gently rocking the creature in my arms. "It's okay. It's okay."

Daniel shook his head. "We'll bag the suit."

"And the cat?" I peered over to him.

"Clark! We got an animal here," Daniel swore as he left the room.

<hr>

WHAT FELT LIKE HOURS LATER, I remained sitting on the curb. I'd been ejected from the crime scene, my white suit taken as potential evidence. Daniel was being fussed at by his superior for letting a P.I. into a violation scene, and I wanted to shoot someone. Most people used their Friday evenings for fun things, like dancing, aerocycle racing, and heavy robotic petting down in the Red Zone district.

Instead, the cat and I had been ordered not to leave. I knew that if each of us took off, one of us wouldn't be found again. The cat had been crated and it sat beside me, glaring at everything that moved.

A kindred spirit.

The regulators finished canvassing in the wee hours of the morn. Worn. Weary. Weathered. They cornered off the apartment and left for sweeter air and on to the warm arms of their families. A stranger death violation occurred so infrequently in these parts; I suspected the victim knew their attacker. Death rolled out of the apartment and above the sickly odor of leftover garbage, vomit, and poverty, as if rising from a thick mist.

"I don't even care about this violation scene. I don't even know why I'm here." I mumbled it just loud enough for the cat to hear, and so folks didn't think I was crazy.

"All right, Lewis," Daniel said from behind me.

I brushed the debris from my pants. "Can I go now?"

"Yeah." He lit his cigarette and peered at me through the haze. "Anything connect to your case?"

"It isn't my case. It's Lynn's." I shrugged. "I don't even know why I came down here."

"You didn't agree to help?"

"No."

"Imagine, you being uncooperative." Daniel hacked out a cough.

"No currency. No case." I spied Daniel's supervisor, a Black man with a bald head and a scowl. He made a beeline to us. "Later."

Daniel bent down and snatch up the cat carrier. "You're forgetting something."

I stopped. "No. I don't do pets."

"You found *her*. Finders keepers." Daniel thrust the cage toward me.

"You got all you need from it?"

"Clark already took hairs and samples." He nodded at it. "She's yours. I mean you heard her, and she marked your face. You definitely belong to her."

I hesitated. I didn't need a cat. My strange hours meant no routine for the thing. Her yellow eyes peered out from the cage. Alert, she watched everything.

I waved Daniel off. "Just let her out."

Before I changed my mind, I hurried to my wauto.

I had the coordinates plugged in for home when I heard it.

Meow.

Damn it.

Daniel stood outside my pilot's side door. He rotated his fingers for me to lower the window. In his other hand, he held the cat's crate.

I did as he wanted. The cat's crying had penetrated the window's protection anyway.

"She'd stop crying if you let her out of that crate." I hovered. The wauto blew air from its bottom blasters. I had to raise my voice. "Just let her out!"

"Look. She needs a home. She had a home and some bastard came in and took it from her." Daniel blew the smoke through his nose.

"Then take her home with you."

"No can do. I'm undercover, remember. I'm not even staying at my place."

I glared at him. "I don't do litterboxes."

"Get a robotic one." He shrugged.

"You aren't making a case here, Daniel."

"Look. I will take her back when this undercover work is done. Okay?" Daniel lifted the crate up to the window. "Babysit her for a little bit."

The ebony cat stared out with wide eyes and hunched down on all fours. She wanted out of there.

"I can keep her until you're done," I said.

He pondered before nodding in agreement. "Okay. Great."

I took the container as if Daniel handed me a miniature nuclear reactor. The supervisor stood behind Daniel.

"Isn't that cat evidence in this death violation?" He approached. His badge name read Jamison Reed.

Tall, thick like a side of fatback bacon my grandma used to have before she lost her farm, and sporting a well-groomed beard, Jamison's voice didn't thunder as one might expect. It was crisp and professional.

Daniel shifted to face him. "Clark already pulled samples and swabbed her."

Jamison looked at me. "I don't want to see you at another violation scene, Lewis."

"You won't." *I shouldn't have been at this one.*

I put the crate beside me in the passenger seat. "Goodnight Daniel. Jamison."

Jamison grimaced. Daniel dropped what remained of his cigarette and grounded it out with this boot's toe. "We'll connect later."

Jamison scowled harder.

Not wanting to hear any more of the ass-chewing Daniel was getting, I raised the window and started toward home. What had gotten into me? Racing to a violation scene that didn't have any connection to currency, cuddling a cat, and now, cat-sitting this one while Daniel was on assignment.

Is this how a midlife crisis happened?

"Meow," the fluffy little furball cried.

"You agree, huh? Well, let's give you a name."

The ebony creature sat in her crate. She'd stopped crying. This *meow* had a different tone altogether.

To my horror, I had nothing. I'd named my smaller laser gun 'pug', but for the cat I had nothing.

Nothing at all.

CHAPTER
FOUR

"What the hell is that?" Jane stood at the alcove where our coffee maker delivered deliciousness. She put down her mug beneath the spout and pointed at the cat's crate with her spoon. With her hair pulled up into a high ponytail, her features sharpened. She wore a black tee-shirt with dark jeans and white sneakers. The shirt's sleeves showed off her hardened biceps.

"A cat." I placed her on Kimmila's desk. "Followed me home yesterday and here we are."

I didn't like, nor was I used to, not having both hands free. Kimmila shot up from the desk as if I'd put down a hand grenade.

"Like an animal? A pet?" Kimmila inched closer. Her delicate face broke into a big smile. She wore big hoop, silver earrings with her dark hair free. She had hair that didn't straighten but wasn't quite curly either. The strands fell in waves, crashing down to her shoulders. She wore a summer dressed adorned with big tulips in soft lavender against a black background.

"Where did you get it?" she stuck her fingers into the crate and cooed.

"You didn't shoot it?" Jane said, smirking as she carried her steaming mug and lowered herself into her chair. "It *is* alive. Right Kimmila?"

"You're still alive, right?" I replied.

She laughed. "And so are you."

"You say something?" "You know you'd be dead without me." Jane slurped her coffee.

"You'd be unemployed," I retorted.

She inclined her head. "Touché."

The soft mewling emitting from the cage interrupted us. The beast had taken a liking to Kimmila. She crouched down in front of the crate and softly pawed at Kimmila's fingers. She'd kept me up most of the weekend, whining and crying. She did manage to eat some food, but most of the time she slept. I kept her confined to my bedroom and the litterbox in my small bathroom.

Seeing as my profession involved handling other people's crap, you would think I would be fine cleaning a litterbox.

I am not.

As a result the weekend blinked by in a blur.

Monday seemed to be up to its usual candor and tricks. *Go me!*

"Does she belong to anyone?" Kimmila glanced up at me over her shoulder.

"Daniel. She belongs to him." I didn't want to get into the backstory.

Jane swiveled her chair to face me. "Why you? You're not good with living things."

I shrugged. "Dunno.

Jane laughed. "Uh huh. You owed him a favor."

"I'm good with people when they're not trying to kill me."

Jane chuckled into her coffee. "Sure."

I disappeared into my office, leaving Jane and Kimmila to handle the cat. As the door to my private office closed, I saw Kimmila open the crate. Soon, little miss black furball would be running all over the lobby.

I sat down at the laptop and opened the email Daniel sent to me with the embedded code. I got the computer to decode it. We had both been in the same regimen in the Army, back during the Moon Colony Wars. We developed a code, one only we knew. The cipher had been locked in my brain.

In theory, Daniel's regulator work had been labeled undercover, but they had pulled him out to go assess the violation scene before Jamison took over. Something political and strange was at work, but I didn't want to know any more than necessary. Daniel promised to keep me in the loop about the victim, despite him being in the outer ring of the case himself.

The audio message unfolded with a paperclip attached to it. I clicked the paperclip, and a document unfolded on the screen along with an image of the victim.

"Nice. A copy of the coroner's preliminary report." Daniel had indeed come through in a big way. "With images!"

I scooted to the edge of my chair.

The victim's name was Henrietta Mayfield. *The* Henrietta Mayfield, prolific activist in The 12. They'd washed the blood from her face, and I could see her more clearly. The bruising and beating she took indicated someone furious with her. Across her forehead and vertically down her cheeks, she had navy tattooing edged with what appeared to be gold. She wore her hair close cut to the scalp, because what scalp slouched off didn't have a lot of hair attached to it.

Despite this, I could see the activist had been someone they wanted destroyed and then discarded. The medical examiner left the cause of death as blunt force trauma. There had been a laser gunshot too. Small one. To the back of her head. It'd been covered by all the blood. Daniel's notes stated the scene might have been staged.

I looked away from the screen. Henrietta Mayfield had been a pillar of Sector 12, an advocate for compassion and dignity, and an absolute outspoken critic of regulator corruption. What little good came from The 12, Henrietta made it happen.

And now she was gone.

According to the report, the markings were digital tattoos. Gold circuits had been applied to them. Digital tattoos were waterproof, flexible, and held information. Tiny electrodes recorded and transmitted data. I found it interesting how her home lacked all but the basic digitalization, but she wore it on her face.

The regulator's reader didn't pull up anything from the tattoos. It could explain why Henrietta's face suffered so much damage. Someone wanted those messages deleted and they tried to beat them out of her face.

Across her chest, tiny scars created a decorative marking around each breast. Scarification, an ancient African culture of tattoos and beautification. No one did this anymore.

Except now I'd seen two people with it. Nico Mars and Henrietta.

What did it all mean?

Why did I care?

I shoved myself back into the chair, closed the laptop, and rubbed my eyes.

"Computer. Play Parker Mao lecture, January 15, 2019."

Without really thinking about it, I spun up the lecture from Parker Mao, 21st century revolutionary and speaker. She'd died in the Moon Colony Wars.

"Victimhood is a state of mind!" a holographic, three-dimensional Parker Mao shouted.

The echo reverberated through my small office. The next-door neighbor pounded on the wall. "Turn it down!"

I ignored them. There are laser gun holes in my wall for a reason.

Parker Mao, motivational guru, hailed from the Southwest Territories. Dressed in authentic Dine dress and complete with shoulder-length black hair, her holographic projection flickered as my private office door opened.

"Jane..."

I stopped and looked down.

"Meow."

Without missing a beat, the cat hopped through the hologram and into my lap. The skinny creature pawed at my hand for petting. I obliged and turned my attention to the window.

The playlist my sister sent via email held more of the same—motivational programs from various speakers across the territories. I admired my sister's enthusiasm to keep me occupied since I didn't have a romantic partner.

If I squinted hard enough, I could spy the remnants of downtown D.C. The older structures that escaped the sacking of 2100 were being rebuilt. I liked the World War II Memorial, even though most of it was a ghost town, former soldiers lingered there still. There was talk about a Moon Colony War Memorial, but the governor couldn't find the currency and tabled it for future discussions

Hallmarks of The District's past sprinkled the ten-mile former capital like hollowed husks of a once fruitful garden. The governor and senate council operated out of a building on Pennsylvania Avenue. The White House had been obliterated and the capitol building, although still standing, had been assaulted and abandoned. They remained as testaments to our past, our violent nature, and our inability to live in peace.

"This is your life! Fight for it!" Parker Mao railed, arms pumping up and down.

I turned my attention back to the hologram.

"Halt program." Parker froze, mouth ajar, her face configured for maximum emotional motivation. "Computer, close program."

Parker Mao spoke true words.

"I need a life." I stood, sending the cat to the floor. "And food."

I stepped into the outer lobby and discovered Jane had left.

"Where's Jane?" I asked Kimmila, who sat with her legs crossed at the desk, laptop lowered, smoking. She had her smoking foghog at the corner of the desk. It sucked the awfulness down into its belly, filtered it, and then sent cleaner air out of the base.

"She said something about going to collect from that one client."

"I'll catch up with her later. I'm going to lunch." I gestured toward the lobby doors. "Cat's okay with you?"

From behind the cigarette, Kimmila peered at me. "You don't like me."

I shrugged. "It's just a cat. You seemed excited earlier."

"It doesn't have anything to do with the cat. Cat's fine with me." Kimmila took a drag. "But, I know you don't care for me. You don't trust me."

"I don't trust anyone," I said. "Don't take it personally."

Her narrow shoulders rose and lowered. "Hard way to live a life."

"You know all about hard living. Don't you?"

She flinched.

"Look, I hired you." I gestured to the lobby.

"That was for *her*, not me." Her voice sounded like broken glass.

"Benefits you, though." My honey-level lowered in steady drops with each word out of her mouth.

For Jane's sake, I'd hidden my impression of Kimmila from her. Some people deserved second chances.

And some people didn't.

Maybe I hadn't hidden it as well as I thought.

Kimmila drew back from my stare. She didn't want to hear about my feelings about her. People often say they want the truth, but what they really want is affirmation of their own ideas. Not the same thing.

"Look. If you want this talk, I can serve it to you." I put my hands in my pockets.

She held up her hand. Scars decorated them. With a smoky wave, she shook her head. "No, no. Forget it." She scooped the cat up into her lap. "But I know."

"You only think you do," I said as I cast a sweeping glance over the office.

As I stalked down the hallway, I noted my still fuming attitude. Kimmila rubbed a raw nerve. Now, my honey levels threatened to bottom out. Monday afternoon pushed on toward sunset. I walked out of the building and into a wall of heat.

July is the undisputed hottest month of the year. The last few days knitted together as a humid, sticky quilt of misery. The damp pressure smothered you and kept its hand around your throbbing throat, applying just enough pressure to leave you tittering on the rim of consciousness. Yeah, southern summer is a sadistic bitch.

A single drop of sweat quickly shot down between my breasts and plowed into my already damp bra's fabric. Overhead the blazing sun stretched out its rays as if enraged that I hadn't fled to the surrounding trees or back inside the building for shade and blessed relief.

My laser gun remained on full display as I refused to wear anything to cover it. Heck, the tank top I sported was a stretch, but public nudity violated the quadrant's decency regulation. Sunglasses hid my eyes, but my weapon stuck out in my shoulder holster. I didn't want to see any more regulators for a long, long while—including Daniel. So, I made sure it had been powered off.

I went three rows over to my waiting wauto. I unlocked the doors, got in, and initiated the flight sequence.

I wanted food and I wanted to know why Agent Lynn thought I would give two damns about Nico. I lifted off and set my mind to autopilot, just like the wauto. The District unfolded miles below me. The elevated lanes threatened to clog up, but I managed to slip over to my section of the territory without so much as a jam.

That should've been an omen right there.

CHAPTER
FIVE

Seated at my favorite table at Big Mike's Jazz Bar, I awaited my lunch special, toast, jalapeno jelly, and coffee, black. The swarm of working professionals buzzed in the bright light that rolled in from windows. Big Mike's was cooler than out in the summer heat. The place provided delicious food and drinks for not a lot of currency. Big Mike didn't have meat on the menu, but not many restaurants did. Threading out animal mutations took time and cost a lot.

I couldn't risk it. I liked how Big Mike still hired human and hatchling servers-no bots and paid his employees a good wage. It worried me seeing so many professionals here. I hope the menu didn't change to include those upscale, revised versions of his traditional favorites. Big Mike came from a southern territory background mixed with some traditional Americana like spaghetti and lasagna.

My server, Bryan, came by and placed the basket of rye toast on the table. He sighed as he set down the coffee and put his hand on his hip. Once he stuck his tray under his other arm, he pursed his lips and tsked me.

"Cybil, this isn't a lunch." He gestured to the toast and the coffee.

"I'm not that hungry." I took out my handheld. "You know, the heat."

"Yeah, I get it. You want a port-in-the-storm? It'll cool you off." He brushed a loose braid behind his ear, revealing a dazzling pair of diamond stud earrings. Those didn't come cheap or from working at Big Mike's. He wore a tight purple tee-shirt, synthetic black shorts, and sneakers. He had great running legs, all lean muscle and smooth skin.

"Nah, I'm good. Thank you for looking out." I booted up my handheld and tried to get my thoughts down.

I pulled my stylus out of my satchel. My tablet allowed me to write. Sure, most people could do the talk to text, or verbal recording, but for me, writing worked out best. Plus, it helped me keep my information private. Talk to text or voice recording always ran the risk of being overheard. Not good for a *private* inspector.

I pressed my thumbprint into the space for thumbs and said, "Cybil Lewis". It booted up and a white, electronic blank sheet appeared. Using the attached pen, I dated the top of the electronic page, July 13, 2147.

My sprawling script translated to legible Courier 10-point font.

As I did with every new case, I started taking notes.

True, I didn't have an active job, but this could turn into one. My memory wasn't foolproof, and I've found over the years taking detailed notes made solving cases easier and more manageable.

Before I could ask, Bryan placed a thin handheld—the bill on the table. I double-checked the tally and settled the tab with a few swipes of my thumb, which drafted funds out of my bank account with speed that bothered me. It took a hell of a lot longer to earn the currency than it did for me to spend it.

I've got to learn how to cook.

Just because it's automatic and computerized didn't make it infallible.

For example, some people trust robots without fail.

I don't.

And no, I'm not paranoid about humanoids, but just the other day, I read an online article about a robotic taxi driver that kept a customer in rotation for four hours around the Washington Monument. The damn thing tried repeatedly to eject the passenger, but the seats malfunctioned.

It saved his life.

Turning my attention to important things, I tossed in some raw cut sugar and sipped my coffee. No dairy sucked.

1. Agent Lynn wants help locating some violator from the Midwest Territories. Nico.
2. Need paying client.

Swell. For once I wished the Fates would spare me a little slack. This inspector business was always feast or famine. A few high-profile jobs kept us from starving and let me hire Kimmila.

I wrote for a while, my pen hardly stopping to ponder before I gave up. The stylus glided as ideas, suggestions, random thoughts poured out from me and into the tablet's active file.

Leaving it alone for a while, I bit into the crunchy toast made sweet heat by the jelly. I chased it with coffee. The day was looking up. Monday might prove to be a rather productive day after all.

"There you are," the chair across from me scraped the floor and I bolted up in my seat, fishing for my gun.

Jane tossed me an uneasy smile as she sank into the opposite seat and signaled the waiter for a beer. Bryan threw his hand up in acknowledgment.

Only a little after two o'clock. I'd been there longer than I thought.

"Been lookin' all over for you," she said, snagging a bronze-brushed foghog from the neighboring table without getting up—a skill for circus performers. "You didn't answer your telemonitor at home. Check Padre's Gym. Finally thought you might be here."

"It's lunch time or well, it was." If I had become predictable, I needed to evaluate my routines.

Jane lit her cigarette with all the grace of a well-practiced user. "You been here since when?"

"11."

Jane squealed in mock sarcasm. "Gods, you're even drinking coffee still."

She pointed at my lukewarm cup of Joe.

"A woman's drink," she accused.

"I am a woman," I said in mock surprise.

Jane grinned.

Though we spoke in kind, polite noise, beneath the headiness lay a coiled snake of stress. Around me Big Mike's had emptied its patrons and diners out into the sweltering Monday afternoon. The earlier patrons had left during my intense journaling.

"Why are you here?"

"Well, two things," she held up two fingers. "One, I sent Kimmila home for the day. Two, she took the cat."

The words lacked any anger or aggression. They were merely statements of facts. She stopped talking as Bryan dropped off her Peck beer.

"Thanks," she said to him.

"I was wondering if you was gonna show up." He laughed and removed his PDA. "Whatcha havin'?"

"A refill." My stomach bunched into tight coils.

"Not you, Cybil." Bryan scolded. "Jane?"

Jane thought about it. "Rigatoni with tomato sauce."

"At least somebody's eatin' and takin' care of themselves." Bryan fixed me with a glare before leaving to go put in the order.

I laughed.

After he left, I waited for Jane, who peeled the labeling from the cold Peck beer, to tell me the real reason she flew down to Big Mike's. The wet ribbons spiraled the length of the bottle and onto the table. Her eyes studied it as if the meaning of life lay within the depths of its hunter green and caramel stripes.

"So, while you were out, Agent Lynn came by the office," Jane said, pulling a cigarette pack from her pocket. The hard-shell packaging kept the fragile tobacco from crumbling when shoved into pockets. Tobacco was expensive. Few areas could grow it naturally and the tobacco-synthetics had a strange aftertaste.

"Oh?" Now, she piqued my interest. "You should've led with that."

I tapped lightly on the table. The metal table gave off a *ping*.

Jane nodded.

"She just asked if you were in. Kimmila told her no, and she left." Jane shrugged.

"She say anything to Kimmila?" I asked. Agent Lynn had tried to arrest Kimmila, so they have a history.

Jane alternated between drinking, smoking, and talking.

"She wanted to know why she wasn't in a cradle," Jane said with a grimace.

"And?"

"I said, because I said so," Jane replied with a shrug. "Kimmila isn't going anywhere."

I peered over my coffee. She said those words with such conviction, it made me pause. Jane's attitude about Kimmila must be dealt with if she was going to be any help to me. With a fast prayer to the Fates, I hoped she'd get over her infatuation with the older woman and former addict.

At the risk of sounding like a disapproving parent, I wanted Jane to move on to someone who deserved her. Kimmila had been through a lot and broken people often broke *other* people.

"Here you go." Bryan dropped off Jane's meal.

He also gave me a fresh coffee before zooming off to other tables.

"Look, Agent Lynn is hovering around me for a reason. Are you sure Kimmila's not selling us out?" I put it out there so it would quit gnawing on my inside.

Jane stiffened. She drank from her bottle of Peck but avoided eye contact. Occasionally, she eyed the patrons, no doubt practicing her surveillance skills.

I waited her out as she internalized the question.

"Aren't you the suspicious one?" Jane leaned her forearms onto the table, making it tilt in her direction.

"You know me, right?"

"No, she's on the narrow."

"How do you know?" I spoke softly, not questioning her as much as questioning *them*.

"I just do."

"How?" I replied, working hard to sound neutral. "You aren't allergic to floatation gel, are you?"

She frowned for a moment. Then the connection lit up her hazel eyes.

"I'm not going to the cradle, and neither are you."

"Agent Lynn is here for a reason. Agent Winsome could've come alone or they could've got the TRU involved. Why is she looking for me?"

Jane's head snapped up at the thick line of sarcasm. "It sounds like she's here for *you*, not Kimmila. There is an escaped violator running lose in The District. It could really be as simple as that, Cyb. Not everything is so damn melodramatic."

"Did she tell you that?" Jane sounded like Kimmila.

She smiled, but it withered fast. "Look, I hear things. You know? Plus, Kim wouldn't do that to me. She wouldn't relapse because she loves her life—her current one."

My inspector instincts went wild. The whole thing was too clean and squeaky. Perhaps it was the expression on my face.

"Why?"

"Why?" Jane frowned.

"Yeah. Why is she doing it? For you? What does she get out of it.?"

"Get out of it? She's living clean. I mean, she gets improved health, complexion, mental care." Jane gave me a half-shrug and smoked. "Okay, see, she told me about the bug in Lynn's hard drive, but she'd been cleared of all violations."

"Just like that?"

Jane nodded. "Yeah. Just. Like. That."

"It doesn't follow." I nearly broke out in hives. "Lynn had her on a ton of violations, especially with her former trafficker."

"Why doesn't it follow?" Jane's voice grew hard. "It follows like a well programed robot."

This line of conversation threatened to erupt into a full fledge row, but I wasn't dropping it. The whole thing reeked to the moon colonies. Jane had lied to me before over Kimmila. I bet my pug she was now, too.

"No, it doesn't. A bot? You put your fucking trust in a former junkie?" I lowered my volume and used calm I didn't feel before continuing. "Why are you trusting what she tells you rather than investigate yourself and make damn sure she isn't a mole for the T.A.? How did she escape those violation charges?"

I bit back my other thought. Jane needed to have time to think on my words and respond.

Jane's eyes left my ever-heated blaze and drifted over to the empty, dark stage.

Kimmila had to get something out of the dropped violation charges. What? I've seen violators, hell, I worked ass deep in them and none did anything without some sort of payment.

Kimmila was no different.

"I trust her, Cyb. She's loves me," Jane whispered, barely clearing the kitchen noise bouncing out from the back. "And I love her."

I sighed, and it seemed to push against the table's tense air. A numbness spilled from my head down to my feet. When all the kind-ness, polite noises, and excuses were stripped and laid bare, the truth remained.

My Jane was in love.

Jane sat still. "I ain't gonna let your trust issues rain all over me. Just cause you shoot down every person who tries to love you doesn't mean I will."

"Fuck this," I swore and got up from the table. I nodded at Big Mike .

As I slipped out of the food-stained air to the sweet, sun-kissed afternoon, I thought I heard Jane call my name. It didn't matter.

A lot happened since the Irving case, and the only thing I wanted to do was put that puppy to bed. I didn't like loose ends and Kimmila was definitely loose. I brought her on at Jane's request, but it was also a bit of payback for us tearing up her life.

That didn't mean I trusted her.

Jane's personal business didn't fit into the day-to-day business. I didn't like it when she prodded into my personal life. So why peak into hers? I'm not denying I yearned to look in Jane's love life; however, some things you just don't do.

Besides, Kimmila had given her testimony for the Irving case against Skip Saunders. She did her part to put him in the cradle.

Why did this bother me so much?

My gut burned in protest, warning me.

I should've listened.

I let out a breath.

Trust.

Jane's deception tore into my faith in her like a toxin through cattle.

Jane and Kimmila.

My protégé had essentially unlearned or turned off all the skills she'd acquired from me because of a love interest.

A beer wouldn't solve any of this, but it would make me feel better.

CHAPTER
SIX

The crunch of minuet gravel forced my hand to my pug before he breathed. I hadn't even thought about it; the practice had become automatic.

"Cybil," called a voice from the space between Big Mike's building and his neighbor. The sound slithered out from the shadows and right into the front of my pug.

"Show yourself!" The hairs on my neck stood in alarm. I searched the area around my wauto, seeking out, and identifying the now gloomy images that sprung from the gloom.

After a few heartbeats, Bryan inched forward, a drink in his hand, and his lipstick perfect. His apron bore stains, but somehow still looked like it was part of his outfit. He waved my pug away as if it had been a magic wand and not a lethal weapon.

"Put that away," he said.

"You shouldn't sneak up on folks." I slipped the pug back into its holster. "Especially in this territory."

"The entire District is under surveillance most of the time, by *someone*, so I don't wanna be seen with you out here. I like breathin'."

Bryan scanned the area before turning back to me and inching further into the alley. "I gotta tell you this."

"I don't talk business on the street. Feel free to come to my office like a normal potential client, and maybe I'll give you some of my time."

"It's important!" Bryan hissed but stopped short of touching me. "It'll be quick."

"Okay. Okay. Speak on." I gave in because he'd given me good intel in the past.

Bryan sighed noisily. "There was a killing over in The 12. Word is the woman was beaten bad."

"The info was in the news files," I said, with a roll of my eyes. I started for my wauto.

"Wait!" Bryan waved me back. "The woman was sector activist, Henrietta Mayfield. Word is one of the breeders had her snuffed, a regulator."

"A reg that's a breeder. You sure?"

"I mean, it's all rumor, but yeah."

Henrietta Mayfield worked as a sector activist in the 12, mainly fighting against human trafficking and drug dealing. She fought to keep the violator element at bay. The District had a thriving underbelly full of sex trafficking, drug dealing, and illegal human augmentation.

Just like the beasts of old, malleable teens who had been trafficked and sold were labeled like cattle, heifers, cows, bulls, studs, etc. Breeders branded them with their unique insignia in case one of them wandered off or tried to escape. They pumped their stock with Ackback, meth, and other drugs. Despite the number of sexbot sales, some people required the warmth of human skin. Breeders filled those needs, and used people like toilet paper.

That's what Henrietta and others like her fought against.

The acidic taste on my tongue turned my stomach.

"Not a domestic violation."

"Nope." His big smile broadened knowing he had, at last, snagged my attention. "That's the word."

"Who is the breeder?" I peered at him. I liked information, but when freely given it made me pause. It also made me question all of it.

"Dunno."

"You're bullshitting me."

Bryan shook his head. "Look, how long I been knowing you?"

"Awhile."

"I know how trigger happy your ass is. I don't mess with you." Bryan drank some of his water. It was clear, and it didn't smell like gin. Probably water.

"Who told you I would be interested?" I closed the distance between us. "Who you working for?"

I slipped my hand around the pug's handle and inched it out.

Bryan bit his lower lip, pulling it between his teeth. He stood rigid and quiet. Arms folded, he rested his drink on his forearm. "Cyb…"

"Jane just wasted all the patience I had left. Tell me." I removed the pug, giving it clear birth to act when needed.

"Do you know how much I'm risking even telling you?" Bryan whispered back, eyes wide as saucers. "Think. A regulator is a breeder on the low. You know how dangerous that is."

I gave a small nod. "You already started. So finish."

"If something happens to me, who will serve you your favorite coffee?" Bryan blinked, long lashes fluttering.

"Lakshmi."

My reply probably appeared on my face, although I remained silent.

His smile waned. "Okay. Sorry. Look, I will give you this, but this is all. Every damn thing I know."

I replaced the pug for the second time in the last ten minutes. "Good."

Bryan pursed his lips, sighed, and then told me what I wanted to know. "Down in The 12, there's a humming about Miss Henrietta's death violation. There's a family member, a big-time violator coming back to settle things and to slaughter everyone who helped send 'em down."

"Who is it?"

"Dunno his real name. Folks keep calling him, Nqobile."

"It's Zulu. Meaning they conquer."

Bryan shushed me. "Not so loud. Sure, the governor runs The District, but Nqobile ran *The 12*."

"What's his real name?" I was skeptical.

Before I could ask any more questions, Big Mike stuck his head out the alleyway entrance. "Bryan! Table 15's order is ready! Break's over."

"Gotta go!" Bryan hurried off.

The door hushed closed, punctuating the end of the strange conversation.

Once back in my wauto, I set the flight sequence. In the long, agonizing history of using people as property, you'd think breeders would be a horrifying practice to The District's citizens. Sex work remained the world's oldest profession. The system dehumanized people, and I hated it. There were empowered people who worked as sex workers and I fully support their business endeavors. It's the breeder system I despised and so did Henrietta Mayfield.

But, like just about everything else, capitalism turned people into profits, and somehow made it palatable. For many, as long as the benefits hit their currency accounts, but the horrible filth didn't, they were good.

I wasn't.

I punched in the coordinates for home and I let myself think about Bryan's clue. Henrietta probably got in the wrong person's face. People violated for less. But investigating anything in The 12 would be daunting. The hostile sector belched up poverty and violations as easy as breathing. I've had cases in The 12 before. I almost didn't make it out. They don't deal well with outsiders either.

I don't take cases in The 12 anymore.

Nico Mars returning to The 12. Could he the notorious Nqobile? I didn't like coincidences. I didn't trust them.

I shifted my thinking about something more concrete.

Jane.

Jane and Kimmila.

My partner-in-training didn't lie when she said I had major trust issues. I didn't choke on regret, though, and the fact I kept rolling forward didn't always sit comfortably with others. Relationships were causalities of my line of work. Collateral damage, if you will. The storybooks never could explain my problem or how to fix it. The happy-ever-after didn't last beyond a few years before it burst into an all-consuming flame and then turned into ash.

A long trail of would-be and former suitors littered the emotional path behind me. I had to go ahead with my life. Jane appeared to be doing the same, but it bothered me who she'd chosen to take with her.

Deciding to switch off my heart's bleating and focus on puzzling out what Agent Lynn wanted, I mentally pivoted again. Jane could be right. Maybe the T.A. was only focused on their escaped violator.

At this my telemonitor lit up. Only a little after three in the afternoon, who could it be? Potential customer? Not on my private I.P.

"Ah, there you are." Agent Winsome's gorgeous skin and flawless make-up appeared in the telemonitor's viewscreen. She smiled like the cat that ate the canary, and leaned in close, like she wanted to whisper a secret.

Co-conspirators, she and I.

"I wanted to update you. I met with the higher-ups today. They've agreed to allow me to bring you on fully to the investigation." She smiled. It stretched from one ear to the other as if she'd announced I had won limitless currency for the rest of my natural life.

"What does that mean, exactly?" I used to be a regulator. I couldn't trust them as far as I could see them.

The skepticism in my tone torched the grin right off her face. She sighed with a huff and leaned back from the screen. Murmurs emitted from behind her.

"It means you are now privy to all the same information I am."

"Does that mean they're going to censor what they tell you?"

She paused with a slight frown.

"So, you don't share it with me?" I don't know what Agent Winsome agreed to or gave up to have me on her team, but one thing was certain-I do not work well with a handler.

"Everyone here is committed to finding Nico and putting him back to sleep." Winsome's words held purpose and it made me sit up straighter in my bucket seat. "I don't do politics. I do my job, Miss Lewis."

"You got an office in The District?"

"Yes. We're set up at Regulator Headquarters."

"Agent Lynn?" I asked.

"Following up on a lead at the moment."

"Look, let's meet for dinner. Bring the case file, and I will consider it. If you got time tonight."

She brightened. "That sounds great. You know a good place?"

"How do you feel about Italian food?"

"Great. Send me the coordinates and I will meet you there. Let's say six?"

"Six." I agreed.

I sent her the coordinates to Big Mike's before logging off. I had about two hours to shower, change clothes, and get myself together before the meeting. Despite my best intentions of not getting involved with anything for Agent Lynn, I couldn't deny the strong connection to Agent Winsome. Her drive, commitment, and nature captivated me. No, she *intrigued* me.

How did Nico manage to escape from a Cradle facility?. The chase was an incredible rush. My hands itched to get active again. We'd talk compensation tonight.

Winsome had cracked open the door and I had no issue walking through it.

Nothing like running face first into the unknown.

CHAPTER
SEVEN

At six o'clock I sat once again in my favorite seat at Big Mike's Jazz Bar and Restaurant. I put my satchel beside me. Tucked into a weathered and ripped leather four-person booth, I had a good view of the stage. A new act set up their instruments. The lead singer was a woman named Raven. Her band called themselves The Wings, and each member had a catchy name, Eagle, Falcon, Crowe, and of course, Raven herself. They sang saucy jazz, spirited and heated from the 20th century, which was why they played Monday through Saturday nights. The other acts had been rescheduled to days or worse, Sunday night.

Bryan arrived at my table, his face grim beneath the fall of bangs and glittery eyeshadow. He pursed his tinted lips, sighed, and asked, "What can I get you?"

"What's wrong with you? Someone forgot to tip?" I gave him my full attention.

"The usual. Mike's upset about the last pan of lasagna. Said he scorched it and when he is annoyed, he gets at us." Bryan offered a small shrug of sympathy. He paused, looked at my blouse. "You meeting someone?"

I nodded.

"A date?" Bryan's face softened. "'Cause good ole Jane doesn't bring out your pretty."

"No. Not a date." I fidgeted.

"You sure?"

"Yeah. I'm pretty sure."

"Your dress and body language are spilling your secrets," Bryan said.

"Not. A. Date. I'll start with a port-in-the-storm." I had a feeling I was going to need it.

Bryan laughed. "Already put the order in with the bartender."

With that he left to go check on other tables and retrieve my drink. On the stage, the Wings struck the beginning chords of the club's favorite, "Mike's Moneymakin' Melody."

I watched the room. Not as busy as lunch time, but most tables and booths held patrons. Low conversations hummed beneath the band's music and Raven's vocals. Some bobbed their heads. Others snapped their fingers to the smooth groove. The place smelled of garlic, mushrooms, and wine. It rolled through the dining area like an invisible tsunami. Each inhaled breath was a meal.

I checked my blouse, an orange cotton tunic, and jeans. I wore the shoulder holster and pug on top of my shirt, but no one gave me any issues. Not here, anyway. Big Mike trusted if I had trouble, I wouldn't bring it in but would take it outside.

This definitely wasn't a date. I crossed my arms and tried to get myself together. Bryan's information about Henrietta bothered me. She'd been attempting to do good. The District squashed her like an annoying bug.

Big Mike's double doors slid back and in walked Agent Winsome.

Except she didn't look a thing like an agent.

She wore white dress pants and white strappy heels. Her soft blue blouse flowed like water over her curves. She pushed her sunglasses up to her hair and squinted against the darker interior. I stood up and waved her over to the booth.

We shook hands. Same firm grip. Callouses. But she'd painted her nails a neutral off white. Her close clipped hair held waves deep enough to make oceans jealous.

"I had a time finding a place to park," Agent Winsome said as she slid into the booth. The seat crinkled as she settled in. Now hemmed in with me, she shuffled a bit until she got comfortable. "That's not a normal problem in the Midwest Territories."

"It takes some getting used to," I said. "We have great public transportation if you have good body armor."

Agent Winsome froze, mouth agape.

"I'm almost kidding."

She gave a nervous laugh.

Not to put too fine a point on it, Agent Winsome stunned. Not a small woman, she moved with the grace of one who loved living in her skin and knew you'd love it too.

Bryan appeared at the table, startling both of us. I didn't quite get my hand on my pug, and if Agent Winsome carried a weapon, I couldn't tell.

"Welcome to Big Mike's. What can I get you?" Bryan flashed teeth, but his normal sweetness had soured. He placed my Port-in-the-Storm on the table.

"Agent Winsome..."

"Anika," she interjected. "Call me Ankia. We're going to be working together so, no need for the label."

Bryan stiffened. He glanced at me, and then back to her. "We can start with a drink."

"That would be nice. What do you have?" Anika fixed her intense gaze on Bryan.

He shrunk beneath it. His shoulders hunched in and hugged his tablet to his chest. She had that impact on people. Once he provided the drink list, he scampered off with her order—an old Scottish whiskey. She picked up the table's electronic menu and scrolled through the entrée choices.

I sipped my drink and put my primary focus on The Wings. I

would wait before talking shop with her. I didn't want to appear too eager.

"Do you come here a lot?" Anika peeked up from the menu.

"I like the food here. It's good." Small talk didn't top my list of mastered skills.

"I think I'm going to go with the pasta, a pesto penne with cherry tomatoes and asparagus." Anika's fingers slid across the screen and once submitted, she leaned back into the seat.

The Wings' song ended. Good timing. I wouldn't have to shout to talk.

Anika glanced at me. "You eating?"

"I already ordered. The special."

Anika smiled. "Okay. Let's get to it."

I inclined my head and continued nursing the drink. This sticky situation required some nuisance finesse. What would she reveal?

And could I believe it?

When interrogating anyone, let them lie.

"Nico Mars was a former regulator. When we put him down in the cradle, we knew people would be up in arms about it. He was not only a rogue regulator, but he also had an entire criminal enterprise. He wasn't too discreet about it either. Some people even wanted him exonerated."

"Where did this take place?"

"Here." Anika confessed. "The District."

"The 12?"

She nodded.

"Didn't know why he was coming back here my ass." I pounded the table.

"We lied. We, *I*, had too. The fact that Nico got out was embarrassing enough for the T.A. The man is nothing short of pure evil." Anika leaned against the table as if she meant to shorten the distance between us. "Look, I'm sorry. I *am*. I wanted to tell you."

"You didn't."

"I couldn't."

"But you can now."

"Yeah." Her voice rose an octave.

"Why?"

Bryan arrived with our steaming deliciousness. He placed the plates down and made small talk with Anika. She spoke freely, but I noticed she hadn't revealed anything of any importance to him.

Time doesn't erase everything. People in The 12 had long memories, like all folks born and reared in poverty and violence. Those with memories like sieves died. The others didn't. They remembered faces, actions, and rumor with a vice like grip. In those places, knowledge meant the difference between ascension and decent into a grave.

Once he left, Anika ate her food with gusto. She chewed, rolling her eyes in delight. "What a taste! Delicious!"

Forkful of pesto-flavored penne was consumed before she reached for her whiskey. I ate my lasagna. Loaded with vegetables and wheat pasta, it tasted divine. The entrée burst with flavor. Damn, Big Mike could cook.

I hadn't been in The District when the Nico Mars incident happened. I had a case that took me to another territory but I do recall when I returned, the protests against regulator violence and corruption were held everywhere both in real life and virtual spaces. It had been years ago and a lot happened since then, so I didn't remember it.

I did now.

After about ten minutes of quiet eating, Anika pushed her plate away and wiped her mouth with a napkin. "Okay."

I put my fork down when she did.

She took out a palm-sized tablet from her purse and slid it across the table to me.

"Some people believe the regulators can do no wrong. They're the authority and thus akin to the governor, especially in the

Midwest Territories. It was hard for us to believe it too, but we followed the evidence. Nico was guilty."

I inclined my head. "Is there doubt he wasn't?"

Anika squirmed. "During the interrogation he came off as guilty. He tried so hard to sound innocent."

"Could it be because he was?" I shrugged. "Just a thought."

Anika released a slow, long breath. "Well, it's all there." She kept her gaze averted to the stage. The Wings played another song and with each passing second, Anika's attention drifted further out of reach. She'd drink, wince at the whisky burn, and hum.

I tapped my fingers against the table when The Wings' song ended. Raven's harrowing and haunting voice echoed a moment after the last musical note fell to a hush.

"What's your role in this?" I broke the quiet.

"How do you mean?" Anika returned her attention to me.

"Is it personal?"

"Personal?"

The calm professionalism I'd witnessed when I first met her returned. She probably did it to mask how unsettled the question made her.

Good. Now we could get somewhere.

"Yeah. Personal." I waited. Most people would rush to fill the silence.

Anika drummed her fingers on the table. She picked up her fork and pushed leftovers around the plate. A cautious silence blanketed the booth. With the tension ratcheting up, she started talking.

"Okay, yes. I was on the original team who arrested Nico. Back then I was a regulator," Anika explained. "If we're going to be partners, you outta know."

"You were friends."

Anika nodded.

"Lovers." I pushed harder.

A slight hesitation, a tremble in her bottom lip, and then an ever-so-slight nod. She met my eyes, as if daring me to judge.

"How are you going to remain neutral?"

Anika blinked. With a cough, she reinforced her professionalism before she spoke.

"The same way I always have, Miss Lewis. I trust my training."

The words held so much conviction I almost shouted Amen.

"How did he end up in the Midwest Territories? All of his violations occurred here."

Anika relaxed. "The T.A. decided to place him outside The District due to his status as a regulator."

"You mean they thought someone would end him."

She nodded. "Well, yes. For his safety, they moved him to the Midwest Territories. We didn't know if some of his victims' families or friends worked in the Montgomery Cradle. One day he could stop breathing."

I shifted the subject.

"You know, as a rule, I don't do regulator ruined cases."

Anika smiled. "Funny, I heard you don't follow rules."

"I don't follow everyone's rules. I have my own."

"I see."

I wasn't sure she did.

"How does Agent Lynn play into this?" I asked, disappointed to find my glass empty.

Anika leaned back into the booth's cushion. "Agent Lynn is working other angles on the case, but not directly with me... and you."

"What's the pay?" I placed the tablet in my own satchel. Tonight, I would delve into Nico Mars.

"The currency will be what a first year T.A. agent receives." Anika put her attention back me. "Plus, your typical retainer."

"No contingency on solving this case or finding the violator? I get paid either way." I would get the details nailed down in writing. Once the transferred currency landed in my account, I would start working in earnest, but I didn't want the Midwest Territories withdrawing the fee if they didn't like how this all turned out.

Anika put both her hands up. "That's what I negotiated. I spoke to Jane, your partner. Right? She gave me the retainer amount and the details of hiring you. If you choose to accept, the Midwest Territory Alliance has hired you."

"My *services*." I corrected. "Not me, but my services."

"Of course." She stabbed multiple penne.

CHAPTER
EIGHT

I got home with Anika's words buzzing in my brain. By the time I had cleared my doorway, I had a plan for the night. Within an hour, I showered and sat on my bed. The cool, air-conditioned streams blew against my damp skin. When Anika mentioned Nico's possible innocence, my lightbulb went off. The wording lit up a darkened area in my sordid history.

Many moon rotations ago, I worked as a regulator. It had been my first job out of the army. The employment didn't last due to me being allergic to authority. It also bolstered my belief that I worked best alone.

But I digress.

Shortly after my first six weeks, a veteran reg got busted for beating a citizen to death in the Adams Morgan neighborhood. Regulator Bruce Keene had been recruited straight from the District's Army and fed into the regulator uniform with hardly an AI mental health session in sight. Blonde. Blue eyes. Tall and fit. He embodied the stereotypical image headquarters wanted to promote despite the department's teeming roster of hatchlings, multi-racial, Black, and other persons of color.

What no one bothered to ferret out or research prior to arming Bruce with a cannon blaster, was how lethal he'd been during the Moon Colony Wars. He'd put so many bodies into the death pits up there, one of them had been named Keene's Crater. By the time all the information about his psychosis and personality disorder came to light, one citizen had been killed and scores more had been injured during routine violations throughout his six-year tenure.

Keene became the face of rogue regulators and the reason why the public didn't trust them. The terror ate at the heart of citizens across The District. I became afraid *for* them. That's why I traveled armed. Violence didn't resolve anything, unless someone ended up dead.

The bastard who killed the governor's daughter down in the Southeast Territories deserved what he got. It hit harder than others because the victim was Jane's niece. I had a niece too, out in the Southwest Territories. My throat closed around the emotional lump. It rose just thinking about her. I solved the case, found the killer, but it nearly cost my own life. Again, trust in those sworn to protect us had been worn thin.

With that lingering feeling, I yanked on a green tee-shirt and my short shorts. The apartment's air conditioning didn't appear to be winning against the summer heat in the living room. The shower's cold streams managed to cool me down, but it was waning fast.

I got up and retrieved my satchel from my sofa where I dumped it. The kitchen's linoleum felt sticky, so I hurried to the living room carpet. I propped up the small refrigerator to cool me off. I had a slender gray stove. It had little wear and tear. The coffee maker did. Once I got comfortable on the sofa, with a throw pillow tucked behind my back, and my legs stretched out, I booted up the T.A.'s file on Nico Mars.

The image appeared first; the exact one Anika showed me on Friday. He looked less menacing than he did angry. A nasty scar snaked across his forehead. Did they reassure him once he came out of the sleep, he'd be a better man?

Some broken things couldn't be repaired.

Only discarded.

The first file held his bio information

Name: Nico Leonard Mars

Birth Date: 2 June 2100

Place of Birth: The District

Tattoos: Digital Blue

Relatives: None

As I troweled through the Mars files, I found confirmation of his menacing explanation for why he'd been detained instead of the "real" violators. They included a video of his interrogation. I clicked play and settled back to watch it.

A younger Anika Winsome stood in the glass and metallic decorated interrogation room. Nico sat, handcuffed to the chair, but still looming as a threat. He stood up, bringing the chair with him. He lifted it as if he hadn't been detained. His naked strength made Anika fall back a few steps. She looked like a bucket of emotional mush.

Not the person beside her, who I can only guess was a supervisor. She remained unflappable. I didn't know her name, but she wore the power suit of a T.A. agent. Beside her, Anika wore a regulator uniform. She folded her hands on the table and faced him. I'd give her credit for that. Facing down the person who betrayed you took guts.

After flipping through the file, I found the T.A. agent's name, Luna Anne Ortega. She commanded a room for sure. I wanted to talk to her. I doubted Anika would be okay with that idea, but no matter. I wanted her thoughts and impression on Nico. Anika had one perspective. I wanted another.

When Ortega spoke, I noted the accent. I didn't recognize it, but it originated outside The District.

Ortega ended the interrogation session with her drawing an index finger across her neck, telling them to kill the recording. It probably wasn't the *actual* end. Knowing what I know about regulators and agents, once the recording stopped, the real questioning began.

And it wasn't all verbal. Over 90% of communication was non-verbal, body language, and tells.

My door announced a visitor with its soft cadence. "You have a visitor."

I don't know what attracted people to haunt my doorway, but here we are. A little after nine, the early evening had slipped by me. Stiff muscles complained as I put bare feet on the floor. I got up, pulled on my robe, a recent gift from Jane who had tired of seeing me answer telemonitor calls in my yellow cami and satin short-shorts. I switched off Nico's case file, shoved it back into my satchel, and went to the door.

I unlocked it to darkness lurking in my entranceway.

"What Daniel?"

He dropped his cigarette and stomped it out. "Let me in."

"Pick that up." I countered.

With a sigh, he reclaimed the cigarette butt, wiped his feet on the rug, and then said, "May I come in?"

I stepped back, allowing him entry, but I scanned the hall behind him. With another visual sweep of the corridor, I shut and locked the door. Daniel stood in the kitchen by the bistro table and chairs.

"I thought you were undercover." I went to the coffeepot. He looked like shit and it meant he needed caffeine.

"I was. But the death violation for Henrietta Mayfield takes priority." He sat down in one of the kitchen chairs. His tee-shirt stuck to his lean torso and his wavy hair was plastered to his head and neck. He tucked the longer sides of his brunette hair behind both ears.

"Where's your tattoo?" His hatchling tattoo at the base of his neck was gone. It couldn't be removed, due to the nanos in the double-helix artwork. It would generate ink for the rest of his life. If he got it removed, the design would appear again. Some people used make-up to cover it. Others tall collars.

Daniel blew out a huff. He reached up and after several attempts, ripped off a thin flesh-colored plastic from the base of his neck. It looked so real, I thought he'd clawed off his skin.

He held it up. "Here. Why you wanna see it?"

"To be sure you're you."

He shook his head. "Right. Like you couldn't tell..."

I placed a mug of coffee in front of him. "What brings you here?"

He smirked. "Can't a friend come say hello?"

"You could've connected for that." I took the chair opposite him with my own cup of java.

And waited.

He smelled like outside—sweat and sunlight. Shorts, tee-shirt, and running shoes completed his athletic look.

"Where you followed?" I asked, choosing to go first.

"No." He drank some of his coffee. "Is someone after you?" "

I snorted. "Someone is always after me."

Daniel rubbed his face and sighed. "I'm not the primary inspector on the Sector 12 violation."

"But..."

"But I still get copied on the reports."

"You wanna talk about it?"

"Yeah. You got the file I sent you?"

"Yeah and decoded it."

"Good. It's weird. So, there wasn't any forced entry at the apartment. She knew her attacker."

"Yeah. I didn't see an indicator of forced entry."

"This reads all kinds of personal intent. The violator slammed her to the floor with such force, it fractured her orbital socket. He also fractured her voice box."

"That's overkill. That's rage." I agreed. "You're thinking a female or a male."

Daniel nodded. "A strong and pissed off one."

"There wasn't anything noticeably missing from her apartment. A thief would've taken her currency cards lying about, or the weapons she had stashed all over the apartment. In her work, I'm sure Henrietta earned a bunch of enemies."

"She didn't get to use a single weapon, meaning she trusted them. We canvassed but didn't find any witnesses. You know how they are down in The 12. No one saw nothing, not even for an icon like Mayfield. The vioTechs collected a lot of stuff, but they're still processing it. The audio techs are on the facial tattoo. The key to her murder is in those markings." Daniel smacked the table. "I know it is."

"It could be an old song or a video clip of her niece." I shrugged. "What else you got? Are you entertaining other theories outside of breaking and entering? Rape?"

"No, that's ruled out, but she was decomposing in the heat so the medical examiner isn't sure. It isn't my case, but it's bothering me." Daniel drank his coffee and made eye contact with me over the cup's lip. "Why are you so interested?"

"I'm not."

"Liar."

I laughed. "You're the one who came over talking about it. Anyway, why the special interest in this one? Death violations happen in The 12 as often as someone breathes. I mean, they pulled you out from your undercover work to go to the scene. That's dangerous. Could've hurt or ended all your hard work."

"It's Mayfield and it's political. Not to add we're shorthanded." Daniel rolled his bloodshot eyes. He'd cut his shoulder-length hair, but it was still long enough to tuck behind his ears. The waves remained too. The sun had already started to turn it a lighter, honey-brown. His medium build placed him at just about the same height as me, but leaner, like a long-distance runner. "You still working with Lynn and Winsome? You know they set up a sort of command room at HQ."

"Anika told me. You'll be seeing me around there."

Daniel smirked. "You decided to help. I'm proud of you."

"They're paying."

"Sure. That's what it is. I know you, soldier, and I know you love a good mystery." Daniel pointed at me. "Don't try to fool me and act all nonchalant. Even if they didn't pay you, you'd still dig into it."

I didn't argue, because, well I couldn't. "The currency is a nice perk."

Daniel laughed.

I explained the case with Nico Mars. When I finished, he frowned. "Mars. That's who escaped the Cradle?"

"Yeah. Didn't Lynn tell you?" I got up and refilled my coffee.

"Why would the T.A. hire you instead of enlisting us? I mean, we took it personally what Mars did. There's still people who want to smash his face in."

"That's the question. Why would the T.A. need me? They claim to want my expertise with the gritty underbelly of The 12, but you know I don't hang out down there."

Daniel took a piece of gum from his pocket, unwrapped it, and popped it in his mouth. He chewed gum when he couldn't smoke. It gave his mouth something else to do.

"You know what bothers me about it?" I stood up and started to pace around my tiny kitchen.

"No, but I bet doughnuts you're going to tell me." Daniel stifled a yawn.

"The best violators keep their mouths shut. No where in the files does it list how The District's regs found out about Nico's violations."

"Someone filed a violation form or they got a tip." Daniel offered.

"All the violations came *after* they arrested him. So, they got a tip, but from who?"

"Should be in the file unless it was anonymous." Daniel crossed his arms. "They'd note the manner it came in."

"It wasn't. My guess is that it was a confidential informant or another regulator." I stopped in front of the microwave and turned to look at Daniel. "If it was, they would protect them by leaving them out of the file."

Daniel's hazel eyes brightened. "Sure. Common practice but the territory attorney would be enraged. You got anything to eat?" He drained the rest of his lukewarm coffee.

"Coffee."

He growled deep in his throat.

That could've been his stomach.

"You do have your own apartment."

"Yeah, yours is closer."

I left him in the kitchen, rummaging through the fridge for something edible. With so many thoughts buzzing in my brain, I wanted to get my thoughts down. I sat on the sofa and pulled out my tablet. I pressed my finger in the spot for thumbs, took out my stylus, and started writing.

"Oh, nice! You have ramen! Spicy tofu." Daniel exclaimed.

"Those have been in there forever."

"Even better."

I had questions for Anika, but I wanted to talk to the T.A. agent who arrested Nico, Luna Ortega.

Every death violation meant the story's end.

I needed Ortega to help me get the beginning.

CHAPTER
NINE

Tuesday morning I found myself clutching a travel mug of coffee, sunglasses, and the wheel, as I flew over to the Pet Worth neighborhood in Sector Three. Luna Ortega agreed to meet me, granted I got over there before it got too hot. I pushed Daniel out of the apartment around midnight, after he'd eaten my ramen, ordered pizza, ate the entire thing, and binged watched the classic horror movies on Terror Telemonitor Tales.

The Pet Worth community behaved better than most of The District's sectors. Known for its community events, cozy stores, and stylish restaurants, people tended to flock here to visit, because no one could afford the currency to live here. Those who resided behind pastel painted wrought iron gates and shimmering force fields had been here for generations. One did not move out of Pet Worth unless your next address was the cemetery.

My wauto dipped lower as I neared the coordinates. Already, bright yellow sunshine poured over the area, drowning everything in heat. No cloud cover to increase the humidity, but it would be a scorcher by noon. The autopilot landed on the street outside a lean, tall building squished together as a result of the tight real estate area. I found building 304. The number emblazed on the front of a bright blue door. The rest of the building had been painted in equally shiny red. The entire block looked like a child had colored the houses with all the primary crayons in the box.

I got out and threw my satchel over my shoulder. I wore a khaki short-sleeved jacket, a sleeveless white blouse, and jeans. The shoulder holster and pug remained in their usual place, my favorite accessory. I wanted to look professional. Luna Ortega would respect that. Territory Alliance agents tended to like processes, protocol, and procedures.

The door slid back as soon as my foot touched the walkway. A stoic Ortega stood in the doorway. Her dark, grey-streaked hair had been cinched back at the base of her neck, revealing a meaty face aged by time and probably drink. With her chunky build, and hunched posture, she waved me in.

"You must be Cybil." Her deep tenor surprised me.

"I am." I called and walked quickly to shake her hand.

We shook. Her hand was dry, and I noted the enlarged knuckles.

She caught me looking. "Arthritis."

"I'm sorry."

"I'm 59, Cybil. It happens. Come on through."

She led me through the shadow-clad foyer, sparse living room, and out to the back patio. In the distance, a microwave hummed. Without difficulty, she slid one of the old-fashioned sliding doors open. The relic took me back. Few manual doors remained, so with her hands so ravaged by age, why wouldn't she get an automatic one installed?

Outside, a short concrete patio held a small, square wooden table, and two reclining patio chairs. She gestured for me to sit in one and she claimed the other. Once she got comfortable, she scooped up her sunglasses from the table and put them on.

"The sun helps my hands and gives me my vitamin D. I want to get it done before it gets too hot." Ortega explained. "Now, what do you want?"

"As I said on the telemonitor, I am a reporter for the *D.C. Mirror*. We're doing a piece on Nico Mars. Since you arrested him, I wanted to get your first-hand account of what happened, your thoughts, impressions, etc." I took out my handheld. I'd elected not to recline in the chair, but it meant I sat perched on the edge of it.

"Funny. Back when it happened, the e-news files brimmed with interviews with him, but not us."

"That's why I'm here now." I smiled through the falsehood.

"Whelp, there isn't much to tell. Nico Mars is a dangerous individual. Despite being a regulator, he wasn't going to be told no, by anyone. Regulations meant nothing to him. One of the victims, he did a lot of bad things to her..." Ortega stopped, her breathing labored. She took several deep breaths before continuing. "What is it you wanna know? I don't like talkin' about this."

"I appreciate you doing this. There are rumors of him being innocent."

Ortega bolted upright, coughing. She snatched off her sunglasses and glared at me. "The hell you say?"

"I..."

"Nico Mars sharked around The 12's neighborhood hunting victims like the predator he was! At first, he was receptive to talking to us, to clear his name he said. Then once we started pressuring him, explaining the evidence we had, he stopped."

All of this I saw in the video. Ortega's passion about Nico remained all these years later, which spoke to something she hadn't told me. So, I poked a little harder to get past the surface.

"I'm sure some of the regs didn't think him guilty. Was the informant credible?" I played my hunch. It could go horribly wrong and she could toss me out on my ass.

No risk. No glory.

She paused, nodded once, and put her sunglasses back on. "We kept it out of the e-news files. So how did you find out?"

"Oh, come on. You know I can't tell you. I protect my sources. I won't reveal your input today." I pretended to type into the tablet. She could hear my nails on the screen. "Confidentiality."

"Your name does sound familiar."

"Thank you."

I should've given her a bogus name, but then, I would have to remember it. I steered the conversation back to the topic and away from me before she became suspicious. Curse her damn T.A. training.

"What did the other regs think about you taking the word of an informant over a regulator?"

"The first violation case stalled out. The informant came through in the nick of time for the next one. The regs didn't want any repercussions for putting a damn predator in the middle of a sector full of prey. At the end of the day, it all fell on my shoulders. I didn't care what The District's regulators thought. They'd let him run rampant for too long."

"He had to be taken down." I added, prompting her to continue talking.

"Yes!"

"Wasn't Anika Winsome, a regulator, partnered with you. Must've been a bitter pill to swallow."

"Anika?"

"Regulator Winsome?" I checked my non-existent notes. "She was assigned to the team working the Nico Mars case. Isn't it strange a regulator was assigned to the case investigating her colleague?"

"It's been so long." Ortega reclined, the fire inside her extinguished.

She didn't talk, and I waited. Contrary to popular belief, I do not like raking up painful memories and events. Sometimes, like now, to get to the truth, horrible things had to be unearthed. It didn't mean I liked it.

Not one bit.

"Nico Mars had a reputation for hurting people. He beat people he suspected of violations. He hurt people he didn't like or if they looked at him wrong. That's why they assigned him to The 12. He's a stone, cold violator."

"Yeah, that's his general reputation, but who blew the whistle?"

She swallowed hard. "All the evidence was tagged and noted. If you have the case files, you know this already."

"Just what I've read in the papers and what I've gleamed from others. But you were there! You brought him in and put him the cradle. How did they know Nico was running The 12? I mean, most violators don't blab about what they're doing, especially one that's a regulator." I stopped talking then. If she didn't want to give me the information, I couldn't risk blowing my cover. She hadn't spoken about Anika. In fact, she acted like she didn't recognize the name.

Ortega reached for the tall glass of water on the table and drank several gulps. A second glass was there, but I didn't follow suit. When she put the glass down, drained of its contents, she pushed her sunglasses up into her hair.

Her eyes looked sad. She met my gaze and with her deep tenor said, "Look, one thing you need to remember about Nico Mars. He isn't like most violators."

"No?"

"No. He's a monster." She stood up. "I'll see you out."

The microwave dinged.

Nothing added up. Arguably, my job wasn't to judge Nico Mars, but to put him back in the cradle for the entirety of his sentence. I couldn't shake the feeling there was more. It rattled me to the bones. Had I missed something, or did Anika hide something from me?

I don't like operating with one hand tied behind my back.

I climbed back into the wauto. Despite our brief chin wag, Ortega hadn't told me anything new. Why? Maybe she didn't trust reporters. I had another option to mine information. I started the vehicle and punched in the coordinates to my next destination—the office.

Just after 10 in the morning, I wanted to get breakfast and get inside. Now I was up, I wanted to get my thoughts down while they were still fresh. At this time, the elevated lanes held little traffic. The tail of rush hour traffic caused some congestion at the popular exits. Where I headed didn't rank in The District.

My telemonitor lit up. Malcolm Moore's Gregorian nose consumed most of the screen. His dark eyes flashed in his excitement. "Cybil!"

I answered. "Malcolm."

"Anything for you. I assume all is forgiven since you called." He smiled as if the remark didn't warrant a slap across the face. He adjusted the zoom and sat back in his office chair.

The last time we spoke I erupted like a volcano due to his attempts to control me via pimping my services. It didn't sit well with me. Recommendations were one thing, but when you get kickbacks out of it, you didn't have my best interest in mind. Only yours. Only currency.

As a reporter for the *D.C. Mirror*, a real one, he had snitches that numbered in the hundreds. So, he was an excellent resource for finding out information. Truth be told, regulators and P.I.s couldn't catch a cold without snitches and Malcolm had access to many. Payment usually meant a roll in the hay, but my patience for sharing my body with him ended.

Don't get me wrong. It was good.

"I need to know what you know about Nico Mars."

Malcolm's dark hair had been cut short. It showed off his strong chin. The new tattoo behind his ear resembled a crow. It made his eyes stand out more. The haircut worked for him. I'd miss pulling on it, grabbing it by the fistfuls, but then, I digress.

"Nico Mars. That's a blast from the past." Malcolm pursed his lips. Behind him, a five-foot screen showed what looked like a map of

The District, with flashing green and red lights all over the place. "He got several years in the cradle. Former regulator. He didn't confess."

"That's him. Who ratted him out?"

Malcolm frowned. "The Territory Alliance took over the case because it was a regulator. They didn't feel like The District's regs could investigate their own effectively and without bias."

Good call.

"They did put a regulator on the case though." I wondered why no one knew Anika had been on the case. What gives?

Malcolm shook his head. His eyebrows made a V as he frowned. The clicking of keys in a flurry spoke to how fast he typed. "I don't remember. Okay. Here's what I can tell you."

I set the autopilot and picked up my tablet from the passenger seat.

"A volunteer spotted something in the water. When she got closer, she spied a young woman, listless, dead in the overflow pond in Sector 12. She had marks on her neck, despite the rest of the bruised body being mangled. The victim had a horrifying death. The medical examiner's words, not mine."

"He dumped the body like garbage in an abandoned part of The 12," I said.

It had been in the report too, but Malcolm needed to warm up. Once he got the bone, he'd dig until he found the information I wanted.

"Yes." He leaned closer to his computer's screen. From the waist up, I saw him in profile. He scrolled, his finger rolling the mouse ball as he'd been doing it all his life. He paused. "Ah, here! Okay, so they couldn't get the victim identified. So, the regulators hemmed and hawed until they got an anonymous tip."

"Who was the tipster?"

"That's why it's anonymous, Cybil." Malcolm chuckled; his attention glued to the computer.

"You know. You always know."

Malcolm glanced at me. "What do I get if I do?"

"Don't be daft. Those days are over. You ruined it."

He pouted. "I don't reveal my sources."

I made a full throat condemnation I won't repeat here. "That hasn't stopped you before."

Malcolm shrugged. "I had motivation before."

"I could trust you before."

"How do you know you can trust me now?"

"I don't."

"That made my stomach hurt, Cybil. Just forgive me already." Malcolm rotated his chair to face the telemonitor. He looked delicious. Blue short sleeved polo brought out the dark brown of his hair. His arrow earring danced across his color. He'd shaved his goatee. He looked younger by about 10 years.

"If the info you give me works out, I will think about it."

"This may come as horrific shock, but I haven't been sleeping. I miss you," Malcolm crooned.

"That's too bad. Next time think before you do stupid shit."

"You made some good currency." He turned back to his computer.

"Jane almost died."

He hesitated. "Yeah. I'm sorry about that."

His apology didn't take away Jane's scars.

Malcolm sighed. "Okay, so here it is. According to my sources, the person who called in the tip was a woman named Anika Winsome."

I wrote it in my tablet, so Malcolm didn't see my alarm. "Who is she?"

Malcolm clicked a few more buttons. "No information on her."

"What do you mean no information? Everyone has a digital footprint." I looked at him.

Malcolm shook his head. "There's nothing on her in the public records. No credit record. No inserted I.D. number, No wauto registration. Nothing. A ghost."

"Not a ghost." The lightbulb clicked, and my anger ignited with it. "Thanks, Malcolm. I gotta go."

"Cybil-what…"

I ended the telemonitor call.

Anika Winsome didn't exist because Anika Winsome wasn't a real person.

She was an avatar.

Damn it.

CHAPTER
TEN

parked in the spot closest to the door in front of my office building, a square ancient structure with weathered windows and worn carpet. The electricity crackled as the front doors slid back onto the empty business lobby. The building contained a semi-circle desk once used to include a receptionist who directed customers to the right office and answered questions. It sat empty, dusty with spiders grabbing the prime real estate. A line of metallic mailboxes, a leftover from the time before the war, lined the wall to the right of the entranceway. They required keys to open, but no one used them. No telling now where the keys resided. No one had paper. Not really. Pulp was too expensive to have it imported from the Northwest Territories..

The rickety elevator took me up to the fourth floor, and I made my way down the stuffy and humid hallway. The corridor lacked air conditioning, and the few businesses on this floor kept their doors closed and their cool air to themselves. There wasn't any point in cooling off empty space.

I pushed into my office's lobby and the waiting arms of artic air. I stopped short, and breathed in it, arms thrown wide to let it coat all of me. I closed my eyes, tossed my head back, and smiled at the ceiling. *Yes! Coolness!*

"Um, you okay?" Jane's snark snatched me back from the brink of bliss.

I opened my eyes and dropped my arms. "Fine. Just hot."

She leaned against her desk, arms folded over her black tee-shirt, and hunting knife strapped to her waist. Her long dreadlocked hair had been pulled up into a high ponytail, but the locs brushed her shoulders.

Seated at her desk, the newest addition to our staff, the cat, purring in her lap, Kimmila typed on the keyboard. The furry beast didn't even acknowledge I'd come inside. I did notice the food and water bowls near the coffee alcove and the hint of a litterbox lingering in the air.

"Hiya, Cybil. It's barely noon and it's already hot enough to fry an egg." Kimmila looked around her computer monitor. "Too damn hot for a jacket."

"I had a business meeting." I offered in way of explanation. "Jane, I need to see you." I walked to my private office and gestured for her to join me.

"Oh, okay. This sounds exciting." She winked at Kimmila, who chuckled in return.

Once the private office door slid closed, Jane's amusing humor dissolved. She took the seat in front of me and sank into it.

"What's up?" Jane asked. "You look a bit peeved."

"I *am* pissed off." I brought her up to speed on what I'd learned about Agent Winsome's Territory Alliance offer. "I wanna know more about her. No, I wanna know everything about her. Follow her. Don't let her breathe without you being able to taste her breath."

Jane inched forward in her chair her hands tented in front of her. "Cyb, you okay?"

"Yeah. I don't like being used like Boo Boo, the fool. I sure as hell am going to find out if that's the T.A.'s intention."

But no. My stomach knotted up the more I thought about the

bullshit Anika tried to pull on me. I should've known something didn't ring true for her. Agent Winsome had been too polite and too helpful.

Definite red flag.

"What did this agent do to you? Date your hatchling?" Jane teased, but her eyes held concern. "You think she lied about her name. She's an avatar?"

The tense atmosphere burst at her corny attempt at humor, and I smiled. "No, she isn't dating Trey, to my knowledge, but if you find out do let me know."

My hatchling didn't belong to me anymore. We broke up months ago. Jane despised hatchling, engineered humans who were crafted in a petri dish, grown in artificial wombs, and raised by adoptive parents.

"There's something you're not tellin' me. You ain't got this upset because the T.A. is puttin' on a full court press." Jane stood up and leaned onto my desk, closing the distance between us. "I don't like movin' in the dark."

"I know." I shrugged out of my blazer and hung it on the back of my chair. Anika got under my skin, and I couldn't rub out the inkling that I'd only just scratched the surface of this situation between her and Nico Mars. "If I knew more, I'd tell you. Why isn't there anything about Anika in the public record?"

"Because she's in the Midwest Territories and we can't access their databases." Jane shrugged. "Could be that she's in the T.A. and they have a whole other security process to keep them safe, including scrubbing the 'net."

"I can buy that for her life *after* joining the T.A., but what about her life *before*. When she lived here, in The District."

"Dunno. Listen, your eyes are bloodshot. You ain't sleeping" Jane reared up to her full height and crossed her arms.

"Look, do me a favor and get what you can on her." I turned to the window.

"Cyb..."

"Just get started!"

Silence.

"All right, boss!" Jane stomped out of the office.

I didn't like keeping her at a distance, but until I had all the pieces on Anika, I couldn't give Jane more. It was early days yet.

Early days.

Plus, I couldn't trust Kimmila hadn't been planted here by Agent Lynn. Paranoia is my middle name. I'd rather be safe than sorry any day. Proactive. Yeah.

I tried to corral my restlessness and focus. I sat back down at the booted-up computer and started entering notes on all I'd learned thus far. When my private office door slid back, I paused.

Jane shouldn't be back so soon.

Kimmila walked in with a cup of coffee in her hand. She placed it on the corner of my desk. I closed the laptop.

"Thought you could use something to pick you up." She put her hands on her hips. "You've been working away in here."

"Thank you." I picked up the cup, blew across the steaming lip, and then put it back down.

"I didn't poison it." Kimmila said with a wet cough. She wiped her damp face with the back of her hand.

It didn't encourage me to drink it.

"That's what the poisoner would say," I replied.

We had a choppy rapport, but she was trying. I decided to put in the effort too—for Jane.

"Have a seat, Kim." I gestured to my visitor chairs.

She sat down in the one closest to the door. "Janey said you sent her out on a job."

I nodded. "Some surveillance work."

"That's good." She rubbed her sweaty hands on her pants. "I'd like to help. I mean, I know you ain't payin' me to just cat-sit. Not that I don't like Zola."

"Zola?"

"The cat. That's her name, Zola." Kimmila chuckled.

"You're from Adams Morgan," I said, and the amusement drained off of Kimmila's face.

"Yeah." It sounded like she spat it out because it had a bad taste to it.

"There was an incident down in The 12, and I know Adams Morgan is one of the neighborhoods in that sector."

Kimmila went still but gave me a slight nod.

"You can help me by telling me about it."

"About what?" Kimmila whispered.

"Life in The 12."

She closed her eyes and sighed. When she opened them, she met my gaze and then swallowed hard. Her whole being slumped. She looked completely deflated.

"I put that behind me," Kimmila said, more to herself than me.

"Kim, I don't know what you've gone through, but if this is too much, we can stop. I'm not going to rip open closed wounds. I have other avenues to pursue."

I didn't have any interest in tearing Kimmila to pieces. The mood I was in, I probably shouldn't interrogate anyone. I wouldn't be gentle. The honey-level in my body hovered in dangerously low quantity.

"What do you wanna know?" Her eyes shined with unshed emotion.

"Well, what was life in The 12 like, when say, Nico Mars regulated it?" I placed my handheld in my lap, picked up the stylus and waited. When witnesses or people talked, I strived to get every detail no matter how small.

She shuddered.

She knew him.

I passed the coffee she gave me back to her. She accepted it with a small nod. With a drink in her hand, Kimmila became braver. She sat up straighter and sipped the coffee.

"I haven't heard his name in a long time. I didn't know him, but I heard rumors of what he'd done. Adams lay closest to The 12's line.

The heart of The 12 held all the hotspots. Most of the time, the rolling chaos didn't reach us, or if it did, I didn't notice. I had my own troubles. You know what I mean?"

Kimmila closed and opened her eyes again. Was she offering little prayers before she spoke?

"One of my friends, Jet, lived down there. He was reserved and modest, mind his own. You know? One of Nico's crew was known to be short-tempered…"

I knew where this was headed.

"…Nico's crew rolled in packs. If you had a problem with one, you had trouble with them all. Jet had mistakenly put a dent in the wauto of one 'em. Can't recall his name, but the man's girlfriend got out of the car. She ain't never met a stranger, so she's all kind and whatnot to Jet. Nico's henchman didn't like it. He got out of the passenger side and stalked over to Jet. Now, Jet's exchanging the insurance info with the woman when this guy stabs him right in the chest. The knife struck a vein or somethin' cause a lot of blood came out. So. Much. Blood."

I knew the pain having been stabbed my Jose Montero. I had a scar to prove it. I'd accept the marking over him taking my life. But it didn't take much for me to visualize Jet's stabbing. Instead of lingering on it, I wrote down Kimmila's story.

"Where you there?" I circled Jet's name.

Kimmila shook her head. "It was online. Someone recorded it."

She paused, drank coffee, and hunched in on herself as if the violator's cold indifference chilled her. Goosebumps appeared on her forearms.

"… The woman screamed. The man pushed her aside, kicked Jet out of the way, and flew off in the woman's wauto. He didn't even bother dumping the body or anything. It was like he didn't care if he got caught."

"Because he knew he wouldn't," I interjected

Kimmila nodded. "That's the first time I knew Nico Mars was dirty. Real dirty."

"Who was Jet's violator?"

Kimmila shrugged. "I dunno."

"But the violator was the one who said he worked for Nico Mars."

She nodded. "Yeah. He ain't have to say it. Everybody knew."

"Any other links or evidence between them? How do you know for sure the violator really had links to Mars?"

"I dunno. I mean, Nico was a regulator. If there had been stuff, he'd gotten rid of it to cover it up or hide it." Kimmila shook her head as I should've thought of that.

And I had. "Who was the girlfriend?"

Kimmila cocked her head to the side. "Um, I think her name was Juicy."

"Juicy?"

Kimmila stood up. "Yeah. She lived in The Bottoms. I think the violator did too. But don't go lookin' for her. They found her a few days later, dead with foam in her mouth, outside one of 'em stripper places."

The Bottoms was also in Sector 12. If Adams Morgan lay on the outer rim of The 12, The Bottoms ringed the sector's heart. That's where Henriette's apartment building was located.

"Tell me about Henrietta Mayfield."

Kimmila visibly flinched. "I don't know nothin' about her."

I held her gaze, letting the disbelief spill onto my face.

She gave me another wet cough and sat back down. "All right. Mrs. Mayfield worked to keep the dirt out of The 12. To me, it was like she shoveling shit against the tide. The whole damn sector is teeming with violators. Drugs. Breeders. Black market augments. All fast currency. Little effort. The legitimate businesses got pushed out, well most of them, to other sectors. If there's limited food and many hungry mouths, everybody gets a smaller piece."

I nodded. A significant swath of The District's economy came from these type of violators. You could say they were the backbone of the territory. The District was partially funded on their backs. The other half on drugs. Capitalism was sickening.

"Some of the cattle down in The Bottoms didn't wait for the regulators to help them. They got themselves out."

"Like you?"

"I wasn't ever a heifer. A bitch, maybe. Yeah. Never a heifer." Kimmila rubbed her free hand on her thigh again.

I waited.

She shifted in the chair. "I mean, it's exactly as they say it is down there. Breeders snatch any unattached woman and abandoned young boys into their homes, pump 'em full of Ackback or heroin, and then let others purchase 'em. If one of them got pregnant, the babe got pushed into one of the breeder's kennels, reared, and sold too. Some people liked 'em little. Real little, you know?"

Those greasy words hung in the air between us. Nothing would make that clean or erase my disgust.

"Mrs. Mayfield fought against it. She'd hold demonstrations, marches, boycotts, you name it, she did it to stop the evil perpetrated down there." Kimmia shook her head. "And they violated her life for it."

"Have you ever seen this before?" I switched gears. I passed Kimmila the handheld with the image of the victim and the facial tattoo.

"This is Mrs. Mayfield." Kimmila glanced up at me.

"Yeah, but have you ever seen those types of facial tattoos?"

"She's fucking dead!" Kimmila shouted.

I took a breath. "But you were a bartender, which means you saw a lot of people. Some of them could've had a similar tattoo. Focus on the tattoo."

"Oh. Yeah. Sorry." She took the handheld then and studied the image.

Bartenders were the best resource in a bar. They paid attention to their customers because their tips depended on it.

I let her shouting roll off of me. I'd been poking in all of her soft and vulnerable spots, so she might have been a little emotionally sore.

She handed it back to me. "No. Sorry."

"Thank you for your help." I stood up and shrugged into my blazer. I put the handheld back in the satchel.

"It didn't feel like I did anything." Kimmila drank more of the coffee as she headed to the door.

"You did." I didn't get a ton of new information. On the other hand, Kimmila and I had made some progress.

"You goin' out?" She turned back to me from the doorway.

"I've got unfinished business. You know how to reach me." I pulled the satchel's strap over my head, so it hung across my torso.

I *still* didn't trust Kimmila. There was something I couldn't put my finger on, but I did appreciate her opening up to me today.

Next stop—food.

CHAPTER
ELEVEN

Once I reached the lobby, the funk bowled me over, a thick, heady aroma of body odor and sweat. Sometimes displaced people used the lobby as a bathroom, a nap area, or safe space. On Thursdays the building owners would send some robotic security guard to chase them out and clean up the mess. As today was Tuesday, I figured I'd find some cluster of the downtrodden finding cool relief in the lobby.

Instead, I found an assailant.

He emerged from the shadows and struck me hard in the face before I could get the pug drawn or step off the elevator. I stumbled back against the now closed metal doors and bounced forward. I shook it off as best I could but damn it freaking hurt! He was tall, not fat but wide.

He knew he was screwed the moment we made eye contact.

I sniffed and wiped. My hand came away bloodied. The man carried something big and bulky in his hands. He hoisted it onto his shoulder and fired.

A cannon blaster!

I leapt out of the way. This man meant to kill me, and not leave enough of me to scoop up with a tablespoon. The blast resounded so loudly; the security lights clicked on. The blackened scorch spot on the elevators' door spoke to his intent.

Dressed in all black, pants and long-sleeved shirt, with a matching haversack on his back, he tried to meld with the lobby's shadows. The security lights made that harder than before. He wore a ski mask (as hot as it was) and all I could make out were eyes. Big brown ones.

Without waiting for the second shot to charge up, I pointed the pug at him and fired. No questions. He made it clear he didn't intend to discuss anything. He ran, ducking behind the old lobby desk. My shot plowed into the desk, not my assailant.

"Come out of there!" I inched up to a thick pillar, but the 20th century open lobby concept left me little coverage. The thick marble pillars held up the ceiling, but they didn't quite cover my round hips. I couldn't subdue him as long as he had the cannon blaster. Those things were designed for war, not gun battles. Now that war was less profitable, you can get them on the black market. And most likely for cheap.

He ignored me (imagine that!) and hopped up from behind the front desk with the blaster. When he fired, the power of the cannon shoved him back where he stumbled and tripped on something behind the desk. I watched him go down, and I pounced, not waiting for him to get himself together or recover.

The blast smashed into the pillar where I had been standing. I moved seconds before he fired, narrowly missing being obliterated. My attacker didn't seem too familiar with the weapon. Again, it hadn't been designed for the casual gun owner, but for soldiers.

Which I used to be.

I raced to the desk and pointed the pug at him. Now I'd be able to unleash the frustration boiling inside me. I found him in a pile of discarded bottles and debris.

"Just a note: Cannon blasters require you to plant your feet before you fire."

I gasped.

My assailant snatched off the ski mask, and there sat a young woman. Tall, wide-shouldered, but identifying as female. Curly hair had been pulled back into a ponytail, but soft short strands framed her face. Elegant make-up and nude lipstick seemed at odds with the gash leaking blood down her cheek. Why the ski mask? Wouldn't it ruin her coverage?

Grunting, she sat up. One arm held her lower ribcage. When she moved, she winced in pain, but it didn't stop her from hoisting the cannon blaster with one hand. Thing was, they took two hands to operate.

"Drop that weapon and put those paws up in the air," I growled.

She complied, almost thankful to be able to put it down. With my foot, I pushed it out of her immediate reach, in case she changed her mind. My face hurt, and my lips itched where my blood had dried.

"Who sent you?"

The problem with being a private inspector was the on-going job hazard, even in the so-call down time. People wanted to snuff you out. Teriad, the dictator of the Northwest, still had a bounty on my head for a stolen aerocycle (it had been a gift). Jose Montano's people wanted revenge for his death (Jane ended him), and my dead ex-boyfriend's wife wanted a piece of me too. I had stalkers. It was like having my own personal terrorists.

I never knew when they'd strike.

"Don't make me ask you again."

In front of me, sat a light-skinned woman, with dark brown eyes, wide nose, and a furious slash for a mouth. She kept her arms up high, but she didn't like it. Not one bit. With a possible rib injury, it hurt. Her menacing look didn't faze me, but she did have a twisted expression. For one, she sat there grinning like she'd consumed a tub of Ackback. She launched herself at me.

We went down and tussled. Heavier than she looked, I found myself at a temporary disadvantage. Using her momentum, I managed to get my knees in her belly. She screamed. Yep, either cracked or broken ribs. I hoisted her with my legs. Damn, she was heavy. I swung her hard into the air and pushed her with my feet. Due to her weight, she didn't go far but crashed to the floor about two feet away. I scrambled up to my knees over to her. To my continued shock, the wench tried to grab my hair, and when she went for it, I got the pug under her chin.

"Don't." I pressed the button and the pug whirled.

The sound made her freeze.

"Do you like your face?" I asked, my tone cold.

She nodded slightly and remained still until I got to my feet. I moved back from her, out of reach in case she wanted more fight. I rotated my satchel to my back.

"Tell me who sent you."

She snatched her chin away.

"One..." I commenced counting. "Two..."

"What number do you get to before..." she asked.

I fired.

She screamed, grabbing at the laser gun wound with both hands.

"That's a flesh wound to your arm." I explained as she rolled around on the ground, holding the injury and cursing me, just tissue and muscles. I fired through the fleshy part of her upper arm.

"Now you know I'm not playing." Despite my anger, I couldn't help but feel sorry for her.

She stared at me with watery eyes. I bet she felt cornered, and I would bet today's coffee she wanted to get away from me. Good, she'd tell me what I wanted to know to be rid of me. A botched hit may cause her more urgency to flee.

"Where you live?" I switched lanes to a less intimidating topic.

"The Bottoms," she spat. Blood leaked through the fingers on the hand she kept clasped to her arm. The laser gun would've cauterized it, but maybe I got a vein.

"Why did you attack me?"

She hesitated. "Somebody paid me."

"Who?"

"I dunno." She threw her head back and instantly regretted it. She roared in pain. "I swear."

I kicked her foot, and she shot up, screamed.

"Fuck!"

I showed the pug. "Tell me who?"

"Don't shoot me!"

"Tell me what I want to know."

Tears spilled.

"That doesn't work on me. You tried to violate my right to live." I made my tone hard. "You don't take jobs to commit death violations, then weep over a flesh wound. Who the hell are you?"

She glared at me. "I'm nobody. Another slug from The Bottoms. I needed currency, so I took a job to take out a target. That be you."

"Who. Hired. You?"

She tore her sleeve and wrapped the shreds around her arm. "This ain't the first time I been shot."

"You don't act like it."

"It still hurts no matter how many times you been shot."

I agreed.

A small rhino was tattooed on her left wrist. Those tattoos belonged to a breeder; those had a certain quality. Other people got tattoos all the time, but I have seen this one before. And his reach went far beyond The 12. Big Game. He saw himself as a big game hunter, finding only the best girls and boys for his clients. A high-end farmer, I couldn't see why he'd send someone to kill me.

"Who's your farmer?"

It startled her. She froze before shaking her head. "I don't know what you talking about."

"I know you belong to Big Game. That's his stamp."

She tried to snatch what remained of her sleeve down to cover it. "I don't belong to no one but myself."

"Did you escape him? Is that why you're freelancing as an assassin?"

She shook her head. "You ask a lot of damn questions."

"It's a personality quirk."

"It's damn annoying. Now I see why he wanted you dead."

"Why does Big Game want to kill me?" I put the pug away. She didn't fear death. Coming from The Bottoms meant she faced dying on the daily. She didn't like being wounded. On the one hand, I could stand there and shoot holes into her.

On the other hand, I wanted food. My stomach rumbled in agreement.

"I didn't say BG wanted you dead." She shot back, caught herself, and snatched away.

"How's your arm?" I asked, shaking my head. Amateurs.

"Sore. What you think?" She snapped.

"This should give you some relief." I reached into my satchel, took out some pain patches and tossed them to her. "Tape up those ribs."

I turned to leave but I picked up the cannon blaster before I left. She sat there, cradled in the indifferent arms of the abandoned front desk. The blaster weighed about fifteen pounds. Not too heavy but running with it during the Moon Colony wars where they created gravity to anchor us to the dusty surface made me hate the damn thing. All the soldiering with a blaster became heavy after a few hours.

I exited my office building and walked into the sunlight. With a little padding, I secured the cannon blaster in the wauto's trunk before I got in. I hadn't had any breakfast, and now, after noon, my level of patience and grace waned.

Did Big Game send this amateur, this poor child to her potential death? I can be lethal. Overhead, the elevated lanes stretched out across the day sky. A couple of aerocycles braved the growing lunch traffic. Down here on the ground, people walked in fast paces, heads down, with eyes averted. As long as it was kept far away from their tables, their doorsteps, their lives, they didn't see the ugly, gross underpinnings of rampant poverty, transitions of human property, or death.

This case had me chasing a ghost, a whisper on the wind. Anika had no solid leads on Nico Mars's whereabouts. According to the case notes, nothing tied him to The District other than the A.I.'s assessment and the fact he used to run Sector 12. Why did she and Agent Lynn believe so firmly he would come here? That's what I needed to know. I stopped at my wauto..

Almost as if hearing her name, my handheld vibrated in my satchel. I fished it out, and found Agent Winsome, Anika's, stoic face glaring up at me.

"Lewis."

"Where the hell are you?" Anika's face smashed into a frown.

"Why?" I didn't want a team of T.A. Agents landing in the parking lot. I scanned the sky and the elevated lanes for possible aerocycles lowering to come get me. She sounded furious.

"You are supposed to be here. You know, for work?" Anika seethed. It sounded like she spoke through clenched teeth. "You missed the team briefing..."

"I must've missed the order last night, because I don't recall you telling me I had to report anywhere, especially to Regulator Head-quarters."

"Come in now," Anika said.

"Please," I countered.

A heavy sigh. "Please."

"I'll be there in about 20 minutes." I climbed into my wauto, and the call transitioned from my handheld to the embedded telemonitor. I lowered the volume.

She glanced around and then leaned into the screen. "Don't come in the front doors. I'll meet you on the east side of the building."

With those cryptic words, she ended the connection.

CHAPTER
TWELVE

Regulator Headquarters took up the block of the former capitol in what used to be the Federal Bureau of Investigations. The building held all the antique precautions it did back when the United States remained one nation and not a scattered puzzle piece of territories. It held the look of authority and crafted fear and trepidation in those coming here for violations. A force field kept vehicles from being able to smash themselves into the building. Traffic flew around the massive beast, so it couldn't touch the building itself. Part of the block had been converted to parking for the Regulator Fleet. A single-entry point forced all traffic through its central entranceways. Each vehicle was monitored with weapons trained on them.

During my brief time as a regulator, the structure made me feel as if I had a connection to something greater than myself. I lost that when I got kicked out of the Army. Now, the place gave off creepy vibes. Wautos and aerocycles took off and landed, like bees among a hive. Cargo crafts marked with The District Regulator logo hauled violators back and forth between headquarters and their final destinations, be it The Montgomery Cradle or court.

My return was bittersweet, but I pushed by the nostalgia. As I flew with others streaming through the flashing alarms lights, warning not to fly outside the designated area. Doing so could lead to immediate death. My wauto stalled mid-flight. A regulator dressed in the navy-colored, one-piece uniform, commonly referred to as a onesie, appeared. Her face remained hidden behind dark glasses, high gloss lipstick, and a fall of thick dreadlocks.

"Purpose?" she asked in a clipped, short manner.

"I'm here to see Agent Winsome." I didn't want to over explain.

"Name?"

"Cybil Lewis."

"ID?"

I raised my arm and placed my wrist against the telemonitor. It projected my credentials onto the telemonitor, and the regulator recorded them.

"One moment."

The beam kept the wauto hovering and it had to be disengaged by them. Every vehicle had a feature that allowed regulators to halt movement. People agreed to this 'safety' feature because the regulators sold it as a method for capturing and deterring violators.

"Cleared." She ended the connection and released my vehicle.

As Anika instructed, I flew around to the side of the building and parked in one of the regulator's spaces. Now, I worked for the Territory Alliance. Once they ran the registration on my wauto, no regulator in the building would dare try to tow it. I walked across the hot asphalt, made a right around a small corner, and to the secured employee door.

Anika stood at the side entrance with her arms folded across her chest, like an impatient mother hen. She wore a light cream-colored suit, with dark brown boots, and an orange blouse underneath. Nothing about her body language said she would be in a great mood when I finally reached her.

"That was fast." She patted her head as if securing flyaways or feeling the waves in her hair.

"You sounded like this was urgent. I skipped breakfast and now lunch, so if it isn't..."

"I will get you something from the canteen," Anika said. She bent down to the security panel and provided a retinal scan to get back into the building.

That's all it takes?

I could kill Anika, and still use her eye to get inside Regulator Headquarters. The front entrance held more security, but they hadn't updated these side entrances since I worked here. Too trusting. Regulators were human beings, and if it's one thing humans do well it's screw up. The badge didn't automatically alter the user's belief system or personality. If they hated hatchlings, the badge wouldn't make them suddenly love them.

"What happened to your face?" she asked.

"I've been struck several times by fists. You could say me and my assailant had a disagreement."

"Are you all right? We can get you down to the infirmary." Anika studied the bruising on my face.

"I'm fine. Let's get this done." For now, the pain patch, a bandage strip that included nanos delivered pain reliever to the bloodstream.

Once the door opened, the roar of work rushed out to greet us. Most of the time in my office, the quiet went on for hours with only short, small talk episodes.

Not here.

Headquarters bustled with activity. Regulators, both in uniform and those in citizen clothes, hurried from point A to point B as if on fire. Organized chaos thundered around us as we pushed through the throng. I followed Anika, but only the top of her head. The din, a mixture of voices, computer noises, bots's whirring, and movement all collided to the point, I stopped trying to respond to her and just followed her to the commandeered conference room she and Agent Lynn shared.

Agent Lynn spied us through the room's floor to ceiling window. The conference room had a long, metallic table with coffee mugs, tablets, styluses, and water carafes on its surface. Agent Lynn looked up from her laptop but didn't speak when we entered. She grunted in way of greeting. The door hushed close behind me.

The floor used to be where they stored paper records and file cabinets stuffed with violator books, records, and equipment. Those items went to an entirely separate building on the other side of The District. Sometime after I left, the landscape changed to established cubicles, interrogation, and conference rooms. I watched as two regulators wrangled a very angry citizen, complete with handcuffs, into one of those rooms. He spat at the window.

Anika flinched.

I didn't.

He met my eyes and bared teeth. One of the regulators snatched him so hard, he tripped and went down. It didn't stop the regs momentum.

Nothing has changed here.

Ahead of me, Anika walked around to the front of the table. She gestured to a neighboring chair as she sank in the other one as if all was right in the world. "Come on over here. Let's show you what we got so far."

Agent Lynn sat at one end of the table, and Anika sat at the other. I would be between them in the middle, closest to the rear wall of the conference room. The arrangement left me without a clear route of escape if something happened.

"I'll stand." I left my satchel in the wauto, and I had no means of taking notes.

Anika hesitated, as if she wanted to force the issue. She glanced down the table's length to Agent Lynn who gave her a one-shoulder shrug.

"Okay." Anika gestured toward the glass where a projection started. "I wanted you to see this. This is CCTV from the Midland Air Station at about 3:00 a.m. Look. Here. See the one in the green cloak. There."

Anika paused it with a tap of her finger on the table's surface. She splayed her fingers and the image enlarged. "That's Nico Mars. Facial recognition picked him up when he deboarded. We can follow him to right about here, but once he exits, CCTV lost him."

"Who is the unfamiliar companion with him?" I pointed at the woman walking alongside him in a matching cloak, hers was black.

Anika closed her hand and the video feed returned to its original size. "Good eye. See, Lynn, she's awesome."

Agent Lynn smirked. "We picked up on it too."

"How does an escaped violator have the currency to take a trip on an airplane?" I ignored Lynn.

"There's been no activity on his bank accounts," Anika said, shaking her head. "Probably a false name."

"And the woman?"

Anika shrugged. "Maybe she funded it. We didn't get a hit on her face, so no violator activity."

"Not in The District. She could be a violator from another territory," I said.

Agent Lynn nodded. "Not the Midwest. We ran her against our databases there, too."

Anika handed me a tablet, this one small, about the size of my palm. "That's who we want you to find."

"The woman." I swept right and the screen lit up. The woman's image from the video had been captured and enlarged. The regulators had video tech people who improved the quality of the video. "This has been reviewed for authenticity. It hasn't been manipulated or layered or overlaid?"

"It's legitimate. Agent Lynn and I are going to chase down any additional video from Midland to see if we can figure out where he went from there." Anika sat back down.

"We've already put in requests to the area businesses, but we'll get agents to do the door to door today," Agent Lynn chimed in. "Be good if we can snag the woman, too."

"Of course." I understood the role they wanted me to play. "I'll see what I can do."

Anika sighed. "Thank you. Check in tomorrow here, at 9. Okay? We do daily check-ins and briefings. Now, about food…"

"Got it." I didn't wait for her to agree before leaving the room.

Agent Lynn's nasal laugh followed me out into the hall before the door closed. She could've told me the information over the telemonitor, but Anika wanted me under her authority. I'd play along until I got my currency or Nico or both.

"Cybil!"

I turned to look at Anika rushing down the hallway after me. Once she reached me, she smiled. "Are you heading to the canteen to eat?"

"No." She could tell from the direction I traveled I wasn't.

The smiled sagged. "I thought you were hungry."

"I am. Starved." She didn't need to know my plans or what I was doing. The Regulator canteen, while they had good food choices, also used robots. Back when I worked here, it didn't, but now it did.

Anika moved over to the wall to allow traffic to pass her on the right. I then realized she expected me to elaborate. I didn't do well with micromanagement.

"Look, if this is going to work, you need to be able to do something for me."

Anika stiffened with her eyes wide. "What?"

"No violations, so relax."

She gave a nervous giggle. "Right."

"I just need room to do the job. Imma need you to stop smothering me."

"Oh, I didn't think I was smothering you…"

"Now you know." I patted her hand, before turning and heading back down the narrow hallways I'd come. With my satchel in my vehicle, the small tablet took up one of my hands. My pockets lacked room for the device.

The truth was it didn't matter if she thought she was smothering me. I thought she was and that was enough. I wanted her to back off because breathing down my neck while I'm working only made me annoyed.

Once I cleared the doorway, I rounded the short corner to the parking lot where my wauto was on fire. Even from the distance between the door and my burning inferno, thick clouds billowed upward. Flames shot high in the air, crackled and snapped as all of my belongs—my satchel included, burned. The cannon blaster in the trunk blew up and the world shook. My wauto had been destroyed inside and out. Without thinking, I rushed to it. Already too late, the heat pushed me back several feet.

From what I could tell, the torched wauto had gasoline poured on the seats and ignited. The fire burned through it. I could see the pour patterns on the pavement from splashes of accelerant. Was there someone watching me? Who knew I'd be at headquarters?

No one other than Anika.

Suddenly, she appeared at my elbow and dragged me out of the way of the firefighters and their crafts lowering to the lot. Someone had called them, but no one told me. No one thought to notify me. They brought out a device to determine of the accelerant. I couldn't have been inside for longer than 20 or 30 minutes at the most.

My ears popped and sound, noise, sirens, and shouts rushed in. I was numb, stunned, and all I could hear was the sirens. All I could smell was fire and burnt leather.

Was the wauto torched to cover up a violation?

Anika grabbed my shoulders and turned me to face her, away from the flames engulfing my wauto.

"Are you all right?" she shouted, but it sounded like her voice came from the other side of a pillow.

I shook her off. "I'm fine."

She searched my face, and dropped her arms. "No, you're not."

"You're right. I'm pissed."

Others would be torn into pieces at such a hateful act.

Not me.

I don't cry on the outside.

I get even.

I stormed back into the building. The door had been propped open by the regulators who poured out to rubberneck at my misfortune.

Not misfortune.

Attack.

My attack.

CHAPTER
THIRTEEN

Seated in the right corner of a beige fabric covered cubicle, I watched Regulator Philips take the property violation report. He looked as if he was born yesterday with tousled curly blond hair and dimples. Perched ramrod straight in his chair, his fingers glided across the glass as I answered his questions. I smelled smoke on my clothing, and my belly grumbled, angry at the continued lack of food.

"Did you have any items of value in the vehicle?" Regulator Philips asked with a side glance at me as if this was a normal conversation.

"The vehicle itself was an item of value." I pinched the bridge of my nose and forced a calm I didn't feel. "My satchel had my hand-held, other important tablets, and my wallet."

"You carry a currency card?" He didn't hide his shock.

Oh, the young.

"I have both a currency card and an imbedded chip." I lifted my right hand and pointed to the scarring where the new chip had been placed after the first one exploded.

"Your identification?" He frowned at the ugly knots of scarred flesh on my wrist.

He ran his scanner across the area with distaste on his lips. He read the chip reader's information, my name, my private inspector license number, and my gun permit. He put the scanner back into its compartment on his desk, where it synced with the computer report, highlighting the identity flags.

He cleared his throat and pushed on.

"Verified. Cybil Lewis. Private Inspector. Resident of Sector 24..." he read off the information for my confirmation.

I didn't trust myself to speak so I nodded.

"Do you know of anyone who would do this?" He turned his seat to face me. "There was accelerant found. It's a fire violation."

"Before you start attempting to dig into my life, I have a few questions of my own," I countered.

He paused. "Well, uh, sure. Of course."

"Where's the CCTV video footage of the violation?" I asked. "I want to see it."

He smiled. The kind of grin that said, 'you-poor-foolish-thing'. I'd seen that same smile on my momma's face when I told her I wanted to marry Stephen.

"Miss Lewis..." he started.

"Now. Or I get Captain Brinnington down here." I stood up. I was sick of sitting, sick of waiting, and sick of being treated like a helpless victim. "So, either take me to the digital vision department or I go myself. I was regulating this territory before you were hatched."

I didn't care that I sounded like an old, angry woman.

I *am* an old, angry woman.

Regulator Philips spoke in soft tones. They taught that skill in escalation training. "Miss Lewis, I understand how traumatic this can be. You *were* nearly killed. Let me get you some water, a coffee..."

"You can get me the non-doctored video," I said back in the same, forced tone of voice.

To his credit, Regulator Philips didn't explode, but rather, kept his nerve despite me stepping all over it. "As a citizen, albeit one that's a private inspector, I cannot give you access to evidence in an on-going case."

"Someone torched my wauto." I offered as way of an explanation.

He nodded like a doting parent. "I understand."

"You keep saying that, but I'm sure you don't."

"A former regulator turned P.I. should know evidence in an active investigation cannot be given out to those not directly involved in the case." He turned his chair back to the screen.

"It's *my* wauto, so tell me again that I'm not directly involved." All of my honey had drained from my body, only hot vinegar remained.

A hush descended over the area as if everyone had heard my volume and froze at the anger seething from it.

"She's not just a P.I., she's an acting Territory Alliance agent," Anika said from the cubicle's opening where I was certain she'd been eavesdropping.

Regulator Philips looked at her with both eyebrows raised in genuine surprise.

"Territory Alliance Agent Winsome."

She allowed him to scan her wrist for identification. Regulator Philips was too young to recall when Anika was a District Regulator.

"She's helping me with a case. That's why she was here in the first place, and if you're done, regulator, I still need her," Anika explained with that short professionalism that she displayed when I first met her.

Regulator Philips huffed out a "well," and then to me, he said, "We're done. I will update you on the investigation. Contact your insurer. I sent you the report number. I have your contact information."

"Sure." I pushed by Anika as I exited the too-small-space.

Anika grabbed my arm to keep me from storming off. Where was I going anyway? My wauto sat smoldering in the evidence lot. I gently shook her off but slowed my pace to match hers. She inched forward, taking the lead.

"I'm so sorry about this, Cybil. Agent Lynn is arranging a temporary vehicle for you right now. As soon as the footage is ready, I'll let you know," Anika said.

I grunted out a "thank you". With my mood so far in the black, I optioned not to talk, but to listen. Someone had the courage to sneak into Regulator Headquarters and in the span of about 25-30 minutes set my wauto on fire. Nothing else had been vandalized. No other vehicles. No walls. No doorways or doors. It had been a personal and deliberate attack.

That left only a few options.

One, the violator was a regulator.

Two, the violator was a T.A. agent.

Three, the violator was hired by one of those two individuals.

It did occur to me Anika could've had my wauto torched so she could provide a vehicle where she could monitor my whereabouts. It was quite a stretch, when a simple tracking device would do the job. The burned wauto also had the case files for Nico Mars in it along with my handheld, which had my notes on the case and previous cases. Good thing I backed those files up to a private server in my office. Now, if someone burned down my office, I may have an issue for the newer files. I hadn't converted them to triple encrypted storage yet.

We reached the elevator and a small crowd waited for the carriage.

"Anika, listen, I'm starving, and honestly, I don't want to be here." I stepped back from the others. "I'm going to catch a cab and head on home."

"Wait, um, we're getting you a loaner." She searched around, a frantic expression on her face.

"Yeah, I'll pick it up tomorrow. Right now, I need to get out of here."

She searched my face. "All right. Stay in touch."

"Sure."

I headed up the nearest stairwell. No one took the stairs, and that afforded me both quiet and solitude. I exit and started up to the third floor, which constituted the main floor if I'd come in through the central entrance. In the rear of the building, behind a sea of cubicles stuffed with regulators processing incoming violators, interrogation all-window rooms, and restrooms, were the closed off captains' and commanders' offices sections.

I weaved through the throng. Once I successfully navigated to the series of automatic doors, I exited regulator headquarters and walked out into the roar of late afternoon. Overhead, vehicles streamed in and out of the parking lots.

None of them mine.

Hovering and blowing hot air from their wautos, bright sunshine-yellow taxis waited in the lane designated for them. Corralled like a fleet of cows, they awaited purpose. Another classic example of supply and demand—released violators normally had to fork over a lot of currency to be freed from citations or holding. They may have enough left for a taxi, because their vehicles had been impounded, if they had one. The District rolled the poor and down-trodden like a violator.

The hot and sticky humidity glazed my body with sweat and made my clothes stick to my person. I strolled along the sidewalk, passing robot pilots. Toward the end of the line, I found a green painted wauto with a male driver. Along his neck, a double helix tattoo and a crucifix dangled from a silver chain. Silver. Despite the vehicle's shabbiness, he had currency or someone loved him. A rare feat for hatchlings.

The passenger door lifted revealing rear seats with USB ports.

How old was this thing?

He leaned over and said, "Where to?"

I climbed in, optioning to sit in one of the rear seats. As I cleared the space, the door lowered. Blessed air conditioning, the interior felt cool. I closed my eyes and gave him the coordinates to my apartment. I wanted to go home, shower, eat and sleep in that order. I exhausted my people quota.

The driver must have understood that I didn't want to be bothered. He turned on some music, light and soft interior classical music, Mozart's last musical, I think. I closed my eyes and let the wind channel's cool air blow over me.

Today sucked hot boiled eggs.

I looked out my window at the land below. Located at the confluence of the Potomac and Anacostia rivers, The District was flanked on the north, east, southeast and southwest by the Southern Territories. There were a few parks sprinkled along the river banks. People boated up the river, water-skied and fished. Unraveling in a cornflower blue canopy with bright sunshine, the day continued as postcard perfect. The air itself roasted beneath the sun's powerful punches.

So thankful to be encased miles above in an air conditioned wauto.

I had to be thankful for the little things.

No matter how small.

It must be the stress and shock talking.

Why did every moment have to be so hard?

I didn't have my handheld, and it felt strange not to be tethered to my device. My hands didn't seem to know what to do so I held them. Though thankful for no more bad news, the lack of access to immediate information forced me to pay attention to other things, like the driver's bald spot. He had short hair, but not shorn.

The sunlight struck the smaller tablet screen Anika gave me. I snatched it up from the neighboring seat where I tossed it when I first climbed in. With a fast swipe, it woke up. The image of the woman traveling with Nico Mars looked like she'd been born into wealth, not like most of us, The District's depraved, dirty, and used up.

Something about the way she carried her head and her shoulders.

Something tugged on my memory, but I couldn't place it. I *knew* her.

High cheekbones, tanned skin, flawless and radiant, happy dark brown eyes, and long curly hair. Could she be having an affair with Nico Mars? Affairs were dirty business. Like violations, these types of engagements created an emotional messiness and it forever altered people's lives, even those not directly engaged in the relationship.

The wauto lowered as we approached. The now humming pilot said over his shoulder, "Almost there."

I scooted up to the rear facing payment console. When I licked my finger and pressed my finger on the oval section for thumbs, the system read my DNA and pulled the currency from my account. Electronics. Some of my clients still used actual coins.

Once we landed, the pilot released the passenger door. Once it opened fully, I slipped out feeling a bit more refreshed than when I entered.

"Thank you." I waved.

"Ma'am," he said, leaning over the passenger seat. "I dunno who beat you about the face, but you should stay away from that person."

I smiled. The fight with my attacker earlier, seemed like a million days ago. "Thank you for your concern."

He waggled a finger at me. "Next time, he may kill you."

I nodded and moved away from the taxi. Who knew what horrors he saw land into his taxi every day?

Same here, brother. Same here.

I made my way up to my apartment where I marched right to my bedroom, shedding clothes like a snake losing its second skin until I fell, naked except for my socks, onto my bed where I slept. My shoulder holster and my pug landed on the bed within my hand's reach.

While I dreamed of delicious meals, the case twisted again.

CHAPTER
FOURTEEN

A long, white tablecloth topped by matching tapered candles decorated a long buffet table. The candles' flames flickered in the soft breeze, as the table itself had been set up on a beach. Most had become so contaminated and polluted they'd been deemed public health risks, but not this sandy oasis. Before me, a juicy steak, medium rare, plated with a heaping side of garlic mashed potatoes, and fire-roasted corn, all displayed in artful direction.

I lifted my fork, full of mashed potatoes, when the closest palm tree spoke.

With a soft, almost apologetic tone, it said, "You have a visitor."

"Tell them to go away!" I moved the fork closer to my lips. The garlic smelled delicious, and the glistening hints of butter promised to be fabulous.

"You have a visitor." This time the palm tree sounded more insistent.

I placed the fork down with careful attention not to spill its contents and then pushed back from the table. My stomach rumbled, threatening to grumble the entire way to see who dared to interrupt my dinner. I'd starved all day long and now, with a feast presented, I didn't take kindly to being interrupted.

Yet, with each step I took, the little whisper in the back of my mind got louder. A dream. Nothing here was real. Cows had severe mutations. Some companies stated they'd successfully threaded the mutations out, but without an independent government body over-seeing those promises, I didn't take the risk. Hell, even if The District declared them mutation free, I wouldn't eat it. So, steak, butter, and corn had all gone the way of the buffalo, as my momma used to say.

Dream.

Gone.

I woke up with a start. I snatched on my robe, tied the belt, and stomped to the door. On the other side, Jane stood on the welcome mat with a container and a grim expression on her face.

"Do not make me pick the lock on this piece of shit door," she threatened. "I know you home."

I punched the release, and the door drew back. In walked my inspector-in-training sporting her trademark cigarette dangling between her full lips, and her hair snatched back into a ponytail. She wore a black tee-shirt that said, "Women Love Better." Today jeans, but not her customary black ones. On her feet, biker boots, black, of course.

"Who tried to rearrange your face?" she asked, with one eyebrow quirked.

"Ambushed in the office building's downstairs lobby." I locked the door and headed to the living room. Jane's demeanor meant she planned to stay.

She followed. "Who are *they*?"

"Dunno."

"Why did they attack you?"

"Dunno."

Jane stopped. "Where the hell was your T.A. partner?"

"Dunno."

"This is bullshit."

"Not now, Jane. The attacker was a woman from The Bottoms. It was complicated." I waved her off.

Jane opened her mouth to further her chastisement but thought better of it. Instead, she said, "I heard about the wauto violation, so I came right over. That piece of medieval hardware you called a vehicle should've been put out of its misery years ago."

"It was a good wauto." I sat down in my favorite spot on the sofa and clicked on the telemonitor. *The Crow* played on the American Film Classic channel. Good. Loved that movie.

"I gotcha some food." Jane handed me a container. The plant-based box released steam through a valve.

"You sure about this?" I asked, looking up at Jane.

"It's tasty. It came from the Cored Apple Restaurant."

This from a woman who refused to eat wheat pasta.

She'd ordered take-out from this new restaurant down on K Street, a place called Cored Apple. Restaurants didn't open regularly so it was a bit thrilling to try some new place. We've passed it a few times, and it had been stuffed with patrons to the point of bursting. Different from Big Mike's Jazz Bar, the place did have one thing going for it—no robotic servers. All employees were human or hatchling.

Shaking my head, I opened the recycled fork that came with the bowl. Inside, pasta, drowning in a moat of lukewarm gray sauce of unknown origin awaited. Good thing we had nice cold drinks. I ate some of the chunks, and realized they were tofu. I would rather eat vegetables in their organic states, not masquerading as something else.

Hell, the "meat" didn't have *any* flavoring at all.

As if reading my mind, Jane got up, went to the refrigerator, and returned with two bottles of cold Peck beer. She passed me one, after opening it with her tee-shirt.

"How'd you know it was my wauto?" I took a long drag of the beer. I didn't think the regulators released the details.

"Eavesdropping on Winsome. She's not expecting to be surveilled. I got real close to her without her knowing. She was flapping her gums to a citizen at The Cored Apple at dinner." Jane perched herself on the opposite end of the sofa's arm.

The weight of things Jane and I had left unspoken lifted. Pride warmed me.

I sat up straighter. "Tell me what you got."

"All right, but don't blast the messenger. It's only been a few hours." Jane took out her tablet.

"For a T.A. agent, she's surprisingly unaware. I'm good, but she just didn't seem to recognize anyone following her."

I put the container on the coffee table.

"Winsome is staying at The Flanagan, room 312, next to Agent Lynn in 310. They're only booked through the next week." Jane paused. "Anyway, she met a citizen at the Core Apple. Don't know him, but I'm looking into it."

"You get a Jpeg?"

She nodded and turned the tablet to me. "You know him?"

I peered at the image. The male had close cropped, salt and pepper hair, short moustache, and a pointy jaw. Seated across from Anika, he wore black synthetic shorts, a tee-shirt, and sneakers. He seemed so comfortable, but his body language spoke to training, either Army or regulator. There was a rigidness in his muscles, which meant he wasn't as comfortable as he portrayed.

"He looks familiar. Maybe he's a former regulator." His face tugged on my memory. I got up and went to the bedroom where I unearthed my ancient back-up laptop. No handheld so back to low tech methods.

When I returned to the living room, I found Jane seated on the sofa, her feet on the coffee table, and a bottle of Peck in her fist. The cigarette had been relocated to the spot behind her ear. "So, you do know him?"

"I feel like I do." I sat back down and booted up the laptop. It shrieked as the internal fans started. Jane raised an eyebrow.

"My handheld got torched along with my wauto."

"Is he her former partner?" Jane asked.

"I don't think so. But old grudges don't fade with age or time. Sometimes, they fester."

"Whatcha mean?"

I brought her up to speed on what I learned about the Nico Mars account and what happened year ago. I included Anika's relationship with Nico.

Outside thunder rumbled. At last, I called up the files from the Nico Mars case. Thanks to the arson I didn't have access to all the notes, but I did upload the videos and JPEGs. I cast the image gallery to the telemonitor so Jane could see too.

"What's this?" Jane scooted forward on the edge of the sofa.

"Anika gave me the case file for Nico Mars. The original tablet is toast in the wauto. These are the images I pulled from those files yesterday."

"I feel like I've seen this man before." I couldn't shake the feeling. Jane jumped up. "There!"

I paused the slow scroll. "What?"

"There." Jane pointed, rising up to get closer to the screen.

"I see it." I zoomed in on the seated picture of them, Anika and Ortega. Behind them, stood the man from Jane's surveillance, except in this still image, he wore a District regulator uniform. "Bingo."

"I knew it." I pumped my fist.

Jane sat back down. "He's a reg."

"Or he was." I collapsed the image gallery.

"What else you got?" I typed some notes on the laptop's Word processing software. It moved like a snail.

Jane drank, swallowed, and then spoke. "All of Winsome's biometrics and historic information checked out. She's who she presented to be."

"Then why didn't the initial sweeps find anything on her? She came up as an avatar. There's few reasons why that happens."

Jane shrugged. "Could be since she snitched on Mars, her info is scrubbed down here or it's blocked to the general public. They protect the whistleblowers. You know some of 'em regs were angry she turned Mars in."

"True. She told me they had to move him to the Midwest Territories due to threats on his life. It could be why she ended up there too."

We sat in silence for several long minutes.

"I'll tell you this. That guy," Jane nodded at the telemonitor, "gave me the chills, like a large icicle had been pushed into my chest. I wanted to end him right there."

"Why?" Those were strong from Jane.

"Dunno. He oozed." Jane fingered her knife's handle as she said this.

"I can't shake the feeling there's more there, between them."

Jane stood up. Once she drained her bottle, she burped. "I've gotta go. Kim's waiting and I need to pick up dinner. I'll get back at it in the morning."

"Okay. How's Kimmila?" I got up, too.

"Fine. She loves Zola. Daniel won't be getting her back."

"Oh, well, now." I laughed. "Daniel may have something to say about that."

"Talkin' ain't gonna get Zola outta Kim's arms. She loves her. Cats pick their owners."

"They pick whoever feeds them." I walked Jane to the door. "Thanks for dinner."

"No worries. Look, Cyb. Stop trying to save me. Stop holding your breath thinking something bad will happen. Me and Kimmila are fine."

"Sure. I, I don't wanna see you hurt. That's all." I couldn't focus on her advice to leave them alone. "Just remember that danger is often closer than you think."

"Got it." Jane stuck her cigarette in between her lips and left. It glowed alive before the door hushed close.

Jane was right. She could handle herself, maybe better than I could. I didn't want to watch her trainwreck, but to her word, that hadn't happened. It was *possible* it wouldn't. But I don't place a lot of faith in luck being in my favor.

Had I let my cynicism spoil all attempts at hope in my life? Maybe.

My partner-in-training had been right. I'd been projecting every worry, every failed relationship, every poisoned promise onto her and Kimmila. And it wasn't fair.

They wanted a fair shot to be happy. That's what I wanted for Jane, happiness. The kind that escaped me.

Perhaps I should give her room to pursue and, if she gets hurt, be here to pick her up.

What was in the bottle of Peck beer?

The facial recognition scan tweeted it had finished. A tense feeling burned in my gut. I returned to the living room and looked at the laptop with growing dread. On the screen, across the jpeg of the mysterious woman with Nico Mars, the word **unidentified** blinked**.**

"Damn." The lack of the results put a craptastic icing on a shit cake of a day.

With frustration boiling to the surface, I sank unto the sofa. I finished my beer and took the laptop to the bedroom. I couldn't let it go. I had to get the ideas buzzing in my brain down where I could see them and the pattern being presented.

I knew I wasn't going to get any rest so I might as well keep working. For there it was again, piling up in my chest like day old indigestion, an acidic reflex that won't let you stop tasting the spicy tofuloaf.

Regret.

Stiff, lumpy, and relentless each night I laid down, I recalled again the would'ves, the should'ves and the could'ves with Trey like other old, ratty-long-be-gone boyfriend.

The certain realization I will someday die, and soon, in my field of play, was scary. I didn't want to do it alone. The added reality I will not die so much as the knowledge I will leave so much undone, unsure, and unmanaged truly made me sad in ways only drinking and thoughts about death could.

The ultimate 'fuck you' from the Fates. I only get one chance to live and make far-reaching and unrealized choices.

If I made the wrong turn at Albuquerque, why couldn't I get a map, check it, and find my way back to the true meaning of life?

Why did I have to be stuck with the decision?

I didn't know but I put all of my heart's aching into a box.

I had work to do, and I did have my notes backed up to my personal server. With a thrill starting to erode the dismay, I searched the server for those files. The notes from my handheld had been transferred to my server, but they most recent ones had been corrupted.

I needed the Fates to ease up on me. I blew a slow breath out and pushed through the rising ball of stress tightening at the base of my neck.

I worked with what remained. It's what I've always done. Working with the pitifully small nuggets of hard truths and resources the world gave out.

I began re-creating the notes based on what I could recall, impressions, and thoughts, into a new file. I copied the previous notes, breaking them down on a daily basis. I started with day one salvaged notes and then filled in what I recalled. Memory didn't mean accuracy. I'd have to cross the bridge when I got there and reconfirmed details as I went along.

After about three hours of filling in the gaps and reconstructing my case notes, I switched gears and picked up the tablet with the jpeg of the unidentified woman.

Jane's mystery man and Nico Mar's mystery woman were two unidentified people connected to Anika and Nico Mars.

I didn't believe in coincidence.

Something or *someone* connected these two individuals.

But what?
I had no idea.
I would find out.
I always did.

CHAPTER
FIFTEEN

The sun was a hazy bloodshot eye as I waited for Agent Lynn in front of my apartment building. She volunteered to drop off my loaner vehicle. The T.A. paid for my replacement until I could get another wauto, but Agent Lynn wanted to rub the vandalism in my face. I would be checking the vehicle for surveillance devices. Nothing came from the Territory Alliance without a price. This loaner vehicle in the face of the destruction of my own wauto made our relationship more complicated.

I had little faith in The District's ability to resolve or find the violator who torched my wauto. I don't think it ranked high on their list of important violation cases. Regulator Philips left a message stating once the vehicle became cool enough for further inspection the firefighters found pour patterns. Thus, confirming the arson. The fire burned fast and hot. The paint job burned off and all the seats melted. What remained, a husk of melted plastic and fiberglass, left little physical evidence. The young regulator promised to keep digging. I didn't sow seeds of discontent, so I wished him luck, and kept my doubts to myself.

Outside, in the mugginess, minutes passed with my arms resembling a bad case of chicken pox thanks to greedy mosquitos. I lifted my baseball cap further back from my forehead and wiped the sweat away. The gun drew weary glances and hesitant smiles from occupants leaving the building and a long glare from a neighbor reading his ebook. They walked past without meeting my eyes.

Hi neighbors!

I slapped the back of my neck hard. The *smack* of my hand on sweaty flesh made a neighboring man look up. The bug juice splattered out on to my palm.

"Gotcha." I smeared what remained of it on my khaki shorts.

The interior lobby didn't have chairs, but it did have air conditioning. A pathetic little stream of cool forced air came with a persistent wheezing. I could go inside, and wait there, but given the choice between waging war against the winged blood-thirsty insects and being somewhat cool, but not quite, I chose battle.

My ongoing fight with the mosquitoes continued as I slapped at my arms. My tank top already contained the smeared marks of their dead, but the winged bastards kept coming. Hunger is one hell of a motivator.

The sleek silver wauto's roar drove them off as it lowered to the ground. The wind turbines blew so hard I fell back a step. I held my arm up against my face to protect it, as the pilot landed a few feet from me. The neighbor snatched up his e-book tablet and stormed off into the building, his quiet reading time disturbed too many times.

The two door wauto's pilot door opened with a soft hush. I dropped my arm and waited as Agent Lynn exited. Her bob swung in her face, but it failed to hide the smear of smugness Dressed in a gray short-sleeved jacket, cream undershirt, and matching gray capris, she came around the wauto's front with glee. She wore cream heels, and I wondered how she would chase down a violator.

Then my brain supplied the answer. She wouldn't.

"Lynn," I said in way of greeting.

"Tell me, Lewis, you feel empty without your vehicle?" Agent Lynn arms crossed across her chest.

"Unlike yourself, I don't need things to complete me. I'm solid."

"Like a brick," Agent Lynn retorted. "You know, if someone had been in your wauto, they'd be dead about now."

"I'd be lying if I said I'm sorry to disappoint you." I closed the distance and opened my palm. "Key."

My vehicle's loss did impact me, but no one would get to see me cry over it, especially not Agent Lynn.

She slapped it into my palm. The roar of another wauto approaching interrupted the strong words I had for her. I turned to see a regulator cruiser hovering directly behind the loaner.

Agent Lynn laughed. "What? You didn't think I'd trust you with driving me back to headquarters? After what happened to your vehicle?"

With that, she scampered off the way roaches did when the lights came on.

After I was sure she'd left, I got in the wauto, closing the sleek door. It rotated down and clamped into place.

Once inside, the wauto announced, "Ready."

The seatbelt automatically locked in and strapped me back into the seat. I had a manual one in my older wauto, but this new tech performed its functions without permission from me. The pilot's seat adjusted to my height before I could swipe the keycard.

Once it was satisfied, I pushed the card into the slot and the rest of the vehicle came alive. Oh, I could definitely get used to this fast engine and smooth, nearly quiet humming. I punched my office's coordinates and off we went. The autopilot assumed command, but I wrestled the piloting away from it. Robots had to gain trust. I flew my own vehicle unless it was necessary for the autopilot to take over.

In no time, I had landed, entered, and got off the elevator on the sixth floor of my office building. I steadied my emotions for the next step in my investigation. Marching past my own office's double doors, I stopped outside the neighboring suite. In previous years, I managed to avoid my neighbor, but today, it had become *un*avoidable.

Across the single, gray door, illuminated in green, was *Yukio Reedburn, Information Broker*. I sighed and pressed the announcement button. The door slipped back revealing a solitary bank of computer monitors and keyboards spread out across a slew of tables. The projected keyboards lit up the glass tabletops. On one wall, metallic shelving units held servers, hardware, routers, and gadgets. They flickered in various colorful flashes as they went about their work. Most of the office space had been consumed by hardware. Blackout curtains cast the room in shadow.

From behind one of the monitors, with her goggles resting on her head, Yukio's big brown eyes squinted against the light's harshness. As soon as he saw me, she stood. Big hoop earrings trapped strands of her long dark hair, which had been parted down the middle and plaited into two fat braids on either side of her head. Multi-colored cords hung from around her neck like technological jewelry.

"You! Again?" Yukio crossed her arms. Her tank top revealed a series of electric tattoos along her right forearm. They resembled train tracks, straight lines in varying lengths.

"Why else would I be here? I need an information broker." I kept my tone light.

"But you don't have to come to me. The District has hundreds."

"You're the best and the closest."

She grunted and lowered herself into the office chair. "So, what's the job?" She glanced up at me, waiting.

I handed her the small tablet containing the mysterious woman's image.

Yukio took it and peered at it. "What is it?"

"I need this person identified."

"You run facial?" She plopped down in her seat, her left hand on a virtual keyboard, fingers moving in a blur.

"Yeah. Nothing."

Yukio nodded as if that had been expected.

"When do you need an answer? It might be a while." Yukio looked up. "600 units."

I stood there with my mouth ajar. "That's…"

"Do you want her found or not?" Yukio asked.

"Yeah." I licked my finger and put it against the POS pad she held up with a wide grin. It held little warmth.

I left leaving Yukio to her work.

If anyone could find out the mystery woman's identity, Yukio would.

CHAPTER
SIXTEEN

After leaving Yukio's, I walked by my office again, headed down the stairwell, all five floors, and out into the humid day. It smelled like rain, and I figured late afternoon showers awaited. Jane should be out following Anika and Kimmila should be seated in the office, answering incoming connect and requests. I didn't check to confirm any of this, because I had my own plate full of to-dos.

I parked the shiny and fast wauto loaner in front of Big Mike's after an aerocycle vacated the spot. I paid for parking. In theory, when I returned to the space, my wauto would be there. Whether or not it would be engulfed in flames, I couldn't say.

What I did know was hunger. Despite Jane's kindness, the tofu mess she said was dinner last night didn't come close to fending off my starvation. I found my favorite seat at Big Mike's and looked around for my favorite waiter, Bryan.

I could go to the Cored Apple. I might spy Anika with her mysterious male companion. But this was my spot, and it had superior food.

When a young girl, rocking a big afro and tight shorts, zipped by my table, I snagged her attention with a "Hey!"

She stopped, turned, and said, "What?"

"Where's Bryan?"

She shrugged and checked her tablet. "I dunno. I think he's off today."

"Okay, can I get a Peck?" I pulled the electronic menu to me from the center of the table.

She nodded and headed toward the bar.

I ordered wheat pasta with pesto sauce, onions, mushrooms, and bell peppers. On the stage, The Blues and Grays set up for the lunch crowd. I'd been lucky to get my seat before the others got to Big Mike's. Barely noon, and already many people came in, boisterous with the latest office gossip or political antics. I missed my handheld, but the server returned to my table. She dropped off the beer without a word and hurried off to the populated tables around me.

I relaxed with the beer. I'd set things in motion. Jane, Yukio, and Anika were out and about, chasing down leads and seeking information. My mind wandered to the dead woman found in The 12. Henrietta. She had a name. A life. Family. Maybe people who loved and missed her. Inspector Jamison took over the violation from Daniel, but I had to be honest, I missed my friend. He kept me looped in with the investigation, but Jamison wouldn't.

None of the threads came together. I'm sure they should but I didn't have enough information to do anything. So, I let myself off the hook and awaited my food. Delicious odors wafted from the kitchen and out amongst us, tickling our hungry bellies and making our mouths water.

In almost no time, the server dropped off my large bowl of vegetables and pasta in pesto sauce. I dug in. It was almost like a black hole opened in my stomach. So enraptured in my eating, I didn't notice anyone until Daniel sat in the seat across from me.

"What the hell are you doing here?" I put down my fork and drank some beer to pushed down the rest of the food in my mouth.

He wore a baseball hat low over his brow, a black tee-shirt and shorts. He looked like he'd come straight from the futbol field, and I wondered again if his undercover work had him in a high school or college athletic program. He smelled incredible, some mixture of sandalwood and musk.

"I heard about your wauto. You all right?" He reached across to me, and I leaned back.

"Of course, you heard about it." I shook my head and started eating again. "Who connected you? Lynn?"

He shrugged. "Yeah, she sent me a message over the telemonitor. She said she got you a loaner."

I nodded. "She's sweet on you."

Daniel brushed it off. "No, she isn't. I'm not here about her. I wanna know if you're okay."

"I need to get a new handheld, another satchel, and eventually a new wauto," I said. "Outside of that, I'm good."

"You need help? I know a place over in Sector 10 that's got a good deal on the latest handhelds."

"Nah, I've got a guy."

He sighed. "Okay, so how's my cat?" Daniel signaled the server.

She brightened when she saw him and made a beeline for our table. He had that effect on people. When she arrived, her attention locked on Daniel and didn't move.

"What can I get you? I mean, I can get you anything." She leaned in, giving him her cleavage vantage point.

Daniel didn't smile. He shut her flirting down with a quick expression of disapproval. He kept his eyes on her face, and said, "I'll have a Peck beer."

"Food?" she asked, her flirty tone a bit deflated, but not gone.

"No," he answered. "But, thank you."

Once she left, he turned back to the topic at hand. "So, how's the case going?"

"It's going." I stabbed the remaining pasta and ate it.

"I can't get near the Mayfield case now." Daniel lamented.

"I heard a whisper the death violator is a breeder."

Daniel's eyebrows rose, disappearing into his ballcap. "Oh? Is that what happened to your face?"

"No, maybe, well, I dunno."

I brought him up to speed on the occurrences since I last saw him. He didn't have a clear idea either of why I was attacked, but he didn't like the breeder angle.

"Big Game is practically legit. There are articles and pictures of him with Governor Lance shaking hands and smiling at babies," Daniel said, picking some risone from my bowl. "All that currency bought him a council member or three."

"Off the backs of children."

Daniel popped the pasta into his mouth. "Yeah."

"Stop that. I don't know where your hands have been," I said. "Anyway, it's was strange. Just because the attacker had his mark, it doesn't mean she was still in his herd."

"True. He ain't known for letting them girls go though." Daniel picked up the menu and scrolled. "All I know is you got close to something and somebody didn't like it. That's kind of a habit of yours..."

"Someone attacked my wauto and tried for my life. It has to be something significant." I finished the pasta before Daniel decided to dive in again without asking.

"That's good pasta. Is that the house pesto sauce?" Daniel licked his fingers, and with his other hand, tapped on the menu's screen.

"Yeah." So much for him not being hungry.

He ordered and put the menu back onto its charging station. Then he got up and picked up a foghog from a neighboring table. In no time, the server returned with his Peck beer and his pasta bowl.

"Fast service," I said, low enough so only Daniel heard. He smirked.

"Here you go, sir. If you need anything else, please let me know." She winked.

"I need another one!" I shouted after her.

Over her shoulder, she said, "Okay."

Daniel ate like he hadn't had food in weeks.

"How are you?" I leaned in to get a better look at him. "Truth this time."

"I'm fine." He snapped, mouth stuffed with food. He made a cross over his heart. "I'm good."

"What's the gig?"

He swallowed and washed it down with beer. "I can't tell you."

"It's me." I made a hand gesture for him to start telling me.

"I know, but I could lose my job. I'm already in deep shit in some circles because of you." He didn't look at me, but he dove back into the bowl of food. He wasn't forthcoming, and his mood had changed.

I placed my thoughts back on the burners. I put my focus on finding the mysterious woman.

"Oh, do you know this woman?" I fished the tablet out of my pocket. Cargo shorts had deep pockets.

He took it and studied it for a few minutes. Some pesto sauce clung to the new growth on his chin.

"I don't know her name, but she's a District upper echelon dweller. Did you do a facial?"

"I did. I got nada." I shrugged.

Daniel didn't appear surprised. "People living in those circles hire staff or companies to scrub them out of facial recognition. She's probably one of those. I've seen her around, at award banquets and balls, but I can't put my finger on her name. Don't quote me, but I think she's the woman whose husband had shot his first wife, leaving the three children scarred and in foster care. When he got out of the cradle, he married her, the mistress. Big scandal."

"It seems she's now hanging out with violent violators. She clearly has a type."

"Yeah."

"Husband still alive?"

"As far as I know." Daniel gave a small shoulder shrug.

"Do you remember the Nico Mars case?" I drank some of the fresh bottle.

Daniel settled into his chair. He took a cigarette from his hard-case wallet. After he lit it, he blew the smoke through his nose. "Yeah. It was a fucking mess."

"Who worked it?"

"Why?"

"Just tell me."

He took a long drag and held my gaze.

I waited him out.

The cigarette calmed him. He looked around, and cleared his throat. "Regulators weren't allowed to investigate because he was one of our own. They brought in some T.A. agents to investigate him."

"Do you remember the two agents?"

"Agent Ortega and Agent Lightfoot." Daniel didn't hesitate.

"No one from The District?" I prodded.

"No. They couldn't let us get involved because they couldn't trust us not to plant evidence to free him or beat the living snot out of him," Daniel explained, shaking his head. "I remember Ortega was tough. She could've found out I cheated on my Year Three spelling test."

"Anything else you can share?" I smiled.

"I'd started around that time, so I don't remember a whole lot." Daniel peered through the smoke at me. The foghog sucked it in, but a brief delay between when he blew it out and when it got captured created a hazy veil.

"Do you know if Nico was guilty?"

"He was convicted."

"Yeah, but do you *believe* he was guilty?"

"The guy should asleep in the cradle. My opinion and beliefs don't mean shit." Daniel took a drag of beer. When he put the bottle down, he burped. "Sorry."

"Tell me as a hypothetical."

Daniel huffed out a sigh. "Nico Mars had this girlfriend. You would know her as Agent Winsome, but she used to be a regulator here. I don't think any of the new people remember her, but the old heads do. Did you ever ask yourself why Agent Winsome went to the Midwest Territories?"

"It had occurred to me." I sat back in my chair too. I drank more beer and waited for Daniel to get to the point.

"A popular rumor around HQ was Winsome had turned Nico in. No one confirmed it. No one denied it. But, once the case was over, the Territory Alliance offered her a job and she got the hell outta there. Straight to the Midwest Territory."

"Maybe she got some threats."

"Or maybe she was guilty too. Listen, I never thought Nico was guilty of every violation they threw at him. Some of it, others were involved, but I didn't work the case, so I could be way off base. The T.A. handled the entire investigation away from us, even on a separate site."

"Others like who?"

He patted the table. "Don't get excited, Lewis. I don't have names or anything that resembles proof. Most of those people are in the cradle or in the ground. I was a new regulator back then, full of idealism and clear rights and wrongs, no grays. I've matured since then."

"That's fair."

Daniel laughed. "All right. I'm surprised Winsome didn't share her history with Mars with you. Anyway, happy hunting out there."

"You too. Being a regulator has a short shelf life."

He nodded.

"You're sure no regulators worked the case?"

Daniel smiled. "You clearly know something I don't."

"Wasn't Nico married?"

"Yeah, but it didn't seem to matter. Winsome had been there longer than me and was an inspector back then. I only heard the locker room talk and you know most of it was overblown." Daniel pulled a face. He ran his fork along the bowl's rim.

"Like what?"

"I'm not telling you. I don't even remember most of it."

"I'm not shrinking violet."

"I know. More like a shrieking violent." Daniel laughed.

"Not funny."

"Yeah, it was." He licked his fork.

"As you can see, the agents aren't sharing everything about Mars with me," I said.

The color drained from Daniel's face along with the humor. "You're serious."

"I am."

"THAT's why they didn't want TRU involved. They're trying to save face." Daniel tapped the ash from his cigarette into the foghog's lower rim.

"There's more to it." I took another drink. "Ego notwithstanding."

Daniel drank too. We swallowed and sat in silence as the enormity of the case landed on our shoulders.

He broke first. "I've got to go. I know I say this a lot, Lewis, but you've got to be careful. The arson violation on your wauto wasn't random. I'd bet my pension on it. Someone's been sent to kill you once. Where's Jane? You need someone watching your back."

"Jane's working on the case with me." I paid the bill.

Daniel crushed the remaining cigarette, paid his bill, and stood. "Where are you parked?"

"Out front."

We walked out into the heady humidity. Thick, full clouds rolled across the horizon. Rain was imminent.

Under Daniel's stoic supervision, I made my way to the loaner vehicle. Once I got inside, strapped in, and got the keycard installed, Daniel disappeared into the crowd of people on the sidewalk.

Just a little after one o'clock, the rest of the afternoon loomed. I pointed the vehicle toward the commercial district, Sector Nine. I had to replenish some things, and I wanted to not focus on the case for a while, just blissful shopping.

My currency account retained credits from the bigger cases I'd worked this year, but I couldn't outright purchase a brand new wauto. Plus, my previous feelings about having a new target for violators to trash remained the same.

As soon as I reached Sector Nine, the sky opened, and a summer shower fell.

It rained in buckets, dumping all the clouds' pent of precipitation onto The District like an angry child pouring sand from a bucket at the beach. Once it finished, the clouds pushed on, allowing the hot sun to return. Groaning, I didn't want to be out shopping in the humid, sticky, and wet soppy temperature.

So, I flew home.

Despite it only being two in the afternoon, my body, my mind, and my soul longed for my bed, for rest. Once I got inside, I took off my shoes and crawled onto the fluffy comforter my grandmama made.

It often provided comfort.

Today was no different.

CHAPTER
SEVENTEEN

"Where have you been? You missed the briefing." Anika's veneer of professionalism crumbled. Her voice bordered on yelling. The usual crisp diction slurred a bit. "Lynn dropped off the wauto first thing."

"Uh, thanks." I pushed myself to a sitting position. My bedside clock said the time was after ten--on Thursday. I'd slept longer than I intended, but clearly my body needed it. Stiff muscles complained about the sudden movements I made to climb out of bed. While asleep, I didn't dream, instead I fought the sheet and the throw pillows. The bed resembled a fluffy, purple battlefield with twisted fabrics and pillows.

With cottonmouth clogging up attempts to talk, I coughed to clear it. I drank a glass of water from my bedside. I sighed and felt somewhat more human.

Anika had waited, albeit impatiently humming, until I returned to the connect.

"I wouldn't need a loaner if I wasn't working for you."

She blinked several times, her mouth slightly agape. Then, "It's not my fault your wauto was torched."

"Not directly, maybe not, but I wouldn't have been down there if it wasn't because you continue to demand it."

"Yes, but..."

"And here you are again. Fussing about my attendance at the very place where someone tried to kill me." I needed rest.

"I did wonder what happened to your face..." Anika gestured to my face.

"It's healing. Look, I'm not coming to HQ."

Anika's shoulders sagged. "We need you..."

"No. I need *you* to tell me everything. Remember?"

"I have!"

"Not. For starters, you didn't tell me you're the one who snitched on Nico. How the hell did the T.A. let you work a case when you're neck deep with the violator?"

Annoyance burned so hot I spat the words out. "I don't like being lied to and manipulated."

I waited for her answer, if she had one.

At 10 in the morning, I hadn't consumed coffee or food since early yesterday.

Silence.

On the telemonitor, Anika struggled to put her agent face back on. She adjusted her collar and cleared her throat.

"You've been busy. Found the identity of the female person of interest?"

"Working on it," I said.

"Maybe instead of investigating me, you could do the job we're paying you to do." She flashed a brief smile. Her cold tone hinted at controlled frustration

I knew it well.

"I can multitask." I held her furious glare. "Does the T.A. know about you and Nico?"

"Of course..."

"Does Lynn?"

Her eyes widened.

"She doesn't." I raised my eyebrows.

"Look, we're close to capturing Nico. Focus on finding that woman."

"I am."

"Thank you."

The connection ended.

I didn't touch a nerve. I fondled several instead.

Anika avoided answering my question. She knew that I knew and the balance between us would be different from here on out.

And folks wondered why I have so many damn trust issues.

The telemonitor announced an incoming connect.

Damn, I just woke up.

"Answer."

Jane appeared on screen. "Hey. Let's get together. I found out who the male subject with Anika is and some other good stuff."

"Come on over. Bring some food and caffeine."

"Yeah, okay, but you paying," Jane ended the connect.

I wiped my face with both hands. No doubt, I had to stay awake and go to work.

One of the reasons my mind resembled a clustered desk could be because I hadn't eaten any good food.

While I waited for sustenance, I showered. The cold tapped out about eight minutes in. The sweat resumed the moment I finished drying off. My bedroom's cooler temperature did nothing to encourage getting dressed, so I laid there like a bloated frog for I don't know how long. The air condition's feeble breezes washed over me. It failed to bring any new ideas.

I managed to dress in cool linen pants, a white tee-shirt, and brown steel toe boots before Jane arrived, but only just.

"It's stuffy in here," she said in way of greeting. She hurried over to the kitchen table and put down three containers and one large carafe. "Is your unit broken?"

"No, it's old. This heat wave is hell on these ancient circuits." I took two mugs down from one of the cabinets. "What do we have?"

Jane sat down in a chair and took out one of the containers. "Oatmeal with blueberries and eggs with tomatoes."

"What's in the third one?" I lifted the lid and inhaled. "Ah, ground grits."

"And eggs."

"Delish. Powered eggs are yummy." I removed the chopsticks from the vase on the table and handed a set to Jane.

"Yeah, and you owe me $27 in currency credits."

"Let's eat first. I can't think on an empty stomach."

"Or with a dry throat." Jane poured from the carafe.

"They learn so fast."

She smirked. "I'm not just a pretty face."

"Indeed."

She ate with chopsticks, scooping the thick bluish oatmeal with practiced precision and in her other hand, held her mug's steaming black coffee. Jane's outfit varied 180 degrees from mine. All black. Head to feet.

The ground grits tasted wonderful mixed with salt and savory p-eggs. The cook got the blend right and the powered eggs didn't have any grittiness.

No pun intended.

"How's Zola?" I sipped my own searing coffee.

"She's settlin' in. You know, Kim is too. They're so cute. Zola gives Kim someone to care for and the cat gives her love, no strings."

"Oh, there are strings. It has to be fed."

Jane paused, drinking her coffee. "Seriously, you think everybody's motivated by selfishness, even a cat."

I pursed my lips, released a breath before continuing. "The need to preserve yourself is hardwired into us, fight or flight. Cats love and bond to people because we feed, shelter, and love them."

I resumed drinking.

"True." Jane inclined her head. "They also survived wars, elimination of their habitat without human intervention."

"Uh huh, you weren't expecting that. Were you?"

Jane peered over her mug. "Fuck no."

I laughed. It spilled over to Jane, who chuckled.

In moments, we dissolved into giggles. Full, fed, and finished with brunch, we took our conversation to the living room. I sank into the sofa's end seat.

Jane's favorite seat, the cobalt-blue, square chair, was adjacent to the sofa. She put her cup on the neighboring end table and folded her legs in front of her.

"Okay, what did you find?"

"First of all, Anika's consistent in her routines. If I had been hired to commit a death violation, I'd be done in about a day. Secondly, she hates Agent Lynn, maybe more than you."

"Really?"

Jane said, "Agent Lynn and Agent Winsome don't operate on the same plane. Like, Lynn is never with her on outings. Agent Lynn's appears to be working closely with Regulator Inspector Jamison. Those two are running something on the side. I spy those two being chummy buddies while waiting on Agent Winsome. Jamison's visited Lynn's hotel room too."

"Jamison and Lynn, two rattlesnakes. Maybe that's why Anika's been so wound up. The last time I was with both of them, I could cut the tension between them like a piece of cake. "

I filed this tidbit in the back of my mind. Maybe Jamison and Lynn worked on the Mayfield case. Why would he bring a T.A. agent into a District death violation?

"Tell me about Anika's friend."

Jane licked her lips. "The regulator's well, former reg's name, is Eric Mann. The lead server at The Cored Apple told me. He's a regular and a lawyer. He doesn't live too far from that place. She either didn't know or wouldn't tell me specifically. I ran his name through the socials.."

I quirked an eyebrow. "A regulator and a lawyer?"

I didn't see that coming.

"He used to be a regulator, but not anymore. He's a lawyer—get this. Out of The 12."

Jane drank more coffee, draining the cup.

"That *is* interesting. When did he resign?"

Jane shook her head. "I dunno. I'm still digging into that. You could just ask her."

"I could."

"You think it's connected to Nico Mars?" Jane went into the kitchen. She returned with a refilled mug of coffee.

"I do. It's gotta be a common thread between the players. There's an escaped violator, a T.A. agent, and a former regulator. All of these people are connected by their relationships." I also thought the dead activist had links to this case, but I wasn't certain how Henrietta fit into the puzzle.

"It's all coincidental. We don't have any evidence. Nothing nefarious." Jane shook her head.

"Nefarious? You've been studying."

She laughed.

"What does Eric Mann know?"

Jane set her cup on the coffee table and crossed her arms. "It could be she's catching up with an old colleague. That's why she's meeting with him almost every night."

I leveled my gaze at her.

"Nah." Her hazel eyes shined in mirth.

"You know the only way to find out for sure..."

"...is to ask," Jane finished.

"Yep."

"We gotta determine fact from fiction."

Nothing like launching my own personal apocalypse.

"Agent Winsome won't like it." Jane gave me a knowing side eye and reclaimed her mug.

"I know."

Jane chuckled.

"Let's go see what they get up to."

THE LATE AFTERNOON burned in a sunny haze. Jane slipped her sunglasses on as we made our way down to the loaner. A light breeze met us once we cleared the building. It died before making a difference.

Same, little breeze, same.

When I got to the vehicle, despite parking it in the shade, it remained hot.

"This the new wauto?" Jane eyed it. "Must've cost all your currency."

"It's a loaner."

We got in and I started the flight sequence while she cranked up the A/C.

"You good with leaving your aerocycle here?"

"Yeah, it's fine. It has GPS. I can summon it to me when I need it."

"That's, uh, new."

"It is."

It didn't surprise me too much as Jane always tinkered with the tech on her aerocycle.

"What's Eric Mann's address?" I lifted into the elevated lanes. The territory traffic remained light.

"He lives close to The Cored Apple."

I punched in the coordinates. "You do have an exact, on the ground addy for him, right?"

Jane sucked her teeth as if annoyed at the question.

I laughed. "Sorry, I shouldn't have doubted."

"No, you shouldn't."

She entered the address into the wauto's GPS.

We spent the flight over to Eric's apartment in reflective quiet. Jane tossed her hunting knife, in its scabbard, in her left hand, a habit she did when bored and couldn't smoke.

"I miss your old wauto."

"Why?" I asked her.

"I could smoke in it."

"Ah, this one doesn't come with a foghog." I scanned the dashboard. "It's a basic model."

"What's the play?"

"I wanna surveil him. Who goes in and out, then we can ask some questions."

I lowered the vehicle as we drew closer to the location. The neighborhood around the capital, downtown, threatened to crumble into dust, like the ideals and lingering hypocrisy of the former country.

Eric Mann's apartment occupied the 6th floor of an aging walk-up. Two blocks over, sleek and shiny high-rises stretched for the stars while blotting out the heavens for others. Such was life in The District.

We landed the wauto. The day marched on to dusk.

Jane tapped out her boredom on the armrest. "How do we know if he's even home?"

I said, "We don't. Let's give it some time."

"What're we waiting for?"

"Anika."

"She usually meet him around this time." Jane's eyebrows rose.

"Right. We should see him heading that way to meet her. Does he fly?"

"No. Since he lives so close, I think he walks or bikes."

"We'll follow him to the meeting and ambush them."

"It's harder to lie when you're both blindsided with the truth," Jane said.

We waited until shortly before seven. Jane pointed at a male exiting the building. She stood outside the wauto, smoking. She leaned down and said into the open window.

"That's him."

I got out and with Jane, we fell into step behind Eric. Jane lit another cigarette and groaned in delight to be in action. The heat threatened to smother us, but it had become cooler. Others must've had smarter ideas because the sidewalks remained empty except for us and the target.

Eric wore khaki shorts, a yellow tee-shirt, and white sneakers. He wore a low-cut fade and diamond studded earrings, which I could make out when he passed beneath the streetlights.

A lawyer and former regulator.

Jane made pretend small talk with me. We fell farther behind him, but we knew his designation—The Cored Apple. The occasional breezes kept me from melting and brought with them the soured District aroma.

Ahead, Eric walked on. He used to be a regulator, but he didn't appear to have kept any of the skills. He had no awareness. He bopped to music, no doubt from ear buds and he would occasionally burst into song.

"I wish I had my buds," Jane muttered.

"No kidding."

When we neared the restaurant, we stopped and basked in the rich, savory aromas wafting through the trees. I pretended to tie my boot, allowing Eric time to meet with Anika and get comfortable in a booth or at a table.

We were about to make him *very* uncomfortable. Jane ran up to peek inside.

Minutes later, she returned. "Agent Winsome's inside already. He's joining her. She doesn't look thrilled to see him."

"Oh, she's probably mad because he's late. Doesn't he usually meet earlier than this?"

"It isn't that serious. He's like 15 minutes late."

I patted her on the shoulder. "Come on."

Lavender scent greeted us as we entered the restaurant. Like most dining establishments, it didn't have a large eating area.

"May I assist you?" The host wore a red shirt and matching slacks. No tie. "Table for two?"

"No, thank you. We're meeting our, uh, friends here," I said.

"Their names?"

"Never mind, I see them. Thanks."

I cleared the host stand before he could snag two menus from the stack of tablets. Jane followed behind me without a word.

We threaded our way through the seating area and reached Anika's table. She stiffened when she saw me.. She looked polished as usual, dressed in a scarlet, sleeveless dress. Eric Mann sat beside her, both facing the windows. We pulled out chairs and Jane sat opposite Eric, and I, Anika.

"What the hell, Lewis?" she said.

"Evening, Anika."

"Why are you here?" Anika glared.

If looks could kill, I'd be a grease stain on the wooden floor.

"Who is this?" Eric asked, his eyes shifted between me and Jane.

"It doesn't matter, because she's leaving. They both are." Anika snapped at him before turning her annoyance back to its source. Me. "Do you have something to tell me?"

"Just the opposite. I believe you have something to tell me," I said.

A server arrived. His young face showing concern. "Is there something I can get you?"

"Two bottles of Peck," Jane answered before Anika could object.

"Yes, right away." He fled.

"I don't know what's going on..." Anika said.

"Me either. That's why I'm here." I adjusted the chair, pulling it closer to the table.

"What do you mean?" Anika crossed her arms, and shushed Eric. The clang and clatter of people enjoying their meals served as a strange background.

"For starters, who's this?" I nodded at Eric Mann. "We haven't met."

"None of your business," Anika said, her tone hinted at raw rage, barely contained, but there, bubbling beneath the surface of her perfect makeup.

"You see, everything about Nico Mars is my business."

"Nico? What does she know about..." Eric started.

"Hush," Anika said to him. Then to me, "I've given you everything you need."

"Uh, no, you haven't. I know you know it too," I said. "For example, I saw the same man on some old video of the Mars' case. Yet, you neglected to tell me about him."

"There's nothing to tell. I've given you all the intel you need to do the one job I assigned to you." Anika paused when the server arrived to distribute drinks.

"Are you ready to order?" He offered a quick, but nervous smile.

"They're leaving," Anika interjected with a head nod at us.

"Not until you answer some of my questions, Eric." I ignored her grumble of protest. "I'm working the other job. It's in hand."

"Ma'am." The server's eyes—wide and round—shifted to me and then Anika.

"I'll have the bowties with red sauce, no tofu." Anika handed the waiter her menu.

Eric ordered flatbread with roasted mushrooms and garlic in olive oil. The aromas smelled delicious as the neighboring table had ordered the same thing.

"For you?" The server turned his pointy features to me.

"I'll have the same as what he ordered. Jane?" I looked at her with a big grin.

"Gnocchi in pink sauce, extra tofu." Jane drank her beer.

Relief washed over him and he gave us another nervous grin to defuse the tension. "Thank you. It'll be right out."

"You're intending to stay." Anika pursed her lips. The tone held nothing but contempt.

Eric used the silence to speak. "I'm Eric Mann, but you have me at a disadvantage as you know me, but I don't know you."

"I'm known for that," I said.

Jane coughed, but I heard her chuckle.

"She's Cybil Lewis, P.I., and a pain in the ass," Anika said. Her precise pronunciation took a dip on *ass.*

"I'm known for that too." I drank my beer.

"This is the infamous Jane, her partner-in-training," Anika said.

"In the flesh," Jane said. "Cyb, I'm infamous!"

"Don't let it go to your head."

"I see," Eric said, and cleared his throat. "A private inspector."

"You obviously know his name, so you must know he's a lawyer," Anika said. "He worked as a regulator, same as I did, but resigned shortly before I left for the T.A—"

"You're right. I do know those things. Tell me what I don't know." I crossed my arms too.

Anika's shoulders slumped. "None of it has anything to do with Nico and finding him. Why do you want to know?"

"Why do you want to hide it?" I countered.

"It's personal," she said.

"Personal circles and incidents of the violator are key to understanding them and building a profile. We always look closely at the victim's social circle. You and Eric are inside one of the closest rings to Nico Mars. You know this from Regulator training."

"Look, I just met you. I don't get to see my Anika often, and well, you're upsetting her, ruining our dinner, and our limited time together. Can't you two get your order to go and leave us alone? Maybe follow up with Anika at work?" Eric said.

I glanced at him, then back to Anika. "Mars. All of it."

"Didn't you hear me?" Eric raised his voice, maybe thinking I hadn't heard him, unable to fathom I had *ignored* him.

He rose and stuck out his hand toward me. A flash of metal caught my eye. Jane's knife was positioned at Eric's wrist, faster than I blinked. She hated hatchlings.

"Don't do that," she said to him. "Unless you wanna learn to jack off with the other hand."

"Put it away." Anika whispered. "Both of you."

I drank more beer. Jane looked at me out the corner of her eye. I nodded. Her blade vanished.

"Tell me what I want to know, and we're gone," I said.

Honestly, I didn't expect all of this, well, stubbornness. At least, I'll get a leftover dinner out of it. But Anika's reluctance only made me more determined to get information.

She stared.

"You know I turned Nico in. What you don't know is how or why. Nico patrolled The 12 and he worked in VV…"

"Vice Violations." Jane whistled.

Anika nodded. "I was the one who discovered Nico's illegal activities…"

"How?" Jane interjected and signaled the waiter for another beer.

She shrugged. "The heifers were all telling me about this breeder, Nqobile. They were scared, like frightened of him, more than any others."

"What scared them so much?" Jane pushed.

"Does it matter?" Anika huffed. "I did some digging, discreetly. Discovered Nico was dirty. I made an anonymous tip off to the detectives in Vice. They confirmed some of the activities, helped us get confessions from witnesses who came forward, and the rest you know."

"Mars never knew it was you?" I watched Eric.

He avoided eye contact.

"No but to be certain, I left the territory. Ortega made sure my previous life with Nico was scrubbed," Anika explained. "I got on with the T.A."

"And you?" I said to Eric.

"What about me?" He looked up at last.

"You resigned. Why?"

"No reason, just didn't love the job. Not a good fit for me." He shrugged again, but his shining eyes said more. "I went back into law practice."

"You're lying," Jane said. "Mars's boys drummed your ass out of the regs."

Eric shot to his feet. "I'm going for a cigarette. Message me, Anika, when the food comes and these people are gone."

He stormed off, bumping Jane's chair in the process.

"I told you to stop flicking nerves," I said to her.

"Was that necessary?" Anika leaned forward; her hands balled into fists. "None of this will get us closer to finding Nico!"

"It might. Was Nico confirmed to be Nqobile?"

"No, he denied it." Anika pushed back from the table. "As I said, we had witnesses, audio, video, and files documenting Nico's corruption."

"But not as Nqobile."

"No."

"And you said it didn't have do to with Mars." I smirked.

"Your meals are on the way," the server said as he approached. "Would you like anything else?"

"We'd like ours to go," I said. "Along with our bill."

JANE'S CIGARETTE smoke curled into the cool evening sky. We sat on blankets beside the Potomac, eating The Cored Apple yumminess from the takeaway containers. The moon, swollen and bright, provided an excellent stream of silvery light. There weren't any blankets or happy families situated near us.

Good. I liked solitude. Jane did too.

"That was fun but what do we really know? Did we get the magic answer?" Jane held a container in one hand. Her chopsticks stuck out like a buoy in a sea of pink sauce. "We knew most of it."

"We surmised but now we have confirmation. We also know Mars isn't Nqobile. The theory he's coming back to The District to take The 12 back doesn't fit. So why is he here?"

"True."

"We also know Eric had much more to do with the situation than she let on. It's like we're chasing a ghost."

"I dunno if I'd be meeting her for meals after she ditched me and hightailed it to the Midwest."

"You think he resents her?"

Jane blew smoke through her nose. "Fuck yeah. That shit probably festered."

"He said he went back into law. Maning was an attorney before he joined the regulators. Why did he leave the regs? He didn't seem like a flighty or wishy-washy person, but swinging between professions on a whim," I said. "Why?"'

Jane said, "I dunno about him. But Mars might be here for revenge. He gets out. He makes a direct route to The District."

"How'd he even get out?"

"No idea." Jane shook her head. "It had to be an inside job."

"For sure. You can't turn off your own cradle."

"And Eric's lying." Jane puffed.

"What if they're both lying?"

Jane shrugged.

I ate.

I missed nights like these when Jane and I hung out, drank beer, and talked theories. She stared up at the star-studded sky with wonder shining in her hazel eyes. She drank her beer, having put her food down.

"Where's Mars?" Jane said.

"He's got to be getting help. I can't see him avoiding capture by chance."

"Well, yeah, but who and why?"

"If I knew that, I'd catch him and be done with this foolishness." I laughed.

"Hell yeah!"

She drank more and then caught herself. "Shit. I gotta fly home. Kim's gonna be worried."

Her face lit up and she packed up and hurried over to her aerocycle. Then she was gone. The cycle's green rear lights rose against the dark.

Alone, I finished my meal and the beer.

I like solitude. Right?

I didn't taste it.

My mind returned to the looming question. *Where is Mars?*

If I could find the answer, I could find him. Desperation was a good motivator.

Here's what I knew so far:

Nico Mars escaped the Midwest Cradle

He used to be in a relationship with Agent Anika Winsome

He obviously had help escaping the cradle.

I groaned. All of this amounted to nothing. I didn't have anything more than when Anika and Lynn walked into my office. No new information and minus one wauto.

Once back in the loaner, I flew over to Eric's apartment building. The private inspector's life and her work were often lonely. You never know what will happen.

Nothing cured my restless spirit like surveillance.

With so many strings, I struggled to focus on one direction. Eric interested me. My gut burned. It could've been too much beer, but something about him niggled at me. I've been doing this too long to ignore it.

The neighborhood settled down for the evening. Dogs barked in the distance. Muffled music thumped from an open window. The bass rattled my windows. The slight opening in my windows captured the occasional breeze. I kept the wauto on. My previous vehicle caused too much noise to let idle. This newer one barely raised any attention. On nights like this, people hung out at pools and played out beneath rattling air conditioning units, wheezing in concert with the weak streams.

Same A/C units.

Same.

CHAPTER
EIGHTEEN

"Hello Cybil." Anika's face came into the camera's view. She might still be sore about being caught off guard last night. The zoom pulled back to reveal her in the conference room, surrounded by mugs, empty glass bottles, and tablets. I must be on the room's big telemonitor. Anika wore a lime green pantsuit with scallop sleeves.

"I'm on my way in. Where do I park?"

She froze, eyebrows raised in alarm. Her lips parted in surprise. "What?"

"Parking."

I got up Friday morning and surprised myself. If I wanted more information, I couldn't keep bullying Anika. Even I can have epiphanies. Plus, I believed she and Eric knew more than I got last night, and another way to get it was to be around them.

"I-I didn't expect you, especially after the stunt you pulled last night."

"I warned you. I needed full disclosure. By the way, is Lynn there?"

Silence.

Then, "it doesn't give you the right to force yourself on us. I haven't seen Agent Lynn so far today. I figured she was out chasing down leads, like you. I've been in meetings with my supervisor and the director about this, *situation*."

I didn't want to believe her, but Agent Lynn's record for honesty ranked lower than Anika's.

I cleared my throat. "It's only 11. What situation?"

"Some of us get up at 6."

"Gross."

She laughed.

"Now, I do have you, I have intel to share."

"Okay." My new slimmer, sleeker, and smaller handheld contained an earlier ping from Yukio. That would have to wait until I had coffee.

"We got an anonymous tip that Nico had been spotted over in the Adams Morgan neighborhood. That's in The 12, right?"

"Close."

"I'm working with The District's TRU unit now to go make a run on the home. Maybe we'll get this damn thing done and we can get back to our lives." Anika sounded full of hope.

That worried me.

TRU, the tactical retrieval unit, hunted humans who escaped from holding cells or who committed violations and have gone on the run to avoid punishment. TRU was the big guns.

"Wouldn't it be easier to get confirmation he was there before activating the retrieval unit? You could give a grandma a heart attack or frighten small children living there . The tip could be false."

"I've already activated them," Anika said. "They know their jobs."

"I'm close to The 12. I can fly by real quick and let you know. How long until TRU is ready to move?"

Anika checked her handheld. "25 minutes."

"I'll get back to you in 15. Send me the coordinates."

Anika sighed and sent it over.

Once I disconnected, I rerouted the wauto to its new destination. I'd been to Adams Morgan before, when I found Kimmila in a community bar doing her best to make her ends meet. I didn't care for the place. An older neighborhood, it didn't keep up with the speed of technology. From the looks of it, most homes still had antique door handles and lacked obvious automation. No oversized, converted warehouses turned apartments here in this part of The 12.

This was a residential area, and the homes struggled, like their residents, clinging to roof tiles, sagging porches, and decaying hope. They rimmed the outer edge of The 12, and so the splashes of violations and poverty washed up on them too.

I passed vacant yards where grass once grew but had been rendered to concrete squares. The area displayed grim reminders of the disastrous effects of neglect. Where other neighborhoods had lush green trees and litter-free lanes, here abandon and outright desperation blossomed with every drug deal, every stolen wauto, and every cry for help. It hadn't changed.

I didn't like it a month ago, and I didn't like it now.

The wauto lowered, dropping to the lowest elevated lane. It stopped and landed at a spot in front of the coordinates Anika shared. The house looked uninhabited. Nothing indicated someone lived there, so maybe Anika's tip about Mars' location was leaked to him. No garage or wauto hanger was attached to the home, but that could've been because there wasn't a vehicle. Many people took public transportation.

I checked my pug and climbed out in a slow manner. I didn't want to move too fast. That would alarm people. No one stood or sat on their porches or along the sidewalk. Still nosy neighbors could be watching from the confines of their cool living rooms. I walked up the path to the house where according to an anonymous tip, Nico Mars hid. When I reached the wooden porch, I stepped carefully. Termites' feast had created gaps.

Suddenly, the door swung open.

A small woman appeared in the entranceway. A long gray-white braid hung down to her shoulders. She wore thick-framed glasses and an orange shawl. I hadn't seen glasses in a long time. Most people corrected their eyes with surgery.

"Whatcha want?" the woman asked.

"I'm looking for Nico Mars," I said. "Is he here?"

"Why you lookin' for him?"

I held my enthusiasm in check. She knew him.

"So, he does live here?" I kept my tone light and non-threatening. I didn't want to spook Nico, but I hadn't expected the woman to open the door. My intentions were to snoop around the front porch to see if I could see inside through the windows.

"No. Not anymore. I don't like reporters. You one of them?" the woman stepped back as if ready to flee into the house.

"No ma'am." I could see through the crack of the door, but not much. Nothing moved inside the house, so perhaps she lived alone.

"So whatcha want?" She snapped, drawing my attention back to her.

"I heard a rumor he lived here. I was doing research for my violation class." The lie rolled off my tongue as smooth as Peck beer into a glass. "Thank you for your time."

She grunted and disappeared back inside the house.

I returned to the vehicle and waited to see if I spied Nico Mars crawling out a window or running out the back door.

After about fifteen minutes, the screen in the wauto lit up with Anika's face.

"So?" She asked. "Is he there?"

"I got a small look inside, but I couldn't see much."

"Oh, for fuck's sake! Is he there?" Anika's hardened tone gave me pause.

"I dunno." I didn't want to sit on the fence, but here we were.

"You dunno?"

"I'm gonna say that he isn't there, but I am only like 75% sure," I said.

"75%?"

"Is there an echo on the connection?" The edge of my annoyance sliced through to match hers.

"I'm going through with TRU. You should leave that area." Anika declared and moved to end the connection.

"Anika, I don't think that's a good idea. If you're not 100% sure he's in there, why give the resident a heart attack by TRU rolling in there? Most TRU events don't happen in broad daylight." I met her heated gaze. Oh, she didn't like me saying that.

"We need to locate the subject," Anika said, voice like stone.

"I know there's a lot of pressure–"

"He's there, now get out of the way." Anika ended the connect.

I didn't realize Anika had that kind of fury, but I knew better now. I got back out of my wauto and returned to the front porch. I pressed the doorbell.

The elderly woman opened the door again. "What you want?"

"Ma'am. There's going to be a raid on this house in about 10 minutes. You should get to safety."

Her eye narrowed. "You a reg? I knew you weren't no student. Too old."

I let that pass.

"I'm not a regulator, but I know, for certain, they're coming." My voice held pleading. I risked alerting Nico. The idea of leaving this woman to the brutality of the tactical retrieval unit didn't sit well in my body. "You got some place you can go for an hour? Maybe two?"

"Yeah," she said with resolution. She closed the door with increased speed.

I returned to my wauto.

Anika's order to get out of there lingered in my ears. Odd, the old woman didn't get rattled, or maybe she did, and this is my first time observing it. She'd probably seen a whole lot of regulator activity around here and if she survived to her old age in The District, she wasn't a fool.

In two minutes, that felt like two months, the woman came out of the house carrying her dog. They walked across the street to a neighbor's house. With relief rolling through me, I turned on the wauto and headed down the block. I parked the vehicle and got out. On foot, I'd blend in better than sitting in the vehicle.

I didn't go down to the house, but rather stayed under the trees of an abandoned corner residence with my shades on. The heat threatened to ruin everything. The trees' coverage helped, but damn, it was *hot*. I wanted to be home under the air conditioning, drinking beer, and napping.

But needs must be met.

The roar of the several aerocycles and wautos flying at high speeds ripped across the sky. The District's Tactical Retrieval Unit had arrived in all its midnight blue glory. In all, six cycles and four wautos were a small team, but it still seemed like too many for one escaped violator. Sure, Nico Mars could be dangerous, but so could any human being.

Just look at me for example.

At Nico's former residence, movement commenced as four TRU regulators in conjunction with those that spilled out of the wautos all converged on the property. They moved in formation, in deliberate steps surrounding the house. The whole point of their dark uniforms were so they could blend in with the evening. Out in the sunshine, they were exposed and somehow less threatening. All I could think about were roaches scattering away from the bright light.

Everything stilled, as if listening, waiting for the shoe to drop. They'd drawn their laser guns and continued their synchronized advance. Standing on the sidewalk, Anika stood with her arms crossed. Her suit jacket had short sleeves and the pants stopped inches above her ankles. She wore cream heels, and I could see from this distance her foot tapping. With her sunglasses on, she looked like the proverbial violation agent, a cliché in every way. Hard, unemotional face. Pursed painted lips. Detached. Professional. Cold.

Something about working with the worst of humanity, eroded your own, carving out hard and hollow places, leaving you empty. I understood Anika's facial expression because I often wore one just like it.

The early afternoon's quiet shattered. A figure moved in the trees beside the house, and the scene ignited. Shouts in alarm erupted at once. The TRU regulators split like a seam, with one half rushing off to the right of the house and the other side flanking left toward the figure in the trees. Anika's arm had dropped, and she took a step toward the house. The shouting continued, but I couldn't make it out. It all sounded like a bunch of people talking at once, which it was.

Time slowed.

The shouting died down to a murmur I couldn't hear from this distance. I wiped my forehead and waited it out. Minutes ticked by with sluggish speed, temporal molasses. At one point I thought to sit down, but then I couldn't see the full view due to vehicles parked on the street.

One of the TRU regulators walked back across the street toward Anika. She had her weapon pointed at the ground, her helmet off, and her hand at her temple. Once she reached Anika, she spoke to her, gesturing a lot and at one point, shrugging. Anika stepped toward her and started pointing her finger at the regulator's laser-proof vest. To her credit, she kept her mouth weld shut while Anika shouted at her, and when she was dismissed, she retraced her steps back across the street. Anika held back and didn't let it out.

My telemonitor lit up, vibrating in my pocket. I took it out. Anika's hot and sweaty face appeared on the screen. I swiped left. "Hello Anika."

"Did you tip him off?" She barked.

Considering she didn't have him, her emotions were appropriate, if not misguided. "No, I didn't. I'm assuming you missed him, if he was there at all."

"I cannot believe you! No, we didn't catch him! You know what I do have, now? A body!"

"I am definitely not responsible for that." I wiped my eyes where sweat had dripped into them. "Look, even though you botched this up, tomorrow is a new day."

"Fuck you. Fuck you to hell!" Anika shouted and disconnected.

Stress can ratchet up intense emotions.

Anika's gruesome discovery piqued my interest, and I wondered if it had any connection to Nico Mars. Who had decided to end the victim's life, if not him? Random death? Nature taking its course or the results of human interference? Among the devasting scene, did a person succumbed to her injuries in the yard? The resident probably never had an inkling of the death violation. No doubt, our escaped violator was on the hook for another death.

The elderly woman couldn't have violated someone's life. She didn't look like she could lift a bag of flour.

Whose body rested there?

For about two seconds I considered going to the active violation scene to get a look at the corpse and to gather intel. Instead, I walked to my wauto, away from the yellow caution beam the TRU agents erected.

I didn't like the heat and it was past time to get out of this kitchen. I'd get the information about the retrieval tomorrow.

CHAPTER
NINETEEN

No sooner had I sat down into the pilot's seat, did my telemonitor light up. This time, the connecter was Yukio. She appeared on the screen, unsmiling, but with news.

"I found your mystery woman," she said. Today's hair had been pulled into one side plait. The number of cords around her neck had increased. With her fingerless gloves, she pointed at the screen. "It took a little bit of digging, but I got her."

"That's fast."

"I'm fast."

"I see. So, send me the information."

"Send over the currency."

"Come on, Yukio. You can trust me."

"No currency. No information." Yukio shrugged. "I can press this delete button right here..."

I held up my hand to stop her. She laughed.

"What's the account number?" I could bring the information to Anika as a peace offering.

Yukio told me, and I used the dashboard telemonitor to pay. In seconds, it beeped and text scrolled across the screen. The mystery woman's name, address, and telemonitor contact I.P. address along with other minute details. I didn't want to know how Yukio got this much on a woman as high profile as Kinnear Von, but she did.

"Are you serious? Kinnear Von?" I glanced up at Yukio.

I was floored.

Yukio nodded. "At first, I had to double check the scrubbing software and the facial recognition app I used, because those deep fakes are a pain in the ass. I went back and pulled her pilot's license and sure enough, that's her. Look, here's the side by side."

I leaned in close to the telemonitor's small rectangular screen. On one side, the pilot's 3-D image of Kinnear Von. On the left side, a still from the video I gave Yukio with the face now visible.

"I went even further and blew both images up to the highest resolution I could get and still keep it clean. It's her," Yukio said. She clicked and both the images disappeared. She leaned back in her chair. "Our business is done. Yeah?"

"Yeah."

"Great." Yukio ended the connection.

Stunned, I sat in the parked wauto as the blistering heat of summer raged on.

Why on earth would someone as wealthy, politically connected be hanging out with an escaped violator? Kinnear Von had charisma. It oozed out of her flawless brown skin and perfect body proportions.

Maybe she and Mars were related?

I started the wauto and lifted up into the elevated lanes. Now that I had the information, I didn't quite want to give it to Anika or the District Regulators. Not yet. This had to be handled with some finesse. People like Kinnear Von had lawyers who had lawyers. Plus, the manner in which I found out it was Kinnear, wouldn't stand up in court as reliable evidence. When the possibility that the mystery woman was someone on a lower rung, Anika wouldn't be too concerned about how I came across the information, but someone with Von's clout, the data would be scrutinized as our dual justice system allowed.

My office smelled like tuna and coffee.

"Why does it reek in here?" I looked around the lobby, having arrived at work.

Kimmila looked up from her computer. Zola sat at her elbow, lazily pawing at her hand. She meowed at my remark.

"Well, I wanted coffee and Zola wanted tuna," Kimmila said. She picked up her cup and sipped.

Coffee does sound good.

"Where's Jane?" I went into the alcove of our lobby where the coffee maker and random snacks resided. I fixed myself a cup of coffee.

"Oh, right. Janey said to tell you she had a hunch and would connect later with you."

"About what?" I came out of the alcove with my mug in hand.

Kimmila scrunched up her nose in thought. "Um, she was going on about last night's dinner shenanigans. Someone named Edward or Evan…"

"Eric?"

Kimmila brightened, snapping her fingers. "That's it. That one!"

"She say what her hunch was?"

Jane didn't run off without telling me. The job had hazards and we tried to keep each other in the loop. Whatever came up must've been urgent.

I sat at her empty desk and searched for any hints as to where she'd gone. The electric sticky notes didn't include anything about her recent tasks. Glass bottles consumed most of the desk's surface area.

"She okay. Right? You don't think somethin' happened to her? To Janey?" Kimmila stroked Zola. The cat sounded like a small engine as it purred.

"I'm sure she's fine. If one thing's certain, Jane can take care of herself."

I tucked my concern behind faux confidence. I *did* trust my partner could handle whatever came at her.

I still didn't like it.

I wanted to go home and shower. Sweaty, hot, and more than a little annoyed, I got up and went into my private office. There, the closed-in space delivered cool air. Seated and fueled by caffeine, I turned on my computer. Part of investigating required research. For starters, who was Kinnear Von?

I typed in her name.

It had occurred to me Anika could be using the regulators' audio and video department to find out the mystery woman's identity too. It wasn't a competition, but the T.A. agent struck me as no nonsense. She wouldn't rely on me but would ensure she got the information she wanted. It had occurred to me, that she kept me tethered to her to make sure I stayed out of her hair. She'd probably heard from Lynn how meddlesome I could be.

The search engine belched hundreds of sites. Von had married wealthy. Her husband, Bradford Von, had been suspected of committing a death violation against his first wife. Kinnear married him fresh off his trial. She'd moved from another territory. I forgot which one, but she swept into the District's elite parties with grace, a shrewd and often biting fashion sense, and political savvy.

If Kinnear was so smart, why was she hanging out with a known escaped violator? It didn't make sense. Perhaps the woman herself would shed some light on it, or maybe she'd tell me to go to hell.

Either way, I had to try.

"Incoming." My telemonitor lit up. Kimmila's face appeared. "Answer."

"Heya, a Daniel Tom wants to see you." Kimmila cut her eyes over to her left.

"Okay, send him in." What the hell did Daniel want?

He strolled in with frequent glances back at the lobby. I wondered what exchange happened between him and Kimmila.

"That's new." He jutted his thumb back at the lobby, and then he sat down. "It's about time you got a proper receptionist. No shade to Jane, but clerical work doesn't suit her."

"You're not wrong. You've seen Kimmila before. Yeah?"

Daniel shrugged. "Oh, sure but I thought she was Jane's partner."

I inclined my head. "She is."

"Ah." Daniel rubbed his hands on his khaki pants.

He wore a light green tank top and matching shoes.

"What's up?" I noted the plain clothes didn't match anything Daniel would normally wear so he must've been still undercover.

"I was near so thought I'd come by."

"How'd you know I was here?"

He squirmed in the hard metal chair. "I didn't."

"But?'"

"But I didn't want to connect. Those aren't always secure."

I sat up straighter and drank some of my coffee.

And waited.

Daniel's warm eyes bore darkened bags underneath. He looked worn, like wrinkled or balled up paper.

"I was at headquarters, checking in with my supervisor, and overhead some conversations while in the second-floor breakroom." He swallowed, and continued, "Henrietta Mayfield is Nico Mars's sister. One of the old IRs who knew Mars also knew the family and was chatting it up with IR Baker about how the family had suffered so much. First Nico's violation and now Henrietta's death violation."

Well, that was one hell of a bombshell. Daniel's fidgeting made sense in hindsight. If IR Jamison found out he'd come here and spilled this intel, he'd put Daniel's career in a jar. No wonder he didn't want to use the telemonitor to connect.

"Wow. A social activist, fighting like hell to stop violations in The 12 is the sister of a corrupt regulator. "Can you imagine?"

Daniel took one long pause. Then, "It wasn't common knowledge. One theory is someone found out and committed the death violation to get back at Nicol. Remember how battered her face was? Almost like they wanted to destroy her face."

"Or the tattoo messages."

"Uh huh."

"Any transfer evidence?"

"There might be. I'm not on the case. Remember?"

"Who knew the connection between Mayfield and Mars, other than this inspector regulator? Maybe the rotten regs didn't all get early retirement."

Daniel glanced around my room. "I know I said this before, but you need to update your office. It's gloomy and depressing."

"It's not worth the currency. I'm rarely here."

Daneil sighed. "Whelp. There may be some older regs still hanging around that supported Mars, but I don't see them letting him out of the cradle. I mean, all the way to the Midwest Territories?"

"It is doable. Could Mars have committed the violation against Henrietta?" I pulled my attention back to Daniel, who tried to divert the conversation.

"It's always those close to the citizen. Isn't it? No one thinks their loved one will be part of a death violation, but if the timeline is correct, Nico didn't escape the cradle when she died. You could ask his ex-girlfriend."

"Anika's not opening up about their relationship." *Or anything else for that matter.*

Daniel tsked. "That's too bad."

"She's hiding something."

"Of course, she is." Daniel chuckled. "Everybody hides stuff. You got your own storage locker of skeletons too."

"You know what I mean."

"Do I?" Daniel teased.

"She knows how Mars escaped and she knows why he's here." I tented my hands in my lap.

"Why hire you? Why not tell you?" Daniel stuck a cigarette in his mouth. "You got a foghog?"

"On Jane's desk."

He left to retrieve it.

I couldn't put it in terms of actual proof. The fact the TA didn't know how Mars escaped the Midwest Cradle didn't sit well with me. The gravity of the situation weighed like stones balanced on my shoulders. I suspected they *did* know but had been gagged by the territory's leadership.

"All right. What are you gonna do?" Daniel returned, smoke trailing him like a gray scarf. "Please don't do something that'll add to my workload."

"I'm going to talk to Kinnear Von."

"Wait. *The* Kinnear Von?" Daniel coughed.

I let him recover before answering.

"Yeah."

I brought him up to speed on the investigation, leaving out *how* I learned her identity.

"You going out there?" Daniel raised both eyebrows. "Today?"

"Maybe."

"You're not thinking clearly. Von is elite. Let the TA handle it."

"How's your undercover going?"

Daniel sighed, pushing air through his nose. "Tough."

"You wanna talk about it?" I went to drink and found my cup empty.

"No." Daniel peered at me before looking away.

Well, no was a complete sentence. I wondered if he remembered the words I said earlier about helping him. I didn't mean to shame him.

"TRU found a body earlier today." While he remained, I wanted to get as much information as I could.

Daniel stood. "The body's battered and crumpled. It's in bad shape. Thanks to the heat. It's going to take time for that one."

"We know who it is?"

"Not yet. Identification will take time, but I can tell you this. It may be a natural death." Daniel put his cigarette out. He picked up the foghog. "Why?"

"You know TRU found it while trying to catch Mars."

He didn't know.

All these links led to a central relationship.

"So that's how the death violation came in. Interesting. If I hear anything, I'll let you know, but I gotta get back." Daniel rubbed his hair.

"Okay." I stood too. "Keep me looped in."

"Don't I always?" He shot me a smug smile before leaving.

"No."

The door sliced off his laughter.

CHAPTER
TWENTY

Kinnear Von's residence lay outside The District's city sprawl and into what was once considered Virginia. Part of it fell along the Southeast Territory, and a swath of land from The District's center as far west as Fairfax, and far south as Springfield now belonged in our territory. During the mad scramble for land after the United States' fall, the District officially enlarged its borders beyond the D.C. metro area. The flight would take time, so I cranked the wind channel up to four, set the autopilot, and reclined my pilot's seat.

I opened my eyes and watched the verdant landscape sweep by. The autopilot cruised with ease. Outside, automation disappeared into the surrounding vegetation and kudzu. Camouflage robots meld in with the roadside clean up, the maintenance of the elevated lanes, and the repair of damaged billboards, signs, and roadside pilot stations.

Here, they didn't stick out.

In the District, the sectors all had various robotic activities. So integrated in the daily coming and goings, people didn't notice them or feel like the bots were something odd. Just everyday items, like a carrying craft or an aerocycle. Yet, the people of Falls Church wanted their robots to be unseen, camouflaged against the environment.

I roused from sleep when the wauto lowered. Lulled to sleep by the smooth flight, I sat up and adjusted my seat to its upright position. Ahead, the trim, multicolored trees, dressed in white lights, and a gate, wooden from this distance, hugged the Kinnear Von estate. As I approached, the gate swung open, allowing entry. No guard or guard shack, so security must be automated. I'm sure the wauto had been scanned or I doubt the gate would've opened. I suspected she had a force field over the estate's acreage including the house.

I took over from the autopilot and flew up the long pathway to the front of the home. I set down the wauto in front of the wrap around porch. The house looked like an old farmhouse from the 20th century, but it had been updated. The hovering white drones waited and watched me as I climbed out of the vehicle. Security disguised as fans and embedded cameras in the railings, painted to look like moss, kept the appearance of lazy lawns and sweet lemonade.

One of the drones, a metal box with tiny antenna and a large singular eye, spoke. "State your name and purpose."

"Cybil Lewis. I'm here to speak to Kinnear Von about her flight." I didn't want to give too much information. I had no idea who operated the drones or who sat in the security room watching. "The one from the Midwest Territories."

The drone hovered, as if submitting the information.

I waited.

The front door slid back, and the drone flew in. It floated just inside the foyer.

"Follow me."

I stepped inside and did as directed.

Lavender scented the air. A long, plush white rug covered the hallway's entirety. Archways led to other rooms, but the drone flew forward. I didn't dare sneak off to explore. I did get a peak of a white, grand piano, and a ruby-red leather settee with an adjoining silvertone table. Large telemonitor consumed the space above the fire-place adjacent to the piano.

The next room I passed held gym equipment. The blinds had been opened, and sunlight streamed inside, highlighting the tread-mill's metallic handrails, and the fingerprints and sweat on the free weights.

Finally, the hallway emptied into what my grandmomma would call a great room. In its center, a large hearth, painted ivory mantel, sat blackened and empty. A fireplace grate, also white, but looked like it was made from wrought iron, stood in front. Along the side, cut logs were stacked artfully. Along the mantel, thick candles flick-ered in the air-conditioned room.

A matching, ivory sectional took up most of the space in front of the hearth. A raven-haired woman stood and turned around to face me. She put what looked like grass onto the mantel as she turned to me.

"Cybil Lewis. Private Inspector," Kinnear Von said and held out her hand.

"That's me."

"I'm Kinnear Von."

I shook her hand, and noted it was draped in diamond rings complete with sapphires, one on each finger. Her wrists sparkled with gold bangles. Her other hand sported more rings and a glass of red wine. With so much white décor, I feared for the red wine and the stains.

"What brings you to me?" She gestured for me to come around and sit on the sofa. She sat down, not waiting for me. "My trip to the Midwest Territories shouldn't alarm anyone in a *citizen* compacity."

I smiled as I sank into the soft leather cushions. "I have a few questions. Would you be willing to answer them?"

She crossed her legs and sipped from the wineglass. Once she swished and swallowed, she said, "I'm not fond of being questioned, Miss. Lewis."

"Few people are, but it won't take long. You can decline to answer the ones you don't like."

She relaxed back against the pillows. "Can you tell me who hired you?"

"Is this a safe place to talk?" I sidestepped her question.

She sipped again. "Yes."

"Can you tell me about your relationship with Nico Mars?" I took out my new handheld and its stylus.

She gave me a closed-lip smile before she spoke. "You know how it is. I wanted an object to crave and to play with. It gets lonely out here."

"He's a violent violator," I countered. "How does your husband feel about it?"

She shrugged as if I had said he made great cookies. "Marriage vows are like speed bumps. Sometimes you have to blow by them. You can't keep a butterfly in a jar."

"Mars isn't everything you think he is. He's a rough-looking character with an extensive violator file." I cautioned her, but none of my words penetrated her beautifully decorated face.

Kinnear crossed her arms, keeping the wineglass close to her chest. "I listened to him. His story didn't tie up with the others arrested at that same time."

"No?"

She shook her head. "They moved quickly to keep him quiet."

"They? Who do you mean?" I've lived long enough to know that not all conspiracies were theories.

"The Territory Alliance. Did you know they let his jaded ex-lover work the case? Talk about a conflict of interest! They should've removed her and then the case would've come to a screeching halt. Without her testimony, her lies, they had nothing." Kinnear drank the rest of her wine, got up and went to a round, linen clothed bar, and poured more red wine from a crystal decanter.

"My source said they had audio, video, and documentation," I said, keeping my tone light and as neutral as possible. She had some good points. Some of those were the same as ones I had.

She smirked at me as if to say 'poor thing.'

"When wrong words enter the right ear, tragedy ensue. The weak, circumstantial evidence came from *her*. They couldn't produce one credible witness. Before you mention the confession, he was under pressure. He talked, but only about the drug dealing." Von pursed her lips.

I couldn't understand what she saw in him. But she was quite informed. Did she believe an angry ex-girlfriend would go through all that trouble to frame him? It seemed like such a waste of energy.

"How did you meet him?" I switched to a different, less combative topic.

Kinnear sat down on the sofa and tossed her hair over shoulder. She cupped the wineglass as if for strength. Something made her uncomfortable.

"We met online."

As soon as she said it, her face flushed.

Switching gears, I asked, "Why would the T.A. go through so much effort to frame Nico? That's what you believe. Right?"

"I dunno." She sighed. "Perhaps not so much the Territory Alliance, but the ex-girlfriend, yes, she would go through that trouble."

"Why? How are you so sure?"

Kinnear laughed. "I'm not P.I., but I have my ways. I know much about *her*."

I wondered how much came from Nico. Why was she focused on Anika?

"They broke up years ago," I said. "You know a lot about her. What's her name?"

Kinnear Von's eyes twinkled. "Anika Winsome. She's the sole reason Nico landed in the cradle. Horrid woman."

Strong language, almost harsh. There's something more but Kinnear wouldn't tell me.

"How did he get out of the cradle?" I asked, switching gears.

She raised her eyebrows in faux surprise. "He told me he was given early release."

"So, you just fly out to the Midwest and pick him up?" I tapped my tablet.

She smiled but did not answer.

"How did he know you'd be available to come get him?"

She gave me a slow shrug. "To many people, I'm a reliable friend. When they need help, they contact me."

"Is he here? Now?" I knew she'd shut that answer down. She wouldn't admit to harboring a violator.

"No."

Short. Firm. No hint of emotion. Complete sentence.

I'd bet the currency in my bank account Nico Mars *was* here, lying in wait.

"Why risk your marriage, your reputation, your status for him?"

"One night with him was better than twenty years with my husband." She scooted closer to the sofa's edge and whispered, "Far better."

"I see. He is a convicted violator, given 20 sessions."

I kept my tone serious. The information I gave her could save her life. Now that I showed up here, Nico wouldn't let her live. She proved a link to him, a connection. He would severe those connections without a second thought.

"All of that's behind him," she countered. "You don't know him like I do. Now, he keeps himself to himself. He's so misunderstood, an aching soul. You make one mistake and people stop seeing your humanity." She shook her head as if disgusted. "He used to be a be a regulator, did you know?"

Kinnear's smile softened around the edges. She stood up, signaling my time had ended. "I did." I brushed off my pants and stood up.

"Well, thank you for your time."

"You never did tell me who you're working for," Kinnear said.

"I can't tell you, but I can say it isn't your husband." I shook her hand.

"Thank you. Andre will show you out." She held my hand a minute longer than I liked, as she stared at me with clear blue eyes. "Don't paint Nico into a corner, Miss Lewis. He's not a pig, but a man. A human being."

"So were his victims, Ms. Von. Good day." I followed the drone back down the hallway in which I'd come.

CHAPTER
TWENTY-ONE

n some sectors, they roll up the sidewalks and put out the elevated lane lights at 21:00 hours. Not my sector. When I arrived home sometime after eight, I found the parking lot full of wautos and aerocycles and a crowd of what looked like teenagers scuffling and pretending to be cool. You could see it in their facial expressions. Music blared from someone's vehicle. Something with a lot of bass and fancy drums. Some of the teens danced; others sat on parked wautos and smoked, and a few more collected into smaller groups and hunched against the frantic atmosphere. A few trashcans had been set on fire, for light, not for warmth. The scattering of functioning streetlights had been out for a few weeks. Whenever the District got around to replacing them help the violation numbers go back down. Our flailing government at work. The weed smell was so strong, I could taste it. It was palpable.

Summer in the District.

I parked in my assigned spot and climbed out of the vehicle. Flying into the space reminded me of my old wauto and the fact someone torched it. At some point, I was going to need a replacement. I hadn't even filed the insurance claim yet. I put it on my mental checklist and headed up to my apartment.

Once inside, I showered, fixed a peanut butter and jalapeno jelly sandwich and grabbed a beer. I sat on the couch with my cranky laptop and the easy listening channel on. All classical music with some jazz tossed in for spice. I transferred my notes from my handheld to the laptop file I started.

I had more questions than answers. Somehow, I thought finding Nico's mystery woman would've paid off in more than confessed sexual attraction and a belief in his innocence. Kinnear Von hadn't been wrong in her suspicions around Anika. Why *had* they allowed her to stay on the case? Especially when they knew she was their whistleblower? Daniel said some in the department thought Nico was innocent. He confessed to the drug dealing charges, but he came apart when accused of two death violations.

I didn't have access to the recordings. Those burnt up with the wauto, and I didn't want to ask Anika for another copy.

I had these questions:

1. Why was Anika allowed to remain on the case?
2. Who helped Nico escape from the cradle?
3. Who hired someone to attack me at the office?
4. What does Big Game have to do with any of this?
5. Who torched my wauto?

There were five questions too many on the list. I ate my sandwich, relishing how damn good it tasted. I drank more beer. Before I could forget, I opened the application for vehicle insurance and started the task of filing a claim. Regulator Philips had sent over the report and I attached it to the insurance form. Once it was sent, I celebrated with another beer and more jazz. I'd switched over to jazz completely at this point and stretched out on the couch. I opened one of the living room's windows and caught the breeze. It contained a hint of weed, but not enough to be annoying.

I closed my eyes and relaxed.

Kinnear bothered me. She swore she knew Nico Mars so well. I'm living proof that you don't know people as well as you think you know people.

But what if I had all this backwards?

Her conviction had sowed the seeds of doubt and piqued my interest.

I'd been operating from the position that Anika and Lynn had been telling the truth. But Anika had already lied to me. Why invite the TRU today, but not earlier on in the investigation, when Nico first disappeared from the cradle? She didn't even have confirmation that Nico had been there in the last 48 hours, which is standard regulator protocol.

Why the urgency today?

Now, there were six questions on my list.

Great.

Tomorrow I'd pay Ortega a nice, unannounced visit. I had to know why she let Anika on the case and why for the life of me, she didn't think doing so muddied the waters. I'm also appalled the attorneys let it go too. Why didn't Nico Mar's attorney argue to have it thrown out?

Maybe they did.

I went back to my computer. The court trials provided entertainment for people. Often they were recorded. I searched the interwebs for clips or full videos to reference. Several files cropped up. The page counter had literally dozens of webpages. My eyes burned. I had my work cut out for me. I'd been spinning my wheels for days.

I stared up at the ceiling fan. It didn't have any answers either.

For tonight, I elected to stop spitting into the wind. I'd refocus tomorrow. My eyes grew heavy, like the burden of unanswered questions weighed them down.

Cooled down by beer and breezes, I dozed off.

Somewhere around three in the morning, I woke up to crisp air and hooting owls. Why those guys still hung around here, I'll never know. My neck ached and my stiff limbs complained as I sat up. I picked up the empty beer bottles and placed them in the recycler. I went about making coffee and finding something to eat. Big Mike's wasn't open at this hour. I needed time to think, to sift through the throng of thoughts piled up in my mind. Pieces of the case didn't have answers.

While the coffee brewed, I went to the living room and opened my home laptop. I had a peanut butter and jalapeno jelly sandwich in one hand. More sophisticated home butlers reigned in the shopping places and everyone and his brother wanted to buy them. I don't trust bots or A.I.s or machine learning. I didn't like my items being stored on the server at work but found it to be a necessity.

I stretched and it was then that I noticed the beeping and flashing greenlight on the telemonitor.

"Play voicemail." I headed to the kitchen to make myself another sandwich, applying way more jelly than peanut butter this time.

"Message one from Inspector Regulator Jamison. Miss Lewis. We need to talk to you about an active investigation. Please report to Regulator Headquarters on Monday, July 13th at 9 a.m."

The connect ended.

Jamison.

I thought about contacting Daniel to see if I could get the skinny on why he wanted me at Regulator Headquarters, but it was too early or too late, depending on your perspective.

But that wasn't my only message.

"Message two from Kinnear Von. You are a difficult person to locate despite being a private inspector. Listen, our visit today will need to be kept between us. I'm sure we can come to an arrangement. You won't be able to return this connect, but please come out and visit for lunch. Tomorrow around four. Tata."

Tomorrow would be Saturday. When did her husband actually come home? Kinnear Von wanted to buy my silence. I may just let her since nothing she gave me helped me find Nico or his whereabouts.

Could he be staying out on the lush, lavish, and large estate she and her husband owned? Sure. It would explain why no one has been able to find him in the District or in The 12. He could be relaxing and eating raspberries out there in Falls Church.

The knot of stress at the base of my neck tightened.

I ate my sandwich, washed it down with cold coffee from the carafe, and headed to bed. It seemed tomorrow and Monday's agenda had filled up all their own.

CHAPTER
TWENTY-TWO

Saturday morning arrived too early and too bright, but I managed to climb out of bed. I landed outside Luna Ortega's blue door home. Ten minutes after ten, I thought I might wake up the retired agent but pushed it aside. Off balanced was how I wanted her. Last time, my ruse boxed me into a certain behavior.

Not today.

I climbed out of the vehicle and into the hushed morning quiet. The dew hadn't burned off yet, but the blue, cloudless sky opened up. It would be sizzling soon, and the humidity would increase.

I knocked on the door.

No one answered.

I pressed the doorbell.

No response.

I stepped back and looked up at the windows. No movement. I walked around to the side of the house, on a graveled pathway, to check if Ortega was out back. It crunched beneath my feet. The security fence blocked my view, but I peered through the tiny spaces in between. The backyard remained empty.

Nope, she wasn't there.

So, I made my way around to the front again. Once I reached the door, I found Luna Ortega standing with her arms akimbo on the tiny porch. Her thin, blue floral robe revealed thick knees and varicose veins. They traveled from her ankles to the robe's hem. She tapped her sandaled foot.

"You again." She smirked. "I didn't think I'd seen the last of you."

She didn't ask me why I was there.

"Can we talk?" I asked. "For real this time."

"I did some digging of my own, Cybil Lewis, private inspector."

"Once an inspector, always an inspector." I offered a smile to ease the tension.

Ortega laughed. "Hell yeah. Come on inside. You ain't gonna leave me alone until I do. This much I know about you."

I liked that she recognized my personality trait. As before, I followed her through the foyer and living area and out to the patio. Once again, she gestured for me to take the empty seat beside her. She sat without waiting and claimed a tall glass of what looked like iced tea. This time she didn't ask me if I wanted anything. She drank her tea and stared ahead at the fence. Her sunglasses remained on the wooden table between the two reclining patio chairs. She cradled a bowl of fruit in her lap.

"What do you want to know?" Ortega didn't turn to look at me.

"I want to know why Anika Winsome was allowed to work the case of her former lover." Since Ortega had come right out and asked, I obliged her.

Ortega pressed her lips together. The color faded around her eyes. With another swallow of tea, she found her courage and answered.

"Yeah, the defense's lawyers wanted to know too. They argued there was a conflict of interest. The territory attorneys believe because she'd come forward and reported Mars' violations she should be protected as a whistleblower. Mars' attorney argued that it was an act of spite and the bulk of her testimony had been exaggerated, if not fabricated.”

“Was it?” I sat up in the patio chair and put my feet on the concrete. She kept her gaze on the fence, as if looking back into the past.

“We corroborated as much of her testimony as we could. Of course, we’re talking about a regulator. Mars knew how to delete evidence. You must understand, Anika was on the fast track to captain. Smart. Capable. Fierce. She would’ve made captain within two years. She risked everything to bring in a dirty regulator, even more so, she loved him.”

“How’d you know?”

She paused. “Huh?”

“How’d you know she loved him? Trust but verify. Right?” I repeated. “Anyone can say they love you and it may not be true.”

Ortega laughed, a wet wheezy bark. “You’re right. I trust she cared. I mean, she struggled with turning him in.

“I admit I don’t know for sure. She acted like she adored him, and he hung the moon. You know?” Ortega paused, then frowned. “You know, you’re right.”

I suppressed the urge to yell ‘huzzah!’. It wasn’t often I heard those words.

You’re right!

Ortega ate a few grapes in quiet reflection.

Minutes ticked by as birds sang and the neighborhood woke up. Saturday morning in July held the promise of adventure.

“Meaning she was incapable of lying? Incapable of being vindictive to the lover who dumped her or wouldn’t leave his wife for her?” I spread my hands wide. “Come on, Ortega. You’re smarter than that.”

“Yeah. You weren’t there.” Ortega drank more tea, and for several minutes didn’t speak. I relaxed a little. Judging her wouldn’t give me the information I wanted, so I held my hands and waited.

When she broke the quiet, her deep tenor rumbled out what

could only be regret. "Hindsight is 2020. At that time, I wanted to make an example of Mars. A dirty regulator sullies every regulator and Territory Alliance agent. And Mars *was* filthy. The drug dealing was the least of it, which is why he confessed to it."

I nodded for her to go on.

"The death violations were vicious. He didn't want those to come to light, to tarnish his propped-up persona. As for evidence, we found Mars DNA on two of the victims, one vaginally. The two women had been stamped and worked as one of his herds. He denied running any type of farm or being a breeder. He said the DNA evidence was because he'd hired them for sex."

"Did the medical examiner confirm rape?" I asked.

"No trauma. It appeared that he had consensual sex; however, that didn't mean he didn't kill them afterwards."

"It didn't mean he did."

"We found his skin under their fingernails."

"Rough sex?"

Ortega snorted. "You sure you ain't a violator attorney?"

"I'm trying to understand how Nico Mars was convicted to 20 sessions in the cradle on the evidence provided at his trial."

"You read the file?"

"I did. That's why I'm here. The evidence is thin at best, no offense."

Ortega waved me off. "You used to be a regulator. You know you can't pick the evidence or the witnesses."

"Truth."

"Mars was convicted of gross violations, include two counts of 187-violations." Ortega continued, but sadness draped her words. "Winsome wanted to escape the blowback in the District. She applied to the T.A. and got in."

"And you?"

"Me?" Ortega drank more iced tea. "I went back to work. Another major case, another territory, another line of human misery to follow. I lost track of her in the shuffle."

The last sounded like regret.

"Was there a male who worked that case too?"

She quirked an eyebrow. "You'll need to be more specific. Back then the regulators were full of men."

"One was named Eric Mann?" I broke the quiet.

Ortega frowned. "Mann?"

"According to him, he supplied witnesses, and other pieces of evidence. You don't remember him?"

Ortega peered at me like I spoke in tongues. She didn't like that she trusted Anika. I can't prove it, but I'd bet currency their relationship went beyond the professional. The career risks she took for Anika spoke to a more significant connection.

Anika had betrayed it.

I knew it.

Now, Ortega did, too.

"Anika was the lead witness. There were others caught on audio or video, but we did have some eyewitnesses, not many, but a few. Could he have been one of those?"

I took out my telemonitor and pulled up the image Jane provided of Eric.

"I saw him on the interview footage. He used to be a regulator."

She peered close. "Oh, yes, him. He didn't work the case, but he was a regulator at the time. Come to think of it, he quit shortly after the Mars case. I believe his name came up a few times in the investigation, but nothing stuck."

"Eric Mann?"

"Yes." Ortega popped in a grape.

"You didn't suspect him of anything?"

Ortega shook her head. "Nah. He liked to run his mouth. He and Mars worked The 12 together. We couldn't get anything on him. But, he's a puff man. All hot air. No substance."

I laughed.

"She and he were close friends."

"She never said."

"If she didn't tell you this, what else did she hide?"

The former TA muttered a "huh."

I made Ortega speechless. I did have that effect on people.

"Is there anything else you can tell me about Mars?" I asked.

Ortega wiped her face. "I meant what I said earlier. He isn't sunshine and rainbows. The man's a cad, a real piece of work. The stuff he did in The 12…"

"Is he a death violator?"

"He was convicted by a three-judge panel."

"That's not an answer."

"But it's *my* answer. The only one you're gonna get anyway. It's over." She set the bowl on the table and pushed herself up to a standing position. Holding her empty glass in one hand, she rested the other on her hip as if getting up fatigued her. "I bet you can start an argument in an empty room."

I let her feeble verbal jab go.

"I'll see you out."

I got up and followed her back the way we'd come. The house seemed empty, as if only Ortega lived there with the ghosts of her cases.

It was eerily familiar.

When I reached the front step, Ortega said, "If you come around here again, I'm going to connect to the regulators. We understand each other?"

"Yes ma'am."

As I started down the pathway to my wauto. I felt her eyes on my back, as if she wanted to make sure I left and didn't linger.

When the wauto's seatbelt clicked into place, I released the breath I didn't know I held.

I took out my handheld and jotted down notes and information while it was still fresh. Out of the corner of my eyes, I spied Ortega standing there with her arms folded, the glass still clutched in one hand. I ignored her while I scribbled. The reality was that I had so much to get down. Ortega didn't have strong evidence about Mars' convictions. So much could've been explained away, but the court and no doubt the public wanted blood from the rogue regulator. All that rush to judgment might have sent Mars down for longer than warranted. Had he been a regular citizen, he might not have gotten such harsh treatment or sentence.

Kinnear Von made similar statements about Anika's role in the initial investigation. Eric Mann may or may not have been involved, but Ortega said he hadn't been. So, why lie to me and Jane about his role? Jane's hunch about him landed. He was forced to depart from the job because they suspected *he* was corrupt.

Anika remained tight-lipped about it. She lied to us. Why?

To hide what Mars had been screaming about for years. He hadn't been responsible for the death violations. Had Mars escaped to come back and clear his name?

For revenge?

No wonder Anika was desperate to capture him.

And she had the District on her side.

Right now, all I had was theories.

I needed to find Nico Mars before they did.

Who helped him escape from the cradle? Was it one of those judges who found his or her conscience? I doubted it.

Spent for now, I slipped my handheld back into my satchel, launched the vehicle, and lifted off into the elevated lane.

Just after 11, my stomach complained about being empty. I also needed to meet up with Jane today too. Maybe she'd found something that would shed some light on the growing list of questions. I didn't hear from her at all yesterday.

"Wauto, connect to Jane Broxter."

In seconds she appeared on the wauto's telemonitor screen, smoking and wearing a white tank top and sweats.

"Hey, you wanna meet me at Mike's?" I put the autopilot on and gave her my attention.

She appeared to be sitting on her bed. The short wooden headboard gleamed in contrast to the black sheets. Her ponytail was tied high and her sunglasses rested on the top of her head. She wore a new necklace, a jagged silver heart at the end of a leather strap.

"Sure. You want me to bring Kim too?" Jane scratched her bicep.

If you must.

Instead, I said, "Okay, yeah. We can call it an office meeting."

It was Saturday after all.

I managed to keep my disappointment from showing.

"See you in 20." She disconnected.

CHAPTER
TWENTY-THREE

We beat the weekend lunch crowd and secured our table at Big Mike's. Jane and Kimmila were already seated, nursing drinks, and listening to a hip-hop artist deliver the latest song blowing up the area's internet streaming joints. They'd taken the two chairs facing the door, which meant my back would be to the entranceway, a position I tried to avoid. My table felt crowded with Kimmila sitting there, but I checked my pout and sat down.

"Took you long enough." Jane scooted her chair closer to Kimmila's. Already smoking, she peered at me through the haze before the foghog snatched it away. "Were you just waking up?"

"No, I flew over from Pet Worth." I spied Bryan moving with ease through the growing throng. I waved at him, and he gave the one-minute hand gesture. "It's been a busy morning so far."

Kimmila said, "Well, it's afternoon, so you can relax a bit."

"That depends on what Jane has to tell me."

Jane had a beer and Kimmila drank something hot from her mug. Jane laughed. "Let's order first."

"You haven't?"

"Waitin' on you." She picked up the tablet to order.

I glanced at Kimmila, who shrugged as she picked up the other tablet and scanned the food options.

"What's good here?" she asked.

"Everything," Jane and I said in unison.

"Jinx!" I laughed.

Kimmila looked up from the tablet at us as if we'd grown extra ears. She shook her head and went back to scrolling. Jane grinned at me and waved to someone behind me. I hated this seat. If I wanted to see I had to turn around, and the people would know it.

As I turned, Bryan tapped me on the other shoulder. "'Bout time you got here."

Despite the fall of well-curved bangs, expert make-up application and coverage, I could see the bruise around his eye. He also moved as if his left arm pained him, but not so overtly others who didn't know him would notice.

"Where've you been?" I smiled. "I haven't seen you around."

"You come here too often, and you still don't know my schedule," he said, while collecting the tablets, avoiding direct eye contact. "Did you order?"

"Yeah, I did." He took my tablet. "You still didn't answer me."

"I don't owe you an answer." He snatched away as fast as he could.

"What the hell was that about?" Jane asked with eyebrows raised.

Kimmila shook her head. "He had scared eyes."

"What do you mean?" I asked. If anything, Bryan could be described as flamboyant bookish. The makeup didn't have any real dramatic flair, except the glitter, but all the folks were doing that.

"I mean, he's scared of something. It's in his face." Kimmila fingered the mug's rim. "Those bruises didn't come from tumbling downstairs either. He's been punched, a few times."

Jane nodded in agreement. "Someone hurt him."

"His partner?" I asked.

"An ex-partner?" Kimmila added.

"None of our business," Jane said, seconds before she took a long drag of her cigarette.

I agreed, but only partially. Bryan could've been hurt because of what he told me. He'd been frightened to death at the time but risked it anyway. It may have cost him. Judging by the short and cold manner he communicated with me, I was certain that was the root of his injuries.

"Here's your Port-in-the-storm." A young woman placed it with care on the edge of the table. She didn't wait for a thank-you. She zipped off to other patrons.

Jane watched her go, taking a deep drag on her cigarette as she did so.

The silence unfolded.

Jane smoked.

Kimmila smoked.

I drank.

It remained that way, each of us in our own thoughts, until Bryan returned with our dishes.

Kimmila had macaroni salad with hummus and lemon juice, brown rice pasta, with green and red bell peppers. It was topped with celery. Beside her, Jane's lunch made me wish I'd ordered today's special, the creamy carbonara. What made it creamy was almond milk and brown sugar. Spinach and bits of seared tofu looked delicious scattered among the penne. My bowl contained whole wheat spaghetti with zucchini noodles, fresh tomatoes, and basil tossed in olive oil.

Big Mike's did food like it wasn't a jazz bar, but some upscale place out in Falls Church or over across the ways where the wealthy ate. Instead, tucked down here among the former capital, his restaurant provided delicious food and good prices to the common citizens. His reputation mattered. In general, food couldn't be trusted. From mutations to poisonings to spoilage, food transport barely counted as safe. People ate at their own peril.

Except here.

We ate quietly, devouring Big Mike's gifts to us. It took me a few minutes to recognize the music had shifted to an upbeat jazz number. The hip-hop artist had moved to the bar and was sipping something from his glass.

The place buzzed with energy, busy chatter, and laughter. It messed with the aromas and crafted this envelope of peace, joy, and electricity. Outside these doors, violence, pain, and life awaited.

It had pounced on Bryan, on the young woman from the Bottoms, and scores more. The sinister underbelly that made people into the living dead. Alive, but lacking in *living*. Zombies craving carnage as a means of survival.

I was more than capable of filling their bellies with laser gun fire.

"Cybil!" Jane shouted.

I snapped to attention, zoodle dangling from my lips. "What?"

"I've been calling your name for like two minutes. You'd left the room."

Kimmila chuckled into her macaroni salad.

"I said, do you want me to start going over what I learned about your favorite T.A. agent?"

More than half of my bowl contained pasta, so I nodded for her to go ahead. She'd apparently inhaled her food. I ate while she read her notes.

Jane took out her tablet and scooted closer to the table.

"Okay, so Anika hasn't been on her usual route. She knows we're following her. She hasn't met up with Eric since our dinner crashing."

I wiped my mouth with the napkin and swallowed. "I'd like more on him. Kimmila when you get back to the office, pull what you can from the public domain on him."

Kimmila broke out with a startled smile. "Me? I mean, yeah. Okay."

"Great. That's Mann with two n's."

She nodded.

I gestured to Jane to keep going.

"What's interesting is that she's supposed to be tracking down the escaped violator, but she went shopping over at the Wells. Then, she's been eating out at those fancy places over there too. She's checked out of the hotel she and Lynn shared and is now staying at The Billings. Where does an agent get that kind of currency?"

"Dunno." The Billings boasted clients from the upper echelons of the District's stars, politicians, and currency-rich. The only person we'd come across with those types of funds is Kinnear Von. I doubted she'd put out any assistance or help to Anika Winsome.

If not Von, then where was Anika getting the funds to spend at The Wells and to stay in The Billings. I doubted the Midwest Territories would allow it. Maybe Eric Mann.

"What is Lynn doing?" I put my fork down.

Jane paused. "They're not working together as far as I can tell."

Kimmila smiled. "I've seen her hanging out over in the Bottoms, a place called Groove."

Jane gave Kimmila a look but didn't say anything. I'd seen that look before from disapproving partners. It asked, *what were* you *doing there?*

Kimmila didn't answer Jane's unspoken question but kept talking. "She's not all dolled up in her suit, but she's just hanging along the wall, watching people. A few times she left with a few folks, but the next night she was back."

"The Groove's a nightclub?" I asked, but I didn't need an answer.

"She could be following a lead." Jane offered. "Didn't you say that Nico Mars was supposed to be headed back to The 12?"

I nodded. "So, if Lynn's following a lead, what is Anika doing?"

Jane shrugged. "Living her life."

"Something's off." I pushed my plate away.

People behaved a certain way for a reason. What was Anika's? She and Lynn hadn't been here for a full week, yet, and they'd already come apart. I put that info in my back pocket for later. It could be a divide and conquer strategy.

Kimmila took out a skinny metallic tube. She pushed the tiny side button and placed the thin tip between her lips. Smoke seeped out of the other end, a seductive curl of foamy white. She inhaled and blew smoke out of her nose. "I wanna know how Mars got outta that cradle."

"How did he get out?" Jane asked me.

"I have my guess," I said.

"We need to follow the circuit," Jane replied.. "The currency. A bunch of people got their cards stacked to make that breakout happen."

"That's a good idea. Who in the cradle got their circuits stacked? We need someone to trace the trail in the Midwest."

Yukio could probably tease it out.

"Shouldn't the T.A. be doing that?" Kimmila said.

"Yeah, but what the T.A. should be doing isn't always what they end up doing," I said. "If they have done it, they haven't shared that information with me."

Jane chuckled. "That agent only gonna give you what she want you to know."

Kimmila sucked her teeth.

I sipped my Port-in-a-Storm.

Jane peered across the table at me. "I know that damn look."

"What look?" I raised my hand in innocence.

"That's the stir the hive look."

I lowered my arms and crossed them to mirror Jane's posture.

"What else we gonna do this weekend?"

As we exited Big Mike's, thunder rolled overhead, threatening to release rain onto the humid city. With a crack of lightning, the clouds parted, and rain fell. I'd parked the rental a few blocks over and hunched against the warm downpour. Jane and Kimmila raced over to her aerocycle, put on their helmets, waved, and then launched upward toward the stalled elevated lanes' traffic.

"They're gonna get drenched," I said to myself and then realized I was in the same boat.

I hated it when my hair got wet. It became a tangled jungle of tiny corkscrew curls. So, I hurried down the sidewalk, but no matter how fast I walked, I couldn't outpace the squall. Darkened and rainy, the day turned to evening in the afternoon. The great thing about being out in a summer shower like this was it's easier to spot someone following me. Unlike sunny days, when the District's crowded sidewalks camouflaged a stalker, no one liked being caught in this mess, thus providing fewer people to hide behind.

Male. Dark hood. Tall, about six feet. Lean. Sunglasses.

Really? There wasn't any sun. *That's not suspicious at all.*

As soon as we cleared Big Mike's, I saw him leaning against the building. I thought he was just waiting for a taxi or AWV, automated wauto vehicle, but he pushed off the wall and trailed behind me like a cat following tuna in my pocket. Even after three blocks and the rain, he didn't deviate.

So, I did.

When a clearing appeared in the street level traffic, I dashed across to the other side. Without looking back, I slipped into a convenience store and stood inside the entranceway. I peered out into the noonday gloom.

A beautiful woman, slender with a welcoming smile, leaned over the counter. "Can I help you?"

Her nametag read, Kenesha, and I thought that was an appropriate name for her. Unique. She had short, bright pink hair, and a warm complexion. The store's tee-shirt somehow managed to look good on her. I wanted to ask her what a woman like her was doing in a dumpy store like this, but I had bigger fish to fry.

"No, thank you." I turned back to the door. The traffic kept the stalker at bay for the moment, but he'd seen me cross the street.

"You sure?"

"Yeah."

My stalker had crossed the street too, but he used the crosswalk. In his confusion, he threw back his hood and searched to see what path I'd taken. I stepped further back into the store.

"I think he's coming this way," Kenesha said from the counter. "If you go down the first aisle, I will hold him up and you can go through the employee section and out the back door. You'll end up in an alley."

Before I could thank her, she waved me off. "About once a week, sometimes more, I have to help women escape these bastards that won't take no for an answer."

She came out from around the counter and shooed me down the aisle.

"Thank you." I took off toward the rear of the store.

A blur of colorful products whipped by as I ran. Once I reached the EMPLOYEES ONLY! sign, I heard Kenesha greet the stalker.

"Oh, I would love to have one of these. Does it come in any other colors?" she said. "No. Humph, where did you get it?"

His sneakers squeaked on the tile flooring. The stop and start of the noise told me to move faster.

I rushed through the back, and out the rear service entry door. As promised, I ended up in an alley, where I made a right, and raced down the tight space between buildings, past trashcans, compost heaps, and deep puddles until I emptied out three blocks from Big Mike's. Almost back to where we started, I crossed the street again and took a different route to my rental wauto.

No sign of the stalker.

No one followed me.

I lost him in the store.

I crawled into the rental wauto, soaked to the bone. My head rested against the steering wheel as I collected my thoughts. Before I turned on the heat, I locked the doors and searched around for any signs of the man in the hoodie. Damn it. I wanted to know who he was and why he followed me. Those questions would have to wait, as the summer shower tapered off. The sun broke through the departing clouds. I lifted into the air and pointed the vehicle toward home. I needed to change clothes, and I had a favor to call in.

I was on someone's radar, again. I'm not sure I've ever been *off* the radar. When you do the work I do, enemies come with the territory. People hire a PI when they don't want to go to the regulators, which meant they had something either 1: immoral, 2: A violation, or 3" both. That put yours truly on the path of some dangerous, crooked, and unhappy folks. Sometimes, they had long memories.

I wiped the water dripping from my face and pushed my hair back. My clothes were plastered to me, and I wanted to strip out of them, in the vehicle. Thankfully, the rental had waterproof seats and flooring. Just thinking about it brought back the memory of my wauto burning. I wondered if the Regulators made any headway on that front.

I doubted it.

The rest of Saturday unfurled in all her rain-drenched beauty. Water glittered beneath the now partially sunny skies in puddles across the pavement. Traffic remained light as I made my way home. I peeled off my pug and the shoulder holster. Once I got home, my first action, after drying off, was to clean my weapon. The second thing? Make a cup of coffee to chase off the chills from being soaked through.

I bet you didn't think I could do homebody.

I can, even for a Saturday.

Just not too often.

It seemed later than it was, but once I hauled myself up to my apartment, I wanted to crawl into bed. Instead of giving in to the urge, I made a beeline for the bathroom. I peeled off the now damp clothes, starting with shoes, and socks. They fell to the floor with a *splat*. I'd left my gun and its holster on the kitchen table. I toweled off my puckered fingers, toes, and damp skin. I washed and conditioned my hair, braiding it into two big plaits to air dry. An hour of detangling and moisturizing would make sure my hair survived the rainfall.

I yanked on a gray tee-shirt and sweats. The air conditioning kept the apartment cool since it didn't have to battle blazing heat. Bra-free and in dry clothes, I made my way back to the kitchen. In the cabinet above the coffeemaker, I removed the gun-cleaning kit. It was secured in a smooth, green, velvet-draped box and safe from dirt and debris. I keep my tools in good shape, because they kept me alive.

"Coffee. One. Dark." I placed my mug beneath the coffeemaker's spout and out shot hot, liquid caffeine.

I carried it over to the table and placed it, and the box down. "Telly, play Sting's greatest hits."

The music wafted up from the telemonitor, and I eased myself down into the chair to begin my work. I removed the laser gun's battery and set it aside. I took out the cylinder next. My hands worked as if on their own powers. Muscle memory made it look easy as each part found its way to the lineup unfolding on my kitchen table.

As my hands worked, my brain did too, returning to the six questions.

I started with the first question. Why was Anika allowed to remain on the case?

Ortega trusted her to keep her role as witness, lover, and Regulator separate. Had she done that? I didn't know, but no one removed Anika.. The judges let her testify at trial. From what I got from Ortega and the violation file, they didn't have much in way of forensic evidence, so they couldn't move forward without Anika's testimony. The others who testified had credibility issues.

I didn't like that answer, but there it was. I drank some coffee, letting the bitter heat sear out the distaste in my mouth. Ten years ago, the District was a very different place.

I still didn't like it.

The song switched, and I moved to the next question on my

mental list. Who helped Nico escape from the cradle? I agreed with Jane's insight earlier. It had to be someone with currency and connections. Kinnear Von fit the bill. Nico Mars most likely hid out at her home. That's why no one could find him in The 12 or anywhere else in the District proper. I would turn her over to Anika on Monday and see what happens when TRU shows up on Kinnear's doorstep. They'd blow her butler drone to bits.

The image of the drone exploding all over the elegant porch and seeing Kinnear's shocked face made me chuckle. I paused the cleaning cloth as the wave of laughter passed.

I'm easily entertained.

CHAPTER
TWENTY-FOUR

God said to rest on the seventh day, and I took them at their word. I laid on the sofa, with Sting still on rotation. The playlist had gone through several favorites. I told Jane and Kimmila to take the weekend off to enjoy, because tomorrow we were going to stir the pot.

Music, good warm coffee, and a cool room rounded out another Sunday. I walked over to the living room window. The watery blood color flushed across the horizon. The elevated lanes streamed back and forth with vehicles. Scarlet and emerald lights illuminating the coming dusk. Out there a violator and a murderer roamed free. I'd begun to believe that those may be *two* different people.

I retrieved my new tablet and woke it up. Using the stylus, I reviewed my notes. I contributed additional thoughts and hunches to the margins, but nothing sprung out in terms of finding Nico Mars. Perhaps my well was dry.

I went to the kitchen and retrieved a beer and returned to my couch.

"You have a visitor," the door announced.

Only a little after seven, I got up to see who it was. I expected Jane or Daniel.

To my surprise, Anika Winsome stood at my door, dressed in a cream pantsuit with matching heels. She had a bag in one hand, but it was out of view. One thing Anika couldn't deny. She was breathtaking woman.

I debated about allowing her into my place. A home is a sanctuary, not a hangout spot for strangers. But, with my private inspector business still hovering in the red, I couldn't deny her entry.

I hit the door's release. "Agent Winsome?"

She didn't come in. In fact, she took a step back. Perhaps it was seeing me in my sweats and tee shirt. It *was* my day off.

"I got your address from the system. Is it too late? Am I interrupting your evening plans?" She tried not to peek inside.

"No. Come on in." I stepped back from the entranceway and waved her in. Maybe she was lonely too.

Or maybe she wanted something.

My bet was on the latter.

"Thanks." She came in and relief spilled over her face.

My apartment didn't have a foyer. Once you cleared the doorway, you ended up in the kitchen area. The door hushed close behind her, and she stood there with the bag.

She reached in and pulled out a six-pack of Peck beer. "I heard you liked this beer. This is only part of my apology."

"Thanks." I accepted the beer and circled around her to the fridge. "You want one?"

"No. Thanks." Anika wandered into my living room. Typical regulator. The training takes over and when you're in someone's residence, you automatically start taking it in and making internal notes.

I spied my gun cleaning kit still on the table, so I collected the pieces and returned it to the cabinet. She didn't sit down until I came into the living room. She chose the overstuffed chair to the right of the window. I took up my favorite spot on the couch, sitting cross-legged with my beer in one hand.

"So, why are you here?" I asked.

Anika inched out to the chair's edge, resting her elbows on her knees. She placed her bag beside her feet.

"I came to apologize. This retrieval has me stretched thin, and I've been snapping at everyone," she said. "I'm not usually this taut."

"Sure, I get it." I drank some beer and waited for the real reason she came over to present itself.

Anika's hands came together and interlaced. "The other reason I came by was to check on the name of the mystery person. Any luck?"

"This could wait until Monday. You didn't need to fly all the way over here." Nothing she'd said warranted her to look up my address and then fly over here. No one came to this sector willingly.

She sat back in the chair. "True, but I'm impatient. I want Nico back in the cradle, sooner rather than later. Tonight, if humanly or robotically, possible."

"Tell me why you turned him in."

She flinched. "Uh, wow. I wasn't expecting that. I don't know why that matters now. Just tell me who he was with."

"I'm nosey. Humor me."

"Why?"

"Because you intrigue me, Agent Winsome." I didn't realize I meant it until I heard myself say it aloud. "I want to know why you turned your lover in to the Regulators. I want to know why you submitted it as anonymous but then willingly participated in his prosecution."

She sat further back in the chair, as if needing it for support. Her gun shifted beneath her blazer. At first, she studied her hands. Then she looked up at me.

"I turned him in because he murdered those two women. It sickened me that the man I loved had been a shell, a fantasy, a fabrication."

"That pissed you off," I said.

"No, I see where you're going. What Nico did disgusted me. I broke up with him. We were *regulators*, and he's waist deep in violations." She laced her fingers together. "I had to turn him in."

"Why did they let you stay on the investigation?" I had her here, so I might as well get answers. My momma always said, if you don't know, ask.

"There wasn't any way I'd let them kick me off! It was personal, true, but I had the information they wanted. I had the inside scoop, as it was." Anika's eyes flashed and she became more animated, sitting ramrod straight, and talking with her hands. "I couldn't risk them screwing up the investigation and him walking free. I had seen things."

"The moment it became personal, you should've walked. No doubt you had tunnel vision," I said.

"Normally, I would agree, but you can't tell me you haven't worked a personal case or two. The Change? That beast murdered your fiancé."

"It did and it was, but as a P.I., I get to choose the cases I want to work. As a regulator, well, you don't."

She hung her head, but she chuckled as she did so. "Right. Right. You got me there. But, even as a reg, you know those cases that get personal, the ones that stick to your underbelly and itch like crazy."

I did. Too well to be honest.

Anika got up and came to the couch. She sat down beside me and turned to face me. This close, her perfume, a clean scent so light it enticed me to lean closer to get a better whiff of it. With her so near, I counted the flecks of honey in her dark brown eyes. I could tell she wore make-up, but I couldn't tell you where.

"I've been feeling stressed," her voice soft against the air conditioner's hum. She shrugged out of her blazer and removed her gun from its holster. She placed it on the coffee table.

"You want a beer?"

This close her nose ring sparkled.

"No. I want *you*."

It took a second for her declaration to register, but then she'd leaned in and

kissed me. She pressed her lips to mine, allowing them to linger like soft pillows. Once her words landed, I gave into the kiss, allowing her tongue to part my lips, gaining entry. She wrapped her arms around my neck, drawing me in close as if she meant to breathe me in. I held her loosely around the waist with one hand. My beer was *still* in the other hand.

She folded herself into me, and I let her. Once our kiss broke, she cuddled in my arms as if we'd been lovers for years. I managed to set the bottle down on the floor. She hugged me. With her arms around me, she looked at me with naked pleading. My own libido rose to add its own voice to the drama.

Oh, how I wanted to stay there, feeling our skin touch, caressing each other as if we'd been doing it for years.

Had she used these same moves on Ortega?

"From the moment I saw you, I wanted to do this," she whispered to the base of my neck. It sent chills across my body, and I shuddered in her embrace.

"I couldn't tell." I laughed into her hair.

"Amber was there, so I had to, you know, be on the job."

"Lynn can be perceptive."

I held her for a few minutes more, enjoying the security of being in someone's arms, of being held. It'd been a long time since I'd been kissed and embraced. I wanted more of it. So, I squeezed her tight and then let her go. As I shifted to a sitting position, Anika did too.

She ran a hand over her close-cropped hair. "I overstepped. Didn't I?"

I cupped her cheek and brushed a kiss across her lips. "No, you didn't. We're involved in this case, and I want to remain objective and focused. You and me, in my bed, would be a distraction."

"It's just stress release. I'm not asking to marry you." Anika took my hand and held it. "In probably a week or two I'll be back in Chicagoland."

"Yeah, I know, but I want to remain clear-eyed."

And I can't trust you not to sting me, you little scorpion.

We stared at each other. Her eyes hungry with need remained focused on mine. They begged me to give in, to let go, to feel her hands on my flesh just once more.

But I couldn't.

When I'm with someone, I want to be able to drop my guard—give in completely, entirely. In my line of work, that took an amazing amount of trust.

"You should go."

"I don't want to," Anika said with a heavy sigh.

I didn't want the issue of us sleeping together to fog my windows. I'd beat back my attraction to her, and this pushed me dangerously close to falling into my bed with her in tow. My gut warned that wouldn't be wise.

"Anika..."

"I see your point." She took her blazer and walked around the coffee table to claim her bag. She didn't make eye contact with me, but rejection stung. "I'll see you in the office first thing Monday. Right?"

"Yeah." I stood to walk her over to the door.

She started toward it, stopped, and turned to face me. Nearly as tall as me, she looked me in the eyes. "I wasn't trying to seduce you. I meant everything I said."

I ran my hand over her hair, stopping at the back of her head. I drew her toward me and kissed her again, as if this may be the last time I got to do so. She didn't break away but gave in to me once more. When at last we parted, breathless, and warm, she swallowed loud enough for me to hear it.

"Damn you," she croaked, before snatching away. She walked out as fast as her legs could take her.

Not quite running.

CHAPTER
TWENTY-FIVE

At nine o'clock, Monday, I found myself seated with a watery version of coffee, in a stuffy conference room, and seated across from Inspector Regulator Jamison. I wore my usual tee-shirt with synthetic tan pants and sneakers. Jamison didn't get the memo because he wore a buttoned up pink shirt, which I know they haven't made since the early 2100s, and dress slacks fit for a funeral. His matching black blazer and shoes spoke to the fact he spent a lot of time on his image. Even his badge, clipped neatly to his waist, shined. If he wore a gun, I didn't see it or its holster.

It was only him and the person on the other side of the glass. I'd arrived early with hopes of getting whatever Jamison wanted over and done with so I could push on to Anika, but the inspector had other plans.

"Can I get you anything?" Jamison leaned forward on his elbows.

"You can tell me what I'm doing here." I tapped on the cup to give my hands something to do. I didn't drink it. No intelligent human would.

"You know what I've noticed about you, Cybil?"

"No, but I'm sure you're gonna tell me..."

"You always think you can handle whatever comes your way," he said with a hand flip.

I picked my new satchel from the chair's back, stood up, and draped it over my shoulder. "I can."

He nodded. "Sit down. Sit down. We haven't started yet and you're running out the door."

"I do have other business to attend to today."

"This is important..."

"Is this about my wauto?"

Jamison shook his bald head. "No, you know I handle death violations."

"I don't know anything about you, except you're the next inspector up for death violations rotation."

He showed teeth, but it wasn't a smile. It was like a tick to keep him from biting my head off, so instead he flashed it as a warning. I sat back in the chair and stared at the interrogation room walls. The less I said, the better.

"Do you know this woman?" He launched a holographic image of the young woman who assaulted me in the lobby.

"No."

"Funny, CCTV puts her coming out of your office building a few days ago, shortly after you. You didn't pass each other?"

I leaned close to the hologram and studied it for a moment. "No."

"Well, she's dead." Jamison ended the hologram.

"I guessed." Rage unfurled inside me. With Jamison working death violations, it didn't take a rocket scientist to figure it out. She must've been the dead body found by the TRU team.

"You may be the last person to see her alive." Jamison tapped the table.

"I don't know who this is." I met his glare.

"I wanna know why this woman is dead."

"People in hell want ice water." I threw up my hands. "I don't know anything about her, not even her name."

Jamison inclined his head, but he didn't look convinced.

I didn't plead with him. Nothing would move him except evidence.

"I left my office. The CCTV should've shown that too. So, why am I here?"

"As a witness, of course."

"You don't put witnesses in interrogation rooms."

He inclined his head again, puckered his lips, and said, "What did you two talk about?"

"We didn't talk. I don't know her." I crossed my arms.

Jamison sighed. "This woman killed in a blitz attack that happened so fast, the victim didn't have a moment to defend herself."

"And that's horrible. It is. But using the violence against her to manipulate me is low, Jamison. Real low."

Jamison smacked the table. "This. Woman. Is Dead! Whatever you're involved in, she paid with her life."

I didn't flinch, but instead burst out laughing. Jamison fell back.

When I calmed down, I said, "I'm not some newbie. Shouting and intimidation doesn't make me quake. It's too early to tell if I'm the reason she died. She's dead. That's unfortunate. You have a violator to find. That, too, is unfortunate. None of that has anything to do with *me*."

"According to one of the witnesses in your office building, you were seen exchanging not only heated words with her, but actual fighting and laser gun fire. They connected to the regulators, but once patrol got there, you'd both left, her with some injuries. Only the burnt blasts and destroyed property remained. In fact, your face is healing up nicely." Jamison spoke as if he hadn't heard me at all. "The person who killed her, shoved her panties down her throat to quiet her. She died from suffocation."

"Using violence against women to invoke some emotion or action from others has been done to death in comic books. It's so 20th century. Don't be a toon villain, Jamison. She doesn't deserve that." I stood up and pushed the chair up to the table. "For the record, I don't shove panties down throats. It isn't my M.O."

Jamison got out of his seat and blocked my exit and as a big, thick man, he tried again to intimidate me with size. Problem was, he was roughly 5' 11". I was 5' 9".

"I know you don't know me, but this isn't going to end the way you want. So please, step aside, and let me, *a witness*, leave." The words sounded flat against my ears. My hands rolled into fists. He could beat the crap out of me, but he wouldn't feel too good afterwards either.

He glared.

I smirked.

After a few moments, his shoulders relaxed. "This is a messy one."

"Violence is messy."

"Look, maybe we got off on the wrong foot. I need your help. Give me something. He stepped aside. "Please. Word is you help Daniel with some of his cases."

"Daniel handles his own." I didn't want everyone thinking I was at their disposal. I needed to make a living.

"I see I've offended you. I'm sorry. I don't like being lied to."

"Then you're in the wrong business."

"Maybe." He put his hands into his pockets. "Just hear me out. Okay?"

"You have five minutes." I walked back around to the table. "But quid pro quo."

He rubbed his head. "You know this is an active investigation."

"Do you want what I know or not?"

He sighed. "You know I can stick you in the hold for refusing to give me vital information?"

"You don't know if the I have information is vital."

I held his gaze.

Judging by his actions, Jamison didn't have many people tell him no. He seemed uncomfortable, like he walked on eggshells. He'd been so used to threatening people and getting what he wanted, he only had that tool in his kit. Seeing him attempt to try other avenues amused me.

He laid the tablet on the table and then pushed it toward me. "Violation scene JPEGs. Her name was Michelle."

The first JPEG showed a bed askew from the wall. Sunshine yellow walls trimmed in white crown modeling had been streaked with cast off blood splatter. Jamison didn't have to tell me. The victim had been stabbed. She'd lived through every one of the knife's plunges. Jamison said she died from suffocation. The second image showed the body. Her torso bore brutal, angry wounds. I could make out a shoe print on her face from being stomped. Her attacker must have taken off on foot. Bloody shoeprints lead up and down the hall. Similar to what happened to Henrietta.

He already stole her life.

Did he have to take her voice too?

"The vioTechs combed the area around the house. A cigarette butt was found." Jamison's deep voice rumbled through the mental fog in which I found myself.

Jamison was right. This *was* heinous. Overboard.

"We don't have a motive or a suspect." Jamison took the tablet back and swiped it off as if I contaminated it.

"She didn't lose her life like it's some misplaced tablet. Someone *took* her life. Stole it." I met Jamison's cool eyes. He didn't smile, but something akin to agreement spread across his face.

"Your turn." Jamison leaned forward, linking his hands together and rested his elbows flat against the table.

"Number one, I don't know her name. I do know she was part of a herd."

"She was a heifer." Jamison repeated. "Whose farm?"

"Big Game."

"Why would Big Game send someone to take you out?" Jamison picked up the tablet, swiped it on, and began typing on the keys.

"I didn't say he did."

"You're certain of the connection. She wasn't his family? Friend? Lover?"

"She wore his rhino brand. She also came from The 12, The Bottoms."

"Shit." Jamison spat. It was such a mismatch to his elegant and refined clothing and attitude. "Not another one."

"Henrietta was from in The 12 too," I said.

"Yeah. So, are these connected?" Jamison peered up from scrambling on the tablet's surface, his dark brown eyes wide and round.

Hadn't he thought of this himself? Surely he saw the brand on the victim's arm.

"How do I know?" I didn't know how much more to tell him.

"Cybil..."

"Look, take it up with T.A. Winsome and T.A. Lynn. I'm a low woman on the rung here." I was ready to be free from the too small space and Jamison's aggressive cologne.

He got up again too. He pressed the door's release and leaned beside it against the wall. He had a strange look on his face as I exited the room. Perhaps it was a smile.

"Hey, Cybil, um, you want to grab a drink sometime?"

Stunned, I tripped walking out the door. Once I regained my composure, I turned back to him.

"What?"

"Never mind." Jamison put his attention back on the tablet and tried to make his big self, smaller.

A chill shot through me, and then I felt warm all over. I could only nod because I didn't trust myself to speak. *What the hell body?*

With nothing further, I hurried out of there and to the loaner wauto. My heart hammered like a mad fist in my chest. I'd ran almost full out. I took a deep breath and let it out.

Michelle. Her name had been Michelle. The poor suffered. The candle that burned the brightest burned the fastest. Many women living in The Bottoms had their sparks snuffed out quick. They lived like the next day would be their last.

Because odds were, it could be.

I closed my eyes and offered a prayer for the young life gone too soon. Michelle fought for her life. My stomach complained, rolling into knots. Nausea threatened to ride my esophagus to freedom, but I swallowed to keep it down. Sickened, I inhaled several deep breaths.

Who hired someone to attack me?

The violent images of Michelle loomed large, staining everything red. I would bet doughnuts whomever sent her to kill me, did the same to her when she didn't complete the job. Her killing wasn't a heat of the moment attack. Why not push her back out to work if she wasn't a death violator?

Because whomever did this was a sick fuck.

My fury didn't tell me who hired her. My anger only made me want to go out right now and start shaking down folks. Someone knew. Someone *always* knew. The challenge was finding said person before the bad guy did. Her death violation couldn't go unattested. Jamison wanted my help. I could lend a hand, but I needed to get him straight on my boundaries before engaging further.

Which led to another question. What did Big Game have to do with any of this? Michelle had his brand, but it didn't mean she still worked for him. So, who did she work for? Maybe Jamison would be able to make some headway.

Damn it.

I had tried to reach out to Michelle that day.

That didn't make me feel any better.

"Damn this city."

CHAPTER
TWENTY-SIX

Only 9:30, I had time to make Anika's 10am briefing. She'd been so insistent I attend, and well, since I was at Regulator HQ, I decided to go. Anika's attraction to me could've knocked me over with a feather, but this wouldn't shift the work moving forward. This morning, my living room held her faint scent. It lingered on my clothes, despite it being a few days later. It could've been my imagination.

I walked to the central staircase. Wide, flat stairs connected the ground floor to the second, where death violations were investigated. My tenure here happened a long time ago, and I didn't recognize the inspector regulators passing me on the stairs. I reached the second floor and made a left. The briefing room hadn't moved. Anika and Agent Lynn sought an escaped violator, not a death violation, but I figured they used the same space.

For one, it was big enough for all the TRU members to fit in.

People passed by with steaming cups and blinking tablets, dressed in black uniforms and heavy boots. At the front of the room, Agent Lynn and Anika stood on opposite ends of a mounted telemonitor, a screen's length apart. Folded chairs with tight, dark gray cushions lined the space in rows.

When I walked in, whispers grew in my wake. I didn't know anyone here, except the two at the front of the room, but I stood out. For one, I didn't wear the uniform, and two, I had a certain attitude. It made people take notice.

Anika saw me first, but she looked away. I thought she'd be thrilled I came to one of her briefing, but no.

Not now.

I touched my lips, recalling how soft hers felt.

Before the others claimed it, I snagged a seat in the back room. Easy exit. Early escape.

Over the next few minutes, the space filled with a small sea of people. I spotted several inspector regulators too. They didn't fit the black-clothed bodies either. I relaxed a little. Being in headquarters made me restless. A cold sweat blanketed my hands. I wiped them on my khakis. I put my satchel on my lap, holding it there to shield me from the onset of too many people around me.

Crowds ratcheted up my anxiety.

"Come in and fill in." Lynn encouraged. "Unit Six, where's Commander Crabtree?"

"He's following up with the captain," someone said. By his grim expression, it was serious.

"Okay. Unit 10, you swept Sector Four." Lynn pointed at one of the black-clad individuals in the front row. "Report."

The woman stood with rigid attention as she spoke. "We did, Agent Lynn. Nothing to report." She sat down.

Lynn used her finger to draw an X on the sectors TRU had cleared.

The next TRU lead reported on their sector sweeps. Each hadn't fund Nico Mars or even a hint of him.

I said, "Has anyone checked the surrounding sectors, A-E?"

The room buzzed at the impromptu question.

In the front, Agent Lynn and Anika met. Both turned their heads in my direction, but I could've been wrong. Several rows of people sat ahead of me.

"Uh, we haven't expanded the search area. Any reason why we should? Stand up whomever said that." Agent Lynn gestured to the crowd.

I remained quiet my question answered.

"Okay, moving on. Did we do another sweep of Sector 12?"

I stopped listening to them rumble on. I had a gut feeling Mars hid in Kinnear Von's home.

At the podium, the two T.A. agents spoke with frequent glances to me before Anika started toward me at last. She made a beeline, ignoring people who came up to her. With a wave of her hand, she dismissed them. Her agent face remained blank, emotionless, but I spied a slight tick she did when angry. Her left eye narrowed a tiny bit.

When she stopped at my chair, it confirmed my suspicions. Yep, she and Lynn talked about me.

"Come with me." Anika gestured for me to stand up. Her voice didn't hint at any issue, calm, and clear. "Please."

"Sure."

I got up, collected my satchel, and followed her out of the briefing room and down the rear staircase to the first floor. The path looked familiar to one I'd taken before. When we reached her and Lynn's makeshift office, I smiled.

Cybil- 2

Anika-0

"Come inside." Anika shoved her badge in front of the scanner and the door slid back.

"You sound upset." I followed her inside as instructed. Until then, she'd been calm but her agent face masked her irritation. I wouldn't play Poker with her.

"What are you doing here?" Anika glared at me.

"You've been fussing at me to attend a briefing and I was in the area so I came. And you're upset."

Anika made a noise deep in her throat. "Fine. You identified the woman with Nico Mars?" Straight to the point.

"Yes." I snapped in return.

Anika's face broke into a smile and softened. "Great. Lynn and I have made some headway too."

"Oh? What?" The entire conference room table had been cleared. They must've made a lot of headway.

"First, who's the person in the video?" She asked.

"Kinnear Von."

Anika froze between sitting in her chair and standing. "Kinnear Von?"

"Yes."

She had the same reaction I did when I learned of Von's involvement. "The question is, who has the connections to bring Mars and Von together?"

Anika's mouth gaped. She lowered herself in the seat.

"I don't know."

"Yeah, but I have another question."

"What is it?" Anika crossed her arms as she chewed on the recent development.

"Do you have any updates on who set fire to my wauto?" I sat down across from her. "I expect the T.A. to reimburse my vehicle's total cost."

Anika shook her head. "I don't think so, Cybil. We are paying your retainer..."

"—and expenses. A new wauto is an expense."

"There's no proof it was vandalized because of our investigation." Anika said.

"Who do I need to talk to because I don't accept that answer. Once you scuttle back to the Midwest, I'll be stuck without a vehicle." I meant those words and they came out hard, like pebbles.

"Midwest Director, Trey Ohornon." Anika raised an eyebrow.

"Shit." I couldn't believe my ex-boyfriend oversaw the Midwest Territory Alliance. *When did that happen?*

"You know him?" Anika asked.

"No," I said.

"Yes," Lynn said as she walked in the door.

"Which is it?" Anika looked from Lynn to me.

"It's not important. Do you have a name for the person who torched my vehicle?" I pressed on. I'd deal with Trey, my ex-boyfriend, later, but now, I wanted an answer about my wauto.

"You'd have to follow up with Regulator Philips," Anika said with a shrug. "We've been a bit busy with Mars. I'm sorry, Cybil."

"It's only been a few days," Lynn chimed in.

"It's been a nearly a week!" My honey level dropped, but I stalked out of the conference room before I reached vinegar-induced rage.

I'd have to approach Trey on my own to get my replacement. I wouldn't even have been at Regulator HQ if it hadn't been for the Territory Alliance agents. Maybe the District would pay me. It was vandalized on their property.

"Wait! We must tell you what we've learned," Lynn shouted. "Don't run off yet."

"Okay." I turned and went back into the room. I sat down in the same chair and growled, low in my throat.

"What's that?" Anika's eyebrows rose in alarm.

"Hunger."

"Ah, then we'll be quick." Anika waved her hand across the tele-monitor's screen, waking it up.

"We've learned a guard at the Cradle, a Hermes Leewood, released Nico from his cradle."

"Inside job. Like I said."

Lynn sniggered. "Any first year agent would've guessed it, Lewis."

"Hermes refused to tell us why he let Nico out. In fact, he continues to deny he did." Anika continued, "We found several currency transactional deposits of over $500 credits six weeks before Nico escaped."

"That's not a small amount. He say where it came from?" I asked

Who would be foolish to not only work at the place, but take the currency deposited for any good information broker to find? They didn't try to hide it.

"He refused to tell us where the funds came from, stating it wasn't our business." Lynn shrugged. "He requested an attorney, and so we stopped the interrogation. He's waiting in the hold."

"Those aren't big amounts for someone like Kinnear Von," Anika said.

"Did you trace those transactions to her?" I looked at Anika.

Lynn laughed, a kind of wheezing snort.

"What's funny?" I didn't see the humor in my question.

"Not yet." Anika rolled her eyes. "Amber feels like this is a bit too neat."

"Because it *is!* You're putting words in my mouth. When we ran a trace on those transaction, we caught a virus." Lynn countered. "It was a set up. Someone's trying to erase all the evidence and they may be creating evidence to frame someone else."

"Things sped out of control," Anika interjected.

Lynn snorted. "It shut down the terminal for hours, and the resources spent to clear, contain, and remove the fucking thing–"

"Doesn't the TA have protocols and fire walls for this sort of thing?" I watched them and both shifted in their seats, avoiding eye contact with each other.

Lynn said, "We do."

"And this virus got by those." I looked at Lynn's pinched face and then to Anika's crossed arms and hunched body language.

"Yes, it did." Lynn threw her hands up.

I stared at Anika. "An inside job."

Lynn swore. "Yeah."

CHAPTER
TWENTY-SEVEN

Home for lunch, and I realized I didn't have a damn thing to eat other than peanut butter and jalapeno jelly. Grocery shopping didn't rank high on my list of To-Do, especially when I worked on a case. I had a habit of getting hyper focused on solving the puzzle. I reached into the cabinet to snag the peanut butter when my door interrupted my thoughts.

"You have a visitor."

"It's open!" I grabbed the jelly and bread from the fridge.

Jane came in, dressed in black pants, dark boots, and a black shirt that bordered on being a blouse. She wore her dreadlocks tied back with an ebony scarf. Tiny earrings dotted her right ear, and a thick collar adorned her neck. If I didn't know any better I'd say she had a date or a special engagement.

"You sure we need to be up this early in the afternoon?" she asked.

"Do you want to be roaming around The 12 at night?" I spread both items quickly onto the slices of bread.

"Good point," she said with an incline of her head. Her sunglasses hung from the scoop of her shirt.

"You sleep last night?" I bite into my sandwich.

"Yeah, but it wasn't restful, if you know what I mean."

"I don't want to know what you mean."

She laughed. "You?"

"It was a quiet evening at home."

"Why don't I believe that?"

I shrugged. "Instincts, maybe?"

She didn't push and I didn't tell. "Let me get my satchel and off we go."

"You flying?" Jane asked from the living room.

"Yeah." I answered around the sandwich wedged in my mouth. I retrieved my satchel from the bedroom. Inside was my tablet, an additional barrel for my laser gun, and pain patches. I hoped I wouldn't need any of these items, but experience taught me different.

"Ready."

Jane pointed at my sandwich. "Eat that already. I don't wanna smell it for hours in the wauto."

"Hey, this smells amazing."

Jane rolled her eyes. "Let go sit on our butts all day."

"Oh, don't be so pessimistic. We might get to run for our lives."

"Joy," she said.

Once we climbed into the rental wauto, I started the flight sequence. "Coordinates?"

Jane punched them and then secured her safety harness. "Kimmila dug up some stuff on our target. This Eric Mann has a lot of problems.."

"Yeah, he's about to have another one if he has anything to do with what happened with those two death violations."

"All we've got on him is he ate lunch with Anika a week ago," Jane said.

"And what Kimmila found."

"And what she found." Jane took out her tablet. Where she kept it remained a mystery. Back pocket? Her front pockets would've shown the outline of the device. "Okay, so Eric Oliver Mann was born in the District on October 25th, 2110. He graduated from Old Montgomery College with a certification in law."

He mentioned he worked as an attorney during our ambush of him and Anika. "Is he practicing now?"

"No, but why not?"

"Exactly. There's something off about that guy What's he hiding?" I honked the horn at the cargo craft butting into my lane without a signal. He nearly took the front of the wauto off. *Jerk.*

"Dunno. Oh, here's a juicy bit Kimmila pulled from her searches. His mom said he had a temper when he was young, but he was given Ackback to help keep him calm. He was like the face of child Ackback use."

"The District banned Ackback like 20 years ago."

"I know, but can you imagine what that shit did to him?" Jane shook her head. "It caused his anger management issues."

"Did it?" I'd read and heard from others that Ackback being used to treat anger management and unruliness in children did not work as well as the researchers initially reported. Over time, the drug created suicidal ideation as well as psychopathy in the children when they became teenagers.

I thought back to Henrietta and how severely beaten she'd been. My mind automatically linked to Michelle. She too had been assaulted in a savage manner that transcended stranger murder. It bled into personal. Eric Mann worked The 12 as a regulator and had a short circuit. Those two things, when combined, would wreak havoc because most folks in The Bottoms had short fuses too.

Outside, the vehicles in the elevated lanes transition from glossy and shiny to shabby and worn. The Bottoms wasn't going to roar back to life and become a thriving District sector. Along the street level, burn piles marred their spots in the center of man-made camps. Heavy cargo crafts fitted with tires trudged down the street, groaning under their loads. A scattering of people hugged various street corners.

"Anything else?" I asked, breaking our quiet.

"No, but she said she'd get back at it today. When I left this morning, she was cuddled up with Zola."

"Remind her, she's only cat-sitting for a few weeks," I said, noting I needed to ask Daniel how much longer he'd be undercover.

"She's named her. He ain't gettin' her back. That's Kim's cat now." Jane stuck a cigarette in her mouth.

"Truth."

We laughed. Once it tapered off, we both became quiet again, allowing the wauto's hush to provide white noise as we flew deeper into the Bottoms. We dropped down to the lower lanes, closer to the street as we got nearer to Eric Mann's *other* residence. It didn't matter how many times I came down to this inner part of Sector 12, the devasting poverty always stole my breath. It also enraged me; the sheer chasm between the lofty life Kinnear Von lived and the way Michelle scrapped for every minute of their existence. Digital signs flickered adverts, with missing eyes, letters, and numbers. Here, the automation occurred slower, so many of the buildings lacked auto-matic doors, windows, or solar panels.

The other thing that stood out about Sector 12 was the number of pedestrians. People walked, cramming the crumbling sidewalks, almost in a trance. Telemonitors, tablets, and smaller contact devices appeared in every person's hand. How many lived a thriving life inside the internet, outside of real life?

"Why does Eric keep a home in the Bottoms?" Jane asked.

"I dunno, but we're gonna find out. The apartment we saw is registered as his home, but this address was listed under his moth-er's name." I pointed at the left corner ahead. "Kimmila did well with finding that out."

We approached a three-story home, complete with wrap around porch, thriving landscaping, and painted a flawless gunmetal paint. It consumed at least 3000 square feet of real estate. I couldn't see much of the actual house due to a serious privacy fence. Kinnear Von's security seemed demure compared to Eric Mann's.

"What a fence."

Jane whistled. "That's not a fence. That's a fortress wall."

We flew around the house and spied the landscaping through the gate before parking further down the road. The iron gate attached to steel walls ran along the edge of the landscaping, encasing the house in a protective barrier. I wanted to get out to see more, but I thought better of it. It probably had surveillance and other additional security, like drones and bot monitoring.

"Why does he need all of that? The governor's house isn't that protected." Jane lowered her window and lit her cigarette.

"Jane..."

"Okay, I'm goin' for a walk." She opened the door, slipped on her sunglasses, and took off in the opposite direction from Eric Mann's home.

I sat and waited. I didn't know if he was home. Many people went out on Saturdays and did activities in the real world. While I waited, I took out my tablet and pulled up what information I could about Eric Mann. Kimmila had secured basic information, but I wanted deeper intel. It meant sneaking into online clusters as my other alias and asking around.

I surfed around, looking for any hits on Eric Mann. Nothing.

Then I entered the coordinate for his massive home.

Bingo!

According to public violation records, the District regulators had to come out to Mann's coordinates for assault and disturbing the peace. No violations have ever been filed, but the number of times they'd come out, there should've been, probably because he worked as a regulator. I couldn't get the case numbers to open, but I kept them to follow up on when I went by Regulator headquarters.

The thought conjured my memory of Anika, her soft lips, her firm embrace. I sighed so loud I startled myself. What they don't tell you about surveillance is that it's boring. That was why I brought Jane with me. Otherwise, my mind tended to wander and well, nothing good ever came of it.

Jane tapped on the window spooking me before she opened the passenger door.

"Hey!" She slid into the seat and locked the door. "I did my walk around."

"Is he home?"

"No idea."

"Did you find out anything?"

"Only that the place is a fucking fortress. Eric Mann's either doing a lot of evil shit or he's overcompensating for something." Jane shrugged. "How long do you want to give it before we try again tomorrow?"

"A few hours."

She nodded. The wauto had tinted windows, and so we wouldn't have to worry about anyone spying inside. We settled in for the long wait and the butt-numbing activity.

"Maybe he's a good person." I offered as Jane reclined her seat. "Emotional straits or financial straits may have caused him to get stressed and act out."

"Or maybe he's a liar," Jane said. "He *is* a lawyer."

I laughed.

JANE TOOK several trips around the neighborhood. On one of those excursions, she scored two cups of coffee. She passed me a paper cup and got into the passenger seat. The java's weakness didn't bother me because I wanted something to wet my throat. While I sipped the lukewarm liquid, I spied Eric Mann's iron gate yawn open.

Out flew an aerocycle, black, slick, and shiny. Its rider wore a helmet, as was regulations, and a dark one-piece bodysuit.

"Is that him?" Jane sat up. "They're wearing a helmet."

"I can't tell. Let's go." I put wauto into flight and flew behind the aerocycle.

I kept our distance well behind the person. Could it be our target? I had no idea, but if it turned out that it wasn't, we'd question them. One way or another, we'd get something.

The aerocycle glided through traffic like a knife through jelly. I kept my distance, but the afternoon traffic made it challenging. It wasn't long before we'd left The 12. The buildings began to look familiar. To our surprise, the aerocycle landed in the front of Big Mike's. I flew by and parked several blocks away.

Jane and I made our way to the restaurant. We looked around for Eric. The aerocyle remained parked close to the restaurant, but the actual individual wasn't.

"You go in," I said to Jane. "I'll hang here."

Jane nodded.

She disappeared into the restaurant. Delicious aromas slipped out. My stomach rumbled in longing. We'd need to break for food, but not yet. It'd been hours but it felt like we had only just started.

I paced around the front of the building. When it appeared no one was watching, I walked over to the aerocycle and placed a homing device beneath the rear wheel well. CCTV cameras would spy me doing it, but it wasn't a violation. What I did with the information, now that, could give me another visit from the Regulators.

When I returned to my post outside of Big Mike's, I watched as people went in and others came out sporting big smiles. I walked over to the alley where Bryan and I talked a week ago. Hot whispers sprung out and voices rose, echoing down the tight corridor. I dipped into the darkened space, concealed by partial shadows, following the shouting and furious hisses to silence them.

At Big Mike's service door, the server, Bryan, with hands on his narrow hips, yelled at a man. I dropped down behind the square, industrial trashcan and peered around it. The odor of rank food forced me to breathe from my mouth. The neighboring compost pit didn't help matters smell any sweeter, but to get any closer risked exposure.

A few feet away, the conversation escalated.

"I'm done. I told you!" Bryan shouted.

Across from him, a man held a cycle helmet under one arm. He stood about four inches taller than Bryan. In a flash, the man snatched a fistful of Bryan's shirt and dragged him closer. The words came out like a series of hisses. Bryan's voice echoed in the alley, but the other person's voice was a low timbre. I couldn't make out the exact words. I just knew he was intensely angry.

I stood up.. I watched as he let Bryan go after delivering some furious words. Bryan fell back a few steps. His body language betrayed his fear. He rubbed the spot on his chest, smoothing his crumpled shirt. A scowl spoiled his usually cheerful face. His hands trembled.

"Not any more, Eric!" Bryan shouted after the figure.

That I heard loud and clear.

The back door slid open and Big Mike stood in the threshold. He rumbled out something, and Bryan raced back inside, squeezing by Big Mike and disappearing into the noisy, bright lights interior.

Eric faced Big Mike, but from where I stood I couldn't tell if words were exchanged. Sometimes there didn't need to be.

I crouched back down as Eric stalked down the alley in my direction. He shoved his helmet onto his head as he passed by me. I pretended to scavenge the dumpster. The great thing about garbage cans was no one paid them or the people searching through them any attention. They blended into the backdrop of an alley.

I watched Eric climb on his aerocycle and bolt upward into the elevated lanes. A few minutes later, Jane jogged down the alley and met me on the sidewalk.

"I thought you were watching the door." She lit a cigarette and inhaled.

I told her about the exchange I saw between Eric Mann and Bryan.

"You're sure it's him?" Jane asked.

"I'm a certain, but we can always ask Bryan."

Jane nodded. "I *am* hungry."

"Me too."

"And we're already here..." Jane blew out smoke.

"We've lost the tail," I replied.

"Might as well eat."

"Might as well."

CHAPTER
TWENTY-EIGHT

When Bryan spied us walking in, his shoulders sagged. We sat in our usual table, in his section, and ordered from the table menus without waiting for him. I hope he didn't delegate our table to another server. While I wanted to talk to him, I didn't want to embarrass him or cause any trouble with his employment. He'd been at Big Mike's for a long time. In the District, currency didn't come easy. Bryan didn't deserve to lose because I'm nosey.

After about ten minutes, he arrived at our table with our drinks in both hands. He placed Jane's beer beside her, and my Port-in-a-Storm in front of me. No joking, no poking fun, nothing sarcastic to say about my outfit. Oh yeah, he was nervous.

"Your orders will be up shortly. We've got a full team in the back so everything's coming out fast." He avoided eye contact and scanned the room around us instead.

"Can you take a break in a few minutes to come talk to us?" I asked.

"Nah, I just had my break, and it's about to get busy." He stepped back, ready to bolt.

"All we need is five minutes." Jane leaned back in the chair. She pointed to something out of my eyesight.

"Please give us a few moments, so we can talk about Eric." I added.

Bryan looked at me then, his mouth agape. When he started to talk, no words came forth. So, he pressed his lips together, nodded once, and fled.

"You pushed too hard," Jane said with a shake of her head.

"Did I?" I sipped the berry sweetness of my drink. This was much better than the watery coffee we had in the Bottoms. "I didn't threaten him with my knife."

"You would've if you had one." Jane retorted.

We drank in silence and waited for both Bryan and our meals. Today's performer sat on a bar stool and sang jazzy songs from the early 20th century. Periodically, she would pick up a trumpet and play. The clear, mournful quality to both her voice and the brass instrument stroked my soul. Beautiful.

Once the food arrived, Bryan removed his apron and sat down at the table with us. He rubbed his hands on his pants and huffed. With a quick glance around, he crossed his arms low. "What do you want to know?"

I stirred my zoodles. "First, I want to know if you're okay."

He shrugged. Thin shoulders pulled against sheer fabric of his shirt. "I guess."

"Why were you arguing with Eric Mann?" Jane got right to the point.

Eric sighed.. He closed his eyes and then opened them. He didn't look rattled.

"When I was younger, Eric Mann was all you heard about in the Bottoms. How the sector's golden boy had grown up and become this wealthy lawyer. Currency connects, right? So, I ended up at this youth camp, working on coding and whatnot. Eric was one of the sponsors. On the strength of the neighborhood gossip, he was some-body. I *wanted* him to notice me. And he did. Over time I left the youth camp, moved outta the Bottoms, and started working at the Del Ray Restaurant while going to college."

I've heard this story before, but I didn't tell Bryan. Grooming is often so innocent looking on the outside, unless you distrust everyone, like yours truly, people don't pick up on it. Once they do, the damage is so extensive, the person is forever changed.

"One day, Eric comes in and we reconnect. He says he has a job for me. So, later, I contacted him, thinking I'd get on at his firm or in the office. You know, outta this type of work. Look, I know it's wrong, but the Del Ray wasn't exactly helping my ends meet."

I didn't even know what he'd done, but it bothered him. His body tensed up the more he talked. His hands curled into fists on the table, and he sat up, no longer leaning forward.

"What did he want?" Jane sipped her beer and kept her tone even. "Sex?"

"No!" Eric's eyebrow shot into his dark bangs. "Never. I have standards."

"Then what?" I kept my tone light.

"What does everyone want? *Information.* I worked for the Del Ray for five, maybe six years. Some of the District's political powers ate there. I mean, its super high end. As a server, I sometimes heard stuff, snippets, and whatnot..."

"And you passed those tidbits to Eric?" I finished for him.

He nodded, his eyes on the table in front of him. "I ain't proud of it."

It clicked. That was how Bryan knew Henrietta was a breeder. Who had he gleamed that little piece of intel from? Eric?

"Even me?" I slipped back in from my musings.

"No, no, Cybil. Never you. You and Jane have been good to me." Eric waved his hands as if scattering the suggestion to the four winds. "That's why he, he..."

"Beat you up," Jane said. "He wanted information on Cybil."

Bryan nodded and hunched back into himself as if reliving the beating. "He—he found out she liked to come here from that agent, the one you ate here with the other night. She told him. Then he wanted me to spy on you for him. I said no."

"And that's what the drama was about in the alley?" I wasn't sure whether or not to believe him. Why would Eric Mann want to know about me?

Big Mike's had been my sanctuary, and to think it could've been infiltrated made me nauseous and more than a bit pissed. Jane and I made eye contact but didn't speak about the thought I was sure we both had.

"Yeah. He said he didn't care what I wanted. I either get information from you or he'll beat the crap outta me again." Bryan looked from me to Jane.

"If not me, then who did you give him information on?" I sipped the drink, but I kept my gaze on him.

Bryan squirmed. "So many people. It's a blur. Whatever little tidbits I picked up. I don't know what he kept or used. He never told me who to spy on, until you."

"I'm going to say some names. You tell me if it rings a bell. Okay?"

Bryan sighed and slumped. "Okay."

"Anika Winsome."

"No, but I know he knows her."

"Nico Mars."

"Only in relationship to what you knew about him."

"Amber Lynn."

"Nope."

"Michelle."

"Surname?"

"She doesn't have one." I replied.

Bryan screwed up his face in thought. After a few minutes he said, "The only Michelle he mentioned was a sex worker out of the Bottoms. He only mentioned her in passing."

I noted that Mann had a connection to her.

"Kinnear Von."

Bryan lit up at the name. "Oh, yeah!. He definitely wanted everything on her. She's been an interest to him since the days I worked at the Del Ray. She's some political busybody."

I didn't confirm or deny it. "Okay, thank you, Bryan."

Jane drank her beer. He shifted in his seat, and then got to his feet.

"Before you two came in I planned to go to my aunt's house in the Southeast Territories. Just pull up shop. You know?" He rubbed his hands on his pants again and checked the doorway.

"That's not a bad idea, if only temporarily. You need currency to get going?" I took out my handheld.

"When are you leaving?" Jane asked.

"After my shift, if I can score the next cargo craft to the SE." Bryan's face relaxed beneath his bruises. The more we discussed it, the more concrete it became and that seemed to make him more confident.

I admired his courage to stand up to his attacker. The fact he'd once looked up to Mann, and he was able to push off the manipulation, impressed me more.

"Give me your currency number," I said, and as he did so, I transferred a few traveling credits for him to get to safety. "Look, you gotta go right after you leave here. Don't go home. Don't go see anyone. Take off your apron and go directly to Union Station."

Jane nodded. "We'll keep an eye on Eric, but the sooner you disappear, the better."

Bryan swallowed hard. "This is really serious, huh?"

"If he beat you this badly once, he will do it again," I said, "and next time, he might violate your right to live."

It was well after 2100 by the time Jane and I returned to the rental. I'd spoken to Big Mike about Bryan's leave of absence, vouching for the danger the young man was in without breaking anyone's confidence. None of it sat well with me, and I wanted to smack Eric Mann in his slimy face.

Jane stood outside the wauto, smoking. I sat in the pilot's seat, hovering and waiting for her to be done. The telemonitor lit up and I answered.

Kimmila's burgundy lips and bright, colorful makeup appeared on screen. She said before I could offer a greeting, "Hiya! Where's Janey?"

"Why didn't you contact her directly?" I waved at Jane to get her attention.

"I knew she was with you." Kimmila grinned, sticking her tongue between the gap in her front teeth.

"You seem in good spirits," I said.

Jane tossed down her cigarette, blew out some smoke, and opened the passenger side door.

"Yeah. I found out something you both are gonna love." Kimmila shimmed in excitement.

I exchanged a glance with Jane, who shrugged as she shut the door.

"What's up, baby?" Jane adjusted herself in the seat.

"Eric Mann, the one you been followin', used to be Nico Mars' attorney..."

"Wait..." I said, "he was Mars' attorney?"

"Yeah, but what I found out after a little digging is that he's been Mars' lawyer since he got convicted of those two death violations. Nico Mars's wife, was Eric Mann's *sister*. There's an official license in the public database, but I didn't connect it at first, cause the sister has a different father and different surname."

"Eric Mann is Nico Mars' brother-in-law." I blinked. "The wife, she's deceased. Right?"

"Yeah. She died, before Mars was convicted of being a violator." Kimmila nodded "There's a little bit more. When she was alive, his wife worked as the social media coordinator for Kinnear Von."

I quirked an eyebrow at Jane. "This is a tight little circle. Isn't it?

Nico marries Eric's sister. She works for Kinnear Von. Nico gets brought up on violation charges and Eric quietly resigns as a regulator, only to turn around and defend Mars on appeal."

"What did the wife die of?" Jane asked.

Kimmila said, "Cancer."

"Maybe Nico was suspicious of his brother-in-law. He raised a lot of hell about those violations. Eric's motive must've been to make sure Nico got convicted," Jane said. "For the TA, there was only ever one suspect, him. No one looked at Eric. Right?"

Kimmila popped her gum. "Dunno. It's interestin' though."

Clearly, she took to the research part of the job.

"If Nico had gotten wind of that, he'd request new counsel." I shook my head. "There had to be more to it than that."

"If he didn't get wind of it, he was a sitting duck." Jane pushed her sunglasses into her hair. "His ex-lover and a vindictive brother-in-law. No way had he got a fair trial."

"No way." I agreed. "The question is, did he know?"

"We'd have to ask him," Jane said.

"Why didn't Anika tell us?"

Jane shrugged. "You gonna have to ask her too."

I didn't like that she still wasn't forthcoming with me. It soured my stomach. I wanted to talk to her. Did she and Eric get involved with each other romantically? If Eric Mann was angry enough and couldn't get over someone hurting his sister, he might have sold Nico a line. And the regulator would've been hooked like a catfish dangling on a line.

"Let's leave Eric alone for now. We can pick him up later," I said to Jane.

"Okay."

At that, a black blur appeared on the screen, blocking Kimmila's face.

From behind Zola's fur, Kimmila said, "I guess that's my cue for gettin' off of here. She don't like it when I don't pay her attention."

"Good work," I said.

Jane leaned in close to the telemonitor. "I'll be home about nine. Make that tofu with sauce, the honey sauce and put it in the fridge. I'll warm it up."

"Okay. Love you." Kimmila disconnected.

"You sure about nine?"

Jane nodded. "Bryan gets off at eight. I'll escort him to Union Station. Hang out for an hour to make sure Mann doesn't follow and then go home. Sound good to you?"

"Yeah." It did. I placed the flight sequence toward home so Jane could retrieve her aerocycle.

"What are your evening plans?"

"I'm going to talk to Nico Mars," I said.

CHAPTER
TWENTY-NINE

ater, I parked the wauto in my numbered spot. Jane got out, reclaimed her aerocycle, put on her helmet, and disappeared into the elevated lanes. She headed back the way we'd come. Her main job tonight—to ensure Bryan got on the train to the Southeast Territories. Right now, he was my only link between Mann, Mars, and Anika. He held the key that locked all these people together. And like all things precious, he needed to be protected.

Once, I watched Jane fly off, I made my way to my apartment. I meant what I said earlier. I wanted to talk to Nico Mars. He must be held up at the Von estate. Her politics and clout would keep him protected. But for how long? Did her partner know about the escaped violator on his property?

Too many questions and only Mars could answer them.

I needed darkness and a plan.

But first, Bryan.

I worked a case for Jane, a while back, in March. Despite the trauma and the death, I made friends with the Regulator captain. It was time to call in a favor.

With my hair down, and my chin up, I punched in the numbers for Tom Hanson. In a matter of moments, Hanson's smiling face dominated my telemonitor.

"This is a surprise," he crooned. "Cybil Lewis."

"Good evening, Tom," I said in my polite voice.

"I was just thinking about you. I'm coming up to the District next month for a conference, and thought I'd reach out to you. Maybe we can get together. You can show me the sites," he said with a twinkle in his eye. He wore a crew neck sweater the color of moss (even in summer and he looked crisp) and a wide smile.

I suppressed the urge to roll my eye at the thinly veiled invitation. I wasn't in the mood to discuss his trip, nor did I care to hear about his reasons for wanting to see me...naked.

"It's been too long," he added. Behind him a painting of the Mississippi River and boats coursing those waters hid most of the background.

It hadn't been that long.

Only five months!

"We'll have to see if I'm working or not," I said as sweet as honey. I could do 'nice' when I wanted.

"Yes, well, things have been so hectic for you since you worked the Irving case. Dreadful. I..I mean, the woman and her death. I met her once at a gallery here and she had to be the rudest, coldest fish I'd ever been introduced to..."

I wanted to tell Hanson that not everyone fell for his southern charm, but he probably wouldn't catch my sarcasm. I let it go.

As Jane often pointed out, I have an issue with authority figures, which was one of the reasons Tom and I couldn't get together. He's a regulator captain and if you've been paying attention to the stories I've told you, then you already know my opinion of regulators.

"... I'll send you the dates I'll be there."

Currently Hanson had set his eyes on making me his next lover. The seventeen years or so age difference between us created quite a chasm. The man was nearly sixty at best, but I had to admit it was an attractive offer. His body was killer, and his face wasn't bad either.

His currency...now that was a bonus.

No pun intended.

I've never truly been motivated by credits, but it didn't stop him from trying to woo me from his mansion in the Memphis Quadrant.

"Absolutely, but it might be a while." I forced myself not to frown at him. "I'm on a case, and I need a favor."

He actually did frown. "You're much too beautiful to be chasing down violation scum. Leave it to the regulators."

"Already invested."

He didn't argue, falling back into his ideal of being a gentleman.

"What do you need?" He sat up taller in his chair, manicured hands folded in his lap.

I explained the situation and how Bryan needed a safe house. In ideal conditions, the Territory Alliance would protect him, a witness, but I couldn't trust Anika not to have him eliminated.

"I think his abuser will know to pick him up at his aunt's. He needs a place where no one will think to look for him," I said.

Hanson sighed and rubbed his forehead. "He will come, willingly. Yes?"

"Yes. Just explain you're my friend. Connect me and I'll vouch."

"I'll bring him here." Hanson's eyebrows lowered across his eyes as he scowled.

"No, I don't want you inviting possible violence into your home. Isn't there a safe house the Memphis Regs use?"

Hanson shook his head. "I don't want to involve my job with this as it is strictly a personal matter. He'll come here, and as for violence, I've got my own particular brand of that."

Well, okay then!

"Thank you." Gratitude pricked my eyes, making them sting.

"After this, we are going to at least have dinner."

"Yes." I promised. A meal was a tiny price to pay to make sure Bryan remained safe.

We disconnected after making promises to visit when he came up next month.

I returned to the kitchen table. On my tablet, I surfed until I found a massive outline of the Von estate. As a celebrity, Kinnear Von was a favorite paparazzi target. And I was right. I scrolled through scores of sites and clips, some were obviously deepfakes and others didn't warrant me clicking on them—I wasn't interested in her skin-care routine. According to the poster, he had been a former employee there and recreated the schematics from memory and regulation violation taken JPEGs. I couldn't confirm its accuracy, but it was better than nothing. The information wasn't easy to find. Trawling the web took time and I had to be careful of the terms I used. I didn't want to get flagged for a violation. The intel wasn't well hidden in the internet's depths, either, but one had to be careful. I didn't want to download a virus, like Anika did when trying to trace the deposit transactions. Whoever was behind this had coding savvy and currency.

I zoomed in on the schematics. Several structures dotted the grounds. From what I remembered, the main house held the most security. The intel from the dark web confirmed robotic dogs monitored the perimeter 24/7. Drones provided aerial coverage and CCTV watched it all. If I got past those measures, the house itself had a security alarm that fed to a private firm.

One bright spot—no force field.

My usual B&E tools wouldn't work here nor would my universal entry key.

I made a pot of coffee and went back to work.

No structure was impenetrable. People entered and left the property all the time—service workers, human security guards, and delivery bots. On my previous visit, I arrived via the front gate, and flew up the long flyway to the main house.

To get through the gate, someone punched me in.

They had a security service. They outsourced it, no doubt. I pulled up all I could find about the Vons. It had been less than I had initially thought, but they probably hired a bot service to scrub their digital footprints, except in those stubborn dark corners of the web.

I reviewed the overall plan once more.

I leaned back and my neck popped. The telemonitor gave the time as a bit after twenty-three hundred. I'd consumed a lot of coffee and information. The virtual scenarios were one thing. I needed real life information.

So, I used the bathroom, washed my hands, grabbed my satchel and hoodie, and headed back down to my wauto. Still too hot for a jacket, but I would need it later. My pug and its holster hid in the satchel.

A wauto hovering near the Vons' home would trigger all kinds of alerts.

They didn't take kindly to unexpected visitors, despite my some-what welcoming first experience and her invitation

I had other ideas.

Thinking back to that first visit, Kinnear had foliage in her hand. It wasn't petals, but more like shrubbery. She didn't strike me as an outdoors gardening type. No dirt under her gel-coated, pink nails.

I got into the rental vehicle and launched the autopilot. I recalled the map's location. A row of shrubs bordered a cottage on the prop-erty. Long ago, the gamekeeper lived there.

Now, I was certain, an escaped violator did.

I GOT fuel outside Falls Church.

While the pump poured in the jet fuel, I pulled on my hoodie. The loaner would appear on CCTV, but the registration would come back to the District's regulators or the TA. The official channels would take time to verify it before it got back to me. If Anika asked, I would tell her I was following a clue.

Soon, I was back in the air. I considered telling Anika and Lynn my suspicions, but part of me wanted to be sure I was right before presenting the intel to them.

I parked roughly a mile from the Von estate. When I climbed out of the pilot's seat, I hated myself for wearing the hoodie. The air was so thick with humidity, even the street signs appeared damp from sweat.

I started walking.

Quiet blanketed the area. Few wautos and traffic flew by as I passed gated homes hidden by huge hedges or tall walls. I stuck out like a sore thumb. A solitary dark figure haunting the late evening sidewalks, I kept my head low, to avoid being facially recognized.

I thought about cool things like ice, cold showers, and frozen pops. I reached the Von home in what seemed like no time, but in reality, it took about twenty minutes. I crossed the street to the opposite side.

I picked up a few decorative pebbles from the landscaping that dotted the street. My initial guess was that the Vons had an aerial force field. Considering how much other security they had, my opinion changed. Why would a businessman and a trophy wife need so much security? What type of secrets did they have?

You had to finish one thing before you start something new, but that didn't appear to be Kinnear Von's thinking. It took balls to keep your lover in your partner's home. Either her partner didn't live at the residence or he didn't walk around the property much.

The estate came into view. Homes on this stretch weren't close. I doubted the Vons saw their neighbors without scheduling it. People of prominence lived here as indicated by the distance between each home and the tall trees and fencing. Unlike Eric Mann's house in the Bottoms, these residences didn't resemble fortresses, but they were no less secure.

Beneath my hoodie, sweat poured. Stuffy and hot, the evening didn't cool off as much as I would've liked. I could reach my weapon, but beneath the holster, the material was damp and irritating. I wanted to strip and dive into a cool pool.

But first—work.

I passed by the Von's massive front gate. When I reached the end of the block, I made a right and kept strolling. The fencing that connected to the gate continued around the property. Initially, I thought it was wood, but upon closer inspection, it wasn't. No, this was smart glass made to look like vintage wood. Probably laser gun proof from the looks of it. I kept walking at a good pace so as not draw attention, so I didn't get a close inspection and I didn't try to touch it.

At the end of the block, I made another right.

I spied silhouettes and heard the soft humming of machinery on the other side of the fence. Green pin-lights sprayed through the fence indicating a lighted parameter. That was my first thought, but then the lights moved. The shadows were about my knee level. Robotic security dogs. They cost a chunk of currency and unlike real dogs, they didn't require food, rest, or waste removal. Faster, smarter, and more lethal, they were chilling machines, the ideal guards.

I hate robots.

My parameter search continued.

The dogs followed.

If they sensed me, then no force field. I tested my theory by tossing one of the pebbles over the fencing as far and as fast as I could. Part of me expected it to ricochet back to me.

It didn't.

The mechanical hum and eerie lights took off in the pebble's direction. Robotic dog confirmed. How many? I guessed three. No force field. This pleased me as it offered an opportunity. My mental plan gelled. With luck, I could get inside the property, over the fence, and right up to Nico Mars, whom I suspected hid out in the cottage.

Like many people, the Vons put their trust in technology.

I started walking again, making two more rights until I arrived back at the Vons' front gate. I crossed the street and kept moving away until I arrived at my wauto.

Once behind the vehicle's tinted windows, I removed my sweat-soaked hoodie. It went *splat* in the passenger seat. My tee-shirt had been soaked through too.

With a grin on my face, I set the autopilot for Padre's gym. I was already a sweaty mess, might as well enjoy it.

I did have a four-mile warm-up.

CHAPTER
THIRTY

Around one, I arrived at Padre's Gym. I walked in to the three-story fitness facility. A few people rode stationary bikes. Their sweat covered faces in black VR masks transporting them to virtual fantasy locales. Others lifted weights at the behest of holographic trainers. Their grunts and groans were a labored soundtrack. The place smelled of old sweat and disinfectants.

I headed to the second floor where Padre's had a tiny clothing shop. My duffle bag with my workout clothes had been in my old wauto. After about fifteen minutes, I left with a Padre's Gym logo-themed short set. I'd wore my sneakers to the surveillance instead of boots because I knew I'd do a lot of walking.

Already warmed up, I stretched, did some lunges and a few crunches on the mat before heading over to the treadmills. Each station had a glass enclosed box with saucer size holes in the surrounding walls. This allowed air to flow through the container. Once good and heated, I began. I climbed onto the treadmill and started the program. My favorite being winter in Colorado.

I pressed the start button, and the machine started. While the smartglass panels turned into brilliant snowcapped mountains and landscape, I ran at a slow trot. It would progress to a job, but right now, I wanted to take it easy. To be honest, I wasn't the faster runner. In my line of work, all I had to do was outlast my assailant. Staying fit helped me stay alive in more ways than one.

Fluffy snow fluttered around me. The air thinned and cool breezes brushed my face and torso. My breath came out in puffs. Travel between territories didn't happen without currency and risk. The further the distance, the greater the chance for violence and danger. Programs like this one, let me visit places that may no longer exist, exotic locales, or fantasy worlds. The immersive experience coupled with the exercise relieved much of my stress.

None of this was real.

My brain knew it. My body reacted to the sensory information it received. Just like this case, I'd reacted to everything that told me, while my brain had teased out the answers.

I'd been too foolish to face the facts. My pace quickened as did my breathing-going uphill now. Each foot slap against the packed snow pounded the ideas in my mind, a cadence, a drumbeat of my next moves.

Facts:

1. One, Nico Mars is innocent of the death violations.
2. Two, Ngobile was Eric Mann, who ran a violator enterprise in The 12.
3. Kinnear Von paid to have Nico extracted from the cradle and delivered to her home.

I suspected Nico remained tucked away at the Von estate.

Why? Their motives remained unclear, but what was certain was that all of the individuals involved wanted to keep their dark secrets to themselves and did anything to keep them from being revealed. The callous disregard for others brought misery and death.

Anika knew Mars didn't commit those death violations and either suspected or knew Eric Mann was the notorious Ngobile. This last was hard to prove. Detaining a regulator on violations was a delicate process. Reversing a death violation would take more than my belief or Nico Mars stating he didn't do it.

After all, it hadn't worked the first time.

All of this tied back to currency and power. Nothing noble or extravagant, only good old-fashioned greed. The trio—Anika, Eric, and Nico—left destruction in their wake and those waves were coming back to gather them.

The victimized women deserved some measure of justice. These four people, Mayfield, Michelle, and the two social activists, had been brutally disposed of, like trash, as if their lives meant nothing because of the sector they lived in.

An address shouldn't determine your lifespan.

I finished my workout and left Padre's around three, the witching hour, dripping sweat with rubbery legs and burning thighs. After most exercise sessions, I rewarded myself with a protein drink. Tonight (today?) was no different. The frosty drink replenished and rehydrated my throbbing and aching body. Good thing, too. I was starving.

My wauto felt good. The wind channel and air condition were new, strong, and powerful. Under the artic breezes, I was in post-workout bliss, on the brink of unconsciousness. I cooled down and sipped my protein shake.

I could order a takeaway once I get home.

The autopilot flew through nearly empty elevated lanes. I closed my eyes, too tired to think. Suspicions gnawed at me, but blessed exhaustion blotted it out. The feeling of foreboding lingered, a mere gurgle underneath the muscle fatigue. My bed called to me and I eagerly awaited the good sleep one only got after a hard workout.

It would be the last decent night's sleep for a few days.

CHAPTER
THIRTY-ONE

Later, Tuesday night, for a brief moment while putting on my socks, I debated whether to take my heavier, laser gun or my pug. The laser gun 350 was a bit too big for my hands. If I needed to obliterate someone, the 350 was the better choice. But, if I wanted to slow someone down, and then maybe kill them, the pug worked out well. It was my favorite weapon, if truth be told. So, my pug would have to do. It was a little gun, but still packed a solid punch. The pug was perfect because I didn't have large hands.

Random thoughts as I prepared for the night's activities. I'd spent most of the day recovering and once awake, planning. I compiled the supplies I needed. All that was left was for Jane to fulfill her end of things.

I put my holster on with the laser gun before I even made it to the living room. Growling at the hour, midnight, I stuck my socked feet into my sneakers and strapped on a new backpack, hurrying. Once I locked up, I jogged down the hallway, four flights of stairs, and outside into the muggy dark. The plan called for the cover of darkness.

I got into the wauto and took off.

First stop was Jane's apartment. Zooming on autopilot, the areas outside The District unfurled in hiccups of urban clusters. Some remained thriving and others were gone—vacated in haste at the decrepit spool of time after the Great War. Farmland mauled by hate and greed carved across the landscape in huge tracks of death. Many turned into graveyards. A once pleasant path with green glades and thickly forested hills along the scenic route, the Seminole Trail had been marred by raw violence and bloodshed. So few green spaces remained in real life, hence virtual reality's and holos' popularity.

Zipping through the partially empty traffic lanes, I made it across town to Jane's place in as little as 15 minutes. The flight was so fast when I arrived I felt unprepared.

I wasn't. It only *felt* like it.

Suspicious of my good fortune, I landed in one of the visitor's spot. Feeling the dread flowing down my neck, I headed into the cool gust of manufactured air. It brushed my damp cheeks as I crossed into the lobby of the Smothers Condo Complex. Like Jane, the five-story apartments building were plain, a tower of beige stone with angry black iron encased windows. Older, it had been refurbished with some newer technology.

I entered the lobby. Each corridor I glanced down, the restaurant, and elevators were vacant. No splashy décor. No fake fruit bowls or paintings. No bots either.

Taking the stairs, I climbed upward to the fourth floor. Cooler than the lobby, the stairwell didn't reek of urine and sweat like my old spot. Knowing my luck, Jane probably paid less too. She was resourceful if nothing else.

This was my first jaunt to Jane's place. Ultra-private, my inspector-in-training didn't like visitors, even me, unannounced. She knew the way to my place and often appeared on my doorstep like a dark apparition, but she didn't want the same treatment. It reminded me of a mother-daughter scenario. My place felt like home. Her apartment was a part of her independence, a no-parent zone.

Somehow I knew showing up on her doorstep wouldn't go over

well. I could feel the tension strumming my taut stress strings like a virtuoso.

Foreign and fuzzy with plush pale blue carpet, and stars the color of lemonade lined the walls on either side the hallway. I had to admit it. The place had better air conditioning than my place and my office combined. Those renovations must have been top-tier.

I reached apartment ten five zero's metallic door. I took in a huge gulp of air, released it and rang. The buzzing echoed through the rented space, announcing to everyone that there was little furniture inside.

The doors slid back and there she was.

"Ready?" Jane asked, her dreadlocks loose and free. She wore an ebony tank top and matching pants. Hell, even her feet were clad in dark boots. But her mood was even darker. "I got the stuff." She held up her small cloth bag.

"Great. Let's go," I said, glad to get moving.

Before I turned away to go back down the hall, a thin light-brown hand slid around Jane's neck a brief moment before Kimmila's face came into view over Jane's shoulder. She must've been standing on her tiptoes because Jane was taller. Maybe in heels, but I prayed she had on clothes.

"Oh. It's you!" With a sharp thread of warning in her voice, Kimmila smiled. "You aren't takin' Janey out again."

"Kimmila," I said.

Jane caught my tone with that one word. She frowned at me, before shooting a big grin to the lioness on her arm. Kimmila's red-tipped hand caressed up and down Jane's exposed arm as if she meant to make love to it.

"I'll be back in no time. Tell Zola a bedtime story," Jane said to her. She kissed Kimmila and without looking back started down the hall.

Her partner retreated inside the apartment, and the doors slid closed behind her.

I hurried to catch up.

When Jane got to the wauto, she stood hunched over, with her hands in her pockets, as if I was about to discipline her. She waited, avoiding eye contact and fidgeting, the way she did when she expected a lecture.

"You sure you ready for this?" I asked from across the wauto's hood.

Her head snapped up; hazel eyes narrowed. "Yeah."

"Let's do it then."

She nodded and got into the vehicle.

Together, we flew over to Falls Church. The misty rain and evening dark provided perfect coverage for our planned antics. After my initial reconnaissance mission, I realized I couldn't do it alone.

"You got the gear." I said over the windshield wipers' hushed sweep.

Jane nodded, her unlit cigarette dangling from her lips. She opened her black cloth bag and removed two metallic balls. They fit in one hand.

"They come with plastic caps covering the detonation buttons so no accidental arming," Jane said.

"Even better."

"They weren't cheap."

"I'll bill the T.A. for it." I glanced at her. "They owe me a lot."

"Like they gonna pay for your black market, violation purchases," Jane said with a snort.

"They should. I've spent so much on this already," I said in reflection.

"Too much for what they could do themselves." Jane inspected one of the balls. "Ain't none of my business."

Why had they been so gung-ho about me helping look for Mars? Agent Lynn didn't give two credits. Anika *did*. She pushed for it.

"You got an opinion?" I peered over at my partner.

She inspected the other ball. "No.."

It bothered me all the way to Vons' estate.

I parked in the same general area but a different side of the street from before. We both covered our faces with mesh masks. These would disrupt the facial recognition software and hide our identity from anyone else who crossed our path. These cost less than the fancier scrubbers and were just as effective. I wore a hooded jacket again, and so did Jane. As dark as our complexions were, we meld with our hoods' shadows.

She exited the wauto first.

I waited ten minutes and then followed.

This time I didn't bother heading to the front gate. We moved down the block to the rear of the house. I doubted that anyone human was out and about in this dreary mess.

"They're here." Jane nodded toward the fence.

The mechanical humming pierced the silence. The dogs had arrived. Swell.

"Ready?" I stood beside Jane.

She grinned. "Always."

She handed me the two balls. "Here."

"Thanks." I shoved them into my pocket. "No longer than 20 minutes. In and out. If longer, you know what to do."

"Yep."

With a fist bump, Jane went back to claim the wauto, disappearing into the foggy rain like a ghost.

I removed the portable ladder from my backpack. The ladder had rope and hard plastic rungs. It stood on its own once extended and supported my weight. I didn't use it often, as I was pretty tall, but it came in handy with taller fencing such as the one encircling the Von's home. So confident in their security, the fence wasn't too high for me to climb over. The moment I touched it, the dogs would alert more security, so the key was getting over it without touching it.

The ladder unfolded in tiny, hard planks. I climbed it and jumped over the fence. Once I landed, I rolled in the soft, wet ground. The robotic hounds charged toward me from a small doggy guard house about 20 feet away. I fished out one of the EMP balls, ripped off the cap, and pressed the button. I tossed it toward the dogs. An electronic pulse bright as a new day erupted. I closed my eyes and after a few seconds peeked.

The three neutralized dogs froze. The glowing eerie green eyes dimmed. Frozen in their stance, the guard bots fell over.

I moved with haste. I didn't know if the robots alerted other security measures, or if the bright light did. That was the risk in using the EMP balls. I slipped on my night goggles as it was dark. I put my backpack back on and jogged in the direction the schematics said the cottage was located.

After a few minutes, a soft glow sliced through the gloom. Thick hedges hugged a residence. Someone was inside and listening to music with a lot of guitar riffs.

Adrenaline made my head pound and my ears buzzed. I let out a breath and forced myself to calm down. I crept up to one of the two paned windows. This one had the blinds opened and I peeked in.

Inside, I spied a full-sized bed that ate up much of the space. To the left, a tiny kitchenette with a miniature two-eye stove and cube-sized fridge stood side by side. A person sat in one of the two folding chairs at a laptop table.

Nico Mars.

He held a bowl in his hand and forked food into his mouth with the other. On the bedside, a telemonitor gave the time as just after one am. I suspected the music came from there too. He was clean shaven, dressed in synthetic shorts, no shirt, and bare feet. His hair looked unkempt. His dreadlocks reached his stomach and begun to gray at the temples. Ten years in the cradle had taken a toll. Wrinkles gathered at the corners of his eyes and around his mouth. The once smooth, dark skin had paled beneath the floatation gel. The scars stood stark like thin worms along his brown skin. Dark eyes gleamed beneath thick eyebrows.

The door opened and I ducked down into the shrubs' coverage. The music stopped. I heard him moving around.

"The fact that you can eat afterward, blows my mind," came Kinnear Von's voice from inside the cottage.

I inched up and looked in again. *That's why his hair is a mess.*

Kinnear stood at the bathroom's entrance.

She walked further into the room, adjusting her yellow sundress as she did so.

Nico chewed, swallowed, and ate another bite.

Kinnear sighed so loud I heard it. "I know you're bored."

"I'm fucking going crazy here," Nico said around the food in his mouth.

It was the first time I heard him speak. His voice sounded rough as if from lack of use. The term was called croak throat. Those who spent more than six months in the cradle developed it. Some people needed complete voice box replacements when they got out.

Kinnear crossed the small room to him and kissed his forehead.

"I know. Be patient a little while longer. The regulators are still searching for you. I told you about the PI who came by here the other day."

Nico snatched away from her, spilling some of the bowl's contents. He slammed it on the table. Kinnear adjusted her dress, turned on her heels, and left. I ducked down and flattened myself against the cottage, hoping she didn't see me.

She paused on the pathway, extended her umbrella, and power walked toward the main house.

She didn't see me.

After all, she wasn't expecting a person to be there.

Once the dark swallowed her up, I went up to the front door. Without waiting, I rapped on the door. I shoved the goggles into my hair but was careful not to mess up the mask.

"...you shouldn't leave mad." Nico rumbled as the door swished open. His eyes widened at the sight of me. "Who the fuck?" he managed.

I pushed my way in before he could secure the door or retrieve a weapon. My own laser gun was in my fist in a flash.

"Sit. Down." My voice promised no room for argument.

Nico sat, too stunned to do anything else. The room reeked of stale sweat and sex. He hadn't kept the tiny place clean or neat. The trashcan overflowed onto the floor, like a refuse waterfall. Dirty clothes formed a path from the bathroom, through the bed space and into the kitchenette.

"Who are you?" he barked.

"It doesn't matter."

He started to argue. I leveled the gun at him.

"If I found you, so will others."

He stopped and then asked, "What do you want?"

"Answers."

I was running out of time. The longer I lingered, the more dangerous it became. Kinnear could return for seconds.

"Tell me about Eric Mann."

Nico flinched. "What?"

"Your lawyer. Your brother-in-law..."

"Yeah, yeah, I know him, but why do you wanna know?" Nico waved his hands to get me to calm down. "Keep your hair on. You here to kill me?"

"No."

"Who sent you?" his voice shook and his eyes darted around the room. He searched for either a weapon or an escape path.

"Be quiet!" I waved him over to the bed.

He sat perched on the bed's edge.

"Start talking. Eric Mann." I growled.

"I dunno what you wanna know. He sold me out to the regs. I trusted him. If you doin' work for him, don't."

"Why?"

Nico swore. "I dunno who you are or why you wanna know..."

"Now!"

"What he believed he verbalized, you know. I fell for it. He was my wife's brother, so you know, I trusted him. Next thing I know I got 20 in the cradle and my girlfriend is providing evidence against me."

"You didn't think there was something at play there?"

That sounded a lot like what Bryan said about Mann. He had charisma in spades.

"At first, he was cool, but then he got all aggressive and controlling." Nico shook his head. "Don't nobody run me."

That also sounded like what Bryan told me.

I switched gears. "How did your girlfriend know of about your violations?

Nicole shrugged his thick shoulders and crossed his arms. "I dunno."

"No idea?"

He huffed. "When I was in the cradle, I had time to think and work it out."

"And?" Getting him to talk was like pulling teeth.

"Can you stop pointing the gun at me?" Nicoe gestured with his hands at the weapon. "You said you weren't gonna shoot me."

I lowered it. "Only if you tell me what I want to know."

"Fine. Whatever. It's boring 'round here," he said. "While in the cradle, I figured out that Ani and Eric stabbed me in back and we're kickin' it."

"Who helped you escape?"

Nico shook his head. "No. Not answering that."

"Didn't your wife work for Kinnear Von?" I changed the subject. He would take a laser blast to protect his benefactor.

"She *did*. Hang on now. I don't mean it like it sounded. Kinnear ran her fuel tank down to fumes, if you take my meaning. Kayla worked herself into the grave. Eric blamed me for that too."

"The affair?"

Nico sighed. "Yeah, he found out about Ani. We were all regs. He'd been observing me for various reasons and periods of time so he saw some stuff. It got under his skin.."

"The affair bothered him, not the drug dealing." I snorted.

Nico shook his head. "I dunno. I was out my head back then. Backed to black."

Ah, so Ackback was his poison. Users could black out from using it. No wonder he committed violations to support his habit and his mistress—neither would be cheap.

"Tell me about Anika Winsome."

He shot to his feet. "You asking a lot of questions."

"You have no options." My pug was in my first and aimed at his heart.

He eyed my laser gun. "You'd shoot me."

"Oh yes." The cold filter had already poured over me, numbing me to the act.

"You said you wouldn't."

"I lied." I waved him to sit back down. "The TA wants you dead or alive. You're a problem they want to go away."

Nico smirked. "Yeah. Ain't nothin' changed."

"Anika."

He huffed out a sigh. "Wish I'd never fuckin' met her."

I waited for more details. I wanted the whole story, but I didn't think I had time to get it.

He sat down. "At first, she was my partner. We'd always been close, but when Kayla got sick, me, her and Eric, got tighter. You know? The job fuses relationships. You see so much shit, only another person going through it with you can understand. See?"

I nodded. My experiences in the Army and in the regulators had been similar.

"Ani and I got together, started hooking up. Eric though, he didn't know about it at first, but he caught us once. He was pissed off. Said I was greedy for going after Ani when I had his sister. He went nuclear, like... like, he was datin' her or something. It was weird as fuck."

"But you let him represent you."

Nico shrugged. "I figured he couldn't do any worse than the District's defensive punks. I'd already gotten 20 sessions for something I didn't do."

"How about now?" I quirked an eyebrow.

"Fuck you." Nico crossed his arms.

I deserved that.

"Eric is Ngobile." I didn't have confirmation, but all arrows pointed to him. "Did you know?"

"Fuck no!" Nico rubbed the back of his neck, visibly upset. He was taken aback because he'd been labeled as Ngobile by the District's attorneys and later the general public. Nico shook his head. "I mean we did some shit together down in the Bottoms. He lived down there so I dunno what he did when I wasn't with him,. He was my partner, but I had my hands full with Ani."

"Ani?" I wanted to be sure we discussed the same person.

"Anika." He smiled, a tiny up turn of the lips. He still had feelings for her, even after the betrayal. "How do you know? No one knew who it was. I... I mean they said it was *me!*"

"Henrietta Mayfield told me," I lied. If he knew she was dead, his response would tell me.

"Miss Mayfield? She still kick' asses in the Bottoms?" He laughed, a big grin on his face. As the news sank in, he sobered. "If she said it was Eric, then it be him."

"Just like that? No proof? Only her word?"

"Look 'ere. Miss M don't bullshit around. She keeps records and her word *is* proof. You know how many violators we put in the cradle because of her testimonies?"

"She wasn't called as a witness in your violation cases."

Nico dropped his head. "I told them not to."

He couldn't face her. He didn't need to say this aloud. His whole body hunched in on itself as if bowing beneath the shame and disappointment.

I changed the subject. Time dwindled and I needed answers to a few more questions. "Did you kill those two women?"

"Nah." Nico shook his head. "I told you."

"Who did?"

He shrugged. "Dunno. I wouldn't be here if I knew."

"Thank you."

"Are you a reporter?" Nico asked.

"No." I inched toward the door.

"Who are you? You not a reg."

"Not your concern."

"You gonna give me over to the regs?" Nico stood up. His tone sounded like he could care less if I did. Maybe he'd grown tired of playing house with Von.

I left.

He called out after me but didn't attack.

I backed out of the cottage, keeping my gun trained on him. He didn't move from the bed's edge, but he kept his eyes on me. The mask hid my identity, but it felt like he saw through it.

Once the door closed, I turned and ran into the dark, snatching my goggles down so I can see in the pitch black. While I hurried, I put my fun away, all while running to the rendezvous spot. Not easy, let me tell you, especially with the rain. The mist became heavier, a shower. It reduced visibility and I slipped and fell a few times. I twisted my ankle. I bit my lip to keep from verbalizing the biting pain. With my heart pounding, I pushed on. Adrenaline numbed the pain and fueled my will to live.

I reached the spot littered by expensive robotic doorstops.

I shouted, "Jane!"

She appeared in the wauto, hovering above the fencing. "Here!"

Without missing a beat, she dropped the portable ladder from the passenger's side. She attached it to the wauto, and climbed over to the pilot's seat. I snatched the bottom rung and climbed up as fast as I could. Jane took off before I secured the door.

I managed to collapse the ladder, detach it, and get it back in my backpack. To appease the blaring wauto alarm, I closed the passenger side door and put the pack on the floor in front of me. With my heart threatening to jump out of my chest, I threw my head back and closed my eyes, removing the mesh mask. It came away wet in my hands. Shaking from the adrenaline overload, I squirmed in my damp clothes and soaked hair for a second time this week. My ankle screamed in agony.

We flew for a while in silence.

Jane removed my handheld from the storage box. "Here."

"Thanks." I didn't want the EMP pulse to affect my device.

At some point, Jane asked, "So?"

I opened my eyes and stared at the sky slipping by through the sunroof. Jane had removed her mask too.

"He's there. I talked to him. He was cooperative and calm, albeit rough around the edges."

Jane nodded, "You had a gun."

"True. I could've been a bounty hunter, there to apprehend him."

"Maybe he's sick of being there."

"Maybe. He said he was a full-on Ackback addict. He trusted Eric, and Eric knew about his affair with Anika and some of the violations because they did them together. Sold him out."

"Learn anything new?"

"No, only confirmation."

Jane stuck a cigarette in her mouth.

"Did you use both EMP balls?"

"No. The one worked well enough." I fished the remaining ball out of my pocket. "I like these a lot. Localized pulse."

"Brilliant and completely against violations," Jane said. "Worth it?"

"Yeah. I think so."

I didn't see what Anika and Kinnear saw in Nico Mars. Whatever drew them to this husk of a man must be hidden, something I couldn't discern in 20 minutes. One thing I did note; Nico Mars didn't commit those heinous death violations. Overall, he appeared remorseful. He held Henrietta in high esteem, or so it seemed. I had no proof, only my gut. Plus, it wasn't my case to solve and it was already a closed thing.

But, I found him.

Nico Mars was desperate and broke. Never a good mix. Now he'd been found, he might run again. I'll let the agents know tomorrow. He wasn't going anywhere tonight.

I promised to tell Anika about the conversation I had with the elusive Mars. All that remained was to turn him in and submit my expense report.

Somehow that didn't sit well with me.

No. Not at all.

CHAPTER
THIRTY-TWO

The morning arrived much too fast for my taste. I managed to capture several more hours of sleep before finally crawling out of my precious bed around nine a.m. Wednesday. Dressed and headed out into the sticky July morning with its cloudless sky and lemon-yellow sun, I wondered why I didn't want to turn over Mars.

The issue was too complicated, and I didn't have enough sleep to process it anymore. Doubts were like bothersome flies—they must be crushed. But they flitted around, annoying me and taunting me with my complete lack of direction. *Which way should I take this?*

About nine-thirty in the morning, the elevated lanes were clear as the, District's workers, those who didn't connect remotely, were already seated behind nice, polished desks tucked into rigid square cubicles at mundane jobs.

Once again, I was seated, this time beside an inspector regulator, at headquarters for the ten o'clock inspector briefing. She had thick, dark hair worn in a fluffy Afro. A spread of freckles decorated her cheeks and the bridge of her nose. She dressed in neutral tones of light gray blouse and slacks with black shoes. She didn't smile a lot but she took notes on the on-going 187 violations in the District as Captain Brinnington spoke.

No TRU regulators were in attendance. Maybe Anika and Lynn felt their talents were best used elsewhere. Either that or the District pulled them off for another investigation or retrieval.

After the briefing, she said, "I'm Fawn Granger."

"Cybil Lewis." I shook her outstretched hand. She had a strong, firm grip and no-nonsense detachment.

"You're new around here? I haven't seen you, but I've been out on medical leave." She tucked her handheld into her front pants pocket.

"I'm a contractor with the TA."

"Oh, right. The PI." She flashed a small smile. "Well, good luck."

With that she turned on her heel and left before I could ask her what she meant by 'the PI.' As I started after her, Jamison appeared in front of me, a finely dressed vision in white shirt and khaki slacks. He looked ready for vacation, not death violations. He gave me a bright smile.

"I was looking for you," he said.

"Why?" It was too early, and I'd had too little coffee.

"Agent Winsome said to bring you to our post briefing review."

I followed him out of the larger inspector briefing room, down the side stairs to the lower floor and around the maze of cubicles to the designated conference room.

Jamison didn't turn back to make sure I stayed with him. He assumed I was there, but the sea of regulators traveling around headquarters resembled District traffic at 8 a.m. But he was hard to miss, and stood out against the tide of black-clad, one-piece clothed regulators.

"Good morning," Anika said with too much cheer for it being so early. She gestured toward the empty seat beside Agent Lynn. She wore a sleeveless yellow blouse and dark pants. Gold hoop earrings and her nose ring all sparkled and cast her in a warm glow. She looked stunning and I lost my breath for a second.

"Found her," Jamison said. The door hushed closed. I didn't know why he was here or what their meeting was about, so I held my tongue and waited. He had nothing to do with Nico Mars or the work the T.A. was doing.

"Good. I'm ready to get started," she said.

At the front of the conference room, where the large, rectangular window looked out over the cubicle maze, Anika touched the glass and it dimmed to black.

"We were able to review the facial tattoo on Henrietta Mayfield." Jamison nodded at the screen. He commanded attention when he spoke. With his usual swagger, he sat on the edge of the conference room table.

On the blackened window, Henrietta's face appeared from the shoulders up. The beginning of the coroner's Y-incision ran in jagged dark lines from each of her shoulders, meeting somewhere off screen. They'd done a good job of cleaning her up, but the gashes, cuts, and abrasions remained stark against her sallow, dead skin.

Anika and Lynn's conference room felt crowded with the four of us.

"There are markings here." Anika pointed to the three neat rows that trailed down the right of Henrietta's forehead, over her eye, and the swell of her cheek. "These tiny circles stand for protection in ancient Egyptian."

Agent Lynn put down her tablet and put her attention on the screen.

"It's raised, like cicatrisation," I said. "So, it is really a tattoo?"

"By design, it's a 3-D tattoo technique," Anika said with the rebuke of a professor.

"The AV techs actually got them to play," Jamison added.

"Well?" Lynn said from beside me, her tone hard. "What did it say?"

"They recorded it." Anika smiled.

"Play it." Jamison nodded at her.

She ran her finger along the glass's side and a flyout menu appeared. She pressed play. The audio started at her behest.

"My name is Henrietta Mayfield. If you're playing this message, then I'm dead. I know the dangers of my work and my adversaries numbers are like roaches. The identity of Ngobile and all the documentation of his violations are in my safe. I kept them for insurance, to stop him from working in my sector. I failed. See that you do not."

We sat in silence.

"Mayfield extorted the infamous Ngobile," Jamison scoffed. "Didn't you put him in the cradle?"

Anika nodded.

"We need to find out who that is," I said after clearing my throat.

"Nico Mars was Ngobile. This is old news. Let's focus on finding our fugitive violator." Anika got up and paced, clearly shaken.

Lynn watched her with careful eyes. Jamison did too.

"Did you search the apartment?" Anika asked.

"Of course we searched the apartment. We didn't find a safe." Jamison threw up his hands.

"If there is a hidden safe, people might have known about it and committed the death violation in order to get it," I said. "Henrietta was severely beaten. Maybe she wouldn't tell them where it was."

Jamison stroked his chin. "The pool for potential violators became a lot larger."

"What connects this to Nico Mars?" Caffeine withdrawal throbbed at the back of my neck. "I mean, Mars wasn't even in the territory so he can't be a suspect in *this* death violation."

Anika nodded. "Right, Cybil. Agent Lynn?"

Lynn pushed back her chair. "The two women Mars committed the death violations against worked for Henrietta Mayfield, well, at her church. As you know, Mayfield was a social activist in The 12. The theory goes that Mayfield had concrete evidence on Mars, and these two women were privy to that intel. Their identities or the information—this is all speculation—got back to him and he violated their right to live, to silence them."

"Why not Mayfield, since she knew too?" I asked. "She must've been a bigger threat than two college women."

"She was, and because of it, she had better security," Lynn explained. "These two women, from what I could gather, didn't."

Jamison shrugged. "Look, I'm working this violation like I do all of them. We started with people close to the victim and we're working our way outward."

"Are you thinking it's the same violator?" I asked Lynn.

Agent Lynn held my gaze. "I do."

"But I don't." Anika interjected. "Nico was guilty of the death violations. He can't be responsible for Mayfield because he was still the in the Midwest Territories."

"Mayfield can't be the motivation for him to escape the cradle *and* be the one to silence her. That doesn't make sense. And since we *know* he wasn't in the District, he couldn't have done the deed." I crossed my arms.

"True," Lynn said, her bob swooping forward like an arrow. "We can at least look into it. There's more in common between those deaths and Mayfield's. The M.O. is the same. The boot prints are a match…"

Anika stiffened. "We're still waiting on the vioTechs to confirm that, Amber…"

I tensed. Anika had called Agent Lynn by her territory name, which meant she was royally pissed. Whenever a co-worker called you by your first name, when you're on the job, it reeked of disrespect if not outright anger.

I recalled the vicious assault on the two women from the case files and the images embedded. There'd been clear intent and malice in their brutal beatings, the same as Henrietta's.

Then I said something I never thought I'd say.

"I agree with Agent Lynn."

Lynn gasped but recovered so quickly the others didn't catch it.

Jamison shook his head. "I've got another body, a Michelle Lore, found by the TRU doing a retrieval for you," he said to Anika. "You don't think that's connected, too?"

Anika remained poised and unflappable. If she felt rattled, she didn't show it.

In an even tone, she answered. "Until we have conclusive evidence linking these deaths to a singular violator, they are separate cases. As far as Nico Mars' victims, that case had been decided a decade ago."

"And if you got it wrong?" Lynn asked.

Anika pursed her lips. Her face remained calm. Then to me, she said, "Cybil, please excuse us."

I scooted my chair back, squeezed by Jamison and left the room. Had Lynn accused her in front of me and Jamison just to get a reaction? I bet she had.

I stood outside the conference room, hearing the muffled words grow louder, become more indigent. The cubicle maze of regulators continued buzzing, never pausing, as violations happened across the District every moment. Like drones, regulators would work themselves and commit themselves entirely to the job until they died young, broken and exhausted.

A few seconds later, the door hushed open, and Jamison stepped out.

"You got expelled too." I stood out of the congested walkway in front of the conference room. People moved back and forth through the cubicle maze, little mice seeking exits.

Jamison put his hands in his pockets. "How do you fit into this? I saw you at the inspector briefing this morning."

"I'm a contractor helping with background intel." I didn't want him in my business any more than he had to be.

"They can't get that on their own?" He raised his eyebrows.

I liked the way his jaw jutted out in his handsome profile. If he knew something he wasn't saying.

"Yeah. Not everyone talks to agents and regs, as I'm sure your experience has taught you."

"Yeah." He shifted around and then said, "I'm outta here. I've got death violations to solve."

"See you."

I turned my attention to the conference room window. The shadows of the two agents moved around the darkened screen like an early, silent picture. The soundproof walls kept their heated discussion contained to only muffles.

Was this why they'd been working apart?

Anika wouldn't want the Mars case reopened. According to Ortega, Anika built her career on it. While he lost everything, she gained. If it came to light she'd been more involved than she originally let on, her world could topple over.

I'd had an inkling Mars had been hemmed up by the rush to justice. Anika wasn't too keen on anyone going back and digging around. Was that why she was in such a hurry to capture him? The longer he stayed on the run, the more digging people would do into the case, opening old wounds, and examining it with the fresh eyes of hindsight.

"Cybil," Anika called from the conference room.

As I entered, Lynn stormed out, plowing into my shoulder without a look back. I watched her go, blazing in the direction of the parking lot, before walking back into the room.

Anika sat at the head of the table. The windows had been flipped to clear. The lingering tension remained despite Lynn and Jamison clearing out.

"You have information for me?" Anika's tone carried a sharpness I attributed to her angry discussion with Lynn.

So, I let it pass without comment or attention.

In hindsight, that was a mistake.

"Kinnear Von is hiding Nico Mars."

Anika burst into laughter. "You're kidding."

When I didn't join her in a good chuckle, she stopped. "You're not."

"No."

Anika tented her hands in front of her. "Wow. I'll follow up on that."

"Who else would have the currency and connections to get him out of the cradle?" I knew the answer.

"Good point." Anika picked up her tablet and began scrolling.

No good job, Cybil or anything like acknowledgement that I'd busted my butt to get the information she wanted. Somehow, I expected more from the woman who wanted to share my bed.

After several long minutes, she glanced up at me. "Yes?"

"Do you really believe Mars committed death violations against those women?"

She lowered her tablet. "Not you too..."

I frowned at her tone. "There's a possible miscarriage of justice here. Why wouldn't you want to be sure?"

"I was sure ten years ago, and I don't see the necessity of retreading a solid ground."

"You're not infallible. Ortega isn't either. There were others working the case too. Any one of them could've made a mistake. We all do. There's no harm in being sure."

She stood up from her seat and leaned onto the table with her hands planted for support.

"Harm is done every time the regulators or agents betray the public's trust. Every violation, every gross misconduct, every convicted violator that was paid currency on our payroll chips away at a shaky foundation."

"And every rush job, like the TRU retrieval you called in, results in someone coming up dead or hurt, like Michelle Lore," I said. "Lives are saved when we aren't in a hurry."

You'd have thought I slapped her. She reared back and licked her lips.

"That's why we have corroborating evidence." Anika glared.

"In the Mars case, it was what? DNA? That only proves he had consensual sex with both victims. The ME couldn't confirm rape."

Anika huffed. "I'm sure Jamison has a strong idea about who killed his victims."

"No one deserves to die like them. The person who did it may have committed more death violations," I said. "He left a long trail of death in his wake."

"Allegedly. And those deaths stopped when Nico went to the cradle. Do you have any evidence?"

"No." Only my gut which wouldn't hold water with the TA agent. I'd reached my nexus with her.

An image of Michelle appeared in my mind's eye. Drag marks in the dirt indicated she'd been tossed aside in the backyard like trash. Both her arms had been shattered. Her left orbital socket had been fractured too. That was in addition to the dislocated wrists. She'd fought hard. Like Henrietta.

Why wouldn't Anika do the same?

"Bottom line. This isn't your problem or even your case. You're done here." Anika rested one hand on her wide hip.

"Got it." I'd been fired in more spectacular ways.

It had become obvious she only cared about what she could get to highlight her career. I wasn't angry, but I was disappointed she couldn't see the people, the human beings caught up in her determined grind.

"I'll submit my expense report."

"By the end of the day." Anika eased into the chair and reclaimed her tablet, a little quirk to be dismissive.

She was angry. Maybe she felt things start to unravel around her. Was that her worst fear? Was this how she tried to keep control by being mean and petty? It tore up my gut with fury, but I didn't let any of that show—not in my actions or tone.

"Sure." I started for the door.

"Oh, and Cybil," Anika called. "Leave the rental's key."

Our eyes met. I was glad I didn't get intimate with her. My instincts were right again. Now, I started questioning all the interactions I'd had with her.

"I see you, *Agent* Winsome." I tossed the key on the table. It skidded to a stop in front of her.

"Don't worry. You'll get your currency," she said, making the word currency sound insulting.

"Oh, I won't be the only one who's going to get what's coming to them." I walked out.

CHAPTER
THIRTY-THREE

managed to limp my way up the stairs, past the inspectors' gigantic briefing room, and the sea of shared workstations. Rectangular box-shaped offices contained places for two inspectors to work. The partners had a choice over how they decorated their shared workspace. Some had standing desks, some had hover-chairs and others had the traditional four-legged desk complete with rolling chair. As I walked through the aisles, I noticed that some had only one inspector in them, and I imagined this was how Daniel worked... alone.

As did Jamison. I found his name attached to a boxy and rather plain space at least on the outside. He decorated the inside with plants in handsome pots, landscape art, and real books. It took me by surprise.

Talk about looks being deceiving.

"You get lost?" Jamison said from behind, making me jump. He chuckled as he came around and entered the room. "Sorry. I thought you heard me come in."

"No, you're not." This close to him, I noted, again, how he struck such a physically imposing figure. He was taller than me, not by much, but two or three inches. He outweighed me. The cologne he wore tickled my nose. It raised a lump in my throat and other places. *Calm down body!*

"What can I do you for?" he said, turning to his laptop. "I'm about to head out."

"I wanted to ask you about Michelle Lore's case. Earlier you asked for my help."

He raised an eyebrow as he turned halfway around to glance at me. "That depends. What do you know?"

"Nothing…"

"Well then no," he said, his lips pressed into a line.

"…yet." I added.

"Aren't you on loan to the TAs? They have their own case despite what they tried to push downstairs." Jamison went back to the screen. "I don't wanna step on their toes."

"That's over." I inched further into his office. "This violator is dangerous."

Stylish and well decorated, the tight space didn't allow for visitors. I bet he took all his guests to an interrogation room.

This time he turned all the way around. He studied my face, before stoking his chin, where a brief bit of beard had started to grow in. Dimples appeared when he smiled.

"You're not satisfied with that." He understood me, the overworked regulator.

"No. And you did ask me to help you," I said.

"Daniel said you're a solid PI, and I'm inclined to agree. The TAs gave currency for your services. I can't."

"Pay?" I asked.

"Pay." He inclined his head. "No funding, no official consulting contract."

"Off the record."

Jamison nodded. "Like an informant."

"Not like an informant. They're violators. I'm not."

"I see." I didn't want currency per se. Not that I would turn down viable credits. After all, I did need a new wauto. "That's okay. I do need a vehicle. Mine was arsoned outside these hallowed walls."

Jamison scowled. "What?"

I told him everything I told Anika regarding my suspicions about Eric Mann.

Afterwards, he shook his head and stood up. "I know a woman who sells used wautos. She doesn't have anything fancy."

"I don't need fancy. I need dependable."

"She's got that. Look, I've gotta go. Can you get back here tomorrow and we'll go get the vehicle? Then we can speak in detail about Mann." Jamison pulled his holster from a peg behind me.

It meant he had to reach across me, bringing his chest right up to my face. Great. I now knew my chin came to the center of his chest. He still smelled like fresh clothes from a dryer. I breathed deeply.

"Sure. I can be here about noon." I cleared my throat.

He chuckled again. "No ma'am. Ten am. After the inspector briefing."

Damn it.

"Okay. Ten it is."

Just after 11:30, the coolness of morning had burnt off to the sweltering heat of summer. Outside Regulator Headquarters, I tried not to scream at the humidity.

I didn't get far before Agent Lynn slithered out from the shade.

"You going home to your dumpy little apartment?" She leaned against the pilot door of her wauto with both her arms and legs crossed at the ankles. She wore khaki pants and a blue collared blouse, which I hadn't paid attention to earlier.

I didn't stop walking.

"At least I have a home. You're here so often I wonder…"

She smirked. In the distance, a dog yelped.

"Hey, Lewis. Lewis!" Lynn called. "Wait!"

"What do you want?" I turned around to see her coming after me.

"You saw what happened back there. I need your help." She winced as if it hurt to say it.

"Yeah, but look, I'm hungry and tired. Take your games elsewhere."

"I'm serious." She reached for me, thought better of it, and retracted her hand. "You know Mars isn't guilty of those death violations."

"Oh, I wouldn't say that. I don't *know* if he's innocent." I corrected her. "Neither do you."

"I guess that's true, but if we solve the other two violations, we'll be capturing the real violators." Lynn's tone held urgency—no—desperation.

"Based on how the last partnership with the T.A. has worked out, you'll understand why I don't wanna do it again," I said. "Especially so soon."

"We could do it." Lynn must have been in a hugely vulnerable place to plead with me.

I adjusted my satchel on my shoulder. "You're a long way from Chicagoland. Leave it to the District regulators. Get Nico Mars. Go back to inside..."

"I don't answer to you," she snapped; her thin lips pulled into a snarl.

"No, but I gave Agent Winsome the woman's name in the video with Mars. She most likely scooped him out of the cradle."

Lynn chewed on her bottom lip. "Who?"

"Kinnear Von and Mars are hiding out on her estate."

"Great. Just fucking great! That complicates everything!" Agent Lynn raced to her wauto, opened the door, got in, and flipped me off before launching.

"Glad I could help!" I shouted after her. It did feel good to scream.

I walked down to the string of taxis. I selected one with a human pilot.

The pilot had short white hair, an equally matching beard, a friendly smile and glasses. It struck me as odd. Few people wore glasses when it cost nothing to have one's sight corrected with laser. As an older gentleman, he may not want to go through the two-hour ordeal. His name badge flashed Darrell.

"Aye, where you headed?" he leaned over to the passenger side window.

I gave him the sector and address. He didn't frown or shudder, so points for his bravery. I climbed into the back and relished the whoosh of cold air against my too-hot skin. With my eyes closed, I tried to ignore the rising pain in my ankle. The numbing agents in the pain patches waned. Good thing Jamison didn't want me to accompany him today. With the ankle, I might not have been able to keep up if something occurred where I had to chase a violator.

Darrell hummed as he flew. The taxi smelled like flowers, and it felt like fall cool but not cold. On his dashboard, two rotating JEPGs of cats flashed. I watched as the images shifted by in a slideshow. It made me think of Kimmila's love for Zola, whom I'm sure she'd already taken a gazillion pictures of.

"You got pets?" Darrell spied me looking.

"No, I don't." I smiled. People who loved pets, and treated them like family, wanted everyone to love pets too. "I like pets, cats in particular, but I don't have the time to manage one."

"Cats don't need managing. They manage you," he said. With a nod at the dashboard, "Those two taught me everything I know."

With that he tossed his head back and laughed.

It made me smile and after my time with the regulators, I needed his humor more than my pilot knew. I closed my eyes again and listened to him resume humming.

I pondered my next steps as I dozed. Something about Darrel's demeanor helped me relax, and I don't trust people as a rule. Encased in the late model wauto, I didn't feel in danger.

I was wrong.

After some time passed, poking fingers woke me.

"Wakey. Wakey." The voice sliced through my slumber.

I bolted awake beneath the cracking threat of danger too late. The laser gun was mere inches from my face. I peered down the barrel and into the crinkly eyes of the taxi pilot. He'd parked someplace remote that I didn't readily recognize. Abandoned dive bars and decaying vehicles meant no active video footage or feed. There wasn't anything here but death by the smell of it. Finding him in the backseat with a gun to my face, in broad daylight too, set me on edge. Add that to the hot air blowing through the open door and I went from rested to furious.

A smile graced his face. "Get up. No sudden moves."

I eased to an upright position, my hands in the air. As I did so, I noticed my shoulder felt lighter, and realized to my horror, my own laser gun was gone.

For once, I'd like Lady Luck to stop giving me the bad shit.

"What do you want?" I asked, voice steady, heart racing.

"I don't want you, but Big Game does."

"You'll regret this." I inched out of the vehicle as instructed.

He chuckled. "How can I refuse 1000 credits?"

"That's it? 1000 credits?" I sighed. Darrell was getting ripped off. "You can't get your cats' food with 1000 credits."

Darrel's kind face became menacing in moments. "Shut up about my cats."

"Or what? You'll shoot me? You'll shoot me anyway."

He hesitated. His index finger was close to the gun's trigger. I looked around. We'd landed in a part of a sector that had seen better days. Trash pooled in doorways and porches. It smelled like life had died there.

"What does Big Game want?" I put my eyes back on Darrell.

"You. Dead."

"Then shoot me or let me go. I'm tired and hungry."

At this point, I spied a glimmer of green zip by behind him. I'm sure Darrell, like Michelle, hadn't done this sort of thing before or else he'd have shot me the moment I cleared the back seat. He would've also asked for more currency.

"This isn't what's in your heart—a death violation."

"Oh, you don't know me!" he shouted and fired.

I tried to jump out of the way, but the blast caught my right arm. The burning erupted almost instantly and surged up my neck and across my body like wildfire.

Damn, I hate being shot!

On the street, I scrambled back from him, as he marched forward, firing at will. My ankle screamed in pain as I managed to twist it the wrong direction again! An issue with laser guns was that after a few shots, they must recharge. He'd clipped me with one shot, and the next two shots were close, but not direct body hits.

He pressed the trigger as he stood over me and fired. The scarlet tip of his gun lit up and no laser beam came. I scrambled to my feet, hurting and angry with both an arm and ankle singing in misery. Blinded by rage, I knocked his gun to the ground with my left hand, and then, reeled back and punched him in the face. He stumbled backwards in shock and pain. Sure, he'd shot me in my arm, rendering my dominate hand useless. That's why I trained with both hands.

His nose exploded and blood shot out all over his shirt. "Fuck!"

Trails of blood raced down my arm, and I felt a little lightheaded. Unlike, Darrell, I'd been in this game a lot longer. I knew the wound would stop bleeding on its own.

"If you're gonna shoot someone, aim for the head and the heart." I hauled off and punched him again, this time in the gut. My left arm uppercut isn't as strong, but it did send him to the ground in howling pain.

With his glasses askew, his nose busted, and his gun on the ground, the taxi pilot fell to his knees, a fresh burst of crimson bloomed in his shirt, over his heart, mortally wounded. He grunted at me, gurgled some nonsense words before falling face-first unto the ground. He hit the pavement like a sack of potatoes.

Behind him, Jane, sat on her aerocycle, sporting her helmet and what looked like my laser gun. She climbed off and walked over to the now deceased taxi pilot.

Once she pulled off her helmet, she said, "You hard to find."

I ripped the bottom of Darrell's shirt and wrapped my injured arm. Jane put her helmet down, on the sidewalk, handed me the gun, and took over doing it herself. Good because I can't tie knots with my left hand.

"Then how did you?" I looked over at her. "Find me."

"Kim. She's been following Agent Lynn and she mentioned you were without a vehicle. I came to headquarters to pick you up, and saw you get in the taxi. I was good with that, going to head on home, when I spotted the Big Game insignia on the bumper. Small. Innocuous unless you know what you're looking at."

"And you did."

"Obviously. Anyway, I followed him. It could've been nothing. Just a feeling I had. When I saw him pitch a gun out the window about a block from here, I stopped to retrieve it. I figured if he'd taken your weapon, he didn't have good intentions. I flew around until I found you."

Instant hero status for Jane.

"Just in time, too." I winced at how tight she tied the bow.

"Don't be a baby."

"You get shot in the arm…" I grumbled.

"How you getting home? Another taxi?" Jane laughed. "You can't ride on the aero like that."

"No, not another taxi. Not with you, either, even if I had two functioning arms," I said.

"I'm a safe pilot." Jane looked offended.

"Still…no." Aerocycles made me nauseous.

We both turned to look at the abandoned taxi parked on the street.

"When there's a will, there's a way," Jane said.

"Amen."

CHAPTER
THIRTY-FOUR

At home, I put on a pot of coffee, made two jalapeno jelly and peanut butter sandwiches, and put new pain and anti-inflammation patches on my ankle and arm. I changed the dressing on the gunshot wound. I'd managed to put on my pajamas and returned to the kitchen to unpack my bag and update my notes. I sat down at the kitchen table with my leg propped up on a pillow in the other chair. Once comfortable, I had dumped the contents of my satchel on to the table. Thanks to my new untethered status, I had to submit an official report of my tenure with the T.A. to Anika and Lynn for payment.

I billed my time with Yukio, and both trips out to Falls Church as "investigative time." Overall, I expected to get a good block of currency back, if Anika honored it. I had a contract with the Territory Alliance, so I expected them to pony up. The currency wouldn't come out of her account.

The commandeered taxi sat in a visitor's spot in the parking hanger. We decided to leave it unlocked with the key. Jane wiped it down. Only the thieves'—if anyone took the bait—will appear if discovered by the regs.

Next, I contacted Regulator Phillips about my case. The youthful regulator answered by connect. When he saw my face, he blanched. His eyes darted to something off screen before returning to me.

"Bonjour, Miss Lewis." His voice cracked on my surname.

"I'm looking for an update. You found the violator?"

He swallowed, his Adam's apple bobbed. "CCTV caught a male figure dressed in dark clothing. The AV department is working on cleaning up the image for identification and facial recognition. We're working on *how* the arsonist breached regulator security to get into the parking lot."

I had ideas.

"The arsonist is a regulator. You think of that?"

Regulator Phillips scowled. His unibrow became a v. "Pardon?"

"I used to be a reg. No one broke into HQ. The place is impenetrable, which means someone there committed the violation."

I couldn't believe he hadn't thought of that.

"I... I assure you, Miss Lewis, we're doing all we can and pursuing every lead," he said.

"I'm not getting a sense of urgency." I began removing the pug's battery and laser. My hands moved on their own; muscle memory. I used my left hand. "There's a huge hole in your security safety net."

"Well, we're doing it. Captain Brinnington's overseeing the investigation."

"What?" Why didn't he tell me that at the start?

He seemed quite pleased with himself as he sat up straighter. "Yes. Due to the, uh, nature of the event, a supervisor's been appointed to lead the investigation."

"Now Regulator Phillips, that's an update."

With reddening cheeks, he said, "Thank you. The captain's committed to resolving the case."

It was in their best interest. The District regs knew me, most of them. But Regulator Phillips seemed genuine. *Rookie.*

"Keep me updated."

I ended the connect. With Captain Brinnington looking into the violation, I had a tiny bit more hope they'd solve it.

While resting, I cleaned the pug and reassembled it. Only fourteen hundred hours, but my body—post adrenaline rush and battle—ached. Exhaustion hung over my shoulders like a heavy blanket.

I went to my bed, crawled gently beneath the covers, and closed my eyes. I tried to force the nanos to move faster. I was bone tired and achy.

Three of the most common causes for death violations were greed, lust, and jealousy. Why did Big Game want me dead? Today's second attempt only made me want to investigate more. Both his hired assassins wound up dead. Did it have a connection to Nico Mars?

I didn't see any connections, but my mind held a haziness from the attack. I couldn't think clearly because of the emotional toll. All I wanted to do at that moment was sleep.

Despite consuming three cups of coffee, my eyes grew heavy, my thoughts sluggish. I couldn't pinpoint a cause for him to come after me, let alone be willing to give currency for it.

Then sleep claimed me.

"You have a visitor."

"Fuck. Off." I shouted through cottonmouth and aching pain.

"You have a visitor," it repeated.

Sore and in agony along my right side, I got out of bed to answer the door's insistence. I didn't want to see anyone, but I had to change the pain patches anyway. Recovery took time. I'd been shot. The time on the telemonitor was after twenty-two hundred hours, and the dark sky outside confirmed it. I'd slept over eight hours. I spied Jane pacing along the short corridor outside my door. With a long yawn, I pressed the release.

She stalked in almost vibrating in her movements. "We've gotta go! Now!"

I frowned at her as I went to the cabinet and pulled out my medikit. "Where are we going and why right this minute?" I gestured to my shorts sleepwear.

She ran a punishing hand down her thighs, a whirlwind of fear made her voice shrill. "Kim's at this club in the Bottoms. Uh, Revolutions or something cheesy. I got the cords. The problem is she's found Agent Lynn there and this time Lynn's caught her!"

I pulled off the old pain patches and slapped on the new ones. I winced. "Caught her doing what?"

Jane paused. "Spying on her."

"Lynn doesn't know Kimmila is spying on her. She *suspects* it. Tell Kimmila to order a drink and tell Lynn she's just blowing off steam. If Lynn keeps bothering her, tell her to get the bartender or bouncer to assist her from being harassed." I took out the materials to redress my wound. "That will buy us some time before we get there."

Jane let out a big sigh. "Okay."

While she took out her handheld to contact Kimmila, I went to get dressed. Everything moved in slow motion because, well, I was working with one hand and one leg. I understood Jane's urgency. The situation between Agent Lynn and Kimmila and their shared history goes back, to the Irving case a few months ago. Back then, Lynn tried to take Kimmila on violations she did with her former boyfriend/drug dealer, to the Midwest Territories. The sooner we got there, the better.

I didn't fuss with my gun and holster. Jane was armed and that would have to do. The shoulder felt lighter and I missed my pug.

By the gods, I prayed it would be enough.

CHAPTER
THIRTY-FIVE

The air inside Revolutions hung like an extra coat in the winter—awkward and smelly. Scanty-clad people and robotic wait staff whirled about the three-story club in a loud, alcohol and drug smear. Happy people bounced in glee. Music pumped from every available cranny. Thunderous and bass-heavy, it drowned out all attempts at talking. Drinks, laughter, and shrieks rounded out the noise.

Jane and I paid to get in the front door sans weapons. The full body scan made me think this place might not be so bad, despite its location. I ditched the thought when I realized many of the partiers were drunk, Ackbacked, and high on other fun uppers. They didn't allow weapons but partyers could poison themselves and each other.

I hadn't been inside a club in a long time. People doused in glitter and glow-in-the-dark paints danced on various platforms that scaled up from the round mirrored floor. The walls stretched up to a giant, circular skylight. The graffiti walls had rainbow arrays flashed on them through what looked like a kaleidoscope.

So, this was how the young and restless killed time? They were in such a frenzy to empty the pockets of their soul—it was head spinning. *Maybe I'd been that way too.*

Youth is wasted on the young.

"Where is she?" I shouted against Jane's ear.

"Second floor!" Jane answered. She pointed to one of the platforms above us. I followed her finger to a well-dressed Kimmila, leaning against the ledge opposite the dancers. She sparkled.

Jane took off. I followed, albeit with difficulty. There weren't any signs of Agent Lynn, but with the packed bodies crammed along the round dance floor, the walls, and the stairwells leading up to the higher floors, I could've missed her.

How does anyone relax here?

We navigate the sweaty throng of swinging elbows and rapid two steps. The noise beat at my temples, like little hammers. I hoped nothing crazy popped off, because my body didn't want any more physical work—not tonight.

Kimmila had dove deep into her assignment. When we cleared a path to her, she spun around on the stool in slow motion. Dressed in what resembled a lacy bra, feathered glittery wings, and diamond-bright body paint on the other parts not covered by clothing, which was almost all of it. Dark-lined eyes and extravagant bold eyeshadow in neon pinks and blues decorated her eyes. She swirled the drink in her hand.

"She gone!" Kimmila shouted above the music. She gestured to the vacant seat beside her.

"Let's go." Jane took her drink and set it down on the sliver of counter that ran along the ledge. It overlooked the dance floor on level one.

Kimmila shook her head.

"Yeah. You had enough and the target's gone." Jane rounded to face her.

My partner huffed, but before she could cause a scene, I stepped in. I got close to Kimmila's stool and then got in her face. She struggled to focus on me.

"What's going on? You get Jane and me down here with a three-alarm fire. So what is it?"

Kimmila reclaimed her drink and sipped. She pointed to the platform directly across from us. Suspended along the packed first floor, this dancer appeared nude with electrodes covering strategic parts of her body. As she danced, the lights flickered. She was mesmerizing.

Kimmila leaned close to my ear and said, "That's Kayla Mars."

Stunned, I looked again. "Who?"

"Kayla Mars."

I stood up. "She's dead."

Jane grabbed Kimmila's arm. "You've had enough."

Kimmila shook her off. "I'm clean, Janey! This is tea!"

Jane took the glass, sipped, and let Kimmila go. "Sorry."

Kayla Mars moved well for a dead woman. She had long dark braids with blonde highlights. The braids had beads and shook as she did to the music. From that distance, she didn't look taller than me, about five feet or so. She had a dancer's body, lithe and strong.

"Good work!" I clapped Kimmila on the shoulder.

I waved Jane closer. "The dancer is Mars's wife."

Jane's face didn't change. She gave me a single nod. Kimmila remained focused on the dancer. Jane guided me out of the way, taking my spot beside her lover.

I made my way back down to the first floor. I wondered if this was how Dante felt as he descended into the various levels of Hell. The numbing ankle pain had receded. Everything blurred along the edges.

Then it happened.

Someone stepped on my bad ankle. *Fuck!*

Fire flared and I bit my lip to not cry out.

Hobbling, I shoved the offender as hard as I could. He laughed when he crashed into the others. He had foam at the corners of his mouth. His hooded-eyes and loopy grin spoke to his medical-induced bliss.

I found an unoccupied corner to prop myself up. I pulled out my pain patches from my pants' pocket. Someone dressed in a bright yellow jumpsuit missing its front, paused. He dug into his pockets and fished out several multi-colored patches.

"You need somethin' stronger?" He remained stoic. "Cheap credits."

"No, thank you. I'm good." I glared.

He shrugged. "Suits yourself."

I resumed reapplying new patches to my rapidly-swelling ankle.

If Mars lied about his wife, he lied about other things, too. Not that I trusted the word of a convicted violator or anyone for that matter, but I didn't consider Kayla Mars a player in this game. I figured the TA had ruled her out because, well, she died. None of the notes from Anika included her.

Who was this woman gyrating to the pounding dance track? Was she the real thing or someone with the same name?

I shouldn't have assumed. The mirror caught my eye and I spied my harrowing expression. No wonder the man asked me if I wanted something stronger. I looked like I *needed* something more. Dark circles hung from my eyes, and I still had light blood splatter on my face from Darrell's demise. I didn't have the energy to shower.

"Would you like a refreshing beverage?" a robotic server asked. Its blue eyes blinked, and its animated mouth smiled. "We have Peck beer, imported soda from Colorado..."

"No."

It moved on.

I may have growled.

Throughout the night, I tried to keep my weight off my ankle. I watched for Lynn, but I also kept my eyes on Kayla.

Packs of people came and went, a sweaty blob of arms, legs, and mouths. Agent Lynn didn't appear as the minutes bled into hours. Time slipped by in a drunken montage of terrible youth decision-making.

At last, Kayla stepped down from her platform. I followed her through the masses down to the first floor. The main dance square flickered with projected strobe in time to the electric music lights. Loud, I couldn't hear myself think. Kayla glided through them like a practiced employee. Synthetic smoke from cigarettes and the smoke machines reduced my visibility. I lost her for a minute.

Panic gripped my heart.

Then Kayla resurfaced, close to the restroom. I hurried to follow. I winced at the bright overhead lights. In contrast to the dark dance club, the restrooms had white sinks, gleaming counters, and shiny chrome doors.

Kayla rushed into a stall. Dozens of clubgoers filed in and out. I didn't want to lose her. There wasn't an alternative exit. *Good.*

I backed out of there and waited at the entrance. The wide mouth allowed a group of people to enter and exit without creating a jam in the doorway. The banging music dimmed this close to the end of the building. I could hear conversations.

Moments later, Kayla came out.

"Kayla Mars!" I pushed through two clubbers.

"I don't know you." She didn't stop walking.

"It's about Nico Mars!" I yelled as loudly as I could.

Ahead she tripped, turned around, and stalked toward me, her eyes narrowed. When she reached me, her finger pointed at my chest. "Leave me alone!"

"Did you know he's out?" I ignored her demands. "He's here."

Kayla paused, her mouth ajar. "Huh?"

She didn't know.

"He's in the District."

"No..." Kayla's hand covered her mouth.

"Let's go outside." I pointed to the exit. "We need to talk."

She rolled her eyes, looked around, and agreed with a nod.

Outside, the night was a wire of activity, but the noise had more space to travel.

I waited for Kayla to talk. She appeared shocked, and me throwing questions at her wouldn't help. I limped over to a bench and sat.

"Who the hell are you?" She paced, pausing only long enough to question me. "How do you know me? Fuck how did you find me?"

She wasn't speechless like before.

"I'm Cybil Lewis, a P.I."

"Who hired you? Nico?" She shouted at me, but her voice trembled. The info shook her to the core.

"Listen. I'm not here for you. Relax." I kept my tone matter-of-fact. I made eye contact. "But..."

"You said Nico's here..."

I held my hands up. "He is. Let me explain."

"Alright."

"In exchange, I want an explanation."

"For what?" Kayla scoffed.

"You know what." I patted the seat beside me. Her feet *had* to be killing her after dancing for hours.

She hesitated, then joined me on the bench.

"You're a P.I."

"Yeah. Nico escaped from the cradle and came straight here."

"That can't be true. I mean, no one gets out of the cradle except through death." Kayla shook her head in disbelief.

"Then you can understand why there's a media blackout."

She crossed her legs. "What's this got to do with me?"

"It'd been reported that you died." I didn't admit the source of the information was her husband's mistress and the man himself.

"I suppose you know about Nico's death violations?" Kayla slumped back and closed her eyes.

I nodded, realized she couldn't see it, and said, "Yeah."

I took out my handheld and turned it on. I pressed the record button and waited.

"Hell, it's been ten years. I had breast cancer. With Nico's regulator schedule and me needing dedicated care, I went to Vanderbilt Cancer Center in the Southeast Territories for treatment. It took ten or eleven months maybe a year. Eric, my brother, told me about what was going on in bits and pieces, but he kept me in the dark. He said I... I should focus on recovery."

"Understandable."

She opened her eyes. "By the time I was completely in remission, Nico was on his way to the cradle. I dunno where or who started it, but everyone kept saying I was dead." Kayla shrugged.

"You laid low."

"I did. I stayed in the Southeast. I came back here three years ago, using my own name, but no one remembered me or Nico." She stood. "What's this got to do with you?"

"I can't say but there's one question I've got to ask," I said. "That was the deal."

"You damn P.I.s. What?"

"Was Eric in a relationship with Anika Winsome?"

Kayla guffawed. "Whoa! You got all the dirt, filthy as it was. I haven't heard that cow's name in a long ass time. Eric, well, I cut him off for his part in Nico's conviction. But yeah, she was my brother's girlfriend before she seduced my husband."

"Before?" I stood up too.

She shook her head. "Oh, there's something you ain't know about."

No. I suspected them to have gotten together *after* Nico went down.

"I gotta get back." Kayla waved. "No offense but I don't want to see you again."

"I can't promise. I go where evidence takes me, but I'll try to keep my distance."

She flipped me off before walking away.

I stopped recording.

CHAPTER
THIRTY-SIX

My handheld lit up. Malcolm Moore appeared, and he was already gesturing with his hands to answer. I walked a short distance from the bench toward my wauto.

"What?" I answered.

"Where the hell are you?" Malcolm sat in his office, with his hair pulled back in its ponytail. He wore jeans and a tee-shirt. It looked like he'd been ordered to work.

"Why?"

"You don't know?" Malcolm gasped. "The news is racing through the net."

"No, I don't know. Today's been...busy."

"Damn it! I need an inside scoop!" Malcolm swore and slammed his fist on his desk.

"About what?" I asked.

Malcolm was normally much more put together.

"The regs are raiding Kinnear Von's estate!" Malcolm shouted.

I stumbled backwards. "What?"

"Fuck yeah! Get this, the rumor is Nico Mars escaped from the cradle and he's been at the Von's home." Malcolm almost levitated, he was so thrilled. "You asked me about him and now this."

"Did they find him?"

Malcolm paused, checked the monitor, and then said, "Not yet. There's a livestream, well, several. Right now they're hanging around the front gate."

"Thanks!

"Wait! Wait! I thought you had some inside information for me."

"I might, but not right now. I gotta go." I ended the connection.

I could hear the blood roaring through my veins. Anike had made her move to capture Nico.

What would he do?

That explained why Agent Lynn wasn't in the club anymore. I thought about contacting Anika. Both agents most likely had their hands full with the media, regulators, and TRU. Going to the scene would complicate matters. I sent Jane a message. Trying to speak to her via the handheld with the noise and club chaos would be more frustrating than simply messaging her.

A few minutes later, Jane and Kimmila emerged from the building. They came to the vehicle. They reeked of closed-in sweat but got in the back. I lowered the windows. It was strange talking to them through the taxi's laser-proof partition. I couldn't wait to get my own vehicle.

"Well,," I turned in my seat to talk, careful not to bang my arm. "The TRU are raiding the Von estate."

"Right now?" Jane fished her handheld out of her pocket.

Kimmila gasped. "It's two in the morning."

"I'm heading there, now." I met Jane's hazel eyes in the rearview mirror. "She's made her move."

"You think she knows about Kayla?" Jane asked.

"Yes." I nodded. "Because Lynn knows."

Jane turned to Kimmila. "Head on home, babe."

"You gonna go too?" Kimmila's whine rubbed my nerves.

Jane kissed her lightly on the lips. "Cyb's in no condition to go alone. Just look at her."

I gave them both my favorite one-finger salute.

"Be safe," Kimmila whispered.

"Gotcha." Jane got out and came around to the passenger side.

Kimmila followed her with a soft 'bye'.

We watched her walk over two rows to Jane's aerocycle. She led since she'd flown it down here.

Jane said, "You ready?"

I shook my head. "No, but I gotta feeling."

The long evening had pushed into early morning. A late-night raid could go on for hours, if the violator took a hostage, tried to flee, or fought back.

Nico Mars could go either way.

CHAPTER
THIRTY-SEVEN

The flight to the Von estate went faster than any other time. It could be down to the extremely early hour or the fact I'd made the trip two previous times. Jane checked her gear—a hunting knife and another smaller blade she kept hidden in her boot. Without my weapon, I felt naked, vulnerable. I didn't lack a defense. I could fight, but with a gunshot injury, even though the laser only nicked my bicep, I couldn't operate at 100%. The muscles and tendons were being repaired by the nanos in the patches.

"You expecting trouble?" Jane glanced over to me.

"There's a TRU team at the location so, no. I don't know what to expect. I want to see how Nico's taken in."

Jane said, "You think Winesome will find a way to make sure he doesn't survive?"

"It had occurred to me. It was the worst-case scenario. I really want to see Lynn. I can't believe I'm even saying that, but she knows Kayla's alive and she may know more." I couldn't find words to describe the feeling of dread and anxiety crawling over me.

"We're here." Jane readied herself to get out of the wauto.

"Hang on." The autopilot landed a block or so from the estate. I doubt we could get closer.

Ahead, blue and red lights splashed across the dark, lighting up the neighborhood like Christmas Eve. Scores of Tactical Retrieval Unit officers sprawled out like an army of ants. Yellow caution beams erected around the Von home and a few neighboring estates. Despite the hour, an announcement blared. A think row of citizens stood around in a daze. Low murmurings and whispered conversations threaded beneath the blaring demands of the regulator teams.

I spied Agent Lynn, with an amplifier to her mouth, telling people to return to their homes.

"For your safety, return to your homes. Secure yourselves inside." Her voice warbled through the other end.

Jane and I reached the caution beam. The neighbors wondered back to their big houses distraught and annoyed about the incident and interruptions to their peaceful evening. Lynn spied us and lowered her device. She came over to us, her face pinched in annoyance, her bob swinging in the wind.

"No! No! Don't come any closer. Turn around. Go home!" Lynn pointed at us, shaking her head, ushering us away. When she reached us, she lowered her volume. "There's nothing you can do here."

"I'm here as a witness," I said.

"The *D.C. Mirror* is streaming!" Lynn jutted at the cargo craft parked down the road. "Leaking it to the public."

"I prefer my own eyes."

A shout and a rustle of boots interrupted our conversation. I looked around her to the movement behind her.

Lynn did too. She left. The TRU regulators mobilized. With a screech, the Von front gate buckled in a cloud of smoke. The stench of explosives singed the air. I put my arm over my nose and mouth. Jane did the same. It didn't stop my eyes from burning and watering. I could taste it. About a dozen black-clad regs with shields and laser guns rushed in, followed by an armed cargo craft. While some disappeared into the dark, a few hopped on hover-boards and flew out.

Jane nodded at the force. "He's one person."

"He's dangerous but all this seems extreme."

The Nico Mars I met didn't appear to be a lethal weapon. The TRU regs moved as they would when capturing a double death violator. Just as Anika and her blind ambition wanted. I didn't like it. Anika's paranoia to bury the truth made me nervous. TRU's purpose was strong force and retrieval. It didn't care if the violator was alive or dead.

Time moved like a slug. Both T.A. agents waited at the rear of the TRU command cargo craft. Inside the Von estate, regulators scrambled through the gloom to find Nico. Their element lights bobbed in the gloom like fireflies.

I knew exactly where he was. No one asked me.

"You think the husband is home?" Jane asked, her gaze focused on the unfolding scene.

"I hope not. If he is, that's one hell of a wakeup call to start divorce proceedings."

"Yeah." Jane nodded.

The tense minutes crept by. Anika paced like a caged animal inside the command center.

Through the ruined gate, TRU regs parted as a cuffed and battered, Nico Mars, was marched forward by a trio of regs. Lynn and Anika left the command cargo. Anika met Nico outside the entrance.

I couldn't hear their exchange, but Nico's battered body spoke to his resistance. In turn, the regulators delivered a vicious beating. Signs pointed to a prolonged fight. The spotlights highlighted Nico's bloodied defensive wounds on his hands and arms. Marks on his legs bore boot impressions.

Anika's body language conveyed her gratification. She practically floated. They once were lovers. Further proof how sometimes passion can turn to poison.

Things were bleak for Nico. Everyone was a victim in this case.

Anika gestured to the regs and they jerked him toward a transport craft. He turned to look at us—at me as he passed. When he lifted his head, his one eye widened in recognition. His left eye had been battered shut.

"You!" he shouted. "You bitch!"

He lunged in my direction. I didn't make a move.

The regulators—caught off guard—recovered in time to hold him. Nico made a few steps before they tackled him to the pavement, still fighting to get to me. It took three of them to haul him back to his feet. A fourth rushed over to apply the down straps. He'd earned a shallow, roughly three-inch slash.

"I said get him outta here!" Anika pointed to the transport craft and made a beeline to me.

Jane whispered. "Uh oh."

Livid, Anika's face was flushed, her brown skin bore a reddish hue. "What the hell, Lewis? How does he know you?"

Lynn joined before I could answer.

"Look, it's late. We shouldn't do an interrogation here." Lynn looked around. "Plus, Kinnear Von's attorney is here."

Anika's luminous eyes bore into me. I utilized my right to remain silent. She jerked down her laser-proof vest with a huff.

"Fine. Detain Cybil Lewis."

Lynn's penciled eyebrows shot into her bangs. "What? Why?"

"As Nico's accomplice." Anika waved a few regulators over.

"Not gonna happen." Jane stepped forward, her arm out, barring me from being taken.

"Jane." I touched he arm, lowering it.

The summoned regs looked confused at Anika's erratic behavior. Lynn rounded on the approaching unit.

"No!" Disregard!" she said to them. To me, she said, "I told *you* to leave!"

"What the hell are you doing?" Anika snatched Lynn's elbow.

Lynn shook off her hand. "We can deal with her later. We have more important tasks right now!"

"This is *my* investigation, Amber." Anika leaned in close to Lynn, nearly touching noses, but shouted at a volume loud enough to be heard in the District.

"It's *our* investigation." Lynn's calm, professional tone made Anika's outbursts appear unhinged and frantic.

I turned and headed back to the wauto. You didn't have to tell me twice. Jane followed.

"Stop!" Anika yelled. "Lewis!"

I didn't hear or care what Lynn said, but no regs detained us or followed us.

Later, I dropped Jane at home to a much-relieved Kimmila.

CHAPTER
THIRTY-EIGHT

On the other hand, I was not so lucky.

Once I pulled into my apartment building's visitor parking space, I climbed out, weary and exhausted from an incredibly long day. Every muscle sang with misery, down to the bone.

Before I had taken two steps toward my home and my bed's awaiting comfort, a laser gun poked me painfully in the back, halting me in my tracks.

"Stop right there," he said, his voice slithering all over me.

"Hello Eric," I said. He hadn't tried to disguise himself. How long had he been waiting for me to return? How did he know where I lived?

Oh, right. Anika. I wondered if he'd flown her over when she came to seduce me the other night.

"You think you're so smart. Turn around."

I did as instructed; cursing myself for leaving the pug at home and for being a creature of habit, a death knell for P.Is.

With Jane tucked into her warm bed at home, she wouldn't be here to save me, like earlier.

I was on my own.

"What do you want? You have to excuse my annoyance. This is the second time I've been at the end of a laser gun in the last 24 hours." I lowered my hands, not out of defiance but fatigue.

"I'm aware." Eric wore black gloves, athletic pants, sneakers and a dark tee-shirt. He didn't bother to hide his face or identity. The act showed his hubris.

He knew, which only meant one thing. He had been behind the hits on my life. Each one said Big Game ordered it and if the would-be assassins weren't lying, then that meant Eric either knew Big Game or *was* him.

"You're doing Big Game's biddings now?"

"Nice try." He smirked.

He gestured with the gun to a wauto hovering a few spots over. "Head to that green wauto."

As a hostage, I was easier to steer into a vulnerable situation.

We walked, and he continued. "Sometimes the hired help isn't as effective as doing it yourself."

Then he and Big Game were one and the same. He didn't have to kill them, Henrietta Mayfield, the activists, Michele Lore, and who knew how many others? But that was street life in The Bottoms.

Death.

I didn't have plans to join them.

"Where are we going?" I walked slowly, dragging my feet.

Eric slammed the gun in between my shoulder blades as encouragement to move faster. Pain bloomed throughout my chest. I gritted my teeth against the flare. I'd been abducted before. Back then, Daniel found me in a compost pile roughly 60 miles from here and rushed me to hospital.

As you can imagine, I didn't want a repeat of that horrid event.

"I need you to do a job for me, private inspector," he said and laughed. "Your retainer will be your life."

He thinks he's a comedian. Ha. Ha.

"So this is a job?" I looked back at him. "Why didn't you just come by my office and hire me?"

Neither of us were telling the truth. I wouldn't have taken his job offer if he'd come by it honestly and he didn't intend to let me live. He held me captive.

When we reached the wauto, he opened the passenger side door and gestured for me to get in. The gun acted as an extension of his hand.

"Look, tell me what you want and I'll do it. You don't have to force me." I didn't think I'd be able to persuade him, but I tried anyway. Eric liked the control, the power, and the agony on my face. I fought to keep it blank and not feed his ego.

"Gimme your handheld." He didn't wait, and reached into my pants pocket, snatched it out and threw it as far and as hard as he could. I heard it clatter and shatter somewhere in the distance.

"I just bought that one." I groaned.

Whack!

I tasted blood in my mouth, and I spat it out at his feet. He shoved me into the passenger seat and slammed the door before I could upright myself. If I had been slower, he probably would've caught my bad ankle in the door.

He climbed inside the vehicle, with the weapon trained on me. With his free hand, he took a piece of what looked like tape from the center console and pressed it hard against my mouth. Further proof he'd preplanned or he kept an abduction kit in his vehicle—a true predator.

"You talk too damn much. Your mouth is infamous for getting people hurt."

"Anika tell you that?" I asked before he secured the left side of the tape.

He glared at me. "See? That's what I'm saying."

As he got closer, I grabbed his hair and tugged with all my might. I punched him in the face twice before his laser gun went off. The beam missed me, plowing into the passenger seat. It was close enough for me feel the laser's heat as it passed.

"You fucking bitch!" Eric shoved the gun under my chin, the hot tip burning my skin. It would leave a mark. "I *will* fucking kill you."

I looked him straight in the eyes., unafraid, but breathing shakily. I muffled out a 'try.'

Whack!

My head slammed against the window, bounced, and nearly headbutted him. Stunned I watched with blurry eyes as he reached into the glove box and took out the clear, force field restraints. Apparently the District Regulators don't make you turn those in when you leave or when you get fired.

He secured my wrists and then used the seatbelt across my upper body and waist to ensure I was sufficiently tied down. Eric launched the flight sequence without another attempt to harm me.

"GET UP! GET THE FUCK UP!"

Rough hands roused me. I opened my eyes to a still blurry window and pissed off Eric Mann. I must've been more exhausted than I thought. I winced as a sharp piercing pain ploughed into my head, igniting a headache. I could barely open my eyes from the pain. Maybe I'd been a bit concussed when my head slammed into the window.

My mouth remained taped; my hands secured. He got out of the wauto with laser gun in hand, hurried around to my side and opened the door. Without a pause, he snatched my shirt and my bad arm and heaved me out of the vehicle.

Where am I?

"Let's go," Eric whispered, waving the gun forward as he searched around.

Henrietta Mayfield's apartment building looked dark at this time in the late evening, early morning. I didn't know how much time had passed, but I started for the steps leading up to the front doors. Sluggish with a pounding headache, I couldn't quite gauge the surroundings. I walked by memory, mostly.

We headed up the walkway and into the four-story building. Eric kept his weapon trained on me. The tenderness between my shoulders hinted at bruising from his laser gun's jabs.

Inside, a hallway stretched forward with four doors, two on each side. The spattering of overhead lights hurt my head and I became dizzy. A couple had been broken. I remembered from visiting the violation scene with Daniel that Henrietta's apartment was on the top floor of the four loft-style spaces.

"Use the stairs." Eric ordered.

We passed the elevator on my left and took the stairs, located in the corridors center. With my hands restrained, I looked for an opportunity to escape. He stayed close. His breath brushed the back of my neck.

Once we reached the second floor, I was soaked in sweat. Exhausted, I stumbled and fell. My kidnapper instinctively tried to grab me, but I pivoted out of his reach. I poured on the theatrics, some real, some exaggerated while I writhed around on the ground. My muffled shouts may have been loud enough to alert an early-rising neighbor.

"Get up!" Eric pointed the laser gun at me. It moved as I did. "Stop fucking around."

Nausea threatened to race up my throat. With my eyes tearing, I kicked out as hard as I could. My feet connected to his shin, but he'd planted him feet when he took aim.

"Ow!" He fired.

If he hit me, I didn't feel it. I kicked again, but he'd stepped out of my path. Instead, he fired a second time, but a clicking and whirring happened instead of a blast. The battery indicator on the side of his weapon flickered and turned red. He frowned in confusion at his weapon.

Then silence.

Remember what I said about laser gun batteries?

My opportunity appeared and I took it.

I scrambled to my feet, bruising my hands on the cement as I struggled to propel myself away from him as fast as I could.

I ran.

"Lewis!"

Sluggish with a pounding headache and raging vertigo, I fell several times but recovered. Powered by survivor instincts, prior experience, or sheer spite, I put distance between Eric and myself.

Recall also what I said about staying in shape.

It had been over ten years since Eric Mann worked as a regulator. He probably didn't keep fit and he smoked.

He wasn't catching me, not with my conditioning and adrenaline cocktail pouring through me.

I raced down the hallway to the second set of stairs and stumbled down to the first floor. I hurried out of the building, through the rear doors. The back of the building had parking spaces, a playground, and a walking path that circled the building. There literally was no place to hide. Eric's laser gun would recharge. Models varied. I didn't know how much time I had before he could start shooting again.

The pain patches on my ankle and arm wore off.

On a screaming ankle, I hobbled and crouched down between two wautos and waited for him to show himself. We'd both been regulators but I also had Army training. Crawling around the wautos left me open to fire, if he found my position.

He'd stopped shouting after me. I took several deep, steadying breaths to calm my racing heart. With my eyes closed, I listened closely for signs of his movements. And it gave me some relief from the headache and dizziness. The roar of wautos launching, a baby crying, and the distant sounds of sirens all spoke to people waking up.

I held the position until my muscles cramped. I took turns stretching each one out. My injured ankle complained—a lot. I closed my eyes again, not intending to, but fatigue landed on me like a ton of bricks.

"There you are!"

I opened my eyes, shot to my feet and flailed; my restrained hands became clawlike.

"Whoa!" Jamison said seconds before I socked him in the mouth. "Ouch! Damn it. It's me, District IR Jamison!"

I stopped.

He took my hands and pressed a button on the restraints that released them. Next, he ripped the tape off my mouth with as much compassion as a cradle guard. With glee he said, "Payback."

I gingerly touched my face. "Sorry. I thought…"

"…I was Mann. Yeah, I guessed." He winced when he smiled.

I wasn't going to tell him that I was frightened because I didn't hear him approach. Most people were clumsy and loud in their actions, but Jamison had been stealth.

"You look awful. Medics!" He shouted to the trio of turquoise-clad jumpsuit people.

It was then that I became aware of the sirens, the dozens of regulator labeled wautos and uniformed regs. The parking lot, the rear entrance to the apartment building, the walking path, and the sides of the building had regulators canvassing.

When had all this arrived?

"How?" I couldn't form words. To my ears, I slurred them. I slumped against the closest vehicle.

Jamison gestured to the transport craft, where Eric Mann, now wearing his own force field wrist restraints, was guided to the rear holding section.

"Agent Lynn and I concocted a plan. We kept Mayfield's place under digital surveillance since we decoded her message. We figured Mann would spy a human team. We also knew he'd come back to try to find the safe again or get someone else to do it, especially since I leaked we didn't find the safe."

He smiled with his whole body beaming in pride.

Jamison studied my face. "We can talk later. You don't look good."

"I might have a slight concussion." The landscape swirled. I gripped the door for support. "Jamison—"

"Medic! Get over here!" Jamison yelled.

The nausea I'd kept at bay would be denied no longer.

CHAPTER
THIRTY-NINE

"You owe Jamison a new pair of shoes," Jane said as she stood at the foot of my suspended medical pod. It floated inches above the cold-looking floor. Thankfully, the hospital's air conditioning worked well.

"I figured." The oblong fiberglass bed didn't feel as cramped or as closed in any more, but then again I had been in the contraption for three days. I woke up here, well, not in this individual room, but in the Emergency Room, carried in by the District's medics. I'd been in and out of consciousness over the past few days. Sometimes when I woke up, Jane slept in the chair or a nurse poked with needles and questions.

As far as my ankle, they wrapped it and injected it with an anti-inflammatory with directions to stay off it for a few days. It remained suspended in a sling above the bedding. "How's everything?" I croaked through sleep.

Jane shrugged and sat down in a chair beneath the wall telemonitor. "You been out of it and during that time, Mann was charged for the death violations for four people and counting…"

"They charged him?" I scooted to a sitting position and manipulated the bed's inner mattress to an upright position. I had to use my left hand because my entire right arm was encased in a nano-rebuilding sleeve. It used nanos to deliver medicine to heal and repair damaged muscles. "They get him to confess?"

Jane shook her head. "No, but they have the documentation in the safe and some surveillance footage too. Oh, and they also charged him with your attempted death violation and abduction."

"What about Von and Mars?"

"I can answer that," came a familiar voice from the doorway. It opened so quietly I didn't hear it, but according to the doctors, part of my hearing had been injured due to a mild concussion. Jamison wasn't stealthy after all.

In walked IR Jamison followed by Daniel. My tiny hospital room filled with too many people standing around trying their best not to look directly at me.

"Who put together this little think tank?" I asked.

Jane said, "Not me."

Daniel laughed and came over to the bed. He thrust a bouquet of flowers at me. But when he leaned in, he whispered into my ear, "Stop giving me a heart attack." He hugged me, smelling like cologne and cigarettes. The always present stubble brushed my face. He gave me one hard squeeze and let go, taking the flowers with him.

"I'll get a vase." He left.

Jamison cleared his throat and stayed near Jane, at the foot of the bed, each of them on opposite ends like unsmiling sentries, she in the chair and he by the narrow bathroom door. Despite it being Saturday morning, he wore his work clothes, collared blue shirt and dark brown slacks. He rubbed his bald head and met my eyes at last.

"Jane said you don't need another vehicle?" He asked.

"No. I'm good," I said with a quick glance at Jane. I had no idea what she'd done but if she said I didn't need one, I didn't.

"I'm sorry about not getting back to you sooner. We got busy," Jamison said.

"I heard." I adjusted my position, careful not to bump the arm or the leg. "You said you could answer my question," I said, keenly aware of my hospital gown's thinness and my lack of a bra. Maybe both of the intravenous feeds would distract his attention from my other assets.

He inclined his head and pushed his hands into his pants pockets. "Yeah. I had already spoken to Jane about a lot of what's happened, but it's still early days, you know. Mars is back in the Midwest Territories and in the cradle. He's got new attorneys, courtesy of Kinnear Von, who are in turn pressuring the District over the initial death violation charges. They're demanding reviews of the death violations. And as a result of that, TA Agent Winsome is under investigation by our Anti-corruption team. She's not going anywhere for a bit."

"Really? They aren't basing that on Mars' word. They gotta have something more than that." I looked from Jamison to Jane, who shrugged.

"They do. Agent Lynn managed to find a witness, Kayla Mars." Jamison beamed. He paused, his gaze shifted between me and Jane. He threw up his hands. "Of course, you already knew she wasn't dead. You could've told me."

"I didn't see the point in uprooting her life or bringing that horrid man and his misdeeds to her lap." I shifted to ease the numbness in my right arm, shifting it like a bag of groceries. My ankle flared in pain.

"Aw, come on, Cybil. Mann is her brother. With her help, we've uncovered his pattern of deception."

"*Half*-brother. And Mars is her husband, who she faked her death to get away from. He cheated on her when she had *cancer*. After he'd escaped the cradle, something that is supposed to be impossible, I couldn't out her. He'd find her." I shook my head. "No."

The problem with regulators was they had unflinching tunnel vision. They only saw their immediate investigations but not the fallout of those violations in the others around them.

"What about Kinnear Von?" I said all I was going to about Kayla Mars.

Thoroughly chastised, Jamison swallowed and hesitated. The muscle along his jaw pulsated. He was mad. "You'll need to give a statement."

I nodded. "Von?"

"I can tell you. It's already in the news. She's back at home with her husband. No violations will be submitted."

"What?" I couldn't believe it. "TRU literally found him on her property."

"She claims she had no knowledge," Jamison said. "And she's friends with the governor."

"The TA has video footage."

Jamison grimaced. "Well, with Agent Winsome under investigation…"

"She cannot deny it's her. She's famous." I couldn't confess to how I came by the identification or how I knew Mars hid at the Von estate.

"That's part of the problem," Jamison said, his shoulders slumped. "She's got a ton of contacts in the District."

"So? You're gonna let her get away with it?" I didn't hide the disgust in my voice. "Over a few credits?"

"It was an order from the Deputy Regulator." Jamison swore. "You PIs…that's why we don't work with you No regard for regulations, order, or authority."

"And yet, here you are. Another devotee that's married to routine and regulations, all black and white, no gray."

Jane sniggered. "Can you two get a damn room already. Fuck!"

"No!" We both said in unison.

"Oh, you should look into a violator named Big Game. That's Eric's newer alias. I think he's been using it since he had to retire the Nqobile moniker. He practically told me," I said.

"Why didn't you tell me sooner?" He threw back his head in annoyance.

"I dunno. It could be because I was trying not to die! I've been unconscious for two fucking days." I yelled and one of my monitors blared in alarm.

"Cyb…" Jane warned.

"I can't with you." Jamison made another noise. "I gotta go. Just wanted to let you know I didn't forget about you." He growled something else under his breath as he stormed out of my room, plowing into Daniel as he did so. I heard yelling before he came all the way in.

"What did you say to him?" Daniel jutted his thumb at the fleeing Jamison.

"Truth hurts, Mon amie." I didn't mean to upset him, but he annoyed the hell out of me.

Jane laughed. "Give 'em time, hatchling. They'll be bumping uglies."

"Don't you need to go smoke or walk or something?" I asked her.

Daniel placed the vase of flowers beside my bed. "When you getting out of here?"

"Hopefully tomorrow. One more night of observation." I lifted my right arm and then pointed to my leg. "I have to wear it for the next four to six weeks. But the doctor said I inject the nanites."

Jane stood up. "She'll need three months of physical therapy… with robots."

I scowled. "If I can find a human therapist I will."

Jane laughed. "That is not what your doctor recommended."

"I'm gonna remove you as my point of contact," I snapped. "You're not my mom."

"Well before that, we got to get you another wauto," Jane said.

"They still don't know who did it?" Daniel crossed his arms.

Jane said, "I tried to get info, but I'm not her partner or family so they wouldn't tell me anything."

Daniel said, "They should've cleared that already. The surveillance around HQ is state of the art. I'm surprised it has taken this long to find the culprit."

"Unless the threat came from within HQ." I met Daniel's hazel, questioning eyes.

He sighed. "There is that."

LATER THAT AFTERNOON, Jane had gone out to smoke and meet Kimmila for lunch.

Bored, I switched the telemonitor to live feed. The local area news had a scarlet ticker at the bottom of the screen. It declared Kinnear Von had not been charged with any violations in big block letters. Von was many things, but innocent wasn't one of them. It bothered me she'd would walk away from her part in the shenanigans.

Above the ticker, microphones decorated a podium. A cluster of journalists waited for the press conference to start. The entire District awaited this moment. Now that the proverbial cat of Mars escape was out of the bag, questions spread like kudzu. The last few days made my eyeballs ache. The politics, the violation's brutal nature, and celebrity gelled into a media frenzy. It managed to lure people from their homes and away from the internet—at least momentarily. Few things did that nowadays.

Privilege, and the way folks used it, crafted a surreal fascination in some viewers.

But even I wasn't prepared for the moment when Deputy Governor Graham approached the podium with Von's attorney, a beautiful but cold looking brunette. Decked out in her finest clothes, she didn't smile but looked serious and stern. I hadn't seen her in years—Nicolena Nelson.

Fuck! I thought she'd scuttled under a rock and had stayed there. I guess the lure of the limelight couldn't be denied.

· · ·

JANE CAME in from the lunch, smelling of delicious food. She stood behind me. "You gonna watch the show?"

"Yeah. I want to witness them wiggling out if this." I pointed at the well-dressed man adjusting the microphones. "Deputy Governor Graham and Nicolena Nelson, head of the Human Rights League."

Jane shook her head. "They'll let anyone become at attorney."

I clicked on the audio as she began to talk.

"Greetings. I am Nicolena Nelson and the attorney for Madam Kinnear Von. She will not be answering questions this morning. We will not discuss the specifics of an on-going investigation..."

She flashed a wide smile.

My skin crawled.

The journalists erupted with questions, drowning the rest of her words in a sea of outrage. Nicolena remained stoic. She commanded attention and awe. I could see how she captured people's hearts and convinced them to do awful things.

"I bet Anika fed info to Eric," I said.

"No doubt," Jane agreed. She leaned back against the wall with her arms crossed. "She probably didn't know what he did with it."

"Oh, I don't know, Jane. TA agents are famous for bullying their enemies and manipulating their friends."

"With friends like her..."

"Right?" I answered. "No wonder Lynn stopped trusting her."

On screen, the journalists calmed down, and Nelson responded to general questions. Many of her answers were, "No comment." Already, she laid the foundation for Mars as a home invader. The groundwork for the narrative being that Mars found the Vons' house accessible and had penetrated it a few days before. After all, his wife worked for Kinnear on the estate. If they hadn't already, they'd cover up the link between Von and Mars's escape. It was perfect.

I'd lived in the District long enough to know those in power had enough currency and influence to avoid any real consequences. The TA would add another wrinkle of inconvenience, but I doubted anything would stick to Von.

The graceless age of raw reality exploded on the screen. Jane shook her head at the flashback footage to Nico Mars's arrest and trial.

It didn't sit well with me. Someone violated their rights to live and then tossed them out like yesterday's garbage. The frustration sank deep into my bones, but it wasn't in my ability to alleviate it.

"She isn't gonna tell them what happened." Jane came around and sat in the other folding chairs. "She's doin' a lot of dodging and deflectin'.

My gun wound tingled at the memory of being shot by a friendly taxi driver and at being attacked by a young woman.

Evil came in all packages.

EPILOGUE

stand corrected. August is by far the hottest month in the District. Or so the weatherperson said last night as temperatures reached somewhere near ridiculous. The air conditioning in my apartment didn't go out, but across town, an elderly retirement home lost power and people were trapped for nearly two hours. Mother Nature netted two more deaths and I changed the channel from news to something more pleasant—the Kungfu film festival on Bravo.

Saturday blared on, frying everything in its wake.

Jane sat at the opposite end of the sofa. "Since you're in PT and it's slow, I needed about two weeks off."

"You ready to take a vacation?"

"Yeah," she shrugged, not looking at me. "A little getaway. You know. Me and Kim."

"Oh, yeah. We're not busy, so I can handle the office on my own." I waved her off. "Where is Kimmila tonight anyway?"

"At home with Zola. She's taking a course on violations." Jane smiled with pride. "She may go into regulation-enforcement."

"She's got the bug," I said. "She did a good on the Mars job."

"Totally your fault." Jane pointed at me.

"No, it isn't. She needed a job, you said. So, I gave her one."

By the way, what was Lynn doing at that club?" I rubbed my laser gun scar on my arm.

"According to Kim, dancing." Jane answered with a laugh. "Hooking up. Blowing off steam."

I filed that away to use later. I doubted I had seen the last of Agent Lynn.

"What about you? Isn't Hanson visiting this month?"

"Yeah. Let's not talk about that. We're having a good time." I didn't want to dwell on the fact I owed the man a date. "Though he did do well with Bryan."

"Is Bryan back in the District?"

"Yeah. Got back last week, I think." I sipped some beer.

"What about your wauto?" Jane nodded.

"Jamison didn't know, but I'm assigning that one to Mann too."

"Sure?" Jane asked.

"I'm not sure about anything."

She picked up her helmet. "We'll tackle it on Monday."

"When you need off?" I asked, going to the door.

"I'll let you know, but not when it's this fucking hot." She shoved on her helmet.

The door hushed closed behind her.

Only a few minutes later, the door announced I had visitor. I looked around the living room and didn't see anything Jane had left. I went back to the door and pressed the release.

"What did you leave?" I turned away To check the kitchen.

"Hello Cybil," Anika Winsome said from just outside the door.

Chills raced over my body. "Anika."

"I... I don't want to come in. I came to say goodbye." She stuck out her hand. "No hard feelings?"

I didn't shake her hand. "Hard feelings here."

She dropped her hand. "I'm sorry. When I'm working I have a laser focus, and I messed up. There. I said it. I'm fallible."

Her luminous eyes, well decorated with make-up, held pleading. She had her purse strapped across her body, and she wore a plum blouse and jeans. Travel attire. Her body language indicated remorse, but then it could've all been wishful thinking on my part.

Is this what you do, Anika? Take advantage of people's trust?

"Like sleeping with your boyfriend's partner. Hiding Eric's alias and that he committed death violations, drug trafficking, vios, and more. You fabricated so much. I don't know if you even know what's true."

She closed her eyes then opened them. "I didn't know Eric had gotten into all of that. Later he told me he was heavily impaired by drugs and alcohol. He claimed he heard the shots in his semi-conscious state. That was his testimony."

"And Kayla."

She opened her eyes then. They glittered. "I said I was fallible."

"She's not dead."

"No, she isn't, but she told Eric to think of her as being dead." Anika swallowed and cleared her throat. "Like I said, I messed up."

I couldn't think of anything else to say. I wanted to invite her in, to make her coffee, and to taste peanut butter on her tongue, but after the way she reacted to me questioning her, well, it soured things.

"Yes, but if Agent Lynn hadn't gone back over the case, we wouldn't have gotten the good," she said. "I screwed it up for us, didn't I?"

"Yeah. You kinda did."

"I'm sorry, Cybil."

"Me too."

"Goodbye."

"Safe travels, Anika." I stepped back from the door and allowed it to shut.

The End

ABOUT NICOLE GIVENS KURTZ

Nicole Givens Kurtz has been called "a genre polymath who does crime, horror, and SFF (Book Riot)." They've named her as one of the *6 Black SFF Indie Writers You Should be Reading, 30 Must-Read SFF Books by Black Authors,* and *The Best of the West: 8 Alternative History Westerns (Sisters of the Wild Sage).* She's a two-time Atomacon Palmetto Scribe Award winner. With over 20 years in publishing, she's written for Pseudopod, Fiyah, Apex Magazine, White Wolf, The Realm (formerly Serial Box), Subsume, and Baen. Nicole has over 50 published short stories and is the author of the *Cybil Lewis* and *Death*

Violations cybernoir series as well as the *Kingdom of Aves* fantasy mystery series. She's written the critically acclaimed, weird western anthology, *Sisters of the Wild Sage: A Weird West Collection.*

Nicole has conducted workshops for Clarion West and is an active instructor at Speculative Fiction Academy. She is the owner of Mocha Memoirs Press. She's the editor for the groundbreaking *SLAY: Stories of the Vampire Noire* anthology and co-editor of *Blackened Roots: An Anthology of the Undead.*

Nicole is professional level member of SFWA and HWA.

NICOLE'S WHEREABOUTS ON THE WEB

Other Worlds Pulp - http://www.nicolegivenskurtz.net

Follow Nicole on BlueSky - @nicolegkurtz

Follow on Facebook - http://www.facebook.com/nicolegkurtz

Join The District fb group - https://www.facebook.com/groups/other worldspulp

JOIN NICOLE'S NEWSLETTER

YOU MAY ALSO ENJOY

The First Kingdom of Aves Mystery Series

The Cybil Lewis Science Fiction Mystery Series

The Soul Cages: A Minister Knight of Souls Novel

OTHER NICOLE GIVENS KURTZ'S TITLES

Dead-End Job Series

Reaping By Numbers

Death Violation Cyberpunk Trilogy

Glitches & Stitches

Immortal Protocol

The Butterfly Nexus

Death Violations: The Complete Trilogy w/illustrations

Kingdom of Aves Mysteries

Kill Three Birds

A Theft Most Fowl

Cybil Lewis SF Mystery Series

Silenced: A Cybil Lewis SF Mystery

Cozened: A Cybil Lewis SF Mystery

Replicated: A Cybil Lewis SF Mystery

Collected: A Cybil Lewis SF Collection

Fabricated: A Cybil Lewis SF Mystery

Minster Knights of Souls Space Opera Series

The Soul Cages: A Minister Knight of Souls Novel

Devourer: A Minister Knight of Souls Novel

Weird Western Anthology

Sisters of the Wild Sage: A Weird Western Collection